SHIFTY

Fanny Valentine Darling

SHIFTY

Fanny Valentine Darling

DMP

Shifty

ISBN 13 p 978-1-897492-94-9

Printed on acid free paper

www.dragonmoonpress.com

For my mother:

Who loved the strange, otherworldly child she'd been handed with all that she had and everything she was. That love allowed me to play and thrive in the realm of imagination, where fiction grows.

I love you, Mom.

SCATH VOCABULARY

RIOCHT (ROCKED): Realms, dimensions

SCATH (SKA): Riocht where sheehairn, banshee, and wraiths reside

RIAN (REE-AWN): Magical markings displayed on scath creature's skin

TALAM (TAL-UH): Human world

SAEMBAD (SOU-DAH): Land of death

CEILE (KEY-LAH): Mate, partner, spouse

SIOFRA (SHEE-OH-FRAH): Changeling

RIOCHTFIOS (ROCKED-FUSS): Ability to use magic in all riocht

AONTUET (IN-TAUT): Marriage/binding ceremony

SCATH FIOS (SKA-FUSS): A scath creature's grimoire/book of shadows

CHEANGAL (CHAN-GUL): A restraining spell

FALT RICH DRAIT (FAH-RI-DRE): A summoning spell

SAOI (SEE): Honorific Mrs.

MEAS (MASS): Honorific Mr.

CEATHAR (KEY-YA-TUR): cousin

SCATH CREATURES

SHEEHAIRN/HAIRN: most common of Scath's magic-using creatures

WRAITHS: darkest magic-using creatures of Scath

BANSHEE: offspring of a sheehairn and a wraith

NAME PRONUNCIATIONS

TRESARA: trey-SA-ra

ELBHLIN: AYV-leen

KATARIN: KAT-ah-rin

ARAWN: ARE-one

CIARDA: SEE-ar-dah

CHAPTER

ONE

The first thing they set up was the stereo, so that it blared through the open windows of their third story apartment. The complex was near campus, and that was about the nicest thing Shifty could think to say about it. The bathroom faucet dripped inconsistently; the dishwasher emitted a foul odor that made her wonder if a serial killer had just moved out—except most career murderers were more careful than that, so the previous tenant must have been a slovenly Ed Gein type. The closet in the upstairs bedroom had a rod that had held exactly three hangers before it cracked and fell to the floor. And she would have been able to notice all its myriad shortcomings if she had been able to see past the fact that it was gray. Gray stucco exterior, gray cement front balcony-walkway to the front door, gray carpet, gray paint, and gray speckled faux-marble laminate in the kitchen and bathrooms.

"We're living in Pleasantville," Paxton said, carrying a box marked "kitchen" into the living room and dropping it in a corner with a clatter of poorly-wrapped cutlery.

"You get to re-sharpen those," Peyton muttered, drooped under the weight of a large duffel bag stuffed to capacity. She paused long enough to shoot her brother a hostile glare before continuing into her room with her burden.

Paxton snorted and muttered a rude reply under his breath. He dusted his hands on his jeans and started to head for the door to collect another load of boxes.

Shifty was standing stock-still in front of the kitchen nook's wide window. There was no curtain up yet, so the glass with the sun bouncing off it made a reasonable approximation of a mirror.

It was her bright blue eyes that had stalled his forward progress. They were huge, and haunted, and totally unaware that he was even in the room. He approached her slowly, but with his usual affection, and placed a hand on her shoulder. She didn't acknowledge him. He leaned his face close to hers and brushed his lips across her cheek, brushing back her chin-length blonde hair, stopping when his mouth was near her ear.

"Are you okay, Shifty?"

Except for her parents, everyone called her Shifty. It had stuck in grade school, not only because it was easier for her classmates to pronounce than *She-oh-frah*, but also because it paid tribute to the strange quality of Siofra's movements. She moved more quickly and with a jerkiness, almost as if her bones and joints worked differently than her classmates'. It was a subtle difference, but enough that anyone who was around her day in and day out would notice it eventually. Siofra loved her nickname, and embraced her unique way of moving; she had never been insulted when it was pointed out.

"Shifty!"

"*Shifty!*" She didn't start at his voice. She seemed to come back into her body slowly, and turned her face to his, smiling. She pecked a kiss onto his lips, and quirked a corner of her mouth up in a way she reserved just for him.

"I'm fine," she said, her voice just a little too cheery. "Are you okay? How'd you get through the beer with my dad last night?"

Paxton shuddered, but his face remained light. Grady Gilbert was far from the worst girlfriend's father he'd encountered in his life. Grady seemed to genuinely like Paxton, and didn't have many unreasonable expectations of what Shifty and Paxton sharing a bedroom meant. Grady had made it clear that he would be disappointed to see Paxton—the oldest member of this new household, not to mention his daughter's boyfriend—fall into old and reckless behaviors. He'd intimated that one of the reasons he and Shifty's mother, Adara, had given their blessing to this relationship was the growth and maturity Pax had shown since graduating high school. He hadn't used any clichés, no "if you hurt my daughter, there's a plot at Mountainside waiting for you." Which Paxton really appreciated. He'd known the Gilberts since he was a toddler, and thought of Grady maybe not as an uncle, but certainly as extended family.

"Your father's all right with me," Paxton said, "and me with him. Really, it's your mom who scares me! She misses nothing. I swear she can read every dirty thought I've had since I hit puberty."

Shifty laughed. "You're scared of my mom? She's like five feet tall. Sheesh, Pax, you outweigh her by about three people." She ruffled the hair at the back of his head in that possessive way that always sent a thrill of excitement up his spine. *Mine*, it telegraphed.

"Yeah." He kissed the top of her head, reveling in the smell of her, "Cause I would totally rough up your mom." He spun her around to face him, chest to chest, and bent to kiss her for real now. When they parted, he had a more sober look on his face. "Seriously, you're okay? You were a million miles away in the window."

"I really am. Stop worrying!" She winked at him again, an invitation to continue the kissing. An invitation he did not decline.

"Yeah, this isn't going to get old," Peyton said, now standing in the kitchen doorway. "I should have thought longer and harder about my choice of roommates."

Shifty jumped away from him, sensitive to her friend's

worry that she'd be a constant third wheel in their household.

Paxton shook his head and smiled at his sister. "Kid, you're stuck with us. We're family. Besides, no one else would abide that horrible gum! I thought Shifty told you to spit it out before entering the premises! You positively reek." There was a Pigpen-like cloud of stink around Peyton with the mingled odors of carob, Valerian root, garlic and a smidgen of asafetida.

Peyton grinned, a wicked slash of her pink lipstick framing her white teeth. "You found the coffee maker yet?"

Paxton groaned. The coffee maker was in a particularly heavy box in the trunk of his car. "I swear, sometimes I feel like your packhorse!"

Despite the complaint, he started toward the door.

Shifty caught him by the sleeve. "Don't go, then, if you're going to complain. No one asked you to carry my water," she chided.

But he pulled his arm free and darted out the front door. "I've got it! You make sure she spits out that gum. In an *outside* receptacle," he added before his voice disappeared into the stairwell.

CHAPTER

TWO

In *Scath*, the grass was never completely dry, and the leaves on the trees sagged with dew. Evangeline loved it. The air always smelled like first light, the days always felt new, full of promise. Though she knew, of course, that *Scath* was allegedly the gloomiest *riocht*, filled with the residue of spells worked from the dark places of the soul, it was the only home she'd ever known. It had never seemed scary to her. To her, it was the place she'd explored as a child, playing with brightly colored insects as they crawled over her knuckles and tickled her skin.

The wraiths, on the other hand, scared the crap out of her. Tall, willowy, and silver-pigmented to the point of having the illusion of appearing transparent, until the black *rian* of their death magic snaked their skin and you could feel their solidity, their power. Even Tresara's mother, whom she had known as long as she could remember, made her want to run and hide behind her own mother's skirts.

Today was no different. Lara Keelin swept past Evangeline and Tresara sitting on the grass and into Evangeline's house. Evangeline was used to being stopped and talked to. Being the daughter—even the adopted human daughter—of the leader of the *sheehairn* made everyone greet you. Of the three types of magical-wielding creatures in *Scath*, *sheehairn* were the most populous in the *riocht*, and held most of the political power. Evangeline wasn't bothered by Lara's indifference personally, but she hurt for Tresara. Wraiths didn't make the warmest parents. Had Tree been full-blooded wraith, her mother's apathy wouldn't have stung, but Tresara's father was a *sheehairn*, so her mother's constant rebuffs were painful to her banshee daughter. Banshees, as the offspring of a *sheehairn* and a wraith—or more rarely, a wraith and a banshee—had powerful magic that could be worked in all *riocht*, but their childhoods were often difficult. Lonely and painful.

Tresara smiled at her best friend bravely. "Wonder what's going on. Wasn't she just here yesterday?"

Evangeline was pretty certain Tresara saw more of her mother when she was at Evangeline's house. Tresara and her father shared a house with Lara, but she had lost interest in both her child and *ceile* not long after Tresara was born. Having an offspring, especially a banshee, was valuable, but raising a child wasn't in a wraith's nature. Tresara was in an unusual situation for a banshee: most had wraith fathers who were uninterested in them, and *hairn* mothers who raised them communally with other *hairn* mothers and their banshee offspring.

"She's been here every day this week," Evangeline confirmed. "When was the last time she was home?"

"We aren't really her home and she can't make herself love us either. This is why I come to your house." Tresara smiled.

"My parents are happy to have you, you know that. But now that you're apprentice to *Saoi* Halloran and not around so much it's probably hard on your dad."

Tresara shrugged. "Probably. But he won't say it. He's too busy trying to make my life all normal and be both parents. He forgets I'm half-wraith, I think. I don't require his parental coddling."

"No, he doesn't." Evangeline shook her head. "He just doesn't know what else to do. He's like my mom. All the politics aren't his thing. Probably my dad and your mom should have been *ceile*."

"Your *dad* loves you, Lenny."

Evangeline shrugged. "Probably."

She laughed, allowing the similarities of their reactions to lay between them. She felt the tears prickle, and swiped at them impatiently. This was where her complete otherness—to her friends, her family, the very *riocht* around her—jumped out in stark contrast. Human tears. Tresara became suddenly enthralled with the blades of grass clinging to her skirt, avoiding Evangeline's emotions.

"Sorry," Evangeline muttered, trying to gain control of her runaway tear ducts. "Where's Igby?" she asked, searching for a change of subject. "I thought we were going to market."

"Coming up the path."

Tresara pointed.

Elbhlin O'Brien appeared around the corner seconds after Tresara's announcement. Igby smiled and waved to them. "Am I late?" she called.

"What else is new?" Evangeline asked, standing up and clapping wet grass from her skirt. The three girls stood together in a loose circle, Tresara still gazing a little absently at the house, a wrinkle of concentration knitting between her eyes.

"You ready?" Igby jostled her friend's shoulder with her own.

"Yeah, let's go."

They started down the path toward the town center and market, chattering happily.

Evangeline didn't remember *Talam,* the realm of her birth, where humans like her were born without inherent magic, whose skin didn't have colorful hues and magical markings that came and went. It was there that her parents had found her when she was only weeks old. Cold and crying, wrapped in a homemade blanket, resting right at the crossroads of the *riocht* on a powerful ley line. She'd been told her human parents couldn't have known where they were leaving her, or that someone would find the child they'd left to the elements and the predators in the woods. Surely, they had not intended Evangeline to make it through the night.

But her parents, her adopted species, *had* found her. Evangeline's mother had not been able to bear a *hairn* child, so Evangeline was a gift, if only she could survive the magic of *Scath*. No other human lived in *Scath*. She'd grown up safely and happily, and while her friends learned to control their magic, earned their *rian*, Evangeline, with no inherent magic of her own, studied the history of the *Hairn*, becoming a scholar and keeper of the history of her adopted world. She knew the differences as well as the similarities between the *riocht* where she was raised and the one where she was born. Most flora and fauna existed in all *riocht*, like the birch trees that lined the path. But the magic was where the *riocht* were clearly different. While humans like Evangeline could learn to use and control small skills, the gift of magic was a birthright only granted to the creatures born of the *riocht*. *Talam* was unique in that no creatures born there could claim magical heritage. "What are we looking for today?" Igby asked. She pulled on a young branch of one of the birches as they passed, denuding it in one smooth movement and coming away with the leaves in her palm.

"I have a list," Evangeline said. "Mom's out of most of her cabinet. And I want to see the totems. They should all be new today—the moon changed since we were there last."

Igby picked at the leaves in her hand, shredding them efficiently and arranging them methodically along her hand and halfway up her arm. Evangeline couldn't tell what was holding them to her friend's skin.

Footsteps ahead of them on the path drew Evangeline's attention from the leaf bits and toward the approaching figures. The fog and mist were thick today, making it impossible for her to distinguish anything but two faint outlines. She peered into the haze, eyes straining.

"It's Locke and Linus," Tresara said.

"Oh!" Igby immediately dropped the birch's remains and rubbed her shirt vigorously over her arm, scrubbing away dirt and leaves. She ran her fingers through her hair and stood up to her full *hairn* height, a few inches taller than her human and banshee friends. Evangeline was sure Igby wasn't aware of the way she changed when she heard Linus's name, but without fail, every time the boy was within visual distance, Igby preened like a decorative bird.

It was on Evangeline's tongue to chide her friend, but the fog parted and the boys were inside their clearing.

"Hi!" Igby said, addressing only Linus.

"Hey, Igby." He smiled, shy and sweet, and then made eye contact with the other girls. "Tresara. Lenny. Going to market?"

"New totems today!" Igby announced, unnecessarily loud.

Tresara barked a laugh, and Evangeline gave her a sharp elbow to the ribs. Igby had never really had a crush before, and as her best friends, they shouldn't make fun.

"We'll walk with you," Locke said, watching Evangeline carefully. "The path's murky today, better to not walk it alone." He moved to stand beside Evangeline, slightly behind her, hovering, protective.

"We're not alone!" Tresara protested. "There's three of us. One more than there are of you, I might add, *ceathar*."

Locke leveled a stare at her, Tresara returned it, with interest— sometimes her wraith heritage was very apparent. She didn't back down. Not even from Lachlan MacNair, who, for all intents and purposes, was banshee royalty. He was also her *ceathar*—their wraith parents were siblings—which was probably why she didn't see him as the rest of the community did.

Evangeline saw him differently, as well. He was taller

than she, though only by about half a head. His skin was the shimmering blue of the banshee instead of the semi-transparent green of the *sheehairn*. She often found herself comparing the skin tones of her friends and family to her own. Really, they were not so different. The sheen on the skin of the *hairn* was not opaque; you could see through their veils to the flesh beneath. Evangeline thought it was beautiful, often she'd wished that color floated on top of her skin. Her own flatly pale flesh didn't shimmer in the light.

But mostly when she looked at Locke, she saw the boy her parents had promised her hand to. In one and a half moon cycles, this man standing on the path with them would be her *ceile*.

The square, home of storefront shops and street vendors with their totems, potions, weapons, and foods, was always bustling during market hours. Today it was downright crowded. When they'd arrived from the relative quiet of the path, Evangeline and her friends had split up to make the shopping easier. She finished her shopping quicker than her friends and decided to stroll the traveling vendors' area. A small table with no tent to protect it caught her eye, its metal wares reflecting the light. She held the parcel that contained her mother's potion ingredients in one hand and she scanned all the objects laying on the bare wood. In the center of the table, one caught her eye. Evangeline fingered the totem carefully. She picked it up, the small round object much heavier than she'd expected, and weighed it carefully in the palm of her hand. She ran her index finger along the symbol etched on its face. It wasn't one she knew immediately. The stone was silver in color, but Evangeline wasn't sure what metal it was made from. It remained cool, even cradled in her hand.

She pulled at the small pouch that rested at her hip, with its cord across her chest. The vendor noticed the gesture and reached out to stop her. When she looked up at him, the kind-faced *hairn* shook his head. He closed her fingers around the sphere and leaned in close to her ear.

"Take it," he insisted. "A protection totem is more powerful when it is given rather than bartered."

Evangeline smiled at the man. He'd always been kind to her, slipped her little presents, a small snack, a charm doll, just trinkets to make her giggle.

"Thank you," she said quietly, sensing from his discretion that he didn't want anyone else to know about the gift.

He winked. "Keep it close to you."

She nodded and placed it inside her pouch. When she turned to leave, Locke was at her side. "Where did you come from?" she asked.

"The knife man."

Evangeline was used to his *hairn* ability to appear out of nowhere. The knife maker was on the other side of the market, but *hairn* and banshee often moved faster than Evangeline's eyes could follow. When Evangeline had asked about it as a young child, her mother had assured her that they didn't dematerialize and they couldn't fly. Sometimes, Evangeline still wondered.

Locked pulled a small dagger from a sheath and ran a finger along the blade, then tipped it toward her for a slightly better view. Evangeline wasn't sure what to say to him. More and more often of late she found this to be the case.

She'd known him her whole life, and their betrothal had been cemented on her fifth birthday, so Evangeline had no reason to be shy around him. And yet, with time racing toward the union, she found herself tongue tied and unable to meet Locke's eyes. Locke didn't seem to experience the same discomfort. If anything, his behavior toward Evangeline had become more comfortable and familiar.

Now she focused on the short, blunt blade he was offering for her inspection, hoping he wouldn't notice that she couldn't look him in the face. "What's on the handle?"

The construction and quality of the blade being much more significant to Locke, she wasn't surprised that he hadn't noticed.

"I can't make it out." He offered the knife to her. "You're the expert, what do you think it says?"

Evangeline took the knife from him, trying not to notice the shiver that traveled up her arm as their fingers brushed against each other, and read the inscription. It wasn't phrasing she was familiar with, but she recognized some of the symbols.

She pointed to one. "This means wraith magic, which would mean worked from the power of death or sacrifice. Nothing unusual about that on a weapon. But this one is strange. It's a symbol that usually means *Talam*. But wraiths have no magic in that *riocht*, not even a corporeal form, so there's no reason to use the two together. A wraith wouldn't be able to wield a sacrificial blade in *Talam*, or call upon its magic." Evangeline shrugged and handed it back to Locke. "Hope you didn't pay much."

Locke returned it to its sheath and slipped it into a pocket of his jacket, and then he slipped an arm around Evangeline. She liked it when he did this. It always made her feel safe. And strangely proud. Evangeline was used to being treated with respect, even honor, but she was a human and she had no magic. As she'd grown, her feeling of isolation from the *hairn* had increased, and her desire to truly belong to the race intensified. In Locke, and in the union with him, she would truly be *hairn*. Not a stray, accepted and raised by a kindly mother, but the daughter of Arawn and Ciarda Wicklow, *ceile* of Lachlan MacNair, heir to the seat of the Banshee leader. Then she would be as close to native as she could ever hope to become. She would have pride of place in *Scath*, and she would be entitled to a say in important decisions.

She smiled up at Lachlan, wondering, as she often did, if he would have picked her on his own. It was an unnecessary mental path to follow. With Lachlan's regal birth, the chances he would ever have been allowed to choose his own *ceile* were very slim. But it mattered to her somehow that he didn't feel stuck with her.

These thoughts and fears were no small part of the reason she felt so awkward around him recently. When their union had been a vague idea, somewhere far in the future, their friendship was free to blossom naturally. Now she belonged to him, he to her, and she couldn't help but worry that he wasn't satisfied with his obligation to be her *ceile*. He was always polite to her, always behaved as was proper to their situation—particularly, as now, when there were eyes all around—but Evangeline always wondered if he was truly pleased with their match.

On her part, aside from the fact that their marriage would make her legitimate, she wondered if *she* was happy with the match. She'd always known Locke, grown accustomed to the idea that he was hers, and because of that, she'd never really been able to decipher her feelings for him.

She supposed it was something they would have to sort out together. They would have a lifetime to work out how they felt, and where they fit in each other's hearts. But Evangeline wanted to know before they were tied.

All she had to do was work up the nerve to ask him.

CHAPTER

THREE

"Okay, just a few more…Oof! Peyton!" Paxton glared at his sister around both the door frame and the end of the couch he was holding. "Maybe you could watch where you're going?"

Instead, Peyton dropped her end. "There," she said, and made the universal *this is no longer my problem* sign of dusting her hands against each other.

"Peyton!" Shifty protested, but Peyton had already disappeared into the kitchen. The sounds of the refrigerator door and then the crack, hiss of a bottle opening.

"That's *my* beer!" Paxton yelled, voice strained under the increased weight of his end of the couch.

"We still have class!" Shifty added. She maneuvered from the middle of the couch to reclaim Peyton's abandoned end and made eye contact with Paxton across the expanse. "Where to, boss?"

Paxton jutted his chin to the last piece of open space on the living room floor. "If we can swing it around through the door, we can put it there."

It took a bit of maneuvering, but they got around the doorway and over the boxes—some piled four high. Just as Shifty was sure her fingers were going to release their dubious hold on her end, they dropped it with an unceremonious crash into its designated place. Before either of them could shake out their hands or relax their shoulders, Peyton was stretched across its length, her primly crossed ankles resting on one of its arms, her beer dangling from the fingers of her right hand, which was hanging off the side of the couch. Her other arm was bent behind her head. She played with her light brown hair. The teal streak in her bangs was the only thing that indicated she had exerted any energy in the move at all—the hair was still plastered to her forehead with rapidly drying sweat. "Freedom feels good on me." She beamed at Shifty and Paxton, apparently oblivious to their indignant glares.

"Don't get too comfortable, Nelson Mandela. We've gotta be on campus in twenty-five minutes."

Peyton took a long draw on her beer bottle. "Do I really need to go to orientation, Shifty? I mean, is there much you can't fill me in on? Aren't you an old hat yet? If you can't show me the ropes two years into your matriculation, you really are just a dumb jock."

Shifty ignored her, but Paxton decided to be offended on his girlfriend's behalf. "Her scholarship is academic, not athletic, and you damn well know it. If you want to slack off, be my guest. There's plenty of cleaning and unpacking to do while Shifty is on the mat and I'm stocking the latest delivery at the shop."

"When did you turn six hundred and three?" Peyton asked, but she sat up and set her beer atop a nearby box. "Fiiiiiinnne, let's go." She was on her feet and at the door, and hoisting her backpack onto one shoulder before Shifty had enough time or mental energy to process her change of mood, though anyone who spent more than a day with Peyton became used to her mosquito-like focus. Shifty patted the front pocket of her jeans to reassure herself she had her car keys. She kissed Paxton on the cheek on her way to her own messenger bag.

"When are you off today?" she asked him. "I've got that

thing off campus after practice, so Peyton's going to take the bus home, but I shouldn't be later than seven."

Paxton was a manager at his parents' holistic health shop. He was senior to three part-time teenage employees, and junior to both his parents. As with many family-run businesses, the hours could be erratic. "I'll beat you home, but not by much. Tuesday is closing tonight, but there's still plenty to do before I can duck out. Go easy on yourself at practice, huh? You've exerted yourself enough today, thanks to my useless sister."

"Just doing my part to keep her fit and competition-ready."

"I appreciate that; you're always thinking of me." Shifty slung an arm around Peyton's shoulder and the girls headed out the door, waving a last farewell to Paxton before swinging the door shut with a definitive slam.

Peyton had gotten over her couch potato tendencies by the time they reached the street, and was positively quivering with first day college jitters when she slid onto the passenger seat of Shifty's car. "What 'thing' have you got after practice?"

Shifty, well, shifted in her seat, adjusted the volume on the radio and cracked her window. "Um…doctor's appointment."

"Isn't the student clinic on campus? I don't mind waiting for you."

"Yeah, I'm not going to the clinic."

"Why? If it's free, it's in our budget."

The volume needed adjusting again, and the wind was suddenly much too strong, Shifty changed both things again. "I, uh, am not, uh, comfortable with their OB-GYN intern, I find him to be…"

"Oh. Gotcha. The female nurse in the room isn't enough to balance out the creep factor?" Peyton nodded knowingly.

"Right. It's worth it to me to pay out of pocket." Shifty smiled, relieved to be free of the topic. "You excited?"

Peyton nodded. "I am, I don't feel so new, though. I've

been here so much with you the last two years, I feel like I at least know my way around. Now, if I'm ready for the academic road? I don't know so much about that." She made a short, nervous almost-laugh noise and her eyebrows disappeared into her bangs, a facial expression that Shifty recognized as a plea for reassurance. She touched Peyton's shoulder.

"You'll be fine. Seacrest certainly prepared me for the workload. And Mr. Smythe's history class taught me how to sleep in lecture without getting caught. Just make sure you have the recorder set on your phone. Also, wait, you snore, maybe you better not try it."

Peyton's jaw dropped in outrage. "I do not snore!"

"Right, I forgot, Paxton snores. You drool."

"Just so long as we got that sorted out."

~

Shifty finished her last pass on the mat with a flawless round off, back handspring, back flip, front flip. She stuck the landing; her legs didn't even waver beneath her.

"Nice yo-yo, Gilbert." Coach Hennessy said, and tossed a towel at her. "You're dismissed."

Shifty ran the towel across her forehead and over her eyes before draping it around her neck. "Thanks, Coach."

She headed into the dressing room, grabbing a bottle of water from the cooler next to the mat on her way. In the empty room, she cracked the seal on the bottle and downed half the liquid before heading into the shower.

She didn't have enough time to shower and make it to Dr. Miller's on time, but she also didn't want to arrive sweaty and smelly to her third appointment with the psychiatrist who'd already diagnosed her with a multitude of body image issues.

She shed her clothing as she let the water go from tepid to mildly warm—the showers didn't go all the way to hot— stepped into the stream and quickly lathered her hair and skin. As always, she kept her eyes shut while she bathed. In the shower, the discoloration was always worse. Soap suds seemed to reveal the light green sheen that Dr. Miller assured her wasn't there. If she didn't look, she could honestly tell her doctor that she didn't see it anymore. The cocktail of pills she'd been sneaking at breakfast, noon, dinner, and bedtime had kept the hallucinations at bay.

She batted at the wall until she found the water control, turned it swiftly. The water went briefly icy before the flow stopped completely and Shifty opened her eyes again. She enfolded herself in a towel and hurried to her locker, where she ran through the combination with a practiced hand.

Sitting on the bench in front of her locker, she was reaching for her clothing when something caught at the corner of her vision. She swiped at the spot on her leg, expecting whatever was there to leave her skin and end up on the ground. Nothing happened. She turned her full attention to her leg. At her knee joint, her right leg took an impossible, unnatural turn. It twisted out at a forty-five degree angle and was propped next to her on the bench. The position of her foot, her toes pointed to the wall behind her was a posture even a double-jointed person should not have been able to assume, and Shifty, despite her amazing flexibility, was not double-jointed.

She stared at her leg. How had it even gotten there? Why hadn't she felt it when it twisted to make it onto the bench? A muscle should have stretched, something should have popped, made *some* kind of noise, but when she'd sat down, the movement had felt as natural as walking. Even now, looking at her body in this impossible position, she didn't feel anything amiss. Her body was completely relaxed, one hundred percent comfortable in the awkward pose.

As if in response to her attention, the color began to swirl.

The opalescent green started at her toes and curled to her knee in slow, lazy circles.

Shifty jumped to her feet and screamed, shaking her leg as if to work out a kink. She closed her eyes tightly and clapped her hands over her mouth. The leg was unharmed, she knew, as she was now jumping on both feet trying to convince herself her body was normal.

"Gilbert!" A voice called from the doorway of the dressing room. "Gilbert? Are you okay in there?" Coach Hennessy sounded only a couple of seconds away from entering the room to make sure she wasn't being attacked.

Naked and hopping up and down on two mismatched legs was not how she wanted her gymnastics coach to find her. "Fine! Sorry. Spider…Really big, scary spider!" It was a lame comeback, but it had been the first thing that sprung into her mind. She silently mimed banging her head against her locker in frustration.

Coach Hennessy muttered something she was sure had to do with her constitution, but he didn't come in to make sure her honor was still intact. Shifty, relieved, looked down at herself again. Her legs were both flesh-colored now. She sighed in relief and carefully sat back down on the bench. When she tried to recreate the strange leg placement, she only got about halfway before her muscles groaned in protest.

"You're cracking up, Gilbert," she whispered. She dressed quickly and darted for her car.

CHAPTER

FOUR

Arawn Wicklow sat the head of the table, with his *ceile*, Ciarda. He stood and evaluated the others seated before him to ensure he had their full attention. They wore the solemn faces of soldiers and for several moments none of them spoke.

Finally, Arawn cleared his throat. He stood, his imposing six-and-a-half foot frame throwing a shadow over the others. Arawn was not a calming force on the best of days, and this was not the best of days.

He knew he could trust Lara Keelin and Cecil MacNair to reinforce his wishes. Once their plans were complete, the wraiths' rewards would be arguably the greatest. Though a banshee, Katarin MacNair would be loyal to this until the end. Her devotion to her *ceile* was unrivaled, and her desire for pride of place for her son ensured her compliance even if her conscience did twinge occasionally.

There was much to prepare, and keeping his *ceile* was in the front of Arawn's mind. There had been nothing else to do but let her become attached to the child, but now the time was drawing a close and he feared she might not have the strength for what must be done.

That Ciarda was touched by elemental spirit was one of the reasons he'd been pleased with her at their *aontuet*, and one of the reasons he'd come to love her eventually—her softness, the way she had with creatures, both living and dead, animal and plant. But she had proved to have little stomach for the wraiths, their magic, and the way his goals must be accomplished. If not for his insistence, and her loyalty to the *riocht*, she would have long ago abandoned the plans of this council.

It wasn't that Arawn wasn't fond of the girl. He was. She lived in their home, sat at the place of honor at their table, was respected within their community. He taught her to walk, helped her learn their histories, to write their spells, and had given her a path in their world. This was not an easy walk for him to take either, but they'd known from the beginning it was inevitable. Once Evangeline had survived the exchange, as the others had not, her fate thereafter had never been in question.

Letting the thoughts twist away from his mind like so much smoke, he placed a hand on Ciarda's shoulder. She didn't meet his eye, though he hadn't expected she would.

"Lara, Cecil, are the wraiths prepared?" When he finally spoke, his voice was quiet but firm; in control.

"Of course." It was Cecil who answered. From his pocket he pulled a small packet tied with a long red frond, and placed it on the table in front of him. Lara silently placed a similar bundle before herself.

Ciarda collected the parcels and placed them in the center of the table. She looked to Arawn, and probably he was the only one to notice the tremor in her hand, the weakness behind her eyes. He passed the packet they'd prepared the night before to her and allowed their fingers to touch, hoping to at least settle her.

He started the incantation, and Ciarda spread the contents of Lara's pouch, then their own, and finally Cecil and Katarin's. She made three close concentric circles, careful not to let the lines cross. Lara and Cecil's chant was rougher and brought a chill around them, making the very air around the table take on an icy blue color. Katarin's keening was the last voice to be added to the ceremony. It had a heartbreaking beauty, and sang of loss and pain.

Arawn knew if anything would make Ciarda break, it would be the banshee's keen, and he paid careful attention to her hands as she created the flame. The outer circle went alight in a bright red flash, running its circumference in an almost angry urgency to complete the course. On its heels, the middle circle flared, orange and lazy, completing its run in twice the first flame's time.

Finally, the inner circle ignited, a high, yellow, transparent wall of almost solid flame. Unlike the other circles, it didn't dissipate as it traveled. Instead, the circle complete, the yellow flame wall reached higher, toward the trees, its crackle joining the voices calling their desires into the night.

Arawn's voice was the first to drop out of the magical symphony. He sat back in his chair, staring into the flame, unable to see the other members of the circle through its brilliance. He heard Lara's voice cease, and then Cecil's, until only the banshee's keening remained holding the flame in place. It seemed to last hours, the high, cold sound, and the bright intensity of the fire, tugging at each other, entering the dark of the sky, overlapping and changing, pulling from the air the might of their will. The icy blue of the dome that encompassed the table flared suddenly purple and shattered. Arawn heard Ciarda's sharp intake of breath as the air whooshed around them, hot and menacing, lifting her hair and the fabric of her shawl. He felt it as well, crawling invasively down the back of his neck. There was something obscene in its touch against his skin. With some effort he quelled the desire to pull his wife from the circle to keep its tendrils from her flesh.

The fire wall finally separated from the table, and as if sucked upward, flew into the night where it extinguished completely.

Katarin's voice ceased and she fell into her chair with a

pained shudder, hair wet and clinging to her face and neck like a strange and awful filigree. Her eyes remained closed, her breathing ragged.

With the air in front of them finally clear, the others stared at the banshee. Just when Arawn was sure she'd been injured by the ritual, her eyes opened. They were bright, though not with pleasure, and she drew a cleansing breath.

"I hope we know what we're doing, for it is done now. The door has been opened, our offering accepted, and I will damn all of *Scath* if we are not successful this time."

Ciarda's resolve apparently could take no more, for she let out a sob and then a sharp cry, and before they knew or could react, she'd run for the house.

"Arawn," Lara's rebuke was swift, her tone harsh, full of warning.

Arawn held up a hand, without need. Lara's single word was all she meant to speak. "Yes. You have no concern, Lara. Ciarda knows what is at stake, and what must be done."

Cecil, now at his *ceile's* arm, pushing aside her slick hair, looked at Arawn and Lara. "It isn't as if she will no longer have a daughter. Surely she must have missed Siofra. Doesn't the thought of her return lessen the loss?"

Katarin placed a hand on her *ceile's* wrist to still his hand, and forced him to make eye contact with her. Only Katarin had the ability to reach the wraith's understanding of things loving and familial, especially when magic or power was at stake. She held his gaze for many heartbeats, and much must have passed between them unsaid, for finally he dropped his eyes, face slightly softened.

"She's sacrificed much, and we ask her to do it again. I will try to be more understanding of the weight that such a thing has for a *sheehairn*."

CHAPTER

FIVE

Shifty made it to the parking lot in record time and vaulted the stairs leading to Dr. Miller's office with seconds to spare.

"Sorry, sorry." She headed for her regular seat and dropped into it, still breathing heavily.

Dr. Miller sat in her own chair, the very picture of calm. She allowed her mouth to quirk up slightly at the sides. "Not a problem. Glad you made it, Shifty. How was practice?"

"Good. Thanks." Shifty picked at the corner of her fingernail. She didn't have a problem with Dr. Miller personally. In their first two meetings, Shifty had found her kinder and less judgmental than expected. No, it was the need for therapy at all that she still objected to, even though she knew that the decision to seek out a sounding board was the only thing that had kept her from going completely around the bend. Finally admitting to someone that she feared she was insane—her hallucinations, her improbable body—had not been the freeing experience she'd thought it would be. In her mind, once she told someone about the shimmering green sausage casing she saw over her pale skin; that her straight blonde hair was actually a mass of curls that were a blinding orange color with purple streaks; that her already gyroscope-like joints could practically double back against themselves, it would become someone else's burden. Like magic. Once unloaded, she would stop seeing these things.

It hadn't exactly worked that way. Instead in the two sessions she'd endured, she'd been constantly asked to talk about these things she saw when she looked in the mirror, and reminded that they were not real. She'd been handed prescription upon prescription of medications the doctor said would keep her "hallucinations"—*Hallucinations! Body Dysmorphic Disorder! Lithium!* Words that practically had the exclamation points and capital letters in their very pronunciation—at bay; keep her "normal." Normal was another word that had a special pronunciation: italics, with an asterisk leading you to an explanation that *normal** was different for everyone, and that was "okay."

"You have a meet on Sunday. Do you feel prepared?"

"Sure." Shifty picked up a wind-up toy from the table and turned its key a few times before setting it down again. She watched as the monkey performed three wobbly backflips, and smiled. "He doesn't exactly stick the landings. I'd give him a seven-three."

"Shifty," Dr. Miller warned.

"I know, I know. I'm creating a barrier. What do you want me to talk about?"

"What do you want to talk about?"

Shifty sighed. "Nothing. I don't want to be here, remember? I feel fine, not crazy at all."

"Can you tell me what you saw when you looked in the mirror this morning?"

Shifty knew the drill. "I'm a perfectly normal, healthy looking twenty-year-old girl. There are no strange colors on my skin, my eyes are blue, my joints are all in the right place, and my hair is blonde, though if my coach would allow it, it would be all kinds of violet."

Dr. Miller nodded, ignoring Shifty's confrontational tone. "And your medications? You're taking them regularly?"

Shifty held up a hand. "Right along with my vitamins. I promise."

"The side effects?"

"Ugh. Stop." Shifty moaned. "Side effects are not bad anymore. Sometimes I get headaches, but no more puking. Really, how much longer do I have to keep coming here every other week? It isn't like I've threatened to off myself!"

"Body dysmorphic disorder is a form of self-harm, Siofra. Looking at your perfectly normal, healthy body and seeing yourself as a monster is—"

"Psychotic. Yeah, I know. I've been told." Shifty reached into the pocket of her hoodie and produced a small plastic box. It held several doses of her medications and vitamins. She shook it at her doctor. "Anti-psychotics right here. Not like I can forget."

"Well, this is going swimmingly. So glad your attitude toward treatment has improved." Dr. Miller's tone was even, but there was a calm threat in her voice. Even though it was only their third session, Shifty already recognized the tone. It meant "impress me, or I'll recommend to the authorities and/or your parents that you might be a threat to yourself." Which would land her in the local psych ward for at least seventy-two hours, alert her already overprotective parents and probably her best friend and boyfriend that she was insane, and most likely get her booted not only from her team, but kill her scholarship as well.

Shifty straightened in her seat. Proper posture always impressed authority figures, and Shifty's gymnast posture was better than most her age. "I've had a long day. Sorry, okay? I'm worried about the meet, and I think Mom's about to go all mental about Pax now that we're in the same bedroom. Perfectly normal young adult drama, not of the loony toon variety. On the upside, we are all moved into the apartment, which is all kinds of awesome. I have keys to my own apartment!"

"Why are you concerned your mother will suddenly begin to find Pax inappropriate?" Dr. Miller picked the one subject Shifty hadn't wanted to talk about. Talking about her relationship to her doctor—the adult parts of her relationship, anyway—still made her insides feel wobbly. Not the most mature reaction, and sure not to ensure Dr. Miller she was handling her latest steps into the real world in a proper manner.

"Well, see, there's these things boys have—they're called penises—and my mother would prefer I not have anything to do with them. So I don't think it's Pax she has a problem with so much as his appendage."

"So, does she believe that though you have moved in with Paxton, you are not having intercourse with him? We haven't actually addressed this. Are you having intercourse with him?"

Shifty stared at Dr. Miller in abject horror. "Seriously? That's none of your business."

Dr. Miller raised an eyebrow. "It's perfect natural, normal and healthy, Shifty. And I would take it further and ask you how you view your body during—"

"Still," Shifty said loudly, a hand involuntarily lifted in front of her chest like a shield, "none of your business! Sorry. Private. Off limits. Safe word. Or whatever!"

"I see. Okay, we can leave that for a future session when our trust has been better established."

"Or not," Shifty whispered.

If she heard it, Dr. Miller didn't think it important enough to pursue. "I see." She smiled, her eyes twinkling suddenly. "Well, I assume you are being careful?"

Shifty's mouth opened and closed under its own power a couple of times before she managed to level her gaze at Dr. Miller. "Yes. Happy?"

"Content, at least."

∼

Twenty minutes later, Shifty pulled the door to Dr. Miller's office closed behind her and looked over her shoulder to make sure no one saw her toss the appointment reminder card into the plant-topped trashcan in the hallway. She hadn't forgotten an appointment yet, and didn't want the card falling out of her pocket to be discovered. Finding a place to tuck her medications was already occupying more of her worry quota than she cared to admit to herself.

She'd sought out Dr. Miller's counsel knowing she was at a pretty serious mental crossroads. She wasn't sure she could remember ever not being aware that she moved differently than her peers, and more importantly, it had never bothered her. Her speed and grace had been cause for praise. By the time she was nine, she was practicing gymnastics with the college team, unofficially, and competing at a national level. There was talk of the Olympics.

The Olympics talk brought with it a difficult dose of reality. Relocation—for Shifty, and most likely her family—far from her childhood home. Living full time with a coach, being removed from regular school, and separating her from the only two friends she'd ever truly bonded with.

It was during these discussions that her skin turned green for the first time. Shifty, extremely self-possessed for an almost-ten-year-old, had known this was not a fact she planned to share with her parents, her friends, teachers or coach. "I see green on my skin" and soon "my hair is orange, except for the purple stripes" became things she would scream inside her own head in an effort not to share the truth with others.

Her parents, not at all eager to send their little girl off to live a life away from them, unwilling to allow her coach to become her *de facto* parent, had been relieved when Shifty, too, expressed no interest in training to be an Olympian. As long as she had a mat, a beam, and a set of uneven parallel bars, she was content to let other gymnasts earn the medals. The feeling of freedom she felt sticking the landing from a dismount, the lift of air under her when she made a particularly high pass on the mat: this was all she required from gymnastics. The gym was where the colors on her skin and hair didn't matter, where she felt most in touch with her core.

When she was fifteen, she was so used to ignoring the strange things she saw on her skin that she could apply eye make-up without a mirror. She liked the still pictures her mother produced. She never saw the strange colors in them. The shower had brought a new curse right around her sixteenth birthday: sometimes, when her skin was wet, an ornate, opalescent white pattern appeared to wrap its way around her ankle and up her calf.

In the four years since that time, the patterns had been few and far between, but the patches of green shimmer on her flesh, and the stripes of purple in her hair increased in her peripheral vision. Worse, when she wasn't able to resist looking at her reflection in the mirror or staring full-on at her skin, they remained.

And she pushed it all down. Threw herself into school and gymnastics, made sure that in every outward way, she was the perfect child. If she could do that, they'd never guess she was crazy.

But, when she and the Devlins had decided to get an apartment, she knew she had to do something about the visions. She would not be able to hide her worry from Paxton. He was too tuned into her emotions, too watchful. Too much of a worrywart. And aside from Paxton, if she was going to be an autonomous adult, wasn't it time to take matters into her own hands? Admit she was facing something she didn't know how to fix on her own, and ask for help? If she wasn't willing to tell anyone else in her life about her trial, at least she could try to defeat it before it drove her over the edge.

Enter Dr. Miller and her prescription pads, the pills bringing with them a whole host of new issues she'd had to disguise for her family. The headaches started first, light sensitivity followed quickly on their heels, and vomiting completed the trifecta. Then Dr. Miller had added Lithium on top of the anti-depressants, bringing with it a stiffness in Shifty's joints that she'd never experienced, and a body jarring weariness. That was as close to calling off the treatment as Shifty had come. Was being free of the colors really worth giving up the only thing that made her feel completely normal and in total control of her every move and thought?

Dr. Miller adjusted the medications, until her body and the chemicals had come to a mutual understanding. A tentative peace treaty between mind and body, and the side effects had ebbed. There was the occasional bout of stomach clenching nausea or blinding headache, but they were less and less often, and their duration endurable.

Shifty pushed open the door and released herself from the office into the glorious sunny day. The salt in the air was thick and caused an instant swell in Shifty's mood; a swell that made her want to blow off any other responsibilities, call Paxton, and retreat to their favorite corner of the beach.

She was halfway to her car when she noticed him. He was leaning against her car, arms loosely folded across his chest, sunglasses pointed heavenward, apparently lost in the sun's rays. She suppressed her first instincts, to smile and run to meet him. What was he doing here? What had she told him this morning? Where was she supposed to have been?

Keeping all the strands of her sanity intact was difficult enough. Throwing in the sticky strings of her tangled cobweb of lies, it was hard to keep her footing. Her calm inner voice started up. *Lies are easier to remember when they border the truth. You told Paxton exactly what you told Peyton: a doctor's appointment. A* girl's *doctor's appointment.* Of course he knew to track her down at the medical plaza. Nothing was out of the ordinary here.

She did increase her pace. She was happy to see him. His smoky lenses leveled at her when she was within a few feet of him. She never knew how he did that. It was as if he had a magnetic field around him tuned specifically to her, and the moment she breached it, it alerted him. He always knew when she was close, and never failed to look up and catch her eyes when she thought she was catching him in a private moment of repose. He pulled his sunglasses lower on his nose with a finger, locking eyes with her now, and grinned wickedly.

She couldn't help but return the smile, but she rolled her eyes at him. "You're gonna get busted, you know. Leaving a couple of stoned teenagers in charge of the store. Closing, no less. Your parents are so gonna fire you one of these times."

He held his arms open to her and his grin upped to devilish. "You aren't happy to see me?"

"Stalker," she mumbled, but allowed him to embrace and kiss her. "Of course I am. But paying your share of the rent and bills, not to mention your beer budget, is going to get old fast."

"Pssh," Paxton scoffed, pinching her firmly on the butt, and burying his head into her hair. "Parental affection. They can't stay mad at me for long."

Shifty stepped back, keeping both his hands in hers. She took him in. At a smidge over six feet, he had a few inches on her. His build was lanky, but deceptively solid. His sandy brown hair hung just above his bright blue eyes. But the true charm was in their twinkle, not their color. In his quick, lopsided half smile. Paxton Devlin *was* impossible to stay angry with, a fact he knew well and used with devastating effectiveness. Without a truly mean-spirited bone in his body, Pax had a quick wit, an easy laugh and a way of making everyone around him feel like he was talking specifically to them. Probably, if he put his mind to it, he could have the world at his feet. Though mostly, he only wanted Shifty. He'd made that clear from the time he was fifteen years old. She had not taken him seriously at first, barely fourteen herself. She'd been unable to take his professions of undying love and devotion with any shred of credulity for years, only realizing the seriousness of his intent, as well as her own feelings for him, right around her eighteenth birthday.

From the moment she'd allowed him to kiss her under the veil of the moon in her backyard, she'd lost all reservations and fallen completely in love with the boy next door, the boy who'd been her best friend as long as she could remember.

Now she quirked her head at him in a considering manner before allowing a full-fledged grin to spread across her face. "Probably not. I can't. I love you, Paxton Devlin."

He shifted slightly, so that his forehead touched hers. "Oh, say it again, it keeps me awake."

"I love you," Shifty said.

"I love you, too. Are you going to let me drive to the beach?"

She kissed him quickly on the tip of his nose and jumped away from him, holding her keys over her head. "Not a chance in hell! And what makes you think I'm going anywhere with you, delinquent?"

Moving faster than she'd expected—usually she was able to evade people, especially when she had the jump on them—he caught her around the middle with the tips of his fingers, and shoring up his grip, pulled her back against him. He pressed his face into her neck, his breath on her skin making it prickle, and his voice was low and husky when he spoke. "Cause I know this little corner away from the wind, and I know there's a sleeping bag in the trunk of this car, and I know it has been more than thirty hours since I've had you alone."

"I'm in training, meet on Sunday." She squirmed just a fraction of an inch away from him.

He redoubled his grip. "That's an old wives' tale," he growled.

She sagged against him, resigned. "Probably. I'm driving. And if we're not home by dark your sister will have the state patrol out looking for us, just for the pure thrill of being a pain in the ass."

"I'll be really quick. Promise." He launched himself over the trunk of the car and was at the passenger door before she could press the button to unlock it.

"Oh. Great. Stunning endorsement."

CHAPTER

SIX

Evangeline watched Igby fiddle with the dial on the face of her radio. Snippets of *In the Mood* and *It Don't Mean a Thing* streamed into the room and were quickly dismissed. Igby's brow furrowed, and Tresara looked up from the pages of the magazine she was flipping through on Evangeline's bed. "Need help?"

"No!" Igby snapped. Her ability to find the sweet spot was a matter of pride. "I'll get it. Just hush a minute."

Linus, lounging in the corner, cracked an easy smile, winked at Locke and muttered a few words under his breath. Immediately, the radio's speaker was clear.

"*...Like we had a clue.*
Never planned that one day
I'd be losing you.
In another world..."

"You got it!" Evangeline said, and slapped Igby's hand away from the dial to prevent further tinkering.

"See? Told you." Igby sat back against the wall next to the radio, satisfied.

There were radios in just about every room of every house in *Scath*, since radio waves from *Talam* were so strong. For some reason that had never been investigated, the normal programming they intercepted was at least five decades from current. The adult members of the *riocht's* population loved the swing music and radio plays. They could be heard floating on the air at just about all hours of the day. But the younger generation found it tiresome. Much like the magazine Tresara was flipping through, more current contraband could be obtained and used in *Scath*. All it took was the right amount of magic, or in the case of items like magazines and books— tangible *Talam* items—smuggling.

Happy now with the selection coming from the speakers, Igby became quiet again. Quiet was Igby's natural state, unless nervous, when she would begin chirping out random phrases and pieces of information with a manic quality. She curled her long body next to Tresara's and lay her head against the other girl's shoulder so she could peer at the magazine. Igby's long, bright teal hair spilled over Tresara's shoulder and fell across the page she'd been reading. Igby's hair was always in the way. Evangeline joked she'd found pieces of Igby's hair growing from her own head—there was no place safe from Igby's shedding. Without comment, Tresara gathered the tresses and placed them inside the back of Igby's shirt, clearing the page for continued reading.

"Ooooh! I want one of those." Igby poked a finger at the middle of the page. The paper crinkled and bent, but didn't tear. Igby snatched her hand back. "Sorry, Lenny." Evangline's magazines were always brought to her brand new and crisp, and usually she would store them flat on her shelf to ensure they stayed that way.

"It doesn't matter." Evangeline wasn't attached to the magazines—not like her books. She was allowed pretty much unfiltered access to reading material from her home *riocht*. It was part of her research and study. Or at least that was how she'd convinced her mother. From the surreptitious way her mother would hand off the packages to her, Evangeline knew

Ciarda probably suspected that at least half the items she requested were not expressly necessary for the advancement of knowledge of *Talam's* history. Though if Evangeline ever did get to visit, she knew how to dress, and that she wanted a Ducati and a tattoo. Her friends had vibrant, beautiful swirling *rian* that appeared on their skin in elaborate filigree. Tresara's were inky black, Locke's bright red. Against the opalescent blue of their skin, it was achingly beautiful. Evangeline longed for *rian* of her own, even if hers would only be decorative.

She noticed Linus pull his sleeve down over his arm, hiding the bright blue swirl that had begun to encircle his wrist. He'd done the magic, made the radio behave, but he'd let Igby believe it was her. Evangeline smiled at him. His eyes could have been poured from molten gold, the color so bright and clear, with only small black pin pricks at their center.

Linus Rafferty was stunning. And frightening. Powerful and kind. Shy and smart. He was a strange combination of strength and meekness. He came from one of the wealthiest, most powerful families in the *riocht*. While he held himself as the eldest son of such a family should, commanding and garnering the respect and notice his position in society expected, he had no interest in political power. Like Evangeline, Linus was a scholar, a believer that true power came from knowledge. His magic had always been strong throughout their schooling. Now his impressive control over his substantial array of spells both ancient and of his own invention had ensured he was recognized as the having one of the most impressive magical arsenals of a *hairn* his age in *Scath*. He had recently been assigned several younger *hairn* and banshee students and they would be learning to cast magical spell, brew potions, and the history and politics of the *riocht* from Linus. Evangeline had heard her father telling another elder what an impressive job Linus was doing. She'd had to suppress her jealousy. While her friends were finding their place in the *riocht*, growing into members of its community, she was still kept "safe" at home, awaiting her *aontuet*.

Along with his golden eyes and the blue *rian* on his green skin, Linus had stark, black curly hair, with a few platinum curls tangled within its thick tresses. Evangeline had resisted plunging her hands into it on many occasions. Its surface was so silky and inviting, but Linus's stature didn't invite playfulness like that. He had a cool standoffishness, even amongst them, his closest friends.

The kindness he'd shown Igby, lending his magic without comment or credit, allowing her the pride of tuning the radio, touched Evangeline. It showed a fondness and understanding for Igby that Evangeline wouldn't have guessed Linus would care to possess.

Locke shut the magazine he'd been looking through with a snap and got to his feet. He opened Evangeline's window and cool air blew into the room.

"Where are your parents?" he asked, flipping himself next to Evangeline at the foot of her bed and draping an arm across the back of her shoulders. She wanted to snuggle back into him, let herself be comfortable there. By all rights it was her place. But she couldn't make herself relax, couldn't move that one extra inch closer.

"I think they are at the table with your parents and Tree's mom." She shrugged. "Something for the...ceremony." She stumbled over the last word, and suddenly the floor of her room was fascinating.

This time Locke didn't politely ignore her discomfort. He caught her chin with the crook of his finger and forced her to look at him. "I seem to have become very hard to look at recently." He smiled at her. "Is there something wrong with my face?"

She sighed, a small, nervous noise. "No. Of course not. It's..." How could she tell him?

"It's just all very real now," Locke stated.

She let out a breath that she felt like she'd been holding for a moon, and nodded. "Right."

"And that makes me hard to look at? I'm still me. You've known me all your life." His voice was low, keeping the conversation between them, beneath the music.

"I know."

"But?"

"It's all very real now, like you said." With all that was in her, she fought the instinct to look back to the floor.

He nodded, though if it was because he understood her words, or that he shared her trepidation, she wasn't sure. "We should talk about that."

"Yes," she agreed.

"When we don't have an audience."

"Yes."

"I'll come get you? We can walk the path and talk."

She smiled. "That'd be good."

His smile lit up his face, and she thought he looked as relieved as she felt. Could this be as scary for him as it was for her? As stressful and confusing? He kissed her, quickly, catching the corner of her mouth near her cheek.

"Soon," he promised her.

CHAPTER

SEVEN

"In a different world..."

Shifty killed the sound on the mp3 player at their heads and groaned. "I hate that song," she said, falling back against Paxton's chest.

He laughed. "I know you do. That's why I keep it on my playlist. You're seriously cute when you're irritated."

Her hand made a satisfying smack against his shoulder. "You're terrible and mean."

"I'm funny," he insisted, pulling her tightly against him to keep her from landing more blows. When he was certain she had no more acts of violence planned, he settled back against the makeshift pillow of their rolled up jeans and kissed the top of her head. "So, you checked out all right?"

She shifted a little in his arms and nuzzled her head into his shoulder. Her hair flopped over his chin and lips, tickling him. He blew out gently to clear it away from his mouth.

She didn't look up when she spoke to him. "What?"

"At the doctor? Everything's fine?"

"Really? You really want to talk about my appointment with my OB-GYN? Honestly?" Her voice was flat but held a hint of a smile.

"It's just..." He brushed the rest of her hair off his face, stalling to try find his words and his calm. "Well...okay.

Shifty. I'm just going to blurt this out…" but then he couldn't. He took a deep, calming breath and he felt her breath pick up against his skin. He could practically feel her heart beat against his side. "Are you pregnant?"

He felt a whoosh of air across his chest, cool and fast. The next stuttered across his flesh and he looked down at the top of her head, which was shaking.

"What?" he asked, befuddled.

"No, Paxton, I am not pregnant. And if that's why I had gone to the doctor, don't you think I would have clued you in?"

"You've been so tired. And the headaches…And, well…the vomiting…"

She looked into his face now, her own alight with amusement. "Silly, silly boy. I had the flu. We aren't going to be parents. Sometimes you should try talking to me before you let your brain take a walk down the dark paths of Fantasy Island."

Paxton smiled at her as she reached up and swept his hair out of his eyes. Then, without meaning to, he snatched her hand. The *rian* were visible. They were swirling on the surface of her pale, green skin. They were white. *White.*

He fought to keep his words calm as his mind raced. "Dark paths? Why dark? I mean not today or even the next decade probably, but it wouldn't be so bad, would it?"

She seemed to consider it, her body tensed against his. She remained perfectly still for a few seconds. "No."

Shifty moved her hand so she could draw a lazy circle near his belly button with a couple of her fingers. Pax closed his eyes, enjoying the stir of emotions, the tickle of her touch. He wanted badly to sink into the moment. But as he watched her trace designs on his skin, he was reminded of the *rian* winding about her wrist. The warmth he felt was doused by icy realization.

White. Jesus Christ. White. His teachings weren't as solid as they should have been, and he rifled through them for a memory of white *rian's* power. Orange was a strong earth and animal bond. Those *hairn* with purple or violet markings generally had a mastery with potions and totems. His mind flitted over several other colors, dismissed them, until he was sure he'd never heard mention of white…

"PAX!"

He jumped and focused his vision back on Shifty, who was laughing. "Huh?"

She ruffled his hair. "My head-in-the-clouds boy. I said, are you ready to go home?"

He wasn't. Not to their home, the home they shared. "Um, I think you better drop me at the store. I should kiss a little butt after leaving it in the hands of the kids today. I'll grab my car and swing by the folks' house to pucker up."

"I could just come with you," she offered.

"Nah, that's okay. Let's get you home. I know you've got a lit paper to finish."

She groaned. "Ugh, don't you mean start? I hate Hemingway. At least in college I'm allowed to hate him, but still." She sighed heavily. "You're correct. I do need to put in some time on that. Probably be easier if I'm home alone anyway. You're kind of distracting."

She kissed him quickly and reached for her hoodie and jeans, separating her clothing from the pile. She tossed him his pants, aiming for his head.

By the time Shifty pulled into the small parking lot behind the Tir Na Nog holistic store and parked next to his truck, the sky had turned a lovely purple. She gave him a quick peck and waved as she pulled away. He watched until her car was around the corner and counted to twenty just to ensure she wasn't coming back. He dug his keys and cell phone out of his pocket. As he unlocked his truck and pulled open the door he dialed Peyton's number.

She picked up during the first ring. "Yo, bro."

"Shifty's on her way home. ETA 15 minutes. Get out of there, meet me at the folks' house." He hung up before hearing more than a syllable of her answer. It had contained a "y" and that was all he needed to hear.

He started the truck with a shaking hand and tried to control his breathing.

It was nearly dark by the time he arrived. The fog had started to drift up the driveway. He let it play at his feet for a moment, concentrating on one specific tendril. In the distance he heard a clap of thunder and it startled him out of his meditation.

When he walked through the door he saw Peyton's backpack in the hallway. He peered to the left and saw her leg slung over the back of the sofa. It was kicking slowly in time to whatever she was listening to through her earbuds. The couch was lightly colored and her green skin stood out sharply against the fabric. Paxton sighed. He slammed the front door loudly enough to override the music in her ears. The leg stilled. As he watched, a pale flesh tone started at her toes and spread until its advancing line disappeared past the hem of her shorts. Her head popped up next to her leg. Her hair, in its chin length razor-cut mass of blunt edges, was bright aqua. Her eyes were their natural-hued purple ringed with orange. They sparkled at her brother. "Hi, Paxton."

"You aren't supposed to drop your glamour, even in the house. You know that." He let go of his jacket and it fell to the ground next to her backpack and walked into the living room.

"It's too much work," she whined mildly. But the hair faded to her "natural" color, leaving only her rebellious colorfully striped bangs to fall over her right eye. Her control over her magic was occasionally tenuous. Allowing her to change the color of her hair frequently throughout high school had been their parents' solution. No one even saw a teenager with costume-colored hair these days.

"You're just lazy."

"It's not me, Pax." She looked at him, her face hard. "Don't you miss it? Looking in the mirror and seeing yourself? Don't you want Shifty to see you?"

"She sees me." He sat down next to his sister on the couch, watching as her eyes returned to the colors that matched his own glamour and made them appear as human siblings. "Are Mother and Dad home yet? We need a family meeting."

"Yeah. I kinda got that from the 911 call. Thanks." Despite her annoyed tone, Peyton's face betrayed her intense curiosity. "What's going on?"

"Her *rian*. I saw them. Her glamour's fading."

He waited long enough for her to lift an eyebrow at him and make an impatient motion with her hand. "And?" she said. "We knew that. And we knew it might get worse. The Lithium, it's breaking down her—"

Paxton cut her off. "They're white, Peyton. Have you ever heard of that?"

She stared at him. She didn't speak, but he could see her mind moving at a frantic pace behind her eyes. Slowly, after a few moments, she shook her head. "No. At least, I don't think so. Maybe they weren't white? Maybe they were yellow? Really light? You know, from the lingering power of the glamour? You might not have seen them right—"

"He saw them correctly."

Both Peyton and Paxton jumped at the voice behind them. Their mother, Nelda Devlin, stood in the doorway. Both her children watched her, waiting for more information. But she remained closed-mouthed and grim.

"Well?" Paxton urged. "Are you going to tell us? Or are you just going to admit you know something and leave it at that?"

Their mother shuffled in the doorway for a minute. She seemed to be considering her next move. "I'll get your dad. We can talk about this."

After she left, Paxton got up and paced the room, manic energy wafting off of him. He went to the doorway, peered up the stairs, returned to the couch, sat down, sprang up, and started the entire circuit again.

"Paxton. You're making me sick. Just sit down. They'll be right back."

He didn't. He completed his odd tour of the living room three more times and was half-way through a fourth when his parents arrived. Both looked grim, but his father at least smiled. Tristan Devlin was a much more lighthearted soul than his wife.

"Sit down, Paxton," his father told him, taking his own chair. Paxton returned to his place on the couch next to his sister and waited for one of his parents to speak.

"White *rian* are, well...unusual." Tristan drew a breath before continuing. "Many times the color of *rian* will run in families, but it isn't a given that all members of a blood line will share the same magical strengths. These colors..."

"We *know* all this," Peyton said, teenage impatience thick in her voice. "Can you fast forward to the part about Shifty's white *rian*? I know for you she's a job, but for me and Pax... we *care* about her, you know?"

Nelda flinched. "It isn't that we don't care about her, Peyton. It's a difficult situation. I—"

"Whatever," Peyton cut her mother off. "I don't want to get into it with you again. Can one of you just spit it out?"

Nelda's face hardened.

Tristan cleared his throat. "White *rian* are very rare and they don't run in families. They indicate a talent that our kind calls *riochtfios*."

"And what the fresh hell is *riochtfios*?" Peyton crossed her arms and sat up straighter. "I mean, doesn't all our magic come from *Scath*?"

"No. *Riochtfios* is magic that can be used in any *riocht* and with very little restriction."

"Are you telling me Shifty could use her magic in *Sambaed*?" Paxton's voice was quiet and almost frightened. "Provided she could get there, of course."

"I'm telling you that she *could* get there. For users of *riochtfios*, *Sambaed* is accessible even before they cross over. She can travel to any *riocht*. And use its magic with total impunity."

"Wow," Peyton whispered.

"I don't like the sound of this," Paxton muttered, trying to comprehend the enormity of such power. He looked at his father, imploring him to confirm that the fears swirling in Paxton's head were unnecessary. Both his parents remained silent.

"What're you talking about?" Peyton argued. "That's amazing!"

"It puts her in more danger, moron," Paxton snapped.

"No way!" Peyton countered.

"Your brother's most correct," Nelda said, cutting to the quick. Both of them turned to her, Paxton grim and his sister confused. "Siofra's situation is perilous. There are creatures who would use her for this magic. The white *rian* also explain much of why the glamour is no longer holding for her. It's much more than the introduction of an alloyed metal into her system. *Riochtfios* is incredibly powerful. Eventually it won't be possible to hold the glamour in place without her knowledge. I'm saying we will have to tell Shifty what she is. Carefully, while we can still control what she knows and when. And sooner, rather than later."

~

She wasn't in the apartment when Paxton and Peyton returned. There was a note on the coffee table. She'd be back soon, with Thai food. She loved them both. And a hastily drawn, somewhat maniacal grinning face with her initials after it. Paxton rounded the corner to their room, flipped on the light, and threw himself dejectedly onto their bed. Peyton was on his heels, but she chose the floor instead. She sat with her back against the side of the bed and her feet sprawled out in front of her. The two of them couldn't have looked more miserable if they'd been soldiers in a foxhole.

"You've been worried. You wanted to tell her." Peyton's voice was small and careful, like she was testing the air to see if her comments would come flying back and hit her in the face.

Paxton snorted. He dealt the mattress beneath him a savage blow and Peyton's head ricocheted against the frame with the aftershock. She scowled up at him, rubbing the spot. He ignored her irritation and stared up at the ceiling as if it had just peed in his corn flakes.

"I wanted her to *know*," Paxton clarified, not at all patiently. "I didn't want to tell her."

"What's the difference?" Peyton asked.

"The difference? Seriously? In one scenario, Shifty knows what she is and we've all grown up together where we were supposed to, as we were supposed to. In the other? She becomes even more of a freak in her own mind, her parents aren't her parents, and she may or may not be in danger, and she blames me for lying to her all her life. Oh, and she has all kinds of freaky magical power she doesn't know how to control. Which one of these do you think I want for the girl I love, genius?"

"You don't have to be an asshole," Peyton muttered. "But I get your point." She grew silent, and he could feel her turning over all the rest of it in her mind; the parts Paxton wasn't talking about. *Their* part. She cleared her throat. "Pax, I love her too, you know."

Paxton flung an arm over the side of the bed and ruffled his sister's hair. "I know that, Place." He used the affectionate nickname he'd given her when they were very small children. He'd recognized Peyton's name on a novel his mother had been reading and he'd wrongly assumed his sister's full name was Peyton Place. At the moment, he wanted her to remember their history, their affection, and their bond. "She and I? It doesn't change your friendship. To my mind? It makes us all even closer. If we were home, where we could be listed for *aontuet*, Shifty would be your sister already."

"You want to marry Shifty?!" Peyton's back was ramrod straight, all the tips of her hair turned a light teal as she struggled to keep her glamour in place.

Paxton sighed. Explaining his feelings for Shifty and his ideas about where those feelings should lead seemed an insurmountable task. He'd known, *known* how he felt about Shifty since he met her. It was so much a part of him that he never questioned it. If he could have somehow allowed everyone else in his life entry into his mind for a small moment, he would, to make them see that his love for Shifty was rooted in the very base of who he was. It had never occurred to him that he wouldn't be with her.

He knew from his parents' teachings that it was common practice in his home *riocht* to arrange the marriages of the powerful families. The politics and power plays involved in the joining of families were too integral to *Scath's* survival to leave unions to the whims of the heart. When he'd first learned this, he'd been so thankful not to have been raised in *Scath*. There, he and Shifty would probably never have interacted, let alone been allowed to date.

"Yes, Peyton. I'd marry Shifty tomorrow if she'd have me."

"You're that sure?" Peyton's voice didn't sound accusatory so much as awed. A little scared by the gravity of what he'd said.

The repercussions it could carry. Her head peeked up over the edge of his bed and she gripped his hand, telegraphing comfort and support. It was another thing they weren't supposed to do in this *riocht*: magic. Even a simple exchange of internal power. But like her inability to hide her true face, Peyton couldn't stop her natural inclination to support her family.

"That sure."

Outside of the window, the sky darkened, and far in the distance there was a clap of thunder. They both jumped and looked out the glass. They exchanged guilty expressions and pulled their hands apart. "Ooops!" Peyton whispered.

"Hey, sports fans!" Shifty's call from the front of the apartment was followed by the slam of a door. The aroma of curry drifted into the bedroom. "Dinner! Hurry down, I'll get plates. Kitchen in three minutes or I'm starting without you!"

"I can hear Mom from here," Peyton whispered, her tone conspiratorial and her words hurried. "There had better be a storm coming or you two are grounded for a week! I'm turning on the weather channel right now, understood?"

Paxton, trying to shake his gloom, stood up and offered his sister a hand. "Yes, Mother. I'm sure it's just a fast moving weather front. Nothing to worry about."

Peyton tried to muffle her laugh, and it came out as a strangled snort instead. Opening his window, she hung herself half-way into the night and inhaled deeply, as if she could reabsorb the magic they'd released. Paxton leaned against the wall, echoing his sister's deep breath. The acrid smell of ozone floated on the air, a scent so connected with *Scath* for him that the very tickle of it on his nose brought to mind the tall and fragile birches on the paths, the mists around his feet as he walked. He sighed. "I want to take her there, Peyton. Show her where we come from. We can't just *tell* her. If we can take her to *Scath*, she'll feel at home. She won't be so afraid."

"You mean, she won't be so pissed."

"Fair point. You think Mother and Dad would let us sneak her into *Scath* and tell her our way? Because I have a feeling their way is just going to be an extremely large clusterfuck."

Peyton scoffed. "Not an easy sell." She was now sitting halfway out the window with her legs kicking into the darkening sky. She leaned back into the room so she could see her brother when she spoke. The posture would have been awkward without the added joints and flexible bones of the *hairn*. Paxton could practically feel Peyton's glamour shifting and whining under the pressure to remain joined to her body while it twisted into more and more unlikely positions. He vetoed the idea of chiding his sister, if only because watching her in this natural state was enthralling. He felt his hold on his own glamour slip, watched the green cover his bare feet and crawl up his legs. He watched his hands as the marks started. His *rian* were yellow, his sister's were blue. Both had very bright and sharp *rian*, a fact their parents had taken pride in.

When he was a child—before they'd found their home, when they'd still moved so often that their belongings remained packed at all times—his parents had been able to teach the Devlin children about the heritage more openly. Yellow *rian* meant he would have a strong control over the elements, not only changing or channeling the weather, but using the power in the very air around them to strengthen his spells. Peyton's blue *rian* meant she would excel at mind magic, misdirection and glamours were where she would excel.

Scath was a dark *riocht*, where the magic came from so-called dark sources, but those who cast that magic weren't evil. These were creatures that loved, lived, thought, and learned. They formed families, had and loved their children. The strength of that realm's dark magic came from the power held by the more frightening things in the universe—death, fear, jealousy, and pain—but the spells could be constructed for any purpose.

He focused on a spell for Shifty, strengthening her glamour. He added calmness and a sense of self. Paxton's hair shined its true cobalt and his eyes shifted to match those of his sister. He twisted and wove his intent and sent it around the corner of their bedroom, down the hallway, and into the kitchen, enveloping the *hairn* changeling he loved. *His*. It was part of the spell. She was *his*.

Outside the window, the sky went nearly black. The clouds blocked the stars, the wind screamed, and the rain raged.

CHAPTER

EIGHT

Evangeline watched the shadows from the high tree outside her window flicker and dance against her wall. The radio was still on, but after her friends had left, she'd tuned it to one of the realm's regular channels. Evangeline enjoyed lying in her room, watching the dark shapes move on her walls and listening to radio plays. Relaxing against her pillow with her arms crossed behind her head while *The Shadow* played gave her a place to go where she wasn't worried. Where she wasn't insecure and didn't feel inadequate. It could have been that the radio's waves originated in her home *riocht* and something in her connected with them on a cellular level. Or it could have been something much simpler: all creatures wanted to be comforted and nurtured. There wasn't much that felt more comforting and nurturing than having a story told to you.

She closed her eyes and joined the voice of the opening announcement: "The harmless blue coloring that identifies Blue Coal is your guarantee of clean, even, safe…"

There was a laugh at her window. She jumped and opened her eyes. Instinctively, she pulled her pillow in front of her, though she had no idea what exactly it could protect her from.

Peering out her window, she saw no one.

"Igby?" she whispered into the dark, but only a light breeze responded. It ruffled her curtains across the moonlight and animated the shadows playing against her wall, like fish jumping upstream. "C'mon, Tree, if that's you. Don't mess with me during *The Shadow*."

The radio had finished its sponsor message, soon Orson Welles would be searching the darkest corners of men's hearts, and Evangeline wanted to hear it when he did.

The laugh repeated. Evangeline slammed her pillow to her side with a frustrated sigh. She inched closer to the window. She expected one or both of her best friends to pop up at any second, ready to revel in her squeal. She straightened her spine, determined not to give them the satisfaction.

When she finally reached the window, she shoved the curtain to the side and thrust her head out into the night. "Ha ha, you're very funny."

She looked to the right, but no one sat on the small overhang that was built over the window on the first floor of the house. No one was hanging from the trellis a few feet further on, either.

There was a tap on her left shoulder and another soft laugh. She spun her head so quickly she barely had time to think about it. Whoever had tapped her wasn't expecting that. There was a sharp pain as Evangeline's head connected solidly with another fleshy object. The owner of the unstoppable object that had crossed into her path joined her in letting out a painful "oof" sound. Evangeline pulled herself back into the room, one hand clapped over the spot on her forehead that had taken the worst of the impact.

"Just come in, before one of us ends up seriously injured." She sank to the floor beneath her windowsill and leaned back against the wall. With her eyes closed, she waited for the pain to abate.

She heard a body hoist itself over the window and a thud of feet next to her, but she didn't open her eyes immediately. The blow hadn't really hurt so much as it had surprised her, and she wanted to gather her wits about her before dealing with whoever had just entered her room.

"Are you all right, Evangeline? Crap. I thought I was being charming and mysterious. I screwed that up."

His voice was light and friendly, but it held more than a small amount of self-deprecation. Evangeline was so surprised by that particular note in his voice that she immediately peeked her eyes open. She found herself looking at a pair of gray wool-clad knees, and suddenly, irrationally felt like she was cowering at his feet. The sharp crease of his pant leg was flecked with small bits of tree bark and a couple of leaves.

She swatted away the debris, collecting herself before she smiled up at her visitor. "Hi, Locke," she said.

"Is your head hurt?"

"No, I'm all right. Are you okay?"

"Yes." He shook his head a little ruefully. "This isn't exactly how I pictured this going."

"Really? I don't know, it's certainly original." Evangeline realized that she was more relaxed in his presence than she'd been in a while, and it was probably because he'd just made an ass of himself.

It was hard to be intimidated by someone when they were embarrassed. She held out her hand to him so he could hoist her up to her feet. He gave her a gentle tug and she was almost face to face with him in an instant. The comfort she'd been enjoying vanished instantly. Her face was so close to his that she could have easily given or accepted a kiss, and there was an awkward moment where they both realized it, but neither moved to close the gap.

Then just as she turned her head to relieve him of the obligation, he leaned forward, catching her cheek with his mouth. She wanted to stamp her foot with frustration. Could she not manage five minutes with him that weren't fraught with discomfort and humiliation? She felt her cheeks grow warm, and she knew they were coloring. This wasn't exactly the skin pigmentation she'd been wishing for.

"You want to go for a walk?" Locke asked.

"What? Now? I was…"

"Listening to *The Shadow*, yes. I heard."

"No! Not that, it's…well, my parents might not think it's the best idea."

"Why?" Locke's look was blank.

Evangeline pointed out her window to the darkness. "First, you came in through my window. Second, it's late. You really think we're going to walk downstairs and announce we're walking the path, see you later? I don't know how things play in your house, but my parents are *hairn*, and their parental instincts are a little more acute than the wraiths'."

Locke nodded, slowly. She could see that he wasn't dismissing her argument, but he clearly wasn't believing it, either. "I will concede that my arrival point might be an issue. Other than that, I don't believe they'll kick up a fuss. So, why don't I go back the way I came and call at the front door?"

"You're going to sneak back out, knock on the front door, and ask my mother if we can go for a walk?"

"I am." Before she could protest further, he slipped back out the window.

Evangeline ran to the sill and peered into the night. She watched him drop elegantly from her trellis, bathed in moonlight as he trotted around the side of the house and out of her line of sight. But then she heard his confident knock at their front door. She heard the muffled tones of her parents, their footsteps, the door and another voice added to the conversation. She strained to make out the specific words, but it was useless. She perched on her window sill, holding her breath, waiting for the outcome of this ridiculous chain of events.

"Evangeline!" her mother called up the stairs.

She vaulted to her door and threw it open. "Yeah?" she yelled.

"Can you come downstairs, please?"

Stunned, Evangeline started down the stairs. She found her parents and Locke chatting comfortably in their living room. Her father, in his chair by the fire, a book on his knee, was smiling broadly at the young banshee, which stopped Evangeline in her tracks with surprise. Her father was a gruff man, a leader. He gave no quarter to anyone, let alone to the youth of their clans, and yet, the expression on his face suggested that he was conversing with, if not an equal of, a person who mattered. Her mother, standing in the doorway between the living room and the front hallway, smiled at Evangeline when she was on the last step.

"You weren't asleep, were you?"

"Oh, no, Mom, of course not. What's going on?" She gave her mother a hug. It was hard to be within fifteen feet of her mother and not hug her; the warmth in her eyes was a beacon of affection to Evangeline, and like a moth, she drifted to her mother's heat. Ciarda seemed to grip her a little tighter and hold on a little longer than usual, and even kissed the top of her head, inhaling the scent of Evangeline's hair. None of it bothered Evangeline. She loved her mother unconditionally and fully and could think of pretty much no place else she'd want to be than encircled in her arms. Her mother released her, but kept an arm around her shoulders. "Locke's here. He thought he might take you for a walk on the paths."

"Yeah?" Evangeline asked, uncommitted. She didn't trust herself to say much more, for fear she would giggle and give herself away.

"It's a nice night," Locke commented, and turned to her father. "If it's okay with you, of course, *Meas* Wicklow?"

Arawn nodded. "Of course it is. I'd like you to have her back before too long, but you two need some time together.

Soon my permission won't even be needed, huh?"

Evangeline kept her jaw tight, for fear it would drop to the floor. Was this her father? Handing her off into the night? Now she almost wanted to refuse just to see what would happen. Would he insist she accompany Locke? She shoved the thought aside. She wanted to go with Locke; why be contrary just for the sake of it?

"Well, okay," she said. "Now?"

Locke offered his hand to both her parents in turn and joined her in the doorway. Her mother went to accompany her father by the fire, and both of them smiled brightly toward Evangeline and Locke. Locke took her hand, smiled a little conspiratorially, and squeezed lightly. "Let's go."

They paused at the door for Evangeline to pick a sweater from a hook by the door, and then they were out in the night air, briskly making their way toward the paths.

Evangeline loved the birches at night, the strange green tint they took when the moonlight reflected off their papery white surfaces. She touched one as they passed it, enjoying the smooth, cold surface. Locke still had ahold of her hand. He felt very similar to the tree—cool, smooth and strong. She smiled up at him. "How'd you know it would be okay with them?"

"It's me asking." He said it like it was the most obvious answer. And he seemed surprised when she didn't nod and drop the subject. "Look, Evangeline. Our parents and Linus's make every decision in this realm. They *are* the power. You and I? They decided long ago that we'd be *ceile*. It would look a little petty to deny me access to my intended a mere moon cycle and half before our *aontuet*. Wouldn't show a lot of trust in me, or faith in my family line."

She never thought of things like this. The moment he said it, it made perfect sense, and she felt foolish she'd been so surprised. "Well, I'm glad one of us is paying attention," she muttered.

He laughed, a light and inviting sound.

They continued walking the paths, the mist forming at their feet, tendrils wrapping around them like smoke. Evangeline waited. Locke didn't speak.

Finally, when she thought the anticipation might cause her to scream or cry, he cleared his throat. He stopped walking, waited for her to stop as well, and for her to turn and look at him.

"I am not unhappy with my parents' choice of *ceile*, Evangeline. I want you to know that, okay?"

"That's good to know. Thank you." She paused. "I think." It hadn't exactly been a ringing endorsement.

"And you? Are you pleased?"

"I am not unhappy, as well," she answered. "It's just, well, we always knew this, right?" She waited for him to nod. "So I guess I never really thought about how I feel about it. It always seemed so very far away, so vague and unreal. Then at the last moon change, I realized how close it was, and…"

"And you couldn't look me in the eye anymore," he finished, when she seemed unable.

"Yes. Sorry," she added when she realized, for the first time, he might have taken offense.

"Don't be. I understand. Look, Evangeline, we've known each other our entire lives. It's silly to dance around each other like this. Our union is our role. Our obligation. It doesn't have to be a sentence as well. Not if we don't want it to be."

"What do you think we should do about it?"

"I think we have a good enough amount of time, and a certain amount of freedom of status to play with. I think you should allow me to court you." He paused and looked at her significantly when she snorted at his choice of word. He raised an eyebrow. "This from the girl who was listening to *The Shadow*? I should think the term would please you."

"Sorry," she said again.

"Anyway, let me court you. Let me get to know you as a…" Now he paused. "Oh, heck, a paramour. I think we might find out we're more than 'not unhappy' about our status."

"I would be open to that," Evangeline said carefully. "What exactly *is* courting?"

"This." Locke waved a hand at the path before them. "Walking, talking. Meals alone. Some time without the gang. A real effort to be a couple. Just because they chose for us, doesn't mean it can't be a good thing."

Evangeline considered the words as he said them. She drew in a large breath of the night air, and for the first time in her recent memory, her shoulders felt light, her heart didn't feel burdened. "No. It doesn't. Lachlan MacNair, I accept your proposal of courtship." She even made a little curtseying movement that made him laugh. He dropped her hand and pulled her into a hug. She willingly embraced him back. They stood under the moonlight, amongst the birches, listening to the night animals making their calls, arms around each other for a long time. The air around them was finally clear. They might not know exactly where they were heading, their relationship hadn't been their choice, but they could, at least, play an active role in making themselves happy with both their union and their future.

After a long time had passed, they started back on the path toward Evangeline's house, tentative conversation of their hopes and dreams passing between them.

CHAPTER

NINE

Arawn Wicklow stood at the ley line, murmuring under his breath as he fished inside his pouch. He produced the totem and turned it over in his hand three times, then stood very still, staring at the ground. The ley line flared and he disappeared from his home *riocht*.

When he arrived in *Talam*, he placed the totem in his pocket and walked with slow confidence toward the edge of the woods. Any animals nearby would see snapping twigs and bowing branches, but the *hairn* himself was cloaked from the eyes of this *riocht*. A ghost. The totem was a strong one; Katarin MacNair had constructed it for him. It was a mask of walking death. Only a banshee, whose magic derived from the power of death, could make a totem strong enough to work in a *riocht* that contained no death magic itself. He emerged from the thicket of trees and considered the road before him. He knew he wasn't far from his destination, but it took him a moment to decide which direction he should walk.

Careful now about where he placed his feet, he made his way up the steep rural road. Once at the top, he continued into the mid-sized town that sprawled in the valley. His glamour was strong, but he still didn't wish to be seen at all. He fingered the totem in his pocket as he walked and he muttered a word every now and then to ensure its strength. He followed the directions he'd memorized the day before. Soon, the house he was looking for came into view.

The two story house was light blue with white trim. A swing rocked on its chains at the end of the full white porch. Trees adorned the front yard. Plants lined the porch, the steps and the walkway. The property was clean and orderly in a way that pleased him.

He climbed the front steps and gave the door a cursory once-over. The knob turned in his hand. He didn't stop to pay much attention inside the house. Instead he made his way to the second floor, assuming he would find the bedrooms there. He could tell her room by the smell. The glamour and spells they'd placed on her as a baby had held. If they had not, the scent of *hairn* would be overwhelming. He could pick up only faint strains of her. Even so, he knew his own blood.

Her room wasn't as neat as the rest of the house. It also had a strange empty feel about it. There was still a desk, some papers scattered across its surface, a book on the corner, and an array of some other vaguely teenage items. The bed was stripped of sheets. A comforter hung off one of the bed posts, a couple of inches dragging on the floor. The walls were hung with all manner of photos, ticket stubs; posters for movies, bands, and several with humans performing a variety of contortions, the poses caught mid-flip or leap. He studied these, and realized with some pride that many of them were not humans at all, but were Siofra. His daughter, it seemed, was an accomplished gymnast. She'd found a way to utilize her genetic talents even far from home and without the guidance of her parents.

The desire to touch her, even while merely standing among these sparse belongings which she hadn't thought enough about to take with her when she'd moved, was so thick he had to push it away. This was exactly why he'd forbidden Ciarda any access to their child over the years. Had he or his wife seen her in the flesh, the plan would have failed in that second. As it was, he'd stood here too long. He must complete his task and be on his way. Soon enough they would have her back. There would be nothing but time to learn who she was.

He was slightly stymied by the fact that she obviously no longer had daily contact with this space, which would impact the effect of the spell greatly. He considered for a moment trying to locate her new residence. But the walking death would never last long enough for that endeavor. Surely she would return to the house soon. He would just have to perform the spell here today, and return to find her another day if they discovered that it had not reached her.

He opened his pouch and pulled out another totem and a jar. He broke the seal of the jar and took to his knees in a back corner of her closet. Clearing a small area of dust with the side of his hand, he poured the contents of the jar in a circle and completed the incantation. He looked suspiciously through the closet door and to Siofra's window for signs that his magic called the clouds, but the sky remained clear. Katarin had been correct: the incantation would take a long time to affect the surroundings noticeably. It took very little power from *Talam*, since it had been constructed and spelled in *Scath*. He placed the totem in the middle of the circle and arranged the few items left on the floor of the closet to hide his handiwork, then inspected it from the doorway, making sure there was no evidence of what he'd done. He pushed some winter clothing further down the hanging pole, sure they wouldn't be retrieved before Siofra was called home, and they nicely camouflaged his work. He shut the closet door confident the circle was safe.

He tried to remember if the door to her room had been closed when he arrived. He'd been so intent on her scent that he'd neglected to take note. Stupid mistake. Surely it had been closed; the parents wouldn't want to see the evidence of their daughter's abandoned childhood. He pulled it shut behind him, noting for the first time the plaque secured there. "Shifty's Room." Shifty? They called her Shifty?

Some things would obviously need to change.

~

Shifty's eyelids seemed to weigh a million pounds. She stared out the window of her European Cultures classroom while the professor lectured about conspiracy theories and their "interesting" place in the world's history. Interesting was a relative term, apparently. While Professor Jordan taught a variety of what should have been gripping and diverse interpretations of the history of conflicts in Europe, usually he might as well have been lecturing on the scientific properties of dirt, for all the excitement his monotonous voice spawned in the faces and minds of his charges.

The minute hand of the clock on the wall lurched to the 10 position and Shifty sat a little straighter in her seat. Five minutes and the torture would cease for the afternoon. European Cultures was her last class of the day. She had no practice or appointments after school, and she was looking forward to an afternoon alone with Pax and Peyton.

When the minute hand finally made it to the 11 and the professor dismissed the class, she barely managed to jot down the next assignment before jumping to her feet and joining the rush for the door.

Peyton, who was sitting propped against the wall opposite the classroom door, grinned and waved. "You in a walking coma?" Professor Jordan's metronome-like tone was legendary even to those not forced to endure his classes for their majors.

"Good lord! That man." Shifty rolled her eyes and joined Peyton in a round of laughter. "He's dead dull. I almost feel sorry for him."

"Not me," Peyton said. "I might, you know, if I didn't have

to take his class next year. Instead, I feel sorry for me."

They reached the front doors of the building and stepped into the sunbeams, pausing to appreciate them for just a second. The air was light with the scent of flowers and it was just warm enough to be pleasant without being overly hot. Perfection.

"So, your parents' house?" Shifty asked once the moment passed. "We're expected in about an hour. Not much else we can fit in before then. I'll beat you at pinball before the feast."

"Crap." Peyton rolled her eyes. "I forgot. Family picnic dinner. Why are our parents so intensely weird?"

"Uh, because they're parents? Oh, and I have to stop by my parents' house first. My mother made cookies or something."

"They aren't coming?" Peyton asked. The weekly picnic dinners were a family tradition that none of them had wanted to discontinue, even after the "kids" had moved into their own place.

"No, Dad's at the office late and Mom had some meeting with a client in Sawyer, so she won't be home until later."

In the car, Peyton took control of the radio and blared the music, until they picked up Paxton at the shop and he complained of eardrum damage in the backseat. By the time she pulled into her parents' driveway, Shifty was ready to smack them both. "I'll be right there!" she called, already half way up to her front path. Paxton seemed about to protest for a second, but he turned and joined his sister on the short walk toward their own parents' home.

Shifty used her key in the front door, stepped into the house, and dropped her backpack in the hallway. She headed straight for the kitchen, barely looking around her. The smell of the baking her mother had done that morning lingered everywhere: vanilla, cinnamon, and brown sugar. It felt comforting. She inhaled deeply, allowing the feelings the scents brought with them to enfold her. On the kitchen counter, wrapped in her mother's expert way and decorated by her sure hand, was a plate of snickerdoodles. Shifty fingered the card, tilting it up so she could read it.

"Enjoy! Wish we could join you! Next time! Adara" *Good lord, that was a lot of exclamation points, Mom.* Shifty scooped up the plate and turned to leave the kitchen. She stopped suddenly, unsure why she had paused. Carefully she put the plate back on the counter and walked to the bottom of the stairs, pausing a moment before starting up to the second floor. She saw nothing unusual, so why was there a chill running up her spine and trickling back down to the pit of her stomach?

She moved quickly and surely, though without any real thought or purpose. It was as if her brain had shut off and pure instinct was guiding her instead, leading her to her bedroom door.

There was nothing out of place, but her feeling of violation intensified. She reached for the door and pulled her hand back with a jerky movement. She had the feeling that she was fighting herself for control of her own body.

With every bit of mind control she had—which felt ridiculous, this was her body and she was alone in her house— she managed to turn away from the door. She rolled her head on her shoulders, did an all over body shake and chased away the last of her willies.

But why? Why didn't she want to go in her room? It was, after all, still *her* room. "Shit. I really love being a mental case," she said to the air. She looked between her room and the stairs several times, feeling like an ass as she did it. She pivoted on her toe, finally steady and found she was pointed toward the stairs. "Trust your instincts," she whispered. It was advice Dr. Miller had dispatched many times.

She sighed and started down the stairs. She darted into the kitchen, grabbed the cookies, and scampered to the door. Feeling ridiculous, she slammed it behind her, leaned up against it, pressed her head into the wood, and closed her eyes. Her heart hammered and her breath came fast and heavy.

She approached Paxton's house. He was on the front steps with a paperback book folded over so he could hold it one-handed. He appeared lost in whatever he was reading. Shifty loved catching him in moments when he didn't know she was there. Paxton in his natural state. She stood still to watch him. He ran the nail of his thumb across the top of his lip, an unconscious gesture she'd seen him make countless times while he read. She knew it meant he was enjoying what he was reading and he was really thinking about it. A breeze caught his hair and it lifted off his forehead, glinting teal blue in the sun.

Her breath caught. *Glinting teal?* She blinked hard and opened her eyes slowly. She refocused on Paxton. His hair had settled back on his forehead. It was light brown, with a streak of sun-bleached blond that fell over his eye. Her mind reeled. Had she taken her meds this morning? Yes, she was sure she had. She'd washed them down with the crappy, too-sweet orange juice from the campus cafe. Besides, she only saw things that weren't supposed to be there on her *own* body. She didn't have hallucinations about other people's bodies. Or she wasn't *supposed* to.

As if he'd heard her mental conversation, Pax looked up from his book. He saw her standing on the path and his face split into a grin. He locked eyes with her but didn't say anything right away.

"You are so breathtaking." He set his book down on the porch and got up to meet her.

She felt the blush come to her cheeks and stifled the instinct to dismiss or deflect his compliment. It hurt his feelings when she did that, instantly deflected his endearments. She never meant to diminish his feelings for her. Only his misguided, in her opinion, appreciation of her beauty, brains, and charm.

She held the plate out to him, and once he took it from her, she folded herself under his other arm. He squeezed her firmly. She relaxed without even knowing how tightly she'd been wound. Inside of his embrace she was safe, from the strange feeling she'd had in her house. She was sane. She sighed into his shoulder. He peered down at her.

"Something's wrong."

"You're my favorite and my best," she told him, smiling.

"And that makes you sigh like your heart is breaking?" His voice was still calm, but she heard the strain running under the lightness.

"Now you're making things up in your head, Devlin." She hoped her own effort to mask her tension was better than his.

He stooped down and scooped up his book. He released her only briefly while he shoved it into the back pocket of his jeans before they entered the house together.

CHAPTER

TEN

Evangeline chewed on the end of her pencil, studying the notes and sketch she'd made of Locke's knife the night before. She flipped the pages of one of the several books she had open in front of her. She wasn't sure why she cared about researching the dagger so much. It wasn't an assignment. He hadn't even asked her to do it. But the idea of doing something for him, something unexpected, appealed to her. She wanted to make him proud. Impress him.

Unfortunately, the knife's secrets weren't revealing themselves to her. She'd deciphered the symbols easily enough when he'd purchased it, but that was all she'd been able to uncover. She hummed under her breath and worked the pencil through her fingers, watching it turn end over end as it passed from one finger to another. She hated not finding an answer when she went looking; she took it as a personal insult. She kept skimming pages, but she could feel her mood turning foul.

Wraith magic was tricky. The wraiths were notoriously secretive and hid their knowledge within their clans. Often they didn't even pass spells to their banshee offspring. Banshees, being the offspring of a wraith and a *sheehairn* union, had different magic entirely. Wraiths hid their most powerful charms and creations from the children they considered necessary to the species, but ultimately inferior because of their more sensitive natures. The wraith, to their core, were dark magic. Cold, calculating, and unyielding. They mated and had children merely for the guaranteed continuation of the species.

And, damn it, they were downright spooky. Evangeline didn't like reading their spells or touching their totems. While these items were not technically evil—nothing was born that way, it had to be made so—they were still dark magic, death magic. And so powerful they made her skin prickle and her breath catch.

She set her pencil down. She ran her hands over her face and weaved her fingers into her hair and pulled it back from her head. She leaned against her chair and tilted it until she balanced on two legs. There was something there, something tickling right on the perimeter of her thoughts. Something she knew she knew but couldn't remember what it was. Something her mother had said to her as a child…

The front legs of her chair clattered back against the floor. She reached for her sketch and jumped up from her chair. She scrambled across her room and scanned the titles on the small bookshelf beneath her window. It wasn't there. She leapt to her feet and ran out of her room, scurried down the stairs, her socked feet going out from under her as she skipped over the last step. She righted herself and slowed to a quick walk as she turned the corner into the library. Her parents were both in the room, a lamp's flame flickering between them. Her mother was sipping a cup of tea and listening to the radio. Her father had a large book open in his lap. They both looked up when she entered the room.

"Hi," her mother said dryly.

Evangeline realized from her mother's appraising look that she must be a mess. She tried to compose her face. She ran a hand over her hair.

"Hi," she said.

"Everything okay?"

"'Course...I'm just...uh...looking for a book."

"That's why you came stomping down the stairs and running in here looking like the *dibhalt* himself was on your tail? A book?"

"Yeah. I need it." Evangeline's response sounded lame even to her own ears. "Sorry for the noise. I got excited."

Both her parents smiled. Her mother let out a small, breathy laugh. She gestured to the bookcases that lined two of the room's walls. "By all means. Have at it."

"Thanks. Sorry...again."

"You've been making loud noises in this house for over twenty years. We've become used to it," her father said. "Sometimes we even like it," he added quietly, his smile concealed behind his mug of tea.

Evangeline started on the shelves behind her parents, scanning the colors of the spines quickly. She ran her fingers along them, muttering their titles under her breath. "Not it, not it. Not. IT." She reached the end of the first set of books and sighed. She wondered if she'd made the memory up, but she soldiered on to the second shelf, even though she was losing confidence that she'd find what she was looking for. Then her index finger caught on a spine. The book under her finger was blue and more ragged than she'd remembered. She pulled it from its place and consulted the cover. The title wasn't familiar. She flipped through a couple of pages and snapped it shut, satisfied.

"Find what you needed?" her mother asked.

"Yep. Thanks. Good night." She dropped a kiss on the tops of both their heads and darted out of the room, excited. She took the stairs to her room two at a time, shut the door behind her, and flopped onto her bed. On the title page was the symbol she'd recognized on Locke's knife. There was a row of other symbols she didn't know, and under that title, a single word: "Siofra."

Evangeline flipped to the first page of text and began to read.

CHAPTER

ELEVEN

Paxton's house was always dimly lit and smelled of herbs. Some days were more pleasant than others. Today it was sandalwood and ginger. Shifty inhaled deeply and smiled.

"What's she making today?" she asked Paxton.

Paxton didn't get a chance to answer. Heavy footfalls clomped down the stairs, and Peyton landed at the bottom, popping up right between them. There was something so charming and childlike about her entrance that it lightened Shifty's heart. She hugged her friend tightly.

"You don't want to know what she's making," Peyton said, as if Shifty had directed the question to her in the first place. "It'll ruin your dinner."

Shifty held up a hand and closed her eyes. "Fair enough. Don't say another word."

"Your mom made cookies?" Peyton's eyes zeroed in on the plate in Paxton's hand with the intensity of a laser. He shifted slightly to make sure they were out of her quick grabbing range. She scowled at him.

"After dinner," he said.

Peyton stuck out her lower lip and made a half-hearted grab for the plate, which Paxton easily evaded. Shifty took a step away from him and watched as brother and sister continued to bob and swipe at each other. Their manner light and easy, their laughter quick. Not having any siblings of her own she wasn't sure if their relationship was particularly special or if most siblings were as close and familiar, but she envied it nonetheless. She would have loved to have someone she could talk to about all the ways she felt different, someone who wasn't parental, or over-protective, or a doctor. A person raised in the same house, by the same people, who could be a partner in crime. Sometimes she was sure if she'd had that, all the craziness in her life would be easier to combat. A person to help carry the load. Someone to whisper her secrets to in the dark. If secrets were shared they weren't so damn scary. If you were able to tell someone "I think I'm losing my mind," maybe you didn't go ahead and lose your mind.

Nelda appeared through the door to the kitchen and caught Shifty's eye over her bickering children. She let out a long-suffering sigh and smiled at Shifty in a knowing and affectionate way. "Do you think maybe you two could contain yourselves? At least until we get outside and my candles aren't at risk? I'd have a hard time explaining to the insurance company that my children burned the house down fighting over snickerdoodles." She deftly relieved Paxton of the plate of cookies, ruffled her daughter's hair, and disappeared back into her kitchen.

"If you'd use electricity to light the house it wouldn't be as dangerous!" Peyton yelled after her. When neither Paxton nor Shifty chimed in with a comment she looked back at them over her shoulder. Her glare was scathing. "Uh, a little back up?"

"I *like* the candles," Shifty said with a shrug. "Sorry."

"Traitor," Peyton huffed.

Lit almost entirely with candles and oil lamps, Nelda and Tristan Devlin's house was blissfully dim. Shifty always felt herself relax within its depths. It was as if she hadn't noticed that the harsh lights of her own home, school, and gym were pressing down on her until she was away from them. This house felt safe and comforting. She'd tried to light her room at her parents' house the same way a couple of years ago. When the visions had become particularly bad. Her thinking had been that at least her room could give her a place of escape. But one little, teensy, tiny curtain fire and she'd been lucky she had still been allowed to use the stove. Which was electric.

"Paxton! Go help your father set up the table in the yard, please!" Nelda's voice was kind but authoritative. Paxton kissed Shifty on the cheek and headed for the backyard.

Peyton tugged on Shifty's arm. "Come up to my old room. I found something to show you."

Once in the room Peyton began sifting through a small bundle on her desk. She turned around with a smile and held a small pendant out to Shifty. "Isn't it pretty?" she asked.

Shifty took the necklace and turned it over in her hands. It was an object with many facets. Tiny, elaborate filigree with slightly thicker borders making up each side. Inside it, something rattled. Shifty raised an eyebrow at Peyton. "What's in it?"

"Mom thinks it's amber. From the smell, anyway."

Shifty sniffed it, it had a pungent, and yet not unpleasant odor. "What's the metal? It's got a weird color." It was nearly black. "Or does it need to be polished?"

"Dad thinks it's hematite. It's neat, huh?"

"Yeah. Really pretty." Shifty held it out to Peyton. Peyton shook her head and pushed Shifty's hand back. "It's for you."

"What? Why?"

Peyton smiled and dug under her shirt collar, coming out with a nearly identical pendant hanging off a single finger. "'Cause there are two of them. I know it's kind of cheesy, but they don't say 'best' and 'friend' or anything. Do you want it?"

"Of course I want it." Shifty assured her. She undid the clasp and ran the chain along her hand. "It's more like a thread than a chain, huh? Wonder how they did that. It's like one solid piece." She held it out to Peyton. "Help me fasten it?"

She lifted the hair off her neck. Peyton secured the necklace around her neck and the pendant dropped beneath Shifty's shirt. It vibrated against her sternum.

Shifty touched it through her shirt. "It's warm."

"That's why dad thought it was hematite. It takes on body heat."

"Thanks, Peyton." Shifty hugged her friend tightly.

Peyton pulled away and concentrated on the lint on a comforter her mother had slung over a chair near the window. She plucked away little bits and tossed them on the floor. "You're welcome."

Shifty knew her blatant gratitude had embarrassed her friend and she fished for a change of subject. She looked through Peyton's window into the Devlins' backyard. "Think they're ready to eat? I'm starving."

By the time the girls made it to the backyard the table was set up and most of the food had been laid out. Tristan was already sitting on one of the benches, reading a book intently.

"A moment without reading is a moment wasted," Peyton scoffed in her snippiest voice. She was the non-reader of the family. Every family had one; the rest of the Devlins had often expressed hope that she would be strong enough to overcome what was obviously a genetic mutation.

Shifty bumped shoulders with Peyton and the two girls giggled, alerting Tristan to their presence. He closed his book and smiled at them. "Hi, Shifty. How's school?"

"Fine."

She and Peyton sat on the bench across from him, leaving enough room for Paxton, who was coming down the back porch with his mother, balancing a tray with a pitcher of something pink-colored and glasses filled with ice. He set the tray down in the middle of the table, poured two glasses, and handed one to Shifty before taking his place next to her. He ran a hand up and down her back.

"Shall we?" Nelda nodded toward the bounty of food and drink laid out before them.

It took no further invitation. All hands reached for plates and food to pile on them. There were the companionable sounds of cutlery clicking and plates passing up and down the table, and a few happy sighs. Nelda was a very good cook.

Shifty took a swallow of her drink. She'd been expecting pink lemonade, but found instead a sparkling concoction that tasted of roses, peaches, and something she couldn't identify. It was cool and light and melded pleasantly with the food. She pulled a piece of bread from the loaf in the middle of the table and dunked it into a small puddle of sauce left from her chicken. She popped it in her mouth and grinned at Paxton.

"It's all so good," she said before realizing she'd not completely swallowed her mouthful. Paxton clapped her on the back as she coughed and the entire table laughed.

"Here." Peyton held out Shifty's glass to her. "Try not to die on us, would ya?"

Shifty nodded and accepted the glass, not trusting herself to speak again. She took a few experimental sips of the liquid, and when it cleared her throat without another coughing fit, she decided she could talk.

"Excuse me! It's all so good, Nelda, thanks," she repeated.

"Glad to do it."

They passed the rest of the meal exchanging tales of the day. Mr. and Mrs. Devlin asked Shifty about her meet on Sunday. Peyton told a tale of protesting the current selection in her literature class, extracting a look that was both amused and disappointed from her father.

By the time Nelda brought out her mother's cookies, Shifty was feeling warm and satisfied. Sated. She leaned against Paxton, enjoying the feel of his arms on either side of her. The sound of his face nuzzling her hair. She reached out for her glass and as it crossed her line of vision, her arm glinted green in the light of the setting sun.

Green.

Startled, she pushed back against Paxton, gripping his arm. His reaction was calm. He tightened his grip around her, bringing her outstretched arm back to her and within his embrace.

"Don't be afraid," he whispered into her ear.

"I think it worked," he said to his family. Then he turned his attention back to her. He maneuvered her so she could look him in the eye, but he didn't let her out of his arms.

"What's going on, Paxton?"

"Don't be afraid," he repeated. "Mom cleared your vision. So you could see past your glamour."

"My what?"

Paxton lifted her hand so it was between their faces, and their eyes locked. Her skin was a shimmering opalescent green.

"You," she halted. Her eyes jumped between her hand, his face, and the faces of his family. She took a long breath that caught a couple of times on its way to her brain. She shook her head slightly. "You can see that?"

"We all can," Paxton confirmed. All around the table the Devlins made sounds of assent.

"Why?" Shifty asked. A tear broke free and started down her cheek. She didn't know if she meant why could they see it or why was it that way in the first place or why hadn't they told her before.

"Because we're like you, Shifty," Tristan Devlin said. He reached across the table and patted the side of her face. "And we want to help you."

CHAPTER

TWELVE

Her desk hadn't gotten any more organized. In fact, she was pretty sure the mess was procreating. Papers rattled in the wind from her window but they were held in place by heavier books. She'd spilled her water earlier, and ink from the page she'd been working on ran in swirls. Evangeline sat in the middle of the chaos, still in her sleeping clothes, her hair unruly and her eyes slightly heavy from lack of sleep. When there was a tap at the door, she jumped.

"Son of a frog! Yeah! Come in."

Igby pushed the door in and peered around it. "You okay?"

Evangeline sagged against her chair, shoulders slumped. "You scared me."

"Alllll rrriiiiiggght." Igby stepped inside the room and nodded behind her. Locke, Tresara, and Linus filed in after her. They spread out around the room. Igby threw herself on Evangeline's bed. Linus picked the reading chair in a corner. Tresara sat on the floor with her back against the wall, wedged in the small space between the bookshelf and the corner. Locke leaned against Evangeline's desk. He peered down at her and one side of his mouth quirked up when he took in her disheveled state.

"Sure. Bring everyone! Why not?" Evangeline said. She leveled a withering look at Igby.

Igby shrugged. She was completely unconcerned by her friend's scorn. "You said you need help." She gestured around the room indicating all their friends. "I brought help."

"I see that. Thanks."

"I am impervious to your sarcasm, Wicklow." Igby held Evangeline's gaze as if she dared Evangeline to push the issue further. Finally, admitting defeat, Evangeline looked away. Igby smiled. She didn't bother hiding her triumph. She cleared her throat. "So, what's the big mystery?"

Evangeline lifted papers and books off her desk, pushed items around, mopped up the last of the water she'd missed earlier, muttered darkly under her breath, and finally held up a small blue book. "This."

"Mystery solved. It's a book," Locke said. He plucked it from Evangeline's hand and riffled through the pages without looking at them. He peered at her over its cover. She snatched the book back from his grasp.

"Again, thanks." As hard as she tried, she couldn't keep the grin from spreading across her face. She ran a hand through her curls, hoping to calm them, and smoothed the front of her t-shirt. It was useless, but she felt better at least having tried to become presentable. "It is what's in the book that I could use some help with. Have any of you read it?"

She turned the cover outward and slowly presented it to each of them like they were children and it was story time. They all took it in, but no one's face registered any recognition.

Linus sat forward when the book passed before his eyes. His palms on his knees, his face intent. "*Siofra?*"

Evangeline nodded. She tossed the book back atop the pile of debris on her desk. "But it isn't the kid's story."

Now they all looked both more confused and more interested.

"What else could it be? I mean, it isn't like changelings are *real.*" Linus snatched the book from Evangeline's fingers and

Shifty

opened the cover. Evangeline scoffed at him. Linus dismissed her scorn with a wave of his hand. "You're not a changeling, Evangeline! Not like in the *Siofra* tales our parents told us when we were little."

"Right," Igby chimed in. She was obviously thrilled to be able to share the spotlight with Linus. "Siofra are whisked away to *Talam*. The way my parents told it, the human families that found them always rejected the new baby. My mother said the changeling died in the snow. I think my dad always used starvation and neglect." She made a sharp laughing sound. "Nice bedtime tales, huh?"

"My dad always used it as a way to make sure I didn't wander off alone. 'Stay away from the ley lines, Tresara. They might just send you to the humans.' As if ley lines just flare of their own accord." She rolled her eyes.

Evangeline looked at Locke. "Are those the stories your parents told you?"

He nodded. "Well, yeah. Pretty much. Stay in your own *riocht*, its safe, the magic here will keep you safe. You know... the standard stuff."

"No. I don't know. My mother used to read me a story about Siofra who went to *Talam*, and a human who came to *Scath*. The human family raised Siofra as their own. They loved her and the human baby was loved in *Scath*. She was happy and healthy. In the end, Siofra came home and they all lived happily ever after."

"Makes sense your mother would tell you that story, now doesn't it? Look how they still shelter you!" Locke reached out and touched a strand of Evangeline's hair. He twirled it gently. "They aren't going to tell you the same gloom and doom they told those of us who were born here. What got you on this anyway?"

"Oh!" Evangeline realized none of them knew what she'd been trying to decipher. They were used to her research projects and history lessons, but this one probably seemed to come out of the blue. She smiled at Locke. "I was trying to translate your knife."

"Translate a knife?" Igby scoffed. "Isn't a knife self explanatory? They cut things, spread things, and some of them are for the slaying."

"And some of them have marks on them and are for very specific rituals or magic." Evangeline kept as much affection in her voice as possible. It wasn't Igby's fault Evangeline had been practically banging her head against the wall for the past eighteen hours. She shuffled through her papers again and came up with the sketch she'd made of Locke's knife. She presented it to Igby. "See that mark? That one is a wraith symbol. It means sacrifice. Or something equally dark. This one? I don't know it. But the more I looked at it, I knew I'd seen it." She turned and snatched the book back from her desk. She turned the cover back to her friends and held her sketch next to it. She remained silent and allowed each of them to look at the symbols.

"They match." Tresara spoke first. She came out from her crevice. She reached for the items, and Evangeline handed them to her. Tresara brought them closer to her face and leaned the books against her knees so she could inspect the sketch with a little more intensity. She even outlined something with her finger. Her lips moved but no sound reached Evangeline's ears. She set the picture firmly on the ground and creased it down the middle with her hand. She opened the book and turned a few of the pages. She looked at Evangeline, puzzled. "I thought you said your mother read you this story."

Evangeline snorted. "Welcome to my world."

"Care to fill us in? The rest of us don't speak your weird best-friend language," Linus snapped.

Wordlessly, Tresara handed him the book. He repeated her procedure with the pages and looked up with an identical befuddled expression. "This book is written in gobble-y-gook." He decided. Only Linus, the scholar, could make "gobble-y-gook" sound technical. If Evangeline hadn't been so frustrated she would have allowed herself a laugh.

"Exactly," Evangeline confirmed. "I think it's mostly wraith symbols. But I don't know them and I have no idea where to go from here."

"Good thing it's totally unimportant," Locke said. "Well, c'mon!" He defended himself against the outraged looks of his friends. "What does it matter? It's a silly knife I bought from the weapons vendor at market because I liked it. Does it really matter what the symbols mean, except that it's a mystery Lenny's got to solve to be able to sleep at night?" The room relaxed around him. Or most of it did. Evangeline remained straight backed and glaring.

"Okay. Even *if* I grant you that. Why did my mother 'read' me a story from this book? Why didn't she just tell me the story? What's with the pretense?"

Silence.

"All right. That's weird." Locke's inflection conceded her point more than his words. He met her eyes and a gentle smile spread across his face. "So, what are we going to do about it?"

"Translate it." Evangeline raised her shoulder. Her eyes flickered momentarily while she wondered if he was going to argue with her. If he was going to deny her this. Or at least bow out of the search.

"How are we going to do that?" he asked. His eyes watched only her, oblivious to the others in the room. She liked it.

"Can you get me into your father's office?"

His shoulders slumped and he sat back further on the desk, knocking the empty water glass over with his hip. He studied the floor and whistled through his teeth. "Wraiths. Not the most forthcoming of creatures."

"Which is why we aren't asking his permission," Tresara said, getting to her feet. "Or my mother's for that matter. If what we need isn't in Cecil MacNair's stash, my mother will have it." She took in all their blank faces. "Well? What are you waiting for? Move!"

CHAPTER

THIRTEEN

Shifty's face felt as if it really had "frozen that way." She let her gaze travel from Paxton's and slowly she made looked at each member of his family, ending with Nelda Devlin. Nelda's eyes were now almost completely black, with a mere millimeter of sea blue outlining the iris. As Shifty watched, even that color faded away leaving Nelda looking as if two pools of oil sat on the white sclera. Shifty blinked but nothing changed. She'd seen eyes like this before.

In the mirror.

She'd been told she was seeing things. Making it up. All in her head. Hallucinating. Crazy. Crazy. Crazy.

But she wasn't. She hadn't been. Or…And this was the big "or." Or she'd finally gone completely insane and was living in the world her mind had created.

She concentrated on the feel of Paxton's arms around her. They'd never wavered, never shifted for a second from their firm but loving grip around her shoulders. She could feel his fingers stroking her forearms. The light, pleasant sensation of his affection transferred from the tips of his fingertips straight to her soul. He was real. She knew he was real.

He was whispering in her ear. Not words so much as calming sounds. Soothing nothings. She allowed them to penetrate the dam in her mind while she stared into Nelda's eyes. They were scary and strange. And yet, they were not unfamiliar. The emotion in them was not aggressive or hostile.

"What am I?" It was as straightforward a question as she could think of.

"*Sheehairn*," Nelda said. "You're a changeling. From a different realm, a *riocht*, we call *Scath*."

"*Sheehairn*." Shifty tried the word on her tongue. From the corner of her vision she saw Tristan nod. Her attention jumped to him, then to Peyton next to her, and finally back to Nelda. "*Scath riocht?*"

"That's right." Her head went up and down but her stare never broke contact.

"Changeling?" Shifty asked. "What does that mean? It kind of sounds like you're telling me I'm not human." She laughed. It was a sharp, manic sound. "And also that I'm not crazy. But I don't know. I think now I wish I *was* crazy." She was aware she was rambling now, going down paths that probably made no sense, but she couldn't keep the words from falling out.

Nelda finally broke her gaze. She straightened and considered the others around the table. She topped off all their drinks from the pitcher and swept away non-existent crumbs from the tablecloth in front of her. "You're not crazy, Siofra. As far as being non-human goes..." She paused and smiled, almost to herself. "We've never found the condition to be so inadequate."

"Gawd, Ma! Can we maybe answer Shifty's questions?" Peyton interrupted. "If you think starting with a terrible joke is going to put anyone at ease, you're wrong."

Tristan's laugh was stifled, though not completely, and it drew a glare from his wife. He held his hands up in a defensive pose. "When she's right, she's right."

"Thanks, Dad." Peyton grinned across the table at her father, who nodded his support again, just barely. Paxton cleared his throat and leveled a serious look at all of them.

"All right. Sorry. Everyone has a valid point. We're playing this a little off the cuff, Shifty. This is not a conversation we expected to be having. But, certain…uh…circumstances made it necessary to accelerate the process."

"Process? Accelerate? Circumstances? You're already going too fast for me." Shifty said, waving a hand in front of her face, and with a slightly frantic look in her eye. "Can we slow down? Maybe go back to the beginning? Like, I don't know, the *sheehairn* and *Scath riocht*?"

"Of course."

"Changeling?"

"That's right."

"Do my parents know? Wait…are my parents this *sheehairn* thing, too? Are they from this realm you're talking about?"

"The Gilberts are human, Shifty."

"Oookkaaay…So, they aren't my biological parents?" Shifty raised her eyes to meet Nelda's and awaited the older woman's nod. "So, why? Why didn't my realm thingie parents raise me? Are they dead?"

"No. They are alive," Nelda said.

"So you're telling me my *Scath* parents didn't want me? Basically, I'm adopted?"

"No." Nelda shook her head. But she stopped suddenly. "Well, a little. I guess. But your parents didn't send you here because they didn't want you. More like…they…exchanged you. That doesn't sound much better, does it?"

"Not especially," Shifty agreed.

"They sent you here because your magic is very rare—"

"My what?" Shifty's words were louder than she'd anticipated. They bounced back at her off one of the nearby trees. She flinched and looked around. "My what?" she whispered.

"All the creatures that are born in the *Scath* have some kind of magic. *Sheehairn* are marked by their magic. The white patterns you've seen on your skin? We call them *rian*. There are many kinds of magic. The color of your *rian* show us which type will take root in you the deepest. For example..."

Nelda lifted her arm between them and a light green opalescent sheen spread from her fingers almost to her elbow. An elaborate purple pattern twined around her wrist.

"Purple. This tells any who would know that I work mostly in potions and totems, amulets, that kind of thing. Paxton's are yellow. He works with the elements, the weather. Peyton uses mind magic. Hers are blue. Tristan is a warrior, you can tell that by his red *rian*."

Shifty's mind swirled and she stared at Nelda's arm. She heard her own voice again in her head: *the white patterns*.

They knew. They knew what she'd been seeing. "Mine are white."

Nelda nodded. "Yes. Paxton told me."

Shifty had two questions lobbying to be the next thing she asked. "What do they mean?" She was actually surprised that *why didn't anyone tell me sooner?* lost the battle, but she tamped down the voice that was now screaming in her head and waited for Nelda's answer. She wondered exactly what was in the pink potion, for there could be no doubt that's what she'd drank.

"White *rian* are rare. They indicate a power over what we call *'riochtfios.'* It means that not only does your magic work in *Scath* and *Talam*, that's here—this realm, but also in *Sambaed*, the summerlands. *Riocht* travelers, or walkers, are exceptional. The *sambaed riocht* is not accessible to most creatures until after death, and none can use magic within its borders. Except for *sheehairn* with white *rian*, and as far as we know only *sheehairn can* have them. It is very powerful. And quite a mystery. Since the power almost never manifests what it can do hasn't been studied very extensively. No wraith or banshee has ever presented with white *rian*."

Shifty choked. "Wraiths or banshee? Those are real things?"

"They are very real. In the *riocht* we come from there are three types of creatures. *Sheehairn*, wraiths, and banshee. If a *sheehairn* and a wraith produce a child, those offspring are banshee. The *riocht* is steeped with magic and traditions. *Sheehairn* make up the majority of the populace and control most of the politics. Banshee are more akin to *sheehairn* than their wraith parents. The wraiths are...well, wraiths are dark. And cold. They don't just use it, they *are* black and dark magic. They're made from it. They crave power and will take out whoever and whatever stands in their way. Which brings us to why you were brought to this *riocht*. To *Talam*."

"Okay." Shifty was unclear if she felt better or worse about the information Nelda was providing her. She'd often thought that anything would have been better than being a freak; than constantly questioning her own sanity. But now that her entire reality was being brought into question, she was unsure if she was in a better position than before Nelda started talking.

"It's a lot, isn't it?"

Shifty barked a laugh and shook her head. "Yeah. Just a couple of tons on my back. And, oh by the way, you aren't even human. Plus, we haven't even touched on how in the world you know I see the *rian* and how much more you or my parents, either set, know that you haven't let on."

"I know. I'm sorry. This wasn't supposed to be the way you found out. But it is important we talk about it now. There are things you need to know in order to help us help to keep you safe. I wish I could break this to you in stages, give you time to deal with it. But we simply can't. We have to get it all out and dealt with. So. Are you okay to proceed? Can I get you something else to drink?"

Shifty nodded. "I'm okay." She took a sip of her half-full glass of sparkling pink. "Let's keep going."

"*Sheehairn* and banshees can use magic in both the *Scath* and *Talam riocht*, but with consequences here. A shift, if you will, in the natural progression of whatever type of magic is being used. A strange bolt of lightning," Nelda shot her son a significant look. He held her gaze steady, unwilling to admit any chagrin. She sighed. "Something like that would be a good sign that a weather magic user is casting...well...let's say...a safety spell?" Nelda smiled at her son this time and Shifty turned in his arms to look at her boyfriend's face. He smiled at Shifty and kissed her forehead.

"That was you at the house yesterday? The storm?" she whispered. He nodded his head. She settled herself more firmly into his embrace without trepidation, and focused her attention back to Nelda. "Go on."

"The magic of *Scath* comes from the power emitted by the darker things in the universe. Hate, jealousy, even death. Banshees are death magic users. Before you panic, that doesn't mean what you think it does. They don't work spells to kill people. Death is a very powerful force and banshees harness that power. This is where the legends of the banshee's keen come from. They do wail, though it is not a harbinger of a person's death, merely the chant of the banshee collecting power for their spells.

"Wraiths are probably the most powerful magical creatures in any *riocht*. They don't have specific elemental magic. Their yield is incredibly strong. But they can't leave *Scath* for more than a matter of moments. Most of them can't hold a glamour or even a corporeal form and they cannot perform no magic in *Talam*. They are restricted to *Scath* for their magic."

"And they don't like that?" Shifty guessed.

"Not by half," Peyton said.

"They don't like that," Nelda confirmed. "Which is why your parents sent you here. Your white *rian*, indicating control of *riochtfios*? In addition to having access to magic in all *riocht* and walking in them…" Nelda paused. Shifty thought she might scream from the tension.

"Let's put it this way: With the proper spells and ceremonies, the wraiths could also have magic in *Talam*. And probably more importantly to them, they would be able to walk in the *sambaed riocht*. Any creature who could travel there without surrendering their mortal existence would have opened a door to an unimaginable amount of power. It's a frightening concept; that kind of power in the hands of any creature. But for the wraiths to have it? It must be prevented. At any cost. Even if that cost is sending your own child away to be raised in a strange land by members of a different species."

Shifty could feel her pulse hammering in her temples. Her throat was dry and her vision clouded again. With every new piece of information, Shifty became convinced her grip on reality would finally snap. Paxton's mouth was close to her ear. "You hanging in there?" His breath moved her hair and it tickled around her neck and cheek.

"So far, so good," she confirmed and was surprised to find she meant the words.

Tristan's smile was grim. "You're a strong girl, Siofra. Together we'll make it through this. We're here to keep you safe. And that is what we're going to do, as we've always done. Do you believe me?" His gentle tone made the small shred of confidence she'd been clinging to swell and grow just a fraction larger. In her mind, she tightened her grip on it. She sat up straighter, separating herself from Paxton for the first time since the conversation began.

"I haven't felt so strong, honestly. But I'll try. I'll do what you tell me I need to in order to keep myself safe." She paused and cleared her throat, looked at the tablecloth, then the sky, and then back to Tristan. "My parents, do they know?"

"No," Nelda said quickly. "They don't know. They've had their memories of their human child taken from them. They were charmed to never question your glamour, to love you as their own. To treat you with nothing but kindness and love. There are a few things that a *hairn* needs to do to survive long term in *Talam*. These things were implanted when their memories were changed. As far as they know you're their child. Their love for you is honest in their hearts."

Shifty let out a long, slow breath. Her relief was so strong she realized she hadn't even been aware how afraid she was that her parents were involved with the ruse. Somehow, the idea that they had all been tricked made it better. Their concern for her, the constant parental hovering, the lullabies and bedtime story, their pride in her; it was real. It was love. Not a desire to keep her true nature from her. Not more lies. They'd all been lied to. They shared that. Unlike, apparently, the Devlins, they hadn't known what she had struggled with for years: Her visions. Her fear that she was insane. If they'd known and let her suffer anyway, that was what she didn't think she could withstand.

She realized that she should be angry not only at Nelda and Tristan, but Paxton and Peyton as well. "You knew," she whispered. She pushed herself out of his arms, creating a psychic border around her space on the picnic bench. "You knew I thought I was crazy. Knew what I was seeing. Knew what I was hiding. But you didn't tell me, Pax. How could you do that?"

He let out a long, unsteady breath and reached for her hand. She pulled it away from him and into her lap. She wasn't sure if she was angry with him, but she was sure she wanted to figure it out before he held her hand again. She was too used to Paxton making everything feel better. If she let herself slip into that comfort zone with him, she might never decide if she was upset with him.

"He didn't have a choice, Shifty," Peyton said. "Neither of us had a choice. Literally."

"What does that mean?"

"It means my mother is very good at what she does. She's made Paxton and me drink a potion twice a month since we moved here. It holds our tongues *for* us. Even if our parents hadn't given us dire warnings about what would happen if we betrayed our true nature or made any hint toward yours, we literally couldn't speak to you about any of it. And she watched us drink it. Like in prison. I have my suspicions about whether or not we needed it that often. But better safe than sorry, I'm betting." Peyton gave her mother a bitter look.

"Once a month probably would have sufficed, but I needed to be sure," Nelda said, earning her hateful glares from both her children. She smiled at them, apparently—like most mothers—immune to their scorn. She patted Shifty's knee. "They truly could not tell you. And they made it very clear on a regular basis that they wished they could—"

Paxton cut her off. "It killed me to do, Shifty. To watch you torture yourself about the visions and not be able to talk you about them. When I knew you'd begun taking the medications for a condition you didn't have I tried to cheek the potion, not easy with a liquid, but she caught me. I knew I was betraying a sacred trust when I reported what those medications were to my parents. I…" he ran his hands up her back and hid his face in her neck, distraught.

"If you want to be angry with someone— and you have the right to be, I won't argue that point—be angry with Tristan and me. We're the ones who've earned it. We made the decisions and insisted on compliance with our rules."

Shifty's hand remained in her lap but she did nod her head to indicate she'd heard the words, even if she wasn't prepared to give up her anger immediately. "You said there was a human baby sent to *Scath* in my place?"

"Yes. She was your parents' birth daughter. I believe her name is Evangeline."

"She's alive?"

"Oh, yes, most assuredly. It's the most integral part of the spell of the *siofra*. The changelings." Nelda took a breath, like a singer about to perform a difficult aria. "One from *Scath*. One from *Talam*. Born on the same day and treated as their parents' own from the time of the exchange. Both will survive and thrive. While it is not necessary for the *hairn*'s adoptive parents to have their memories of the exchange taken from them, exchanges have failed horribly when that step was not taken. So, as a precaution—you must see, Shifty, that this exchange was crucial—it was decided to alter the minds of your human guardians."

"Parents," Shifty murmured.

"Parents. Of course."

Shifty bobbed her head, somehow mollified by the speed with which Nelda had agreed. Though there was interstate of tangents running through her mind: the one that whispered questions about what would now happen in *Talam* was one of the more disturbing. Was Nelda implying that she must now return to a family, a home, and an entire reality that she'd never known? Shifty knew what it felt like to be just a little different, a little weird. If she went back to these parents, this *riocht*; on one hand she would be with creatures that were like her and live in a world she'd always been meant to inhabit. On the other hand, she would still be the different member of her community. There she would be able to have green skin, white *rian*, eyes that shifted from the strange, slightly golden orange all the way to black. There her hair would be orange and purple. Her movements would not be strange and she wouldn't need to control them. All of those things were overwhelmingly appealing.

To fit in and be a part of a community that didn't think she was odd, didn't shove medication and therapy sessions at her? That idea stirred something deep at the core of her being. A place that called to the most elemental part of her.

On the other, very large hand; once she got there and dropped her glamour? Then where was she? With her family? Maybe. Technically. But really she would be in a land of strange creatures, unknown customs, magic, and quite a bit of darkness. If what Nelda was telling her was to be believed. This lane of the interstate was a scary one and Shifty didn't want Nelda steering down it. She didn't want to discuss a possible future tonight. There was plenty new and frightening information from the past to mull over first.

"So, they didn't know. Help me understand something else?"

Nelda nodded, but said nothing.

"Well, you seem surprised by my white *rian*. If my parents sent me here to protect me, why didn't they tell you about it?"

Nelda was silent for a few minutes. Her eyes, which had begun to show a ring of color, had now turned completely black again. "While they didn't tell me outright, there were signs at your birth. Signs they kept hidden from all but their most trusted circle. They knew you were important and that the wraiths would come for you. I think we all made a kind of unspoken agreement not to discuss it. To believe what your parents told us and proceed. As I told you, your parents are *hairn* leaders, so running with you was not an option. They have political business with the wraiths, angering them or bringing about their suspicion was not a risk they could take. Not with their child. Not with their *riocht*. So they created a ruse: a reason for the exchange.

"They knew a human baby shared your birthdate, knew the exchange could be made without either of your deaths. A human changeling in *Scath* is a valuable thing that can be used for powerful magic. So the wraiths were anxious to make the exchange. It had to be done quickly once the decision was made; it happened before you were even a week old. They did this for your safety, Shifty. They gave you up in order to keep you from being a pawn in the wraiths' quest for magical power. I believe your parents saw the signs of possible *riochtfios*, but *rian* don't usually appear until a child is five or six, so they wouldn't have seen them. I also believe they had no idea how powerful your marks would be."

"Why?"

"Because of the glamours and the spells they placed on you. If they had any idea how powerful your magic was, I think they would have used very different spells. Ironically, the main reason your glamour has faded almost completely is probably due to the medications."

"Okay, I'm lost," Shifty admitted.

"There are things in this *riocht* that will negatively affect us, either physically, or by impacting our magic in all its forms. Some of those things are certain metals."

"All right."

"Lithium is an alkali metal."

Wide-eyed, Shifty nodded in understanding.

"I suspected your glamour might continue to fade when Paxton told me what you were prescribed. We considered replacing your medications with placebos, but it seemed too risky. We didn't want your doctor to run blood tests and accuse you of not taking your meds. We assumed that would only go further in convincing you that you were crazy. We decided that since you were already being treated for 'visions,' it couldn't be much worse." Nelda paused and laughed a little ironically to herself. "But you managed to prove us wrong. In the long run it is better we didn't. Knowing you're a *riochtfios* user explains why your glamour didn't hold in the first place. Your magic is simply too strong."

Shifty finally took Paxton's hand back. She was still unsure if she'd forgiven him. Even though he'd been literally unable to share anything with her, emotionally, it felt like what he'd done was a betrayal. But she needed his hand in hers, needed to know he was there. And real. So she concentrated on his warmth, and the firmness of his grip on hers.

"So, what's your part in this?" she asked the table. "How'd you come to live next door to me? This isn't coincidence. Are you part of keeping me safe from the…" she paused, trying to remember which creatures were which. "Wraiths?"

"Yes, from the wraiths. Your *hairn* parents tasked us with watching over you. Making sure their spells held. Ensuring your human parents did all the things necessary to keep you safe. Probably our most important duty was to make sure they treated you with all the love of a true parent. We were to make sure you were healthy and happy and growing normally. And that your glamour held."

"Epic fail," Peyton said. She was silent for a second, but the laughter eventually made its way past her lips. When it crested it was loud, clear, and joyful. Everyone at the table turned their attention to her as she laughed until tears streamed down her face. She slapped her thigh and rocked back and forth, laughing until the hiccups started. Paxton pounded her on the back and she pushed his hand away, reaching for her drink to try and quell the spasms. When she'd finally regained control of her faculties, she slumped against her brother.

"Peyton's got an excellent point," Tristan said. "We have the same task now as we did before your glamour faded. We can't drop our guard or neglect our duty. We will just need to teach Shifty to help in the task." He looked at Shifty. He still had the eyes of his human face and a deeply serious cast to his expression. "Are you able to do that, Siofra? Are you able to trust us to keep you safe?"

Was she? Could she admit, even if only to herself, that she believed she wasn't human? That finding this information was the first time since she was a small child that her world had made sense? That knowing she was *sheehairn* made her feel special and somehow complete? But it also made her feel abandoned and scared, like she'd been betrayed at a very basic level. Sorting out who to trust and what path to take, it wasn't going to be a simple task. She'd always trusted her instincts, her inner voice, even in the face of diagnosed insanity. And she'd always trusted Paxton and Peyton to walk with her. At times their home had been her refuge. Had that been the comfort of home calling to her? It turned out her inner voice had been truer than anything else in her world. That part of her had seen what everything else had said was impossible. She searched for the voice's counsel now. She realized it was the only thing she truly trusted, at least in this instant. Slowly, but with confidence, Shifty nodded her head. She looked at each person at the table. She stopped at Paxton. His eyes searched hers.

She knew he was looking for forgiveness, understanding, or fear. But most of all, he was looking for the love he always found there. She let him search, hoping her inner voice would push her feelings into her gaze. When he smiled and his shoulders lost some of their tension, she knew he'd seen it. They had much to discuss, to settle, and to try to make right. But in the end, her love for him and her trust in his love for her were untainted. Just as he was physically real, her love for him was the touchstone of her sanity.

"I'll trust you. But I want to help. I don't want to be locked away in a protected tower. Let me use all this power you say I have."

CHAPTER

FOURTEEN

Evangeline was by the altar behind her house when she heard the noise. It was high-pitched, reedy and unfamiliar. It wasn't a banshee's keen. Not the incantation of a wraith. She spun herself in a slow circle, trying to pin the sound to a general direction. Something about the bleating stirred in her a need to find and assist whatever was making the noise. Somehow she was it was a sound of distress.

But the night air was conspiring against her. The sounds bounced to points at once behind and in front of her, and then to her left and immediately to her right. She whipped her head around and tried to follow the cascading noises until she felt dizzy and a sick.

Finally, frustrated, she sat on the ground, tilted her chin toward the sky, and closed her eyes. She allowed the sound to drift to her and penetrate her being. The crying started again. Or maybe it had never stopped? She rose without opening her eyes and allowed her inner-self to follow the sound. Her feet were sure under her as she made her way closer to the whimpering, its determination and volume increasing with each step she took. She moved more soundlessly than she would have thought possible. It was almost as if she were a hairn, native to the riocht. As if something in the air didn't want her discovered.

She felt the scratching of birches against her face; branches clung to her hair as she passed them. She didn't open her eyes. The crying grew louder, clearer, and closer. And it was becoming more *urgent. It pushed on some part of Evangeline's stomach that made her feel the need to vomit. Under the wails another sound had started to emerge.*

She opened her eyes and stood, planting her feet to reorient herself. At first she was sure it was the wind rattling the branches, or the mist rustling the leaves at her feet. But there was no wind, and the fog—though thick tonight—was still. It was soupy and opaque, full of magic. Then she knew what it was, the wind-like noise. It was a wraith's chant, low, guttural, and harsh. The wraith chants didn't sound so much like words; they were more like breaths being pulled from somewhere deep by a series of painful blows.

～

The wood was cold and a little damp with condensation. The corner of the house bit into her side as Evangeline crouched carefully under the window. While she waited for Locke to signal the coast was clear, she watched the stars and tried to stop feeling like a criminal. The wind had picked up, chilling her to the point that her teeth had begun to chatter by the time the window above her finally cracked open. Locke made a ridiculous attempt at a bird call. She bit back most of a laugh. His hand appeared above her, a grin hiding behind the finger he had pressed to his lips. "Hush! This is a stealth mission, remember?"

She hopped down from the ground, a heel catching on the hem of her skirt and she had to steady herself on the rough wood of the house. The impact of her hand made a hollow smacking sound. Her eyes held a guilty glint to them when she smiled up at Locke. "We're really bad at this!"

"We?" He leaned from the window and offered her his arms. It was only a few feet from the ground to the base of the window, but he bent further out of the window and gripped her beneath both arms, hoisted her over the frame, and brought her into the library where he stood. The movement was quick and sure. And silent. He set her on her feet and winked at her. "Speak for yourself."

"Are your parents home?" Evangeline asked. Mostly she meant was his father home. His father the wraith. His father the creepiest creature in shadow, with the possible exception of Tresara's mother. Unconsciously, she fiddled with the ring on the cord around her neck that her father had given her when she was a child. She ran it along the length of the cord, and tried to draw bravery out of it. How was it that two of her favorite friends had the scariest parents?

Locke nodded. "Dad isn't here, but in town, apparently. Mom's in the kitchen cooking. She likes to have a meal ready when he gets here. We've not got a lot of time."

"Better get started." Evangeline stepped to a bookshelf and started scanning the titles.

"What are we looking for? You know, I mean…exactly?" Locke asked, stooping next to her and started scanning.

"Any sort of translator. I guess. Or anything with mythology based on the history of *Scath*. Something that talks about Siofra or the *riochts*. Any large text written entirely in wraith. If I can get a good sampling, I might be able to translate effectively. I've never had much access to the wraiths' written language, just the symbols used in their magic. They are super possessive of their history and their language."

"Wraiths are weird," Locke muttered, touching the spine of a particularly old book and pulling it out to skim through its pages.

Evangeline peered at him from the corner of her vision and cracked a devilish smile. "Forgetting something about yourself there, banshee boy?"

"Doesn't everyone think their parents are weird?" he countered. He put the book back in its place on the shelf, obviously dissatisfied with its contents.

"I guess."

Evangeline moved more quickly through the titles than Locke and was already onto the next bookshelf across the room. She glanced at Locke over her shoulder. He was engrossed in his task and didn't feel her watching him. He trusted her, she realized with a sudden warmth in her chest. He was helping her search his father's belongings for items they knew Cecil wouldn't want them to have. Secrets of his kind, secrets of a world she was never supposed to belong to. She couldn't help but wonder how many times Locke would take her side and how far she would be able to push his alliance. His sense of honor was so strong, so noble. The fact that she was his assigned mate would carry quite a bit of weight, but the reason she'd been promised to him was because of his family and hers. Eventually, she feared, his loyalties would not be with her. She only hoped she had no reason to expect to be on a different path than their elders. But the knot in her stomach and the strange feeling that niggled in the back of her mind told her they'd only just begun to diverge from those who held power over her and her friends.

"Evangeline! Look at this." Locke's voice brought her back from the valley of her own thoughts. She turned to him and the book he was holding. He flipped through the thick, yellowed pages for her. It appeared to all be written in the same language as the *Siofra* book: Linus's gobble-y-gook. Evangeline nodded her head.

"Yeah, this is good. Not going to get me anywhere fast. But…" She flipped through a few more pages and grinned. "See this? There are drawings here. If I can connect the text with the sketches, I can get an idea was what the symbols mean. From there I can work out the rest of the language. Probably Linus can help me with that."

"Isn't there some kind of spell we can cast?" Locke asked, his voice showing his impatience.

Evangeline punched him lightly on the shoulder and leaned her body against Locke's father's desk. She tucked most of her hair behind her ear in an unconscious movement, and turned a few pages of the book more slowly than before. "No, we can't throw a powder on it and make the pictures translate themselves. There are clarity draughts and things like that, but all they are going to do is open your mind and make the job of learning easier. I'll solve this one the same way I always do: with my nose pressed firmly onto the grindstone." She hefted the book up. "Can we take this with us? Will he notice?"

Locke shrugged. "Only one way to find out." He took the book from her and shoved it into the bag they'd brought with them for this specific purpose. "Keep looking?"

Distracted, Evangeline nodded and turned to walk back to the shelves. She stopped short, staring at Cecil's desk. Locke looked up from securing the book in his bag. "What is it?" he asked.

Evangeline took a couple of steps toward the desk and leaned over it, chewing at the corner of her mouth. She reached out and turned a piece of paper with two fingers, so it faced her, and outlined something on the page with her pinkie.

"Evangeline!" Locke barked as loudly as he dared. Though his mother had seen him enter the house, she didn't know Evangeline was there. She certainly didn't need to know they were in Cecil's study.

"Sorry," she hissed. "Here it is again." Locke came to stand next to her and looked over her shoulder.

"Oh, wow." They were looking at a sketch, quite obviously drawn in his father's hand. Also obviously, it was unfinished. The drawing was of an altar, and had blank spaces that were apparently meant to be filled in with text. In front of the altar was a small kneeling bench, long enough to accommodate half a dozen creatures or so, by the scale. The altar itself was a raised platform, with two wood pallets connected adjacent to it. Small poles holding long scrolls stuck out on either side of the pallet. The beginnings of a symbol had been sketched in a light and unsure hand, but the scrolls were what had grabbed Evangeline's attention. On each of them, in a heavy red hand, was *the* symbol. The symbol from Locke's knife. The one on the book Ciarda had read to Evangeline. The symbol Evangeline had come to think of as *Siofra*. The symbol in this drawing did not invoke a warm feeling. It did not put one at ease. A shudder ran down Evangeline's spine and she leaned against Locke, hoping to feel safer. He put an arm around her shoulder and pulled her even closer. There was something visceral in the image of this symbol on the scrolls. Something that made Evangeline push the page away from them and turn ever so slightly more into Locke's chest.

"We have *got* to translate that symbol. And *fast*," she said into his shoulder.

She peered up at him and found him unable to form words as well. He managed only to nod his head in agreement.

"I suppose we should stop? With your dad on his way and your mother in the house?"

"Probably the wisest choice. Do you think you have what you need?" Locke asked.

"For now. We'll meet up with the rest and see if they came up with anything."

"They got Linus; they'll find *something*," Locke assured her. She stepped away from him and pushed the window back open. Locke squirmed. "I feel funny pushing you out of a window."

"Then give me your hand and don't leave me in the cold too long."

He held out his hand and helped lower her back out the window. "I'll be there as fast as I can get away." He watched her critically for a moment. She stood in the growing mist of the evening. His forehead crinkled. He set the bag with his father's book inside of it on the ground and shrugged out of his jacket and hung it over the sill to her. "It's freezing out there. Take this."

She draped it over her shoulders. "Thanks. Just hurry."

One second he was framed in the window and the next he was gone, presumably making excuses to his mother for missing the evening meal. She turned away from the house and walked a little way toward the woods and the path. The wind and mist had picked up in the time they'd been in the MacNair house. She pulled Locke's jacket tighter around herself, slipping her arms into the sleeves. The wall of mist was so thick she couldn't see her feet as she moved and the tendrils drifted around her knees. She was so hypnotized by the mist that the voices from in front of Locke's house made her jump. After pulling herself back together she moved toward the noise without even meaning to, her innate curiosity taking over.

"Lachlan." Cecil MacNair's voice always sounded cold, but there was an extra icy current running through it tonight. Evangeline burrowed even deeper into the coat, creating a barrier from the chill in the night air as well as in the wraith's tone.

"What are you doing out here?" Cecil barked. "I'm sure your mother is almost ready to put food on the table. Come inside."

"I'm not eating with you tonight," Locke said.

"I see. This is becoming a pattern with you, son. Your mother doesn't like it."

"I know."

Evangeline strained her ears, but that was all he said. She peered around a tree, trying to get a look at the banshee and his father. Through the mist she could make out their shapes. They both stood ramrod straight and were practically toe to toe. Between them was a wall of unspoken confrontation and anger. Evangeline took two involuntary steps backward, easing away from the conflict.

"The Gathering is soon. I trust you will have swallowed whatever problem you have with me by that time and can be in attendance with the rest of your family? There are important matters to discuss and decide. The *aontuet* approaches as well." Cecil's voice ended abruptly, even though the thought seemed unfinished.

Evangeline strained both eyes and ears, but it seemed nothing more was passing between them. The mist parted suddenly and Locke was in front of her. She jumped back, startled by his sudden appearance. She hadn't even known the conversation with his father had ended.

He smiled, but brought a finger to his lips, urging silence. She nodded. He took her hand and they started down the path. When they were a good clip away from his house Locke finally spoke.

"My father and I have some, uh, problems communicating."

Evangeline nodded her head and then realizing that he might not be able to see her clearly, said, "Yeah. Sorry."

"Don't be sorry. He's a difficult man to be related to. No one else should even have to try to understand."

Evangeline considered his profile. She'd expected a little anger, some bitterness, maybe a even like he was going to make a joke to divert attention from what she had heard, but Locke looked dejected and sad. She applied a small amount of pressure to the hand she held in her own. He turned to catch her eye and offered half a smile. She wouldn't push. She couldn't expect him to admit all his family secrets, his most guarded feelings. She only wanted him to know that she'd be next to him. If he decided he wanted to tell her those things, that would be fine too.

"He's not happy with me," Locke said. His voice was so quiet, Evangeline wasn't sure he'd even spoken. "There've been fights at my house lately."

"Oh?" Evangeline prompted.

Locke laughed, a rough horse's snort of a sound, through his nose. The cold air clouded even more around his face. "He thinks I dishonor them. Our family. Their choices."

Evangeline watched her feet as they proceeded down the path, the small puffs of mist that lifted around them when she placed her foot down. She thought she knew what the fights were about. Her. He didn't want her. He was only being kind to her, trying to figure out a way to make their *aontuet* work. A way to keep the peace. It was an attempt to reconcile what he wanted with what he thought was his duty. She didn't want to be his duty.

"Did you hear me?" His words were jarring, though not because of his tone, which had been soft. She'd been lost in her thoughts and in fact, she hadn't heard him.

"Sorry, I didn't."

"My father doesn't understand why I wouldn't want all they chose for me. You know, when I was born. Before they even knew who I was. What I might dream about? What I might be good at? Not taken into consideration."

"I won't expect you to love me," Evangeline whispered.

Locke's feet stopped moving and Evangeline took a couple more steps before their hands had been pulled to their limit and she was jerked back toward him. She found him staring at her, forehead creased and his eyes intense. "Is that what you think I mean?"

"I know duty is important to you."

"It is. You're right. I'm not talking about you or our *aontuet*. I believe we can make that work, Lenny," he paused, smiling at her. He hardly ever used the nickname that her girlfriends did. She knew he'd chosen it now specifically to show her that he was earnest in his intent. "It's the way of *Scath*. It is tradition. I am not unhappy with our parents' decision. You and I? We can make a place in each other's hearts. I believe that. What I don't want, and what I've made very clear to my father I *am* unhappy with, is a place at the Leaders' Table. I don't wish to sit on the Council."

"I see," Evangeline said, cheeks blazing and mind reeling. "What do you want?"

"I want to join the *Hairn* Guard," he said. "For real. Not the ceremonial appointment I'd receive if I took a spot on the Council. I want to join the rank and file, stand shoulder to shoulder with the blues and greens who protect our borders. As a banshee I have the right to join. My father is violently opposed. I don't think it helped when I insinuated that his opposition was a direct result of either his cowardice or that fact that wraiths can't join the Guard."

"Locke!" Evangeline's jaw hung open for a few seconds longer than she'd meant for it to. "You did *not* say that to your father!"

He nodded, looking equal parts ashamed and defiant. "I did. I also reminded him the *reason* wraiths aren't allowed to join the Guard is because their magic is restricted by the boundaries of our *riocht*. That his very *shape* dissolves at its borders."

"Mist over the moon," Evangeline whispered.

"Yeah. That's about right." He sighed. "He responded about how you'd expect."

"Mist over the moon," Evangeline repeated, still stunned. One just *did not* speak to wraiths like that. Even if they were your family.

"Would it matter to you?" Locke asked.

"Afraid you lost me again, Locke." She touched his cheek lightly with her free hand. She hadn't meant to, but she'd found she was unable to stop herself from wanting to comfort him. He placed his hand over hers. They stood that way for a moment.

"If I joined the Guard. If I didn't assume my role on the Council. Would it matter to you?"

"Oh." She was flustered.

He was worried about her reaction to his plans for the future? Unsure if she would think it was proper for him, as her mate, to be only a soldier. She was struck suddenly with the realization that he was used to the confident human girl with pride of place in her community. The child who usually didn't think twice about issuing a request of her elder. Someone with an air of privilege. He didn't know she was afraid she'd never truly be a part of the world she'd been raised in. That she looked at their skin and their marks and she wanted so badly to be one of them. He didn't see the little girl with a crush on the boy who was already betrothed to be her *ceile*.

She leaned forward and kissed him very quickly on each of his cheeks.

"No, Lachlan, it doesn't matter to me." She smiled, trying to show him how much she meant what she told him. "I would be proud of you."

CHAPTER

FIFTEEN

The tray of snickerdoodles was nothing but crumbs. The sparkling pink mixture had been consumed. The night had grown dark around them. The stars and moon were shining down on the table of *sheehairn* shrouded under a canopy of trees. The candles on the table flickered in the wind, and the voices spoke, low and earnest. Eventually, the words slowed. And though the very world had changed around them, it also moved forward.

Paxton wondered over this as his parents stood to retire for the evening, their arms laden with used plates, empty glasses, and dirty linens. How the foundation of Shifty's world had become an unbelievable fairy tale, and now, a mere two hours after the revelation, everyone needed to get some sleep or finish their homework. They would brush their teeth and dream their dreams. The world didn't falter on its axis simply because Shifty Gilbert had discovered she wasn't human. It soldiered on. Somehow, this was comforting.

"Want to stay here tonight?" Paxton asked, yawning widely.

"Is that stuff legally intoxicating?" Shifty rattled the ice in her glass.

"I don't think it would register on a breathalyzer, but probably better to be safe than sorry. A ticket is the least of the consequences of driving under the influence," Peyton said.

"You think Mom and Dad are going to let her sleep in your room?" she teased her brother, leveling a kick at his shin.

Paxton moved his leg easily and caught her foot, pulling it up and over in a way that should have thrown Peyton off balance and knocked her off the bench backward. Instead, the girl remained comfortably level on the bench with her leg bending toward her body. Her skin was still "flesh" tone, the surface unmarred by any colorful pattern, but the joint moved in the way of a *hairn*.

Shifty stared.

"Not such a special little gym star now, are you?" Peyton grinned.

Shifty shook her head, mute. Her face showed what her words were having trouble conveying. Paxton watched it all play out on her features. She wasn't alone, wasn't a freak, there were other creatures who moved the way she did. She was so grateful. All she could do was grin stupidly at her friend, jump to her feet, and fling her arms around Peyton's neck.

Peyton's laugh was quick, fast, and light. She reached up and rested her hands on Shifty's arms, squeezing her friend lightly.

"See? Where's your competitive spirit? You aren't supposed to want to share the spotlight. Gut check time, Gilbert."

"I'll do that tomorrow. Remind me to get super jealous. In the morning."

She disentangled herself to stand next to Paxton again.

He smiled up at her from his seat and she ruffled his hair.

"Well, if there's a chance I'm going to get booted from your room shortly, maybe we could go talk?" She winked at him.

Peyton's eyebrows disappeared into her hairline at the word "talk," but she remained silent as Paxton and Shifty walked through the back door and disappeared inside the house.

Once inside and behind the closed door of his room, Paxton flopped onto his bed and pulled Shifty next to him. They lay with arms wrapped around each other's waists, just living in the new reality, soaking it in and trying it on.

"I want to see," Shifty said.

"See what?" Paxton asked.

"You."

He kissed the tip of her nose and both her eyelids. When he pulled away, her eyes remained closed. "You see me all the time."

"You know what I mean."

"I do." He cleared his throat. "I'm not used to dropping my glamour. Peyton's terrible about it. She can barely keep hers on once she closes the door. But I've never dropped mine."

"Your hair is teal," Shifty said.

"Yeah. Wait. How'd you know that?"

"I saw it. When you were reading on the porch. But I thought I made it up, or the light did, or something. Now it makes sense."

"I didn't drop my glamour, especially not outside." His breathing was sharp. "Damn, Shifty. Your magic is strong. You can break through glamours without meaning to. I've never heard of that. I mean, I'm hardly an expert or anything, but if it was common I'd probably know at least one instance of it."

"How do you drop a glamour?"

"Glamours are mostly mental spells. They're placed with an incantation, sometimes helped with a potion or a totem to make them stronger. They're released the same way. A lifting incantation."

Shifty, eyes still steadfastly clamped shut, moved closer to Paxton. Her mouth quirked. "Teach it to me," she whispered in the general area of his ear.

He did. He taught her the verse. It wasn't complicated, but some of the words were unknown to her. She stumbled, and stuttered, and laughed. She rested her head against his chest, facing him, but her eyes remained closed. When the incantation was done, she sighed, pressing herself further into his arms, hiding her face in her hair. She seemed frightened suddenly by what his reaction to her would be.

"I don't feel any different," she said, the words traveling through him more as a reverberation on his skin than as sound to his ears. "Tell me when I can look."

Before moving again, he closed his own eyes. He reached down and lifted her face from his chest, adjusting their bodies on the bed as he did. He made sure they were now a few inches apart. He held her face in his hands. He studied her breathing, making his own match hers. He lay there with her, her face warm in his hands, her cheeks the only part of her body that touched his own. A deep calm took him over. He could easily live in this pocket of time with her forever—this sweet, wonderful moment right before everything changed. The precipice of true revelation. True discovery.

Her faith in him was palpable and intoxicating. "Whenever you want, you tell me. I'll wait," he told her.

Her exhale lifted his hair. It was warm and carried with it the faint remnant of his mother's summer sun mead. It sent a shiver all the way through him.

"Ready?" Shifty asked, and then without waiting for him to answer, "Now!"

Her orange eyes met his deep purple ones. She blinked once, twice, and a third time before letting her gaze travel from his face down. Without breaking her stare, she slipped a hand beneath his shirt, and with a graceful move that rolled him onto his back, pulled the garment over his head. She let it drop to the floor as she placed herself above him. Her hands roamed his chest, across his stomach, his shoulders. Shifty smiled when his breath quickened. Finally, she shifted her eyes to his face and studied his expression. With one finger she gently, ever so gently, traced the yellow *rian* that swirled along the side of his throat and curled just to the edge of his jaw. Her other hand found its way to his head and she twined her fingers into his bright hair. She laced its strands between her fingers.

"You're amazing," she whispered.

"I can't believe you're watching me." His voice was as low as hers.

"What do you mean?"

"You've believed for how long that what you've seen isn't there, that who you are isn't real. Your glamour is gone, you can see for yourself what is really there, and you're still looking at me."

"You're amazing," she repeated. Then her shoulders sagged slightly. "And I'm scared."

"What are you scared of?"

A single tear traveled from the corner of one of her eyes and rolled, unnoticed, across her cheek.

"That it isn't real. That when I look, I'll still be me."

"Don't be afraid." He smiled. "I'm looking at you, I'm here. You've always been you, Shifty. The green and the white, orange and violet? Do you know what they mean to me? They mean you are everything I ever knew you could be. Everything I knew you were. You're a *sheehairn*, Siofra. You're powerful. You're gentle. You believe in the right things. In amazing things. And, well, you're mine. I'm so lucky. And not because of the color of your skin, and your marks. Because of you, Shifty. What I see when I look at you is the *hairn* that I am in love with. A kind creature. We come from a dark place, but we are not evil. Cold? Sometimes. Calculating and harsh? Yes. But the *hairn* are proud and intelligent, good, and even loving. We are. And you, you are proof of that. Proof that just because our magic is derived from the darker things in the universe doesn't mean our species is destined to be lost to the drive of the wraiths. You can be nervous, my love. But please, *please* do not be afraid of what you are."

"You're amazing."

"You're stalling."

She took a huge breath and pushed herself away from him

and off the bed. On the back of the bedroom door was a full length mirror. Shifty walked to it, her eyes once again closed. She stood still for three more breaths, which he counted with the rise and fall of her shoulders, before her eyelids slowly lifted. For several beats she didn't move. In her eyes there was no emotion, no shift of recognition, but no rejection or tears either. As if in slow motion, she moved closer to the mirror and touched the face in her reflection. Her other hand touched her real cheek. Her orange eyes blazed wet and bright and she blinked at herself. She was there, a tall and willowy *hairn*, her shimmering green skin bright and beautiful. Her white *rian* blazed a trail across her skin from her neck to her clavicle and disappeared under her shirt. She touched her hair, blazing purple with orange streaks. *Sheehairn.* She was *sheehairn.*

He knew she didn't see him rise from the bed, but she didn't jump when he appeared behind her in the mirror's reflection. He watched his arms wrap around her middle, hold her arms around her as well, securing them together. His chin rested on her shoulder. His eyes stared into hers in their reflection.

Their colors swirled and it was a celebration. There was magic in the mirror. Happiness. Love. Discovery. Truth.

"I'm not crazy."

"This is true."

"I'm not human."

"Also true."

"I'm in danger."

"You are."

"I'm not helpless."

"No."

"I'm scared. But not of who I am."

"And that's okay."

"I love you, Paxton Devlin."

"Say it again. It keeps me awake."

CHAPTER

SIXTEEN

Evangeline and Igby sat side by side barricading the door to her room with their backs. The *Siofra* book and the items they used to decipher it were spread before them, but had been forgotten for the moment.

"You should just say something to him!" Evangeline squeezed her friend's shoulder.

Igby didn't answer, but she made a strange, strangled noise and her eyes bulged.

"I see." Evangeline giggled. "Tell me how you really feel about it."

"I feel that's the worst idea you've ever had. That's how I really feel about it. You've seen me! I chirp when he's around."

"No!" Evangeline said without any true conviction. Chirp actually *was* a pretty fair assessment of the way Igby's voice jumped when Linus was in their presence. "It's not that bad."

"Whatever. I don't want to talk about that. Tell me more about Locke and his plan to alienate his father."

"I don't think that's the reason for his plan."

"Maybe not," Igby said sagely, "but the outcome will be the same. I wouldn't tell Cecil MacNair I had a different idea about anything than he did. Let alone if I was his child. And about the Council! Is Locke planning on mentioning this to his parents before or after the *aontuet*?"

"I didn't ask," Evangeline said. "It didn't seem important. What he does or doesn't do politically doesn't matter to me."

"If his father kills him on the spot, you might feel differently."

"Don't be stupid. That isn't going to happen." But as soon as Evangeline dismissed the idea it seemed all the more possible. You didn't go against Cecil MacNair. Well, not without a good plan. Evangeline made a weak attempt to smile. "Maybe I should ask him to wait until after the ceremony at least?"

The two girls laughed with more abandon, which made the book on Igby's lap fall to the floor with a slam. Evangeline picked it up and turned it over in her hands. "This is frustrating. I have no idea where to start. Any translations I've done before, I had some kind of a key. Something to give me a hint."

She opened the book on her own lap and turned the pages roughly. It was the book she and Locke had pilfered from his father's office and the longer she studied the strange characters, the more they blurred together. None of them were familiar. She knew just a few of the wraiths' symbols, but had never been exposed to their language as a whole. The spiky, harsh black characters written in a heavy hand only mocked her from the pages.

The door shook at their backs, three sharp knocks. Both girls jumped and began shoving books under Evangeline's bed.

"Just a minute, Mom!" Evangeline yelled.

"It's not your mother," Tresara whispered harshly through the heavy wood. "Open the door and let me in!"

Igby, closer to the door, threw it open and motioned the banshee through. Evangeline pushed the books back into the center of the floor as the door closed again. Tresara looked around the room, apparently decided on the small table Evangeline kept next to her bed, and shoved that in front of the door. The lantern atop it wobbled and rattled. Tresara grabbed and caught it just before it crashed to the floor. All three girls sighed in relief.

"Did you find something?" Evangeline, suspecting that Tresara had a parcel stashed under her jacket, felt excitement growing in her stomach. Tresara's mother was a wraith and one with not a small amount of power and knowledge. If any wraith would have ancient secrets hidden in her home, it would be Lara Keelin.

"Wait for it!" Tresara laughed. She double-checked the door over her shoulder and shrugged out of her coat, producing a small book and holding it out to Evangeline. "The key to translating *Siofra* isn't going to be in that book you found in Locke's father's room."

"What?" Evangeline asked. She took the tome from Tresara but didn't look at it. "Why? If I can find enough similar characters I should be able to translate and move from there. It is just a matter of—"

"It's not going to happen, Lenny," Tresara interrupted. "Because the key is hidden in magic. Wraith magic. Look."

She reached for the book again but Evangeline held it out of reach and opened it on her own. She perched on the edge of her bed with a friend on each side, reading over her shoulder.

"Whoa! Go back, go back. What was that?" Igby's hand was suddenly in front of the book, waving frantically in a gesture that seemed to indicate Evangeline should work her way back several pages. Evangeline obeyed. She flipped the pages back until Igby slammed her palm against the page. "*There!* What in *anail laghairt* is that?"

Evangeline looked at the page. Her breathing was sharp and short. "That's a spell. A revealing spell. What is this book, Tresara?"

"I found it in my mother's room. It was with her journals. As far as I can tell, this is her *Scath Fios*."

At the words Evangeline dropped the book between them. She'd never held a book of *Scath's* spells before, let alone the knowledge spells of the most powerful wraith Evangeline knew.

Her hands began to shake. She wiped them on her thighs but found she could do nothing to control her breathing.

Igby stared at Evangeline wide-eyed. Evangeline knew her behavior was scaring her best friend. Something in her voice, her manner, was setting the very air around them on edge.

"You have to take this back to her, Tresara. She'll notice it's gone." Evangeline nudged the book closer to Tresara. Tresara shoved it back.

"Copy down what you think we need, then I'll take it back. We have time before Mother returns home. She's with the Council planning the *aontuet*. Move quickly and we'll be fine."

Tresara sounded much calmer than Evangeline felt. Having the *Scath Fios* in her possession made her sick to her stomach. The book of spells was powerful and frightening. Every creature of age in *Scath* had one. They were not books that sat on a shelf and collected dust; not books to go unnoticed if they went missing, even for a day or overnight. If Tresara's mother returned home early for any reason she'd know the book was gone, and she would go looking for it.

Evangeline reluctantly picked the book back up and began rifling quickly through the pages, muttering the titles of spells as she went. The ones she could make out, anyway. Most of them were in a language of *Scath* that Evangeline was familiar with. Some were a strange combination of the wraith symbols she knew and the *hairn* words she'd grown up with. None of them covered the exact spell she was looking for as well as the one Igby had originally noticed. It contained only the one wraith symbol that had caught Igby's attention—the *Siofra* symbol they were all now so accustomed to. The rest of it was in the language of *Scath*, which Evangeline had learned as a child. She could easily copy the spell, list its ingredients, and lay out the instructions for its casting. Having not a shred of magical blood; she couldn't work it on her own, but she had help.

She scribbled as fast as she could, making sure she was noting all the specifics, checking and double-checking her words for clarity. Sweat collected on her lip as she worked. She wanted nothing more than to get the book back to Tresara's house safely. But the scholar in her made her go slowly. Her calculations had to be correct, the formulas accurate, and the phrasing exactly as it was on the page of Lara Keelin's *Scath Fios*. Finally when she was satisfied, she let out a long breath and shoved the book into Tresara's hands.

"Go. Get it back to your house. Igby and I will go collect the boys. Meet us at the birch cove near Locke's house when the moon is high."

"Tonight?" Igby's eyes bulged, but Tresara didn't question. She tucked the book back in her waistband, threw on her coat, and was out the door. Igby turned back to Evangeline. "Tonight?"

"Has to be." Evangeline pointed to her paper. "According to this, we have only until the sun rises on this day in the cycle to cast the spell, or we have to wait until the next cycle. I don't think we can wait."

"Why?"

"Because what if this has something to do with the *aontuet*? I want to know what it is before Locke and I arrive at the ceremony."

CHAPTER

SEVENTEEN

In the end, Shifty snuck down the hall and joined Peyton on the inflatable mattress on her floor long after midnight. Even though the Devlins probably wouldn't have minded, she just couldn't sleep in Paxton's room while they were home. She awoke to the smell of coffee a few hours later.

"Get up, sleepyhead," Peyton whispered, lips close enough to Shifty's ear to raise the surrounding hair. She jostled the mug of coffee so the liquid inside slopped dangerously, but not quite enough to splash the stuff all over Shifty's face. The aroma swelled.

Shifty reached for the mug but didn't open her eyes immediately. "Is it a *sheehairn*," she struggled to make the word sound natural when she said it, "thing? This creepy early morning happiness?"

"Don't say '*sheehairn*.' Only old farts say that. Say '*hairn*.' And, no, I'm just naturally a pain in the ass."

Shifty sat up carefully, the mug still in one hand, and rested her back against Peyton's bed. She took a sip. "Manna from heaven." She smiled and finally opened her eyes to look at Peyton.

She flinched unconsciously and the coffee splashed into her face, dripped off her nose, and ran down her chin, spreading quickly across the sleep-shirt she wore. "Christ! Warn me if you're gonna do that!"

"Do what?" Peyton feigned innocence while running a

green hand through teal hair and grinning mischievously.

"You really are a pain in the ass," Shifty confirmed. "I love your hair, though."

"I know, right? I hate covering it up."

"Which is why you don't." Shifty took a long draw on what remained of her coffee. She peered at Peyton over the rim of her mug. "How much does that piss off your parents?"

"The stripe? Not as much as when I first started doing it. My mom…she's stricter…sometimes we still get into it. That's when Dad can usually be heard muttering about 'hill you wanna die on, Nelda?'" Peyton shrugged. "Apparently there are more important hills to die on."

Peyton settled next to Shifty on the air mattress. They sat in silence for a few minutes while Shifty finished her coffee. When the mug was mostly empty Shifty set it on the floor next to her foot. "Pax is really worried."

Peyton rolled her orange eyes. "Pax is an old woman. All he does is worry."

"Be nice to your brother. You're talking about the boy I love."

"Gross." Peyton made a gagging sound.

"Why do I have the feeling this conversation is about me?" Paxton asked, coming through the door to Peyton's room. He was weekend-ready in a pair of shorts and a t-shirt he must have slipped into his mother's laundry basket the night before. His hair was wet from his shower and slicked back from his forehead. His feet were bare. And green.

"Missed a spot," Peyton said, pointing.

"Oops!" Paxton stared at his foot and the green was slowly replaced with a peachy color, complete with a flip-flops tan line.

"Attention to detail," Shifty commented, running her hand over her boyfriend's foot as he took a place next to her. She rested her head against his shoulder, allowing the warmth that still lingered there from his shower to flow around her like a shield. "What's on the agenda? I get the feeling it isn't a 'matinee and floor routine practice in the backyard' day like usual." She tried to keep her voice even, but she heard it catch and knew she wasn't fooling either of them.

"It's okay to be a little freaked out, you know." Paxton ruffled her hair and chucked the end of her nose with the tip of his index finger.

"If I allow a little, I'll lose control altogether and I don't know if I'll come back from it."

"Okay, so complete calm it is," Peyton said.

Paxton nodded but his eyes showed more concern than Peyton's. "Well, we need to help you get better control of your glamour and teach you a few other basics. Right now only you are seeing through your glamour. But if we don't do something soon, it's possible you can lose it altogether, and for the whole world to see. Thanks to modern human meds. Lithium! It's not just for depression anymore."

"I wasn't depressed," Shifty whispered. She looked at her hand on Paxton's knee. "And now it turns out I wasn't even crazy."

"Okay!" Peyton said, slapping her hand against the mattress and plastering a smile on her face. "Still bitter. Got it. So, that's a betrayal you're not yet willing to put in the rearview. Good to know."

"It's a pretty big one, Place," Paxton admitted.

Shifty was frustrated to feel a tear tumble down her cheek. It joined the coffee on the front of her shirt and she glared at it.

Peyton sighed. "I know it is."

Paxton reached to wipe another tear from Shifty's face, but she caught his hand and stared into his eyes. "No more lies. Promise. You find a way to tell me next time, if there is a next time. Both of you. Promise. Right now."

"There won't be a next time," Paxton said.

"Okay." Shifty paused, settling the new agreement between them, and nodded. "Now, teach me to glamour."

CHAPTER

EIGHTEEN

Evangeline didn't want to go any closer. She didn't like witnessing the wraith rituals, no matter how many times her mother reassured her that death magic was no darker than any of the spells cast around her every day, Evangeline couldn't shake the chill that ran down her spine when she saw the magic being worked, the expression on the face of the wraith twisting the power of death into a workable spell or totem. Somehow the banshees' keen didn't bother her in the same way. All the banshee did was collect the power. Witness the death. Evangeline had always felt it was almost noble, the banshee's wail. To stand vigil as the last breaths were expelled, to assure that the power released would be given back to the riocht, *it seemed a memorial.*

Not so, the working of death magic. She would never get used to it, no matter what her father said. She was ten years old already and she knew, just knew, she would never want to stand witness while it was performed.

But she did begin to walk again— toward the noises, not away. And a third strain of sounds began to weave its way into the melody. A single wailing voice. There was a banshee with the wraiths.

This was not how death magic was usually wielded. Banshees collected the power and provided it to the wraiths for their magic. Or, if they had black rian, *used it themselves when it was needed.*

The ritual of the Death Keen was generally a solitary one. The banshee and the wraith, sheehairn, or dying banshee were usually the only participants. A banshee would be summoned when the time was close and the final act of the dying was to give back to the riocht *and provide powerful magic.*

Why was a banshee performing the Death Keen in the middle of the woods behind Evangeline's house? Who was dying? What were the wraiths doing there? And what was making the heartbreaking wailing noise that was drawing her ever closer?

She was much too close now; all the sounds invaded the air around her, assaulted her senses. The mist was rising around her with each footfall, to her knees, her hips, her waist. The wail became ever more clear and familiar. She couldn't make out the wraiths' chants as individual voices, but the banshee's cry she knew. The memory was living somewhere in a corner of her brain.

She could see the clearing now, or what she knew must be the clearing, behind the wall of mist growing up around it. The instinct to turn and run had never been more urgent, but still she kept on. There was something so familiar in the cry, something that called to her in a way nothing ever had in Scath.

Two more steps and she reached a pocket in the mist. It made a window into the clearing perfectly at her eye level. Evangeline closed her eyes and breathed in through her nose then out through her mouth as she'd learned to do when something scared her. She did this five times, letting the keen, the chant, and the crying surround her as she did.

And then she opened her eyes.

And bit down hard on her lip to keep from screaming.

∾

Tresara was the last to arrive at the birch cove. She was out of breath and sweaty, but in one piece, which meant to Evangeline that she'd managed to return the book unnoticed. Tresara approached their circle without a word, but several head-nods confirmed all was well…so far. The loose grouping they'd assumed waiting for Tresara's arrival scattered, Igby rushing to Tresara's side and Linus staying with Evangeline.

"Gee, your nose looks extra sharp, Lenny," Locke said indignantly. "You've been pushing it real hard to the ol' grindstone?"

Lachlan stood behind Evangeline and wrapped his arms around her shoulders. When she squirmed, he called out, "Linus! You heard her, yesterday right? Lecturing me about shortcuts! 'Absolutely not going to be revealed with a spell! This will only be done with me in a dark room; toiling away behind a stack of books with my huge brain, my amazing work ethic, and research skills,'" he said, using a dramatic, but not inaccurate impression of Evangeline's "serious" voice.

"So cocky," she muttered, glaring. "How was I supposed to know?"

Locke's laughter crested and he lost his grip on her. He bent double, holding himself against the peals of laughter by locking his hands on his knees.

Linus and Evangeline watched him as he lost all his composure. They exchanged glances.

"Let him have his moment," Linus said. His eyes were riveted on the laughing, shaking, joyful creature in front of them. "His brute force is so rarely victorious over our superior intellect."

Evangeline sighed. "I know. But that? That is just... irritating. Honestly. It's behavior unbecoming a MacNair." She hid her smile behind a lock of her hair, but the affection was still clear in her voice.

Locke held up a hand, still unable to get words out through his laughter. It looked like he was attempting to regain his composure, though apparently he wasn't trying very hard. As soon as he put the hand down another wave of hilarity overtook him and he actually had to sit on the ground. Legs crossed, hands over his face, he rocked back and forth.

Acting disgusted, Linus and Evangeline left him to his

own devices and walked to join the rest of the group while he gloried in his victory alone.

"Once Locke decides to join us, we can start," Evangeline told the girls who had begun to stare at Locke with unabashed amusement. "He's a little too busy being pleased with himself," she informed them.

"I see that," Tresara said. "Do you think it will stop soon?"

"We can only hope," Linus said. He turned his head and directed his next to Locke. "Any chance you're almost done? We sort of have important business to attend to."

Locke held up a hand again and nodded his head enthusiastically. His shoulders still shook but the noises had stopped. "Almost," he finally gasped. He regained his feet shortly after and joined the rest of them, cheeks twitching over a broad grin but otherwise in control.

He took Evangeline's hand and squeezed. Despite the seriousness of their situation she felt a warm tingle run up her back. She returned the gesture and was rewarded with a smile and a wink.

"Floor is yours, boss. We are all your humble magical servants." He made an elaborate motion with his hand that included them all.

Reluctantly, Evangeline began rifling through the bag she'd brought, laying out items in a line before her and consulting her notes. She circled the items slowly and then considered the group of volunteers who were watching her. A scrap of paper was handed to Linus, an envelope of fragrant seeds to Locke, a small bundle of dried herbs to Igby, and a glowing ember sitting in a glass jar to Tresara. She pointed to Locke. "Go stand next to Tresara. Banshees together. *Hairns* opposite." She jabbed a finger at Igby and Linus and then at the section of grass across from Locke and Tresara. Silently they all complied.

Evangeline consulted her own paper for the next steps.

"Tresara, after Linus starts the incantation, you need to light Igby's herbs and join the chant. That should start the process. Two complete verses, okay? Then Linus, you drop out. Tree stays in on her own. Locke, then you pour the seeds on Igby's flame and get out of the way—it's going to go up, and that will make the full translation clear. I'll be able to read it as long as the fire burns, with the seeds in it. So, Igby you have to hang onto it as long as possible. We've got one shot at this. I don't have enough supplies to do it again tonight."

"I got it," Igby said. Her eyes didn't look as sure as her voice sounded but Evangeline had faith in her friend's courage.

"Linus, you start. I'll give as much direction as I can but I want as much time with this," Evangeline held up the *Siofra* book, cover turned back so she could hold it in one hand, "as possible. When the flame goes out, that's it. I won't be able to see anymore."

She reached back into her bag and brought out a couple more items. Positioning herself against a nearby sturdy tree, she set the book next to her knee and propped her own version of a *Scath Fios* in her lap. She licked the end of her pencil and looked up at her friends. "I'll write as fast as I can."

"Everyone ready?" Linus asked.

Each of them made a noise of assent. Linus cleared his throat and made eye contact with everyone in the clearing before dropping his gaze to the page. Slowly and deliberately he began to recite the words on the paper Evangeline had given him.

When he was nearly at the end of the verse he nodded to Tresara who walked slowly, hand guarding the flame in her jar, toward Igby. Igby's eyes grew huge and her mouth opened and closed but she stepped forward and allowed Tresara to light the end of the bundle. Once the flame caught, Igby placed the flame into her own small jar and watched as Tresara stepped back, added her voice to the chant, and looked over Linus's shoulder to read the words.

As soon as the flame took to the herbs the words on the book next to Evangeline began to shimmer and move on the page. Evangeline's breath caught in her throat and she almost forgot to start her notes. When there was only a single voice uttering the incantation Evangeline heard Locke's footsteps approach Igby at a tentative but steady gait. She heard Igby's breath quicken in anticipation of the contact of the seeds with her flame. Evangeline's pencil flew across her page as the words became more and more crisp, easier to transcribe. She didn't even pause to understand them as she copied them down.

Evangeline knew the instant the seeds hit the flame, and not just because of the flare in her peripheral vision; the page next to her blazed to life, the translation so vivid that the text practically jumped from the page. Evangeline's fingers flew and her vision narrowed. She saw only the words she copied into her book.

And then the page went black.

Evangeline's eyes snapped to the circle, expecting to see that Igby had dropped the flame. But the *hairn* held fast to her flaming bundle, her eyes huge. Her fingers shook, but still she stood. Evangeline, sure she'd seen wrong, looked back to the page.

The page was black.

She picked it up and turned it over in her hands, sure there was some mistake, but the page remained stubbornly black. She consulted the notes she'd made. The translation seemed to contain a full verse. Terrifying and unsettling, but full. Maybe she'd reached the end of the translation?

"Uh...Lenny?" Linus called from his place in the circle.

Evangeline looked up, surprised to see them all there. She'd forgotten the circle existed.

Igby's hands shook, and the fire was creeping up the sides of the glass toward her fingers. Her face was illuminated by a strange shade of red. Her eyes watered with exertion. Her orange *rian* snaked up her arms and around her neck like serpents sent to strangle her.

"Oh!" Evangeline leapt to her feet, sending both books flying in opposite directions. She ran to Igby's side, slightly frantic. "Igby! Put out the fire!"

With a sound of relief, Igby dropped the small jar of flame at her feet. Linus scooped up a handful of dirt and dropped it over the flame, extinguishing it. Purple smoked drifted from the jar. Igby's eyes were still wide. She slumped where she stood, but Linus jumped and caught her before she collapsed. Evangeline could tell from the look on his face that Igby was not in control of her body and he was supporting dead weight.

She tried to lend a hand but Locke beat her to it. He grabbed Igby's other side and the two boys walked her to a nearby tree and lowered her to the ground. Once settled, Locke walked back to Evangeline, but Linus remained at Igby's side. He whispered to her, coaxing her slowly back from wherever the enchanted flame had taken her.

"Well, that was..." Locke said, his gait slowing as he approached the girls.

"Terrifying?" Tresara supplied, eyebrows disappearing into her hair. "Horrific?"

Locke stopped in his tracks, stunned. "What are you talking about?"

"Were we in different circles?" Tresara spat the words at him.

He blinked at her. "We must have been. Because I have no idea what you're talking about."

"You didn't feel that?"

He shook his head and gave a look to Evangeline. She had straightened next to him and was fixated on Tresara.

He made a gesture of surrender with his hands. "Guess not. You going to fill us in?"

"Tree? What happened?"

Tresara took a couple of deep breaths and let them out slowly. Evangeline thought she would shake the banshee if she didn't answer soon. The tension coursed through her body. Finally, Tresara looked up, her *rian* still a stark black against her blue skin. Her eyes flamed their amethyst fire. She was pure magic. "There was death magic in that spell. Or from it. Or interfering with it. Wraith death magic. It burned Igby. I could feel it. See it. Like I was watching from her eyes. She was screaming. You didn't hear it?"

Locke shook his head. "No, I didn't feel or hear anything. I'm a banshee, too. If there was death magic, I should have felt some of it. At least an inkling. I felt the spell...I could tell Evangeline's book was producing results, but—"

"You don't have black *rian*, Locke. I'm the only one in the circle with those. The wraith magic, it must have been tied to the flame and death *rian*—"

"Don't call them that!" Evangeline spat.

"Why? There's power in death, Lenny. These are just facts. The rest of it, the keen, it's all just stupid superstition. It's what they are. Death magic *rian*. How we use the magic is what matters, not where it comes from. This is *Scath*, all the power is dark. Can't escape it by calling it something else. Sometimes you're so human, Evangeline."

She didn't know how being human haunted Evangeline, couldn't know. Even Tresara didn't know her choice of words were a knife to Evangeline's carefully constructed front. To Tresara, Evangeline's species was just a fact. To Evangeline it was what separated her from everyone she loved. Being human was what had nearly killed her as an infant. It was a part of her she tried very hard not to hate and reject. And Tresara's words cut her, and seemed only to point out exactly what Evangeline felt: that her human nature was something to be pitied and misunderstood.

Even with Tresara, who had been one of her closest friends since Evangeline could remember, Evangeline would not reveal her weaknesses, especially emotional ones. She'd learned early, learned well, how to project confidence, dominance, even superiority. She put that mask on now, smiling at Tresara and constructing the proper response.

Locke saved her the trouble, though she was sure his assistance was as unintentional as it was unassuming, by stooping and picking up the *Siofra* book from the ground. He dusted it off, smacking it roundly against his leg a couple of times, and held it out to Evangeline for inspection.

"What happened to it?"

Evangeline spared a glance to Linus and Igby, who were still huddled against a tree. Igby had most of her normal color back and her *rian* were fading, crawling back into her skin. Feeling that Linus had the situation well in hand, Evangeline took the book from Locke and peered at the page.

"Tresara's right," she said. "The book was spelled against the revealing magic we performed. Once the last step was done, the book protected itself, both by obliterating the page and by attacking Igby's call, it appears."

"So, what? We didn't get it?" Locke's eyes turned dark and he kicked at one of his feet with the other. He looked, to Evangeline, about ten years younger and pouty. And she knew why his mother spoiled him so. Looking at his discontented face, she had an overwhelming desire to just make it better. Luckily, she was able to this time.

"I got it."

Even Igby and Linus heard her and she regained their full attention. She held her *Scath Fios* up. Her scrambled, tight, untidy scrawl covered the page.

"All of it?" Linus asked.

Tentatively, Evangeline nodded her head. "Pretty sure. It went up fast, but I think I got all of it. If I missed anything, it was a line or two, and surely we can reconstruct that from what I did get."

"Do you need any help?" Linus asked. He still had one arm around her shoulders, but both Linus and Igby faced forward and engaged with the group. His scholarly urges were obviously becoming stronger than his impulse to prop up Igby now that she seemed to be coming around from whatever the spell had done to her. "Sure, if you want. I don't think it will hold many surprises, but I'd never turn down an extra pair of eyes or an additional brain."

Linus pushed himself to his feet and smiled down at Igby. He offered her a hand up. She took it with a sigh and seemed a little wobbly on her feet when they walked up to the rest of the group. Linus kept his hand on the small of Igby's back once they came to a stop. Tresara noticed and raised her eyebrows at Evangeline. Evangeline hid her face behind a curtain of hair, a common sight to anyone who spent a significant amount of time with her.

"I'll walk you home. It's late," Locke said, beginning to gather up all the items Evangeline had spread around the clearing and load them into the bag.

"That's all right. You go with Igby and Tresara. Linus and I can make it to my house, I think."

Evangeline was gratified to see disappointment on his face, even if it disappeared quickly into an expression of understanding. Igby had a slightly more difficult time re-shaping her countenance to neutrality.

Locke finished packing up Evangeline's supplies and handed off the bag. He shifted on his feet and scattered leaves with his foot before finally glancing up and touching Evangeline's sleeve. "Come over here for just a moment?"

"Of course."

She followed him a few feet into a thicket of trees. They stood facing each other for a moment. Evangeline tried to imagine what he could want to say to her that he felt needed to be so private. He remained silent long enough that she began to wonder if he was angry with her for some reason, though she couldn't for the life of her think what that reason might be. Finally, he took a step and closed the space between them. He cupped her face in both of his hands and gazed at her for a few seconds. Then without a word, he placed his mouth firmly on hers. She was so surprised she almost jumped away from him, but he moved a hand to the back of her neck and secured her more firmly in his in his grasp. She lost her surprise and leaned into his kiss. His lips were soft and warm, but his movements were intense and insistent, in control. He parted her lips with his tongue and she felt a strange quiver in her stomach as their mouths became one and the kiss deepened. She went up on her toes and wrapped one arm around his neck, the other around his waist. His arm found the small of her back and pulled her entire body tightly against his. She felt the sigh escape her lips and pass into his mouth, a shared whisper of intimacy inside of their already intensely romantic encounter. She didn't know how long they'd been lost in each other, and probably they would have stayed locked together much longer if Tresara's irritated voice hadn't traveled through the trees to them.

"We really need to leave!" she called.

Embarrassed as if they'd been seen, even though still completely hidden, Evangeline squirmed and squeaked in Locke's arms. He lifted his mouth from hers and offered her a rueful smile. "Apparently we really need to leave."

"Apparently."

"Did I overstep?"

Evangeline flushed, but she shook her head. "No."

Locke kissed her again, quickly and much less intimately, but somehow it was instantly Evangeline's favorite part of their stolen encounter. "I'm glad."

They spent a second readjusting hair and clothing, and Locke took her hand as they walked to rejoin their friends. Evangeline realized that for the first time she was relaxed with her hand in his. It wasn't like the times before, when she'd felt a variety of confusing emotions: the pride of others seeing, the duty to her parents and their wishes, the worry that he was doing it only for his own duty. Since Locke had begun to court her, as he called it, she'd slowly begun to trust her feelings for him were just that: *for him*. He'd made it clear to her that she was the one thing about his future he didn't fear. They stepped now, hand in hand, as partners. Evangeline felt as if she walked on the fog. There was so much left up in the air and it seemed as if some very frightening things could be standing in their path, but the heat of Locke's hand steadied her.

"As soon as you know anything, come and tell me." He squeezed her hand.

She nodded, not trusting herself with even a single syllable.

Their friends waited in the clearing. Evangeline joined Linus, and Locke took a step between the girls. They all seemed unwilling to part, each with so much invested in the translation; it seemed unfair that they all wouldn't be there when the answer finally came. But Locke would be missed at home and Igby and Tresara wouldn't have much to add to the work Linus and Evangeline needed to do.

"Guess we should go. Igby? You're really okay? Locke could take you to the Seer's cabin."

Igby shook her head. "I feel fine now. I'd rather just get this figured out."

"Okay. But if you change your mind, we'll go with you."

Igby nodded. Evangeline smiled. Linus raised a hand, waving to the other three and taking a step down the path that led to Evangeline's house. Locke stepped over to Evangeline and kissed her quickly on the mouth, pulling away before either of them could get lost to it again. He squeezed her shoulder. "Talk to you soon. Be safe," he said.

She nodded. "Get them home that way, as well."

Then Locke and the girls started down one path, while she and Linus took the other.

CHAPTER

NINETEEN

"Wow. You are surprisingly terrible at this." Peyton cleared her throat in an obvious attempt to cover her laughter.

"Shut up!" Shifty said, her voice straining with concentration.

She was leaning forward, staring into the mirror. Her brow was wrinkled up in that way that made her eyebrows knit together, and her eyes were intent with strain.

Paxton, up until this point, had been every bit the supportive, caring boyfriend. But the look on Shifty's face undid him once and for all. He turned his head and sputtered a series of chortles. When Shifty turned to glare at him he kissed the end of her nose.

"You're going to pop a blood vessel or give yourself an aneurysm."

"Isn't an aneurysm basically a popped blood vessel?" Peyton asked seriously.

"Uh...you guys? Do you mind? Kinda in the middle of something here," Shifty said sourly.

"Sorry, sorry." Peyton mumbled. "But it's just...well, glamours are super easy, Shifty. We didn't expect this to be so difficult. Here, have some of my gum!" Peyton pulled her pack of gum from her pocket and shoved it at Shifty.

"Is that what it's really for?" Shifty said, incredulous. "It's not an antidote for your coffee addiction?" She crammed a piece of it into her mouth and chomped on it in a determined manner for a moment. She shuddered and resisted a strong urge to expel it from her mouth as far and as fast as possible. It tasted even more vile than it smelled. Then she tried to pull the glamour back on. Nothing.

"Damn, sorry, Shif. Really thought that might help, always has me. I just can't see what the issue is! Pax says you dropped it easily enough."

"Gee, thanks. That's almost as helpful as the gum," Shifty said.

"Well, how'd you get it back on last night?" Peyton asked. "Just do that again."

Shifty's face darkened and she studied the tip of her sneaker.

"Uh…well, yeah. That was me. Shifty fell asleep in *hairn-skin*. I put her glamour back up," Paxton said.

"More information than I needed. That'll teach me to ask questions," Peyton said.

"This really isn't supposed to be hard?" Shifty asked with a withering look at Paxton.

"No. Here," Peyton held out her palm and wiggled her fingers. "Give me your hand." Shifty placed her wrist on Peyton's palm. The girl stared at Shifty's skin for a couple of seconds, while her mouth moved slowly and her fingers worked on the spell-stone in her pocket. Almost immediately, Shifty's pale green opalescent *hairn* skin began to shift and swirl, replaced by the alabaster of her human glamour.

Shifty's sigh betrayed her frustration. "Maybe there's something wrong with me."

"No—" Paxton started.

"We should talk to the folks," Peyton said, cutting him off.

"Glad we could all agree," Shifty said.

"She's got a point, Pax. There could be something wrong with her." Peyton held up a hand to ward off Paxton's outraged retort. She smiled at Shifty with a conciliatory look. "We don't know what funky things have been worked or spelled on her. There may be a reason she can't produce a glamour, and if so, it could stop her doing other magic. We need to bring in the experts here. Phone a friend."

Paxton didn't look happy about it, but he took Shifty's hand and the three of them tramped up the hill to the back door in search of the older generation of the Devlin family.

Nelda and Tristan were in the kitchen washing the breakfast dishes. Tristan passed a dripping plate to Nelda, who waited with a towel. She dried it efficiently and placed it on the stack inside the door-less cabinet next to the sink.

"What's up, kids?" Tristan asked, an affectionate smile spreading across his face.

"Well, it seems that Shifty can drop a glamour, but she can't put it back up," Peyton said.

"She looks fine to me." Nelda said. She dried her hands on her towel and hung it carefully on the small rod in front of the sink.

"Sure, because I placed it."

"I see," Nelda said slowly. Her eyes traveled Shifty's face from hairline to neck. "Shifty? Can you drop the glamour for me?"

Shifty closed her eyes, nervous, and tried to call the words to mind. She stumbled on the first three or four, but by the second line a regular cadence had begun. It worked faster this time. Her skin and her hair color shifted and she heard Paxton take a sharp breath.

"Your *rian*," he whispered.

Her *rian* indeed. The white marks roped her wrists and climbed her arms, encircling her throat before disappearing into her hairline. Shifty could make them out in her reflection in the window. They'd appeared so quickly, had taken up so much real estate on her skin, it was stunning.

"Okay. Now, quickly say the glamour spell," Nelda instructed.

Shifty switched her mental gears as quickly as possible, calling to memory the glamour spell. And when the entire verse had passed her lips...

Nothing. No change. Her skin was green. Her hair curled around her shoulders in violet ringlets, and her *rian* flared a brighter white, almost painful to look at.

"Keep trying, Shifty," Nelda said.

Mrs. Devlin stepped closer, studying the air around her charge. As Nelda raised a hand, swiping in through the ether in front of her, Shifty's voice faltered before picking up the incantation once more. Paxton and Peyton nodded their encouragement.

Nelda made two more circles around Shifty, and then stood very still for a few minutes, her concentration practically palatable. Her lips moved, but no sound made its way to the surface.

Without warning, Nelda bolted from the room, calling for Shifty to "keep going" as she stomped up the stairs. She returned quickly with a small amber colored glass bottle in her hand.

Paxton stepped forward, but he was immediately stopped with a hand signal and a sharp look. He fell back next to his sister, but he didn't appear to be happy about it.

They watched Nelda with anxious eyes. No one spoke, save for Shifty, who was sweating from the effort and concentration she put into her spell, without any result. Nelda unscrewed the black cap of the bottle and unceremoniously dumped the contents over Shifty's head.

Shifty sputtered and coughed, and—more than a little irritated—spoke the first line of the spell.

And the glamour went up. Immediately.

Nelda beamed a satisfied smile, and her husband was the only other person in the room who didn't wear a mask of confusion.

"Why did dumping water on Shifty work?" Peyton asked.

"Well, my child," Nelda laughed, "had that *been* water, it probably would have done nothing. But, since it was an elixir of my own making, it produced the effect I was looking for. Namely, it lifted the additional spell on Shifty that was keeping her from performing magic. A very advanced spell, too. I couldn't spot it."

"And yet, you dumped an *elixir*," Paxton's word dripped with false composure as he addressed his mother. "Over her head. You know, what? Just for kicks?"

"No." Nelda's voice was dangerously calm. "I made an educated guess, proceeded accordingly, and I was right, wasn't I?"

"Can I have a towel?" Shifty asked, stopping the argument before it could reach a crescendo.

It was Tristan who moved first. He grabbed a kitchen towel and passed it to Shifty. She took it with a grateful smile and rubbed her soggy head. "Now. Can we skip the righteous indignation and focus on the fact that there was yet another thing done to me that was meant to stop me from being or knowing what I really am? I'm getting a little tired of this, honestly. So, if liquid on my head lifts it? Fine. Bring it on."

"Okay, she has a point," Peyton conceded.

"Can we all just sit down and discuss this? As a family?" Tristan asked. He motioned to the chairs crowded around the kitchen's island.

Everyone took a seat and in an instant all eyes were on Nelda again. She smiled. "It's what I do, kids. I protect us in *Talam*, make sure our magic doesn't draw unnecessary attention. I ensure that the rules of *Scath* magic and the laws of our *riocht* are followed in this one. Is it so strange that I would think to look for cloaking spells that most of our kind might not even know existed, let alone how to perform?"

"It's strange that you didn't know this one had been placed on Shifty. If, you know, they really sent you here to protect her. Why didn't they tell you?" Tristan spoke the words, but from the nods around the table, he seemed to have verbalized his children's questions perfectly.

"I'd like the answer to that, as well. Though, I suppose it shouldn't surprise me. The consequences if the wraiths were able to control Shifty are extreme. Her parents would have done all they could to ensure that her location remain a secret." Nelda made eye contact with Shifty and gave her a gentle smile. "I know this is all a lot to take in, but they did have your best interests at heart."

Shifty lifted her eyebrows incredulously, but didn't protest. "So, what you did, the elixir dumpage, did it take all the spells off of me? And why could I drop my glamour?"

"I'm not sure. On either point," she added quickly. "As we discussed, I think the medications with their metals removed much of the power of the sight spells placed on you. The 'vitamins' your parents have fed you all your life are also a product of *Scath*. They were necessary to keep you healthy in this *riocht* without going back periodically, as most *Scath* creatures must. They also suppress your magical ability. I've been supplying them to your parents since we took this post, when you were only a few months old."

"With their knowledge?" Shifty asked.

"Oh, no. Of course not. We've used spells and potions to bend them to our will." Shifty raised an eyebrow and Nelda smiled. "They just decided to indulge their wacky, well-meaning neighbors at first. Then as you and the children became close, Adara and Grady came to trust Tristan and me. We only did what we had to, to ensure your safety and keep our promise to the Wicklows."

"Wicklow?" Shifty said the word slowly and carefully, working the syllables over her tongue as if they were made of honey.

"That's your family name. Siofra Wicklow."

"Well, that's…different."

Shifty rubbed her hands together in her lap, watching her fingers as they intertwined. She played with their flexibility, made shapes that would have snapped the bones of a human. Finally, accepting the newest piece of the puzzle that was her life, she tried to allow it to lift from her shoulders. When she looked back up at Nelda, her face was carefully composed.

"Okay, so, the Lithium made me see through glamours. We don't know why I could drop it on my own and we don't know what else has been placed on me. How do we find out?"

"A lot of trial and error, I'm afraid. What I used on you should have lifted any suppression spell. Unfortunately, it probably removed any cloaking spells as well, so I should probably put those back in place. And I want you to be careful. Magic in *Talam* always produces an after effect to the environment near where the magic is wielded, like an aftershock if you will. Even to *Scath* creatures. Small, easy spells, like glamours, their impact is slight and hardly noticeable. But larger, more powerful spells will cause a reaction, usually with whatever type of magic your *rian* represent. Your beloved over there, for instance." Nelda indicated her son with the lifting of her chin and a wry smile. "I mention again a certain violent but quick-moving thunderstorm?"

Paxton cleared his throat, but he maintained eye contact with his mother.

"I am going to continue to hear about this, apparently. But I was worried, Shifty. It seemed like the reward was worth the risk."

"So, how am I supposed to practice without attracting attention?" Shifty asked. She avoided the bigger question: what would the after-effect be?

"Carefully," Nelda said. "There are ways. The kids know them, even if they don't always employ them. They'll teach you.

We should go out into the woods so I can work a cloaking spell."

"Why the woods?"

"Part of the not-attracting-attention thing. In the cover of the woods, the aftershocks of my magic will be far less noticeable."

"But it won't stop me from learning more magic? Using my *hairn* nature?"

"No, no, of course not. Just keep you away from the eyes of any wraith who might have a way to search for you in this *riocht*."

"Would that be a difficult thing for them to do?"

"Yes. And no. The magic would not be difficult, but it would have to be done in this *riocht*. Since a wraith has neither a physical form nor control of magic here, it would have to be working with either a banshee or a *hairn*. Your parents are very powerful, Shifty. I don't see any *Scath* creature agreeing to help a wraith bring harm to you."

CHAPTER

TWENTY

Evangeline's mother was in the study when she and Linus arrived at the house. When she heard them arrive, Ciarda appeared in the hallway, a casting rod in one hand and a book in the other. To Evangeline she looked exhausted, but she smiled at them and warmth radiated into Evangeline's windblown core.

"Hello, children," Ciarda said. "It's a little late for visitors, Evangeline."

"I know, Mom. But it's important. It's for lessons." Strictly speaking, of course, this wasn't the truth. Linus was beginning to lead *hairn* instructions, but with students much younger than Evangeline. But learning was learning as far as Evangeline was concerned. She tried to let the lie roll off her tongue, as her mother was most accomplished at picking even a half truth off the tongues of the young.

Her mother sighed. "Not long. Agreed?"

"Sure, Mom, whatever you say."

"Thank you, *Saio* Wicklow." Linus, always proper and well-trained, nodded to Evangeline's mother.

"I wish you wouldn't call me that, not in my home, not when you are here as a friend of my child. You should call me Ciarda, at least under these circumstances. I won't tell, so you can stop looking so aghast." Ciarda laughed, walking past them on her way to the kitchen. She paused and pushed a piece of hair from her child's forehead, and kissed her cheek. "You're flushed, child, and your hair is a mess. Are you unwell?"

"I'm fine, Momma. It's just very cold out tonight."

"You're sure?" Her brow knitted and she cocked her head to the side.

"I am, truly. Can we go up to my room to work?"

Ciarda nodded and gestured to the stairs. "Run along. Not long, agreed?"

They both nodded their assent and hurried up the stairs. Once inside Evangeline's room they closed the door and Evangeline sat on the floor with her back against it, just to ensure they were not interrupted suddenly. She placed her *Scath Fios* between them and smoothed the pages flat. Her dark, unusually untidy scrawl stared up at them. Evangeline blew a ragged breath out and looked up. She caught Linus's eye and gave him the weakest of smiles. "So, I'll take the top half, you the bottom, and we'll meet in the middle?"

"Sounds good to me."

Evangeline lit her lamp and placed it on the floor next to the book. She handed a pencil to Linus and he pulled out his own *Scath Fios* to make notes in. For quite a while the only noises in the room were the scratching of graphite on paper, the occasional shifting of weight, and the wind blowing steadily outside, scraping a branch against Evangeline's windowpane. The shadows from the flame elongated and morphed, taking on the face of things both fascinating and foreboding.

"I don't like the tone of this spell," Linus said. He pointed to one character on the page. "In particular, I don't like that this keeps showing up. And from what I know of the meaning it isn't being used correctly. It doesn't make sense in an *aontuet* ceremony."

"Have you ever been to an *aontuet*?"

"Well, no. This will be my first, but I have read about them. And I know our language, Lenny." Linus sounded a little defensive.

Evangeline studied her hands in her lap, watching the light play on them. "I didn't mean that," she said, her voice quiet and tentative.

It took Linus a second to understand. "Are you scared?"

Linus and Evangeline had known each other all their lives. They had always gotten along, studied well together, understood the love each of them had for knowledge. Linus had been central in many of the plots to obtain contraband from *Talam*. There wasn't much that she felt shy sharing with him about being human, from a strictly technical standpoint. But her feelings for Locke? What she thought about the *aontuet* and where it would place her in Locke's life afterward? Not to mention her role in the community as the mate of a MacNair? No, she didn't think she could talk to him about those things.

He wouldn't be cruel. Probably Linus would be more suited to conversations like this than either Tresara or Igby; his analytical mind matched her own, and he was able to see things as clear-cut facts and figures. But he was still Locke's best friend. He was still male. And Evangeline didn't think her mouth and brain would allow her to express to him her deeply conflicted feelings.

"You're turning red," Linus noted.

"I told you years ago. I looked it up. It's called 'blushing.' It's a human trait: the involuntary reddening of human's face due to embarrassment or emotional stress, though it has been known to come from being lovestruck, or from some kind of romantic stimulation. It is thought to be the result of an overactive—"

"Sympathetic nervous system," Linus finished for her. They all knew the recitation by heart. "Yes, Lenny, I know that. So, why are you embarrassed? Because we are not in a romantic situation here."

"I'm uncomfortable talking about this." Her cheeks still flamed, but Evangeline kept her voice even.

"Fine. Let's get back to the translation. But, can I say for the record? I happen to know that Locke is not at all displeased or nervous—"

"STOP!" Evangeline whispered. "Seriously, I can't talk to you about this."

Though she'd cut him off, secretly she was glad he'd said it. Hearing the words from Linus, who had nothing to gain from them, meant more than hearing them from Locke, as earnest as he may have been.

Evangeline jabbed a finger toward their papers. "Tell me why you think this is an odd symbol."

"Well, what we are looking at here is clearly a spell for the *aontuet*." He pointed to several characters while he explained their meanings. "We've got 'accord' here, 'pact,' 'covenant,' and even 'to seal.'" Evangeline nodded her head. She agreed with his assessments; their notes had matched on the translation thus far.

"But, this symbol? It's darker than the others. It's for rooting…binding…and not the kind used for *ceile*, it's for holding the subject in place. Controlling them. It's called a *cheangal*. I've only ever seen it used for creatures being subdued for wrongdoings, being held to account. It doesn't have a place in the kind of binding you and Locke will participate in."

"Maybe they fear Locke will run?" Evangeline quipped, though the thought made her blush reappear.

"I don't think so. This spell appears to be about you, Evangeline. Its purpose seems to be in holding you here, making sure you complete your *aontuet* with Locke. With or without your consent."

CHAPTER

TWENTY-ONE

Once the children had departed the house, Nelda and Tristan Devlin slipped out the back door and into the woods behind their house for the second time that day. They didn't speak on their way to the ley line. The only sounds were the animals in their trees and bushes, wings of birds of prey slapping against the wind in their pursuits, foxes and other small animals rising from their daytime beds to run for the night. The moon and stars filtered through the leaves and branches to provide plenty of light for their procession.

Without consulting the other, they both stopped at the ley line. Tristan remained silent as Nelda said the words that caused it to flare and they both placed a foot on the other side. A strange wobbling of the light lifted from the line, traveled over their forms. When it was gone, they stood in *Scath*, their glamours shed, rian prominent across their skin. Tristan smiled at his wife.

"I almost forgot how lovely you are."

"Not the time." But she touched his cheek and gave him a weak smile just the same.

"I know." He took her hand in his and they started to walk. It wasn't far to their destination, but as they weren't expected, they made the steps as quick as possible. Once through the gate and behind the house, they relaxed slightly. It was Nelda who went to the back door of the house and knocked firmly three times. She stepped back to join her *ceile*.

Though it took longer than she'd anticipated, the door did finally open, and Ciarda and Arawn Wicklow walked into the fog and approached the Devlins.

"We didn't have a meeting scheduled," Arawn said.

"No. But there are some changes and they couldn't wait to be discussed," Tristan said.

"Oh?" Arawn crossed his arms over his chest.

"Is she all right?" Ciarda's voice was much softer than her *ceile's*, and her concern was clearly for the child she'd sent to be raised by another.

"She is," Nelda said.

"Then what's the problem?"

"Something we should have been informed of at the start of our assignment. Something that you clearly knew, Arawn. The girl has white *rian*."

"I see. And how did you discover this?" Arawn asked, without admitting any deception.

"Because she took herself to a psychiatrist. A doctor who can prescribe medicines for illnesses of the mind. She went to this doctor because she thought she was having hallucinations. Seeing her skin as a different color, and her hair. Watching as her body moved in ways that it couldn't possibly be able to. How did she see through the glamours placed on her? We thought the spells to be at fault, but once she began taking her medication, it became worse. She saw glimpses of our Paxton's true form and her own *rian* became clear. White. You had to have known. And further, you had to have known that your spells and concoctions wouldn't have been able to conceal them in *Talam*. What have you not told us about this exchange, Wicklow? I don't like being put in a position where my entire family could be targeted, not without full knowledge of what I am being asked to protect."

"Most unsettling," Arawn muttered. "Do you think you can keep her safe for another half moon?"

"Possibly. If we have all the information."

"It is imperative, now more than ever, that Siofra's human family not suspect a thing, that they continue to provide unconditional love and treat her just as they would their own child."

"They don't know she *isn't* their child, Arawn."

"And they can't know yet. We are in the final days, and afterwards it won't matter what they know."

"What matters now is what we know. Why didn't you tell us about her *rian*? Why withhold information so important to keeping her safe, shielding her?"

"Because I feared you wouldn't help us. I worried that she would present too large a danger for your own family and you might refuse. I know now, after all these years, that my fears were unfounded. I owe you a debt, and an apology. Please accept it, as I offer it now."

"I will accept your apology, and the debt, but only if you offer me a full explanation. We knew the exchange was necessary to keep Shifty—"

"My child's name is Siofra," Arawn snapped.

"Was necessary to keep Siofra from wasting away in *Talam*. Without frequent visits back home, the love and acceptance as a human from her parents was the only way to ensure her health and well-being, as well as the human's in *Scath*. But we were told this was a permanent exchange, because you'd been threatened by the wraiths. We believed ours to be a mission of defense of all *sheehairn* against them. I believe now that this is not the case."

"You knew she would come back eventually."

"But after we'd suppressed their power."

"I do not believe that is our best option now."

"Did you ever?"

"You are walking a precarious line, Nelda. Be careful where you step. You were told what you needed to be told as faithful servants of our *riocht*. You are a talented caster and a valuable member of our counsel. But you are not an Elder. You have not earned the right to all our decisions, nor even our discussions."

"Apologies. I did not mean to overstep. As you can imagine, we have suffered quite a shock in the last few days. I may have let my emotions get the best of me. Please tell me your plan."

"We only require that you keep Siofra safe for another half a moon. She can be returned here for the *aontuet*. Lachlan MacNair is a devoted banshee. I am sure, though it may be a shock to him, he will agree to the change. His sense of duty is strong. And once the human is no longer available to him, he will do what he is expected to do."

"You plan to go through with a summoning ritual?" Tristan spoke again and his voice held the fear of a soldier facing a firing squad. "A *sheehairn* with white *rian*, with *riochtfios*, tied to the banshee child of a banshee. You're going to give them what they have spent all of time searching for."

"And in the process, open vast new worlds to the *sheehairn*."

"And the human girl? What of her?"

Ciarda's sob was almost imperceptible. Only another mother could have noticed it. But when Nelda looked up sharply to make eye contact with the other *sheehairn*, the woman was staring into the fog at her feet, her face a blank mask, her eyes wide, and she gave the smallest of shakes of her head. Nelda returned her eyes to Arawn.

"The human girl will no longer be our concern. You know of the ritual, why ask me that?"

"You know that our son cares for your daughter. Deeply."

"And I know that you should never have let that happen."

"Had we been fully informed, we would have known not

to allow it. As it was, allowing the children to become friends was our best way to grow close to the family, gain their trust, and ensure Siofra's safety. If I knew I was signing my boy up for this kind of heartache—"

"Nelda! The boy is a *sheehairn*; he will do his duty. Heartache is for *Talam*. Once this is done, he can return to his own *riocht*, his own kind, and he will have his pick of mates. You sound as coddling as the humans you are living amongst."

"Again, I owe you my regrets. We've been there for so long."

"I forgive you, Nelda. I look forward to the return of you and your family after the ritual. There will be cause for much celebration."

Arawn stepped back with a look of expectation on his face. Nelda and Tristan both bent at the waist, then the knees. They remained there until Arawn made a gesture with his hands for them to rise.

"Until the moon is clear of the mist, then we will see you again," Nelda said. She knew what was being asked of her now, and what they must do for their kind.

CHAPTER

TWENTY-TWO

Grady Gilbert watched his daughter ascend the front steps up to the house. Her eyes were sleepy, her hair stood up strangely in the back, and she was still clad in sleep pants and a tank-top. She reminded him of the three-year-old she'd been seemingly only moments ago. The small blonde girl who'd stood at his knee holding aloft a book much too large for her little hands and asking him to read it to her for her bedtime tale.

"Siofra," she hadn't been Shifty yet, "that's a dictionary. It's not a fairy tale. You won't be entertained by what you hear."

Her blue eyes had grown wide. "What kind of tale is it, Daddy? Maybe I do want to hear it."

He'd relieved her of the book, and her little arms sagged back to her sides. He'd set the book next to him on his chair and scooped his daughter onto his lap. Sweeping her bangs from her eyes, he smiled at her. "A dictionary is a book about words and what they mean."

"All the words?" She reached up to play with his eyebrow, a habit she'd had since she was a baby.

"A lot of them," he confirmed.

"So, it has all the stories. Just out of order."

How he'd laughed. He loved the way she saw the world they lived in, and the depth of understanding that seemed greater than her years should have possibly allowed. And she had seemed to understand that his laughter wasn't cruel, that somehow they had shared a special moment, had created a memory.

"Yes, Siofra, the stories are in there. They are just out of order. Shall we try and sort one out?" He picked up the dictionary and maneuvered both it and her so that they could share his lap.

Siofra laid her head on her father's shoulder and sighed happily. "I think we shall." Then her forehead knitted. "How shall we?"

"I'll show you."

They'd picked words at random, reading their definitions and discussing the best one for their story. Building a story from the dictionary had become a weekly event in the Gilbert house after that, the most beloved bedtime of the week. For both of them.

Grady tried to remember when they'd done it last, when the childhood ritual had died. He found he couldn't, and it made him simultaneously nostalgic and amazed. His daughter was twenty, she was a woman, and he wasn't sure he'd stopped recently to really appreciate that.

There had been so many other concerns in the last few years. School, her gymnastics, her friends, high school, college, teaching her to drive, the list was too long to contemplate. He got to the door before she could use her key and swung it open for her.

"Morning, Shift. You appear well rested. Sleep well?"

"Shift, alt. Delete." She stepped past him into the house and flopped onto the couch in the living room. When she pulled her legs up under her, her feet disappeared completely.

"May I assume you forgot something here in your former abode, and that's why you're gracing me with your charming early morning presence?"

"Kinda. One pair of my mat shoes is here, but I think I'm just nervous about the meet and I didn't want to drive Pax and Place crazy. You're coming, right? Where's Mom?"

"She went out to run an errand, but she'll be back in plenty of time. You hungry?"

Shifty made a face. "Ugh, no. Hey. Do you know if Mom cleaned my old room or something?"

"Right, sure. Mom cleaned your room. Does that sound like your mother?"

"Well, no. Did you?"

"I have been nowhere near the inside of your room since the day you moved out. Too busy. Now, why the interrogation?"

"I don't know. It's weird. My door was closed the other day when I came for mom's cookies. And it smells funny in there. I thought maybe Mom got a room freshener or something."

"Smells weird?"

"Yup."

Grady stood up and started for the stairs. He didn't want to say anything to Shifty about it, but if something had died in her room he wanted to find it before the strange smell turned into a problem throughout the entire house. Shifty followed behind him. When they got to the room, he stepped inside and sniffed. Then he just stood there looking blankly at his daughter.

"I don't smell anything."

Shifty raised an eyebrow. "Seriously? You can't smell that?"

"Is it bad?"

"Well, no. It's just, well, it's not how my room usually smells. It's, I don't know, earthy or something. That's why I thought Mom had put a stink bomb in here. She's on that organic kick. I can't believe you don't smell it."

Shifty turned in a circle, sniffing extravagantly while she spun. Not for the first time, Grady admired his child's grace, and wondered where she'd gotten it. Neither he nor Adara were particularly graceful or elegant, but their daughter was both. She was a natural athlete.

"I don't smell a thing, kiddo."

He joined her in the room and they began sniffing corners and fabrics. He lifted papers to see if there was a plate of food or a forgotten flower hiding under them. Shifty followed his lead. Together they had made pretty solid progress throughout the room, but no source of the phantom smell turned up. Shifty opened the door to her closet and reared back before she could even stick her head inside.

"You find it?" Grady asked, noticing her extreme reaction.

Shifty closed the door and turned to face him. "No, nothing in there either," she said.

But there was something to her voice, a tone just slightly off, the words a little too slow. Grady knew she was lying and he was about to call her on it until he saw her face. She didn't look as if she was about to be in trouble or frightened. He knew that expression, the veil of shadows that hid her eyes and took away her expression.

She looked embarrassed.

And Grady didn't think he wanted to know what made a twenty-year-old embarrassed when it came to her closet and an earthy smell. He didn't need to make that father-daughter memory.

He made a big show of shrugging his shoulders, and then he walked to her window and opened it a few inches. "Well, here. Maybe it'll air out?"

"Sure, Dad. No worries anyway, if you don't smell it. It's not like I sleep in here anymore. Thanks for looking."

"No problem." He ruffled her hair on his way out the door. "Okay! Pre-meet ritual, kiddo. Let's get some orange juice and vitamins in you. Maybe a slice of toast? Gotta have something to make you leap higher than a skyscraper, right?"

"Sure, okay," she said again.

He was aware of the many times she looked over her shoulder on their way back down the stairs. He made a mental note to mention it to Adara so she might ask Shifty about it, if necessary.

He'd meant to do that. By the time they reached the kitchen, the rest of the day had already swept the strange smell right from his mind.

Like magic.

CHAPTER
TWENTY-THREE

In the center of the clearing were several wraiths. All were familiar to her, though she knew some of them better than others. There was also a single banshee and an infant. A human infant. Evangeline had no doubt it was human, for the pale peachiness of its skin looked very much like her own. The tufts of hair on its head were light red. A wraith held the squalling baby across its outstretched forearms. The infant's vocal cords seemed to be the only part of it that could move. Its body was still, despite its cries.

The banshee stood at the baby's head, her face hidden behind her long hair. Her keen was haunting, beautiful, and familiar, but Evangeline was now too terrified to force her brain to process anything else.

A human baby in the center of a ritual. How could that be? Hadn't she always been told how rare a human was in Scath? That it was a miracle she had even survived crossing into the riocht? What was this baby doing here? How had it survived? Where had they found it? Had it been abandoned like her? Had its parents also thrown it away in the forests of Talam to be eaten by animals?

Evangeline felt the blood rise to her cheeks, the dreaded blush. Her eyes filled with tears, hateful tears, betrayers of her nature, and she bit down ever harder on her lip. She wanted this baby to live. And she wanted it to die. She was special. She was valued. She was one of them. If another human was brought here and survived, what did that mean for her?

She wished she could flare the ley line on her own and throw the baby back to the riocht *it had come from, back to its human family or the hungry animals in the forest. Either one, she almost didn't care. Just away. Away from here where it might become more than her. Where her parents might love it more than they loved her.*

Another wraith stepped next to the banshee. He held a small dagger in his hand. Cecil MacNair, Lachlan's father.

Cecil placed his empty hand on the banshee's shoulder, leaned in, and whispered something in her ear. Then he added his voice to the chant and reached for the infant's arm. He held it gently, loosely. Evangeline could tell by the way it seemed to dangle across his palm.

And so quickly she didn't see it he slashed the knife across the baby's wrist. Evangeline didn't know it had happened until the beads of bright red liquid began to form on its flesh. Another wraith's hand appeared and held a wooden bowl out to Cecil. He placed it on the ground beneath the baby's wrist. The rivulets of blood flowed downward, and the first drops hit the bowl in a swirl. Cecil stepped to the other side of the child and repeated his process with the second wrist. Another bowl appeared and was placed beneath to catch the blood.

And still the banshee keened.

Still the wraiths chanted.

The baby bled.

And Evangeline stood on the edge of the mist and watched. As much as she'd been unable to stop moving when she'd first heard the noise, summoned by it, she could not lift a foot from the earth to flee now.

Cecil MacNair stayed by the banshee, near the baby's head. But another wraith, one Evangeline had seen in her father's study but whose name she didn't know, took his place near the feet of the baby. He placed two more bowls on the ground under the baby's legs, and soon those bowls were stained with their own swirls of thick scarlet. The mist swelled around Evangeline, like she was in the center of a lung that was contracting around her. The chill filled her.

The banshee Keened, half the wraiths chanted, the others wailed. The mist grew thicker. Evangeline stood and felt her teeth break the skin of her lip. She tasted her own blood as she watched that of the infant fall into the bowls. Its crying grew weaker, stalled while the infant tried to catch a breath, or maybe as it became resigned, Evangeline couldn't be sure.

A female wraith, Tresara's mother, approached the baby. She placed her hands onto its naked chest and added her wail to the cacophony. The crying stopped, save for the spare, halting whine. Evangeline could see the baby's eyes were still open, staring into Lara Keelin's face. Its wounds slowly closed, and Evangeline had the feeling that this was a result of Lara's touch.

The wailing wraiths stopped their song, then the chants died out, and all that was left on the air was the banshee's Keen.

The child's eyes closed, cutting off its silent communication with Lara. Silent, its little chest raised one time, and fell, and didn't move again.

Evangeline felt the air rush out of her, and with it a small sob. Just enough to gain the banshee's attention. Evangeline saw her straighten and stiffen. She performed the closing movements of the keening ritual, a beautiful series of hand motions, a clearing of magic, a welcoming of death, a containing of power. And then she turned to lock eyes with Evangeline.

Katarin MacNair smiled at her.

~

Evangeline sprawled with her head hanging over the edge of her bed, playing with the charm around her neck and studying the walls. She had been doing this since she was so young that her hair barely reached the edge of the bedding. Now it pooled on the wood floor beneath her like a lake of dark curls. She stared at her wall and ran the charm along length of the cord, passing its smooth surface along the top of her upper lip, studying her room from her skewed perspective. Something about the flipped reality often helped shake loose the answer to whatever problem she was working over in her mind. This morning, though, it wasn't helping.

Why would *Scath's* elders care so much about her binding to Locke that they would use wraith magic? Did they believe her human instinct would be to run from her duty and her adopted home? She'd never shown them one bit of resistance. Her entire life she'd done as she was told. Studied what they wanted her to study. Believed what they told her to believe. Befriended who they told her to befriend. Even loved who they told her she would love.

Love? No, that wasn't what they had told her to do. The *Scath* creatures would not speak of love, it would not come into matters as important as politics, magic, and the growth of *Scath*. How human she was to think of the *aontuet* as a ritual of love. The joining of two hearts into one for an eternity. As if it was like in the books she'd had smuggled back to her from *Talam*. Like Elizabeth and Darcy, Buttercup and Westley. Or even like the voices from the radio plays, love that was not romantic, like Little Orphan Annie and Daddy Warbucks.

The *Scath riocht* didn't work on love, it wasn't run by emotion.

And Evangeline had never given them one reason to think she expected it to, or to think she expected special treatment just because she was human. Now they planned to keep her compliant by force? She wasn't sure if she was more hurt, angry, or embarrassed. Embarrassed that they thought she might fail them; that as a human she would not be able to contain her emotions. Angry that they would consider taking away her free will. Hurt. Hurt that if at the last moment she *did* have a doubt, *did* wonder if she could be bound to someone she might not ever love, they would force her to go through with it anyway. The hurt that came from knowing that her parents consented to the *cheangal*: that was the hurt that grew in her mind and clawed its way to the front of her thoughts.

She sat up quickly, hoping to shake the ache from her heart. She knew this hurt was unacceptable; there was no one she could explain it to. She was all alone with her emotions and her humanity. She had so many feelings, and explaining the depth of them to any of her friends would be like telling them what blushing was. Scientifically they would understand it, they would even be sympathetic, but in the end her inability to squelch her feelings would be one more thing that made her different.

There was love in *Scath*, there was caring, and affection. Warmth. They all existed here, swirled together and suppressed in the fog that was a constant presence above the earthen floor of the *riocht*. And they all had their place. But much like the magic here, the strength of the *riocht* came from darker things. Working with those elements made being in constant, cold control a trait that was not only admired but required. Especially if you interacted with the wraiths on any type of regular basis.

Evangeline questioned whether the wraiths did have the capacity to love. Evangeline had wondered many times if wraiths were bound to *Scath* because of their lack of emotion; if the *riocht* recognized in them a force so dark even the ley lines knew it must remain contained.

Or did being unable to travel to places where love was considered important, even an asset, rob the wraiths of an ability to allow light, love, and empathy to take root in their beings?

Evangeline had no answers, and more frustratingly, she had no one to talk to about her questions. How would she admit to any of her friends that she wanted to hear that her parents loved her? That she wanted Locke to tell her she was pretty.

That she wondered if there was true evil and if so, was that evil taking the form of wraiths? Were they barred from leaving the darkness of *Scath* because the light of *Talam* snuffed them out like a candle in high wind if they tried?

Sighing and feeling like her insides weighed three times more than they had when she'd started thinking about it, Evangeline opened her bedroom window and let the cold air lift her hair. She wanted it to clear her head and heart.

Did it really matter if they planned to hold her by magical force during the *aontuet* ceremony? She'd had no plans to refuse Locke before the spell had come to light, what difference did it make now? Why did knowing that they didn't trust her make her want to withdraw her compliance? Did it really change so very much?

Yes, she decided, *it does*.

If she stood with Locke, as she had always planned, she did it completely of her own free will. She did it without invisible, magical ropes on her wrists. She gave herself to the service of *Scath's* political machine and to Locke out of her love for her parents, her community, and because of her belief that she could love Locke. That being his *ceile* was what she believed was best for her as well as for her home.

She latched her window and hurried down the stairs. Her mother was just starting up the stairs as Evangeline reached the bottom. Her mother smiled at her and it struck Evangeline that her mother was always quick to do so for her. Ciarda's smiles for Evangeline always reached her eyes. It was Evangeline's favorite thing about her mother.

"Are you going out?"

Evangeline nodded. "I'm going to see Igby."

"Your father and I will be leaving shortly. We have counsel with the Elders today. If we are not here when you return, that's where we shall be."

"Okay. Is it about the *aontuet*?"

She knew she was over-stepping, that she had no right to ask, and her mother certainly had no obligation to provide the information. She was sure, in fact, that she would be scolded for her presumptions.

"Yes. It's coming up quickly and there is much to prepare." Her mother's face flickered and then went cold. It happened so quickly that Evangeline could almost tell herself she'd imagined it.

Evangeline turned everything over and over in her mind while she walked the path to Igby's home, playing through different scenarios. She didn't want to disobey her parents' wishes. She didn't want to cause trouble, to turn her back on all the things she'd spent her life believing were right and true.

When Igby answered the door, Evangeline still hadn't found her solution. "We need to find a protection spell," she said by way of greeting.

Igby looked back over her shoulder before stepping outside next to Evangeline and pulling the door closed. They walked few feet away from the house and finally Igby spoke. "For who?"

"For me," Evangeline said.

She watched her friend's eyes grow wide and fill with a kind of terrible awe. Evangeline hadn't even gotten to the worst part.

"I need to stop the elders, the wraiths, and my parents from keeping me in *Scath* against my will."

CHAPTER

TWENTY-FOUR

Because of her visit to her parents' house, it took hours before she could get to Peyton and Paxton alone, and Shifty's performance at the meet suffered for it. Distracted because all she wanted to do was sit around their living room and make a plan to hide her from the creatures that may or may not be coming for her; her landings weren't as rock-solid as they usually were, she even hit a stumble-hop at the end of a mat pass, something she hadn't done in years. Though she took home a medal, hers was not the top score.

Coach was more befuddled than angry. She listened to him stammer around, asking her if she felt okay, did she think she was coming down with something? Had she gotten enough sleep? Eaten a good breakfast? Was she having a fight with her boyfriend? Did she have something weighing on her mind?

Shifty stifled a grin and a laugh when she considered telling Coach exactly what she had on her mind. The look on Coach's face would almost be worth a trip to Dr. Miller and the seventy-two-hour psychiatric hold the monologue would bring with it. Almost.

"I don't know," Shifty lied. "I felt fine all the way here and I didn't do anything that should have taken away from my performance out there today. I'm really sorry. I didn't mean to let the team down."

"No, no," he softened immediately in response to her chagrin. "Everyone has an off day, Gilbert. Just bring your A-game next time. We're still ahead for the season. That's the important part!" He thumped her on the back and rumpled her hair. "Go home and rest up. There's practice in a couple of days. We'll run the floor routine a few times and see if we can find out what went wrong out there today. Tighten it up. That's all it needs."

"Sure thing. Thanks, Coach."

Shifty scanned the crowd making their way down from the stands and out into the gymnasium proper for the faces of her friends and family.

They were all together, her parents and the Devlins. They chatted amiably, Paxton's mom laughing at something Adara said. Shifty lifted a hand to wave at them, but only made it halfway to her shoulder before she let her arm drop to her side. She wondered...If she concentrated, could she see through their glamours? She found it didn't even take much concentration. She focused on them, separating them from the crowd in her mind, and their coloring began to change. Knowing what they looked like under the glamour helped, sure, but it wasn't only that.

The magic was getting easier.

Whatever spell Nelda had lifted from her had been powerful. Now that it was gone, her instincts took over and using her gifts felt as easy and natural as a back walk-over. Once she knew which muscles did what, everything fell into place. For the first time since the big talk with the Devlins, everything made sense. While using her sight as a *hairn*, she felt normal. If only for a fraction of a second.

Her heart soared. Then she waved to the group of people she loved. Her wave was exuberant and excited. Maybe a little too excited for a gymnast who had just placed third in a competition she'd been heavily favored to win, but she couldn't care about that. She knew who she was. She knew *what* she was. And not only was she not crazy, she was good at this.

"You'll get them next time, tiger!" her mother said, embracing her tightly.

"Thanks, Mom." Shifty hugged her back, and for an instant all the good feelings she'd just been wrapped in wavered, slipped an inch. Had her mother ever known what she was? Nelda had been pretty confident that her parents had been spelled. That their memories had been taken from them. But what *exactly* had been altered? Had Adara and Grady been tricked into taking her from *Scath* to raise as their own? They couldn't possibly have given up their own child, could they? The Gilberts couldn't have been the loving, attentive, and caring parents she'd known her whole life only because they were in service to the *Scath* creatures. And unthinkable; colluding with the wraiths, raising her to be handed over to creatures who wanted only to use her for their own power. Surely they couldn't have been that cruel, or even that accomplished as liars. They were too caring, too *parental* to be faking it. She knew they loved her. Knew it. Didn't she?

Paxton reached her first of the Devlins. He placed a chaste kiss on her cheek.

"Can we eat now?" Peyton whined.

"Yes, please," Shifty said, and she realized as she said it that she was starving. Her stomach let out a series of grumbling noises, telegraphing it louder than words.

They agreed to meet at the Italian restaurant not far from the gym. The kids set off for their car, the parents in the other direction for their own vehicles.

"What's on your mind?" Paxton asked the moment they were out of ear shot.

Shifty's shoulders sagged and she tried to organize her

emotions enough to pick one thread. "There's something weird in my closet at my parents' house."

"I've always hated those bunny pajamas," Peyton offered.

"There's a weird smell in my closet." Shifty amended.

Peyton whispered something that sounded suspiciously like "bunny pajamas."

"There's always a weird smell in my closet, and it's usually my shoes," Paxton said. "I assume you've checked your shoes?"

"It's not a shoe smell," Shifty said. She wasn't going to admit that she hadn't checked her shoes. "It smells like something that would be in your mom's kitchen."

"It's a totem," Peyton, now serious, said. "Who would put a totem in her old room?" She turned to her brother and smacked him across the chest. He stumbled and rubbed the spot, probably wishing Peyton would learn her own strength… or care.

"I don't know." Paxton's voice dragged as he spoke, slowed down so his thoughts could catch up. "Obviously it wasn't our parents or they would have told you about it—or, you know, know where you live now. It's got to be a *Scath* being. No wraith could get it into the *riocht*. We need to know what kind of totem it is. If you can bring it over, my mom could tell us in a heartbeat. Then we'll have a better idea of who put it there and why."

"It won't be hard to find. The damn thing reeks! I can't believe my dad didn't smell it."

"Good. You and Peyton go back to your house after dinner, find it, and bring it over. Mom will tell us what it is. No problem."

CHAPTER

TWENTY-FIVE

As soon as Evangeline's feet were free from the worst of the fear that had rooted her to the spot, she broke away from Katarin's stare, turned, and ran through the woods in the direction of her house. This time she was not quiet. This time the earth and plants did not seem to part for her as she ran. She stumbled and fell, was cut, and bled.

When she finally arrived in her own backyard she had only one shoe, and her dress was torn at her right shoulder. She clamored up the rear stairs and threw open the door, letting herself into the safety of her mother's familiar kitchen, and slammed the door behind her. Pushing herself against it, she tried to nail it shut with just the sheer force of her will. Her shoulders heaved as she gasped for breath. Her lungs burned inside her body.

"Evangeline? Can you come into the library please?" It was her mother's voice, and it acted on her like a balm. Her breathing became more regular, her scrapes hurt less, her panic was tamped down. Without thinking she started toward the library, ready for the warmth of her mother's embrace.

On the other side of the door were both her parents. And Katarin MacNair. And Lara Keelin.

"Sit down, Evangeline, please," her father instructed, indicating a chair by the fireplace.

"Yes, sir," she said, but did not drop eye contact with her mother. She crossed the room and sat where she'd been told.

"*What you saw,*" *Katarin started.*

"*I'm sorry!*" *Evangeline blurted.* "*I didn't mean to.*"

"*Hush, child,*" *her mother said, concerned. Evangeline closed her mouth.*

"*What you saw was probably very confusing and quite frightening to you. We're sorry that you experienced that. We'd like to explain it. Do you think you are calm enough to hear what we have to tell you?*" *her father asked.*

Her mother placed a hand on her shoulder, the one that was still covered by her dress, and squeezed. Evangeline nodded her head.

"*We found another human on the ley lines today,*" *Katarin said.* "*It wasn't strong like you, Evangeline. It had been on the line when it flared, and was sent to this* riocht *by accident. By the time it was discovered it, it was too late to send it back. The elements had been unkind, and the magic too much. The human was going to die. It didn't matter what we did. The death of a human in* riocht, *you know that power is worth much. It couldn't be wasted. It wasn't a task any of us relished. But it was for the good of the* riocht *that we acted. We witnessed its death, we performed the ritual, the binding of death power.*"

"*Do you understand?*" *her mother asked. Her father looked up sharply at the words. Evangeline thought she saw him shake his head sharply. She knew not to answer the question. She sat straight in her chair.*

"*The* riocht *comes first,*" *her father said.*

"*I know that,*" *Evangeline said.* "*I'm sorry that I got upset.*"

"*You were confused, you didn't know what you were seeing.*" *Lara said, but her words were not comforting.* "*It won't happen again.*"

Evangeline, only ten, understood the threat in Lara's words and she moved slightly closer to her mother.

"*No. It won't happen again,*" *she said.*

"*And it won't ever happen to you,*" *her mother said into her ear, oh so very softly.* "*I promise.*"

Evangeline leaned into her mother. She let but one tear escape, though she hoped very much that no one else in the room saw it. "Here, Evangeline, take your tea into the kitchen with your mother." Her father held out a teacup and a saucer. She took it with a steady hand. "Say goodnight to our guests, then up to bed with you. Understand?"

"Yes, Father. Goodnight, Meas *MacNair,* Meas *Keelin."*

"Evangeline," Katarin said.

Lara only nodded.

With her mother closely behind her, Evangeline retreated to the kitchen to have her tea.

He'd come up to tuck her in that night. He never did that. The tea had made her extra tired, and she was snuggled down in her bed, nearly asleep. He sat to her side and stroked her head.

He must have seen Mother do that, *she thought.* Even at ten she could tell it wasn't a natural action for him to take.

"Are you all right, Evangeline?"

She nodded her head, and her nose rubbed the covers as she did. She couldn't remember exactly why he would be asking. She was so heavy with weariness.

"You were very brave today. I'm proud of you."

"Why?" What had she done? She wanted him to be proud of her, but she wanted to know how she'd earned it so that she could do it again.

"You acted like a sheehairn child. You denied your human instincts and sensibilities. You did our family proud. There were many human ways you could have reacted to what you saw. You contained your nature and performed as a member of this riocht. *You've learned well."*

"Thank you."

He raised the flame on her lantern and the light flared a little brighter in the room around them. He reached into the small pocket on the front of his vest. When his hand reemerged a length of cord dangled from his fingers. It was weighted by a small, wooden charm. He held it out to her and when she hesitated he smiled at her. "It's for you, Evangeline. You can take it. It's our family's seal."

She reached out and took it, examined it as it sat in the palm of her hand, her chest bursting with pride. All the things she'd been so afraid of—that the human would take her place, that her parents would want the new human more than they wanted her—it all left her head. That baby had been a stupid, weak human. It had stupid, weak instincts. She was strong. She was practically a sheehairn. She didn't have those sensibilities. And if she did, she would fight them, push them away. She pushed herself up in the bed and allowed her father to place the totem around her neck.

Her father kissed her on the top of her head and pulled the covers back up around her. "Good night, Evangeline. Have a good rest."

"Good night."

By the time she woke up the next morning she didn't remember the baby or the wraiths. But she loved her new necklace. Loved wearing the mark of her father's pride. Whenever she felt particularly weak, or very human, she would run the charm across the cord and remember she was a Wicklow. She lived in Scath. She was strong and brave.

～

"You want to do what?" Tresara asked. She shook Evangeline's shoulder and pulled her from the memory that had eaten her brain and taken her from the reality of the moment.

"Your eyes grow wider each time you ask me that question. They're going to take over your face when you get to double digits," Evangeline joked in an effort to push the unsettling feeling even further from her mind. She pulled the piece of cord over her head and shoved the charm into her pocket. "I think you've heard me by now. Oh, and you can't tell Locke."

"Oh! Of course," Igby said. She cocked her head to the

side and her stare bored a hole into Evangeline. "Why can't we tell Locke?"

"You wouldn't get it."

"Try us," both girls said.

"You won't get it and you'll hurt my feelings when you don't get it. And that's part of the problem. You don't understand that hurt feelings…" Evangeline's words stopped slowly. "Well, they hurt. That's all."

Locke's parents. They'd been there. They'd helped kill the baby. Tresara's mother, too. A wraith was a wraith, Evangeline knew. In her mind, this excused Tresara's mother and Cecil MacNair. But the banshee in the clearing had been Locke's mother, and that along with all the other personal reasons she had meant they couldn't tell him.

"I don't get it. As it stands right now, could it really be worse? And I don't know how we can accomplish what you want without help from Linus and Locke," Tresara said.

"If we tell Locke, he'll think I don't want to go through with the *aontuet*. He'll think I'm changing my mind and turning my back on the ceremony, the *riocht*, and him. That's not it. I just want to be free when I stand up there. I want it to belong to me. You see?"

"No," Igby said.

"Not really," Tresara admitted, though it was clear in her face she was trying.

Evangeline made a frustrated noise and threw her hands in the air. This was going just about as poorly as she'd envisioned. "Can't you just trust me and help me anyway?"

"Lenny, we're going to help you. But, the way I see it is that you don't have a problem with the *aontuet*, you agree and even want to go through the ceremony with Locke. So what is the problem with the casting of the *cheangal*? It isn't as if you're being compelled to complete a task you find abhorrent, you see? Evangeline, we don't have to understand all you're telling us; we will never understand all your humanity. And you have to stop thinking that means there's something wrong. Either with you, or with us, or with the *riocht*. Just because we're different doesn't make either of us wrong. Look," she paused to compose her thoughts. "It's like my black *rian*; something about them and what they do, where they gain power, is upsetting to you in a way I will never understand. I hear your explanation and I see that you really believe what you're saying, but it will never resonate with me. Does that make you wrong and me right? Or the other way round? I don't think so. You're human. We are *Scath*. It's really just that simple."

Evangeline reached out and placed her hand over the banshee's. A moment later, a green hand settled on top of hers. The three girls locked eyes over their stacked hands.

"We still need to tell the boys," Tresara said, not breaking eye contract. "We might need their help, especially Linus. And Locke deserves to know, if your plan really is not to attend the ceremony if we can't prevent the spell. It is a very real possibility that we won't be able to stop them from casting it. If you aren't going to participate in the *aontuet* unless you aren't under magical restraint…if you're going to flee…Locke needs to know that. Don't you agree?"

She didn't want to agree. But she thought about Locke—not as Lachlan MacNair, heir to the banshee leadership, but as *Locke*. She remembered the interaction she'd overheard with his father about duty and honor. She thought about his own plans for his future and his idea for her part in them. Maybe he would understand her reluctance to be bound in magical participation more than she was giving him credit for. Even so, working up the courage to nod her ascent took longer than she'd expected. She finally did it: worked her chin down to meet her chest, once up to the sky, then back to center.

"I'll tell him."

"Igby and I will go get Linus. You find Locke and talk to him, and we'll all meet in the clearing?"

"Now? Right now?"

Somehow Evangeline had imagined she'd have time to work on the spell before telling Locke anything. If she had the spell completed, if she knew she could still move forward with the ceremony unfettered by magic, then telling him wouldn't be so hard. Even if they'd started the process so she could explain that she was looking for a way to go through the *aontuet* on her own terms, so he knew her reluctance wasn't about him. Telling him before any of that, and asking for his help, it seemed daunting.

Tresara removed her hand from the bottom of their pile and nodded to Igby to follow. "Yes, Lenny. Right now." Her tone was firm, her look cool. She was allowing for no trepidation on Evangeline's part, no backing down, and no negotiation.

Evangeline lowered her hand back to her side and dropped her eyes to her feet. Without a word she turned and started toward the path to Locke's house.

She watched her feet in the swirling fog while she made her way through the birch trees. Some steps, it was so thick that it seemed to swallow her feet when they touched the earth. Other steps just stirred eddies that floated away from her body, licked at the air, and then drifted to the ground, wispy and white. The air was cold, with a hint of moisture that made the trees' scents thicker. The woody, earthen aroma sat on the air around her as she walked on. Night was falling, the moon and stars just beginning to cast their light.

Evangeline walked as slowly as she dared. She knew the others would be expecting for her, knew she couldn't keep them waiting for too long. She dreaded explaining to Locke her reasons for taking this stand. She doubted he would understand any more than Tresara had. Characters in the books she'd read and the advice in the silly magazines all said the same thing: never, ever tell a boy (or a girl, for that matter) "it's not you, it's me." That was almost as important as not asking someone to "stay friends." There were also many articles that touted consent; that "no meant no." But, as Evangeline had already found out, since she hadn't ever been planning to say no, her friends (and probably Locke) didn't see the same line that she felt she was being tricked into crossing.

But what else could she tell him? It truly wasn't him. It *was* her. Her humanity. Her otherness. She wouldn't be this way if she had a choice. She'd be *hairn* in a second, if it was possible, shedding her human skin for the green sheen and swirling *rian*. She wished she could get rid of the human instincts that made her so different from everyone she loved. Then they wouldn't even consider the *cheangal*. They wouldn't have to.

Long before she was ready, she arrived at Locke's house. It seemed to just appear on the hillside, its dark wooden frame looming like a nightmare. The tall, heavy pickets of the fence jutted angrily into the air. Despite the cold fear and panic that inched up her spine and told her every fiber to run in the other direction, she soldiered on, and didn't pause until her fist was poised to knock on the door. Once her presence was announced there was no turning back. Only that she would have no way to explain Locke's absence to the group at the clearing kept her from backing down.

Locke responded to her knock too quickly. She'd barely removed her hand from the door when it opened.

"Evangeline? What are you doing here?" His face registered surprise, but he didn't seem to be scolding her unannounced arrival. If she had to guess, he appear pleased. Which only made her feel worse.

"Are your parents home?" she asked, suspecting the answer.

His parents were most likely at the same meeting attended by her own family.

He confirmed as much with a shake of his head.

"Can I come in? I really need to talk to you."

He stepped aside. As she moved past him, he reached out and took her hand. Locke lifted it to his mouth and kissed her palm. He didn't release it, and they stood facing each other in his doorway. Every second that passed between them made Evangeline want to run away faster, change her mind, and allow the *cheangal* to be placed on her. She could feel her brow knit and she didn't catch it quickly enough. Locke's free hand rubbed a soft line between her eyebrows and along her nose, and his eyes took on a hint of worry as he looked into hers.

"Is something wrong, Evangeline?"

"I need to talk to you," she repeated.

"So you've said. Shall we sit down?" He closed the door, finally. Still holding her hand, he led them to the small sitting room in the front of the house. There was a fire crackling in the hearth. Locke chose a small settee that held them both, if they sat close together with the sides of their bodies touching. "Tell me what's wrong," he said, when it was apparent that Evangeline was unwilling to speak first.

"Do you know what a *cheangal* is?"

"I do. My father uses them to ensure compliance with punishments." He seemed to be choosing his words even more carefully than usual.

"That spell we uncovered in *Siofra* is a *cheangal*. The elders want to force me to participate in the *aontuet*."

"I know that. My father told me this morning before he left for his meeting with the Council. I told him I didn't think it was necessary…"

"You *knew*?" Evangeline was sure that she had heard him incorrectly.

"But you never said you wouldn't be my *ceile*." Locke's voice was even, but his face showed the first hints of anger. She hadn't missed that he'd refused to answer her question.

"I know. And that's why," Evangeline took a deep breath and held it until her lungs protested. "I want to cast a protection spell." The words rushed out with her breath. She felt both relieved and horrified now that they hovered between her and Locke, like tiny accusations.

His face changed from anger to confusion and he released her hand, but didn't drop his eyes from hers. "Why?"

"So they can't force me participate."

"So they can't force you to be bound to me." His voice was even, and soft, but deadly quiet. Now it was his turn to look at the floor.

"Locke, no." She reached for his hand, but he moved it away, placing it in his lap, and she didn't try again. "I will still be bound to you. I'll be at the ceremony. I just can't be there like that."

"Like what? I don't understand, Evangeline! What difference does it make?"

"They are treating me the same way they would treat a deserter! That doesn't seem wrong to you?"

"Not if you were going to do it anyway!" He spat the words out and they hit Evangeline like a slap in the face. "What's the difference? Or were you lying to me? Were you never going through with it from the start?"

Evangeline had known this wasn't going to be a smooth conversation, but the depth of his anger surprised her. "No, Locke. Of course not. I didn't lie to you. I wouldn't do that. I...I...I just can't have my will taken away from me. It's like they don't trust me. I'm not being treated like a *sheehairn*."

"You're not a *sheehairn*, Evangeline."

She wondered if he knew how much that would hurt her, if he'd done it on purpose, used the words to cut her. But that would be an emotional play, and very unlike a *Scath* creature to use. More likely, he was just stating the facts.

"So why would they treat you like one? Doesn't the fact that you're here now and telling me that you won't go to the *aontuet*, won't do what you already planned to do, if a spell is placed on you—and only to ensure you will do what you said you would do, by the way—doesn't that prove their point? If you had never known about the *cheangal*, would there be a reason to question the *aontuet*? For you, I mean?"

Evangeline could feel her face growing hot. She knew she was blushing and she knew he had noticed. She swiped her cheeks with a hand. It came back dry, but she could feel her eyes prickling and knew tears of frustration wouldn't be far away. It made her angry, her body's betrayal. She felt weak, exposed and naked in front of him while her tears stung her eyes and ran a path down her cheeks. He sat watching her, closed-up and blank-faced.

"No, Locke. Of course I wouldn't have changed my mind. I made a promise to my parents, to you, to the *riocht*, and the elders. Duty is just as important to me as it is to you."

"Apparently not."

"So you're taking your seat on the Council?" She glared at him, hoping to make a dent in his emotional armor. Wanting to wound him with her words. She wanted to do it even as it made her ashamed. But he didn't even blink.

"I've never promised anyone that I would. I'm not shirking a duty I've already agreed to. My honor is intact."

"And mine isn't?"

"I believe your honor is at risk."

"You would have me take your hand, be bound to you, promise my life to yours...You would have me make those choices without knowing whether I was under the spell of the wraiths?"

"My father is a wraith."

"And you've stood up to his wishes before! I've heard you! And you were right. You honored your duty, but your way. By doing what you think is right. Or is that privilege only granted to creatures born to this *riocht*?"

"Evangeline."

Oh, was his voice cold. And calm. And cruel.

She shuddered.

"You agreed to the *aontuet*," he said. "While we courted, you seemed more than happy to accept me—"

"We courted for two days, Locke," Evangeline whispered, cutting him off.

"Don't be myopic, Evangeline. It's only two days," he mocked her whisper, "plus our *entire lives*. Maybe we only gave it a name two days ago, but you didn't just meet me! I fail to see why the *cheangal* has changed anything for you. It seems to me that you have discovered something which offends your human sensibilities, something you see as an injustice. So you've come to me to stamp your foot and be outraged. You expect me to indulge you. If you choose to not to be at the *aontuet*, that is a decision you make on your own, and you will have to suffer the consequences that way as well."

"Alone?" she whispered.

"Quite." He reached for her hand again and stroked her palm with his thumb. His face softened ever so slightly. "Really, Evangeline, can't we just carry on as we were?"

He leaned toward her, and with his free arm he reached out to embrace her and pull her closer. Perhaps he planned to kiss her as he had in the clearing. She wanted to let him. With all she was, she wanted to melt into him, to let him convince her that the *cheangal* wasn't something to worry about and that it didn't change their situation. His lips were on hers. He was gentle and soft, warm and inviting. Giving in would have been the easiest thing in the world.

"Don't, Locke." Her words were muffled against his lips. She felt him freeze in the act of the kiss, but he didn't pull away.

"What's wrong?"

"I won't be bound to you under the *cheangal*."

He did pull back then, and dropped her hand. He pushed himself as far from her as the seat would allow and crossed his arms over his chest. There wasn't much physical space between them, but it might as well have been the vast darkness of the night sky.

"You are backing out."

"I didn't say that. I said I won't be bound to you under the *cheangal*, and I mean it."

"This is so human. I thought you were stronger than this, Evangeline. I thought this *riocht* meant more to you."

"This *riocht* means *everything* to me, Locke. Doing right by my family and our name? That means as much to me as it does any other creature of *Scath*. But you don't see that. I'm just a human to you, in the end. It almost seems like you'd be relieved if you're not saddled with a human for a mate."

"Self-pity isn't a pretty trait, Evangeline."

"Why are you being so cruel?" She cracked again, and more tears tumbled across her cheeks.

"I'm not being cruel, I'm stating the facts. If you don't like them, you can easily come to your senses and change your stance."

"You won't help me?"

"I don't see why there is a need for help. Either you want to be bound to me or you don't. I hope you'll change your mind, I honestly do. And despite that look on your face, I hope you'll believe me. I mean everything I've said to you about our *aontuet*. I hope you will find a way to live with the *cheangal*. Because you won't find a way to prevent it, Evangeline. Even with Linus's help."

She stood up. Emotions like she'd never felt ran through her body, made her blood flow hot and fast. She felt out of control, angry, sad, and profoundly misunderstood. She'd believed she could love Locke. Since he'd begun the "courting," she'd even let herself fancy that she already did love him a little. Had she been so wrong? Was he more his father than she'd thought? She stared at him, very still on the settee with his lovely silver hair covering one of his eyes as he looked back up at her. He was so beautiful, and so cold, so different from her.

She did love him. She knew it suddenly. Shockingly. She loved him.

She placed a finger under his chin and tilted his face up so that their eyes met again. She still had tears streaming down her face.

"Listen to me very carefully, Lachlan MacNair. I won't say these things again. I want to be bound to you. Not just because it is the right thing to do. Not because our parents decided when we were small this was the way it should be. And not to bring honor to *Scath*. I want to be bound to you because I love you. I didn't even know that until right now. I love you. But I will not have my free will taken away from me. I can't do that. Maybe you will never understand it. But if I let them do that to me, I lose everything. I won't do that. Not even for you. So, I am going to fight this and I am going to find a way to prevent the *cheangal*. I have very little time and I hope you'll help me even though you don't understand it. But that's something you will have to work out for yourself."

She took a sharp breath. "If I am successful, I will see you at the *aontuet*. I will stand next to you and I will try to find a way to understand why you couldn't help me. Because I love you, I will try and understand. That's what love is, I think, or at least part of it: trusting the needs of the one you love, even if they make no sense at all. However, if I am unsuccessful, I will go to my father and I will refuse the *aontuet*."

Evangeline leaned down and kissed him very gently. She was about to pull away but his hand was on the back of her head. He pulled her to him, urgent, winding his fingers into her hair. She broke away and stepped out of his reach. "Goodbye, Locke."

She turned and left without looking back at him. It took every ounce of strength she had. Right before she closed the door she heard his voice, though she couldn't make out the words for sure.

And she couldn't allow herself to go back to find out what he'd said.

CHAPTER

TWENTY-SIX

"Oh my gaaawd! It does reek, doesn't it?" Peyton's voice was muffled. She was on her hands and knees, waist deep in Shifty's closet. After a series of thuds, scrapes, and at least two mutterings of "ow," she made her way out again. She held out what looked like a burlap bulb, tied at the top with some kind of string to Shifty with a wide grin across her face. Taking it from her, Shifty rolled the object over in her hands a couple of times, and brought it to her nose. She flinched.

"It's not unpleasant."

"The hell it isn't, it's downright overpowering!" Peyton said.

"But it wasn't that bad when I was in here earlier. It was noticeable, but it didn't smell like," she shook the bundle at Peyton, causing a fresh wave of scent. Both girls wrinkled their noses. "Well, earth and death, I guess."

They broke into involuntary giggles. "Well, I am certainly glad we get to bring it to my parents' house," Peyton said when she'd caught her breath. "That's a treat. I can only hope to be in its presence longer."

"Don't say I never did anything for you, Peyton. At least now I have something to threaten you with if you keep chewing that horrible wad of gum in the apartment." Shifty looked a little closer at the object. "Surely my parents will be able to smell it now. So how do we get it out of here?"

Peyton plucked it from Shifty's fingers and chucked it out the open bedroom window which overlooked the backyard. "There, we'll just pick it up on our way, if some unfortunate squirrel doesn't snag it first."

"We better hurry. I'd feel kind guilty about that."

"My mother would be thrilled. They're leaving persimmons in her herb garden again. It's driving her nuts."

The girls hurried down the stairs and through the kitchen, where Shifty's parents were pouring a nightcap.

"Found what I needed in my room." Shifty held up her spare pair of mat shoes. "We're going to head on home." She dropped a kiss on both their cheeks and Peyton followed suit.

When they ducked out the back door, Peyton spotted it first, laying in the grass. She scooped it up and they hopped the fence into the Devlins' backyard, unable to suppress the need to take a final look over their shoulders to ensure they weren't being watched.

The rest of the Devlins were in the living room. Paxton stood leaning against the doorframe with his eyes locked on the front door. His parents were more relaxed, but neither of them were seated. Tristan was building a fire, while Nelda had a large book open across her left hand and was flipping through the pages with her right.

"We didn't use that door," Peyton said, coming up next to Paxton and giving him a gentle nudge in the ribs.

"Did you find it?" Paxton asked, not giving her the satisfaction of acknowledging her jab.

Shifty had more compassion for his anxiety. She slipped herself under his arm and squeezed him in what she hoped was a reassuring manner. "Easy, peasy. Peyton's got it."

Nelda's head snapped up and she shut the book, setting it aside. She reached a hand out and Peyton dropped the totem into it. Nelda held it up to the light, then dropped the totem from one palm to the other, almost as if she was weighing it. It looked like nothing so much as a rough, brown fabric pouch, tied with a piece of leather cord. The top of the fabric was sealed with bright red wax. The whole thing was the size of a Barbie doll's head. It surprised Shifty that something so small could produce such a stench.

"Well?" Peyton urged. "What is it?"

"A totem," Nelda said, her voice far away. She wasn't trying to be obtuse, Shifty knew. She'd seen Nelda go to this place before. When she was reading, or elbows deep in some new concoction at the stove. If they just gave her a minute, Nelda would snap out of it and share her discoveries with the rest of them. Tristan, the most unfazed by his wife's lapses into her own reality, continued to poke at the fire.

Peyton shuffled her feet and toyed with her hands, sniffing her palms to see if the pouch had befouled them, pulling her fingers back toward her wrist, one hand and then the other. Paxton stood almost completely still, his only movement was the rhythmic grip and release of his hand against Shifty's shoulder.

They didn't have to wait very long before Nelda looked up.

"So? What is it? Is it wraith magic?"

"No, Paxton. Of course not. Please, you're going to scare Shifty if you keep jumping right to that conclusion. This is a summoning totem. A kind of beacon."

"For what? To where?" Tristan asked. He stood and dusted ashes from his hands.

"I'll have to take it apart to be completely sure, but I think Shifty is being summoned home. To *Scath*. Shifty?" When Nelda addressed her, every other head in the room snapped to look at her as well. But no one interrupted. "Have you had any strange urges?"

"What kind of urges? What would they feel like?"

"You would know if you'd had them." Nelda was picking at the wax seal on the totem, wearing a hole in it. When she'd made a large enough slit, she sniffed at the opening, and peered into the contents of the package. "Everything seems to be right. I don't know why it…didn't…maybe because you weren't around it enough. But…"

"Aaand there she goes again. Great." Paxton slumped back against the doorframe again, his shoulders sagging into Shifty's back.

"Give her a break, Pax. She's just trying to figure it out," Shifty scolded. It was always easier to be patient with someone else's parents.

Nelda motioned for Shifty to come to her, and took each of her arms and pushed her shirt sleeves up to Shifty's elbows. Shifty's glamoured skin changed, but she must have found nothing out of the ordinary because Nelda gave a jerk of her head and Shifty's skin went back to what she had begun to call in her mind "pale human." Nelda then lifted Shifty's hair to look at her neck. Her fingers were so gentle that they tickled when they danced around her ears.

"I think…I'm pretty sure that when I removed that spell from you earlier and gave you back control of your own magic, I also blocked the power of this totem."

"Well, that's good, right?"

"Yes. It's good. Whoever was trying to call you home can't do that now."

"Then why do you still sound so upset, Mom?" Paxton asked.

"Because now they'll have to come looking for her."

CHAPTER
TWENTY-SEVEN

Evangeline walked home from the clearing without noticing anything around her. They would still help her, her friends, but they didn't understand. If she wasn't unhappy with the *aontuet*, what did it matter if the *cheangal* was in place? If she wanted to do the right thing anyway, why did she care if the *riocht* had a little extra assurance? Linus agreed to help for the challenge of it, Tresara because her mother wouldn't like it, and Igby...well, because Igby believed in friendship and loyalty. They'd hit the books, try to find a way to block the *cheangal*, but in the end they thought Evangeline should walk the path to the ceremony either way. They made their feelings very clear: Evangeline was being silly, childish, and sentimental. She was being human.

She pulled at the leaves on a low hanging branch until one snapped free. The ricochet hit her on the cheek and swept over her eye, which began to water immediately. Great. She was crying for the third time this evening. She didn't swipe the tears away this time. There was no one around to see them, no one to act brave for. She let out a strangled sound deep in her throat, an involuntary sob.

She just wanted to run to her room, turn on *The Shadow*, and have time reverse back to a time before any of this had come to light. She wanted to see Locke at her window and hear his cocky banter with her parents, secure in the knowledge they wouldn't deny him her company. She wanted him not to have been disappointed in her. In her humanity and her will. And, if she was going to let herself be completely honest, she wanted him not to have disappointed her.

She threw the leaf to the ground and obliterated it into the fog with the heel of her shoe. It should have made her feel powerful, or at least burned off some of her excess emotion, but all she felt was small. Insignificant. Alone. And scared. Scared they wouldn't find a way to lift the *cheangal*, scared that her parents would force her to carry on under its weight, scared of the only home she'd ever known.

She was on the last step of her porch when the door opened. Her father stood in the arch and his expression was the same one he wore at important meetings, or when the wraiths came to call. Not a hint of parental compassion. All business. Evangeline knew then: someone had told him she'd discovered the *cheangal*.

She was glad her tears had stopped. She squared her shoulders and tried to look him in the eye.

"Come inside, Evangeline."

"I wasn't going to back out. I'm going to be bound to Locke, Dad. You don't need to do this."

"Come inside, Evangeline, please."

"Can't we talk about it? Don't you trust me?" She took another step closer to the front door though every fiber of her being was screaming to run the other way. She wouldn't do it. She wouldn't prove them right, that she was an impulsive child who needed to be controlled with magic in order to behave. "It's just not necessary. Really."

"I won't ask you again to come inside."

She stalked past him and into the house. Her feet stopped, her body sensing the danger before her mind could comprehend it. Her house was not empty, and she had been too focused on her next argument to notice.

There were dozens of them. Not just the elders, but members of the powerful families as well. *Hairn*, banshee, and wraith. They lined the walls of the rooms downstairs. Evangeline scanned their faces. These were the creatures she'd grown up with. She'd shared meals at their tables, traded at their shops and stalls. She had played with their children. But right now, there wasn't a single smile or gentle face in this crowd. They were of a singular being and purpose. Evangeline felt a chill run up her body and her stomach lurched. She was suddenly sure she was going to lose the last meal she'd eaten and she started for the door, if only to have a place to be sick without all these eyes on her. But they'd closed in to block her path the moment it had closed behind her. Her face grew hot, pushing the cold terror to the side. Fear and anger competed for space in her brain.

"Please," she whispered to the wraith and banshee who were guarding the door. "Please, you don't have to. Oh, oh..." she fumbled for words. She had to get the emotions under control if she had any chance of reasoning with her captors. Her panic would only convince them she was too unstable to proceed under her own free will. "I just needed some fresh air...my stomach...I wasn't going to run. I'm not going to run," she clarified. "You don't have to do this. Just listen to me, okay? I'll be bound to Locke. Willingly. I'll be there at the *aontuet*, I swear. Put a guard on me until the ceremony. You'll see. It's not necessary...what you're planning."

"Evangeline. Quiet. Please." Cecil MacNair stepped from the center of a small grouping of wraiths. He laid a hand on her shoulder and its weight made her feel as if she'd sunk two inches into the floor. "Don't force us to make this any more unpleasant."

He could, too. She knew it. The hand he wasn't using to hold her in place held a casting rod, and Cecil MacNair was a talented caster. She would be bent to his will no matter what. Doing what they asked was the only way she might be able to convince them the *cheangal* was unnecessary. She tamped down her panic, reminding herself that she knew the MacNairs, the O'Briens—Igby's mother and father—and finally the Raffertys, Linus's parents; that she didn't need to be afraid. They all only wanted the same thing: for the *aontuet* to be successful. "Okay, I'm sorry. What do you want me to do?"

"We need you to go to your room. Dress for the ceremony."

"The ceremony? But the moon—"

"The *aontuet* will take place tonight. That's all you need to know. Go to your room. Lara Keelin is there to assist you."

"Where is my mother?"

"So many questions," he said dismissively. "Your mother will see you later. Lara will be attending you. She will be placing the *cheangal*."

"It isn't necess—"

"Stop telling us our ways, child. You only need to do as you are told. Now." He removed his hand but his glare was just as much a push. He stepped back and allowed her access to the stairway.

She did as she was told, though slowly, one foot in front of the other. Each time it felt as if her shoes were gathering more lead. She scanned the faces in her home as she ascended, hoping for just one face that could be an ally. As she reached the top of the stairs one person made eye contact with her, but there was no salvation in his eyes. His face was a canvas painted only with duty and resolve.

Lachlan MacNair would do as he was told.

CHAPTER

TWENTY-EIGHT

"Why do they want her back in *Scath*, Mom?" Paxton crossed his arms, dropped them, wrapped them around Shifty's shoulders. "It doesn't make any sense. They sent her here. They sent *us* here to keep her out of *Scath* and away from the wraiths. Why would anyone but the wraiths send for her?"

"Or someone working for the wraiths," Peyton said from the corner. She crouched, small and scared. All her tough pretense had vanished and her glamour was completely dropped. She gripped her hair on either side of her head and stared at the floorboards beneath her. "There's something really bad happening, isn't there, Mom?"

"We don't know anything yet. Let's not get ourselves all worked up." It was Tristan who spoke. Tristan, who was so often the more compassionate parent. They'd raised their children in *Talam*, trained them to appear human, to allow their emotions to show, and Tristan had taken to the *riocht's* lightness more easily than his *ceile* had. Comfort and reassurance came more naturally to him.

He ruffled his daughter's hair and offered her a hand. She took it with a smile and he pulled her to her feet and into a brief hug.

"Here's what I think," he said. "Your mother needs to spend some time with the totem and consult her books. Let her do that tonight. You kids and Shifty go home. Everyone get some rest. Tomorrow when you girls are in class, Paxton can mind the store while your mom and I cross a ley line and talk to someone we can trust. We'll find out what they know."

"I don't like it," Paxton said. "Why can't you go now? We'll wait here. What is a couple more hours with the totem going to—"

The sound seemed to explode from the back of the house. All five of them jumped, and Peyton actually let out a yell, burying her face in her father's chest. The second time the noise came, it was apparent it was only someone knocking on the backdoor. Knocking urgently, sure, but it wasn't grenades being launched through the windows.

"Who on earth…" Nelda's voice seemed to fade into itself and she started toward the back of the house. "Probably your parents, Shifty. I'll ask them to stay for a nightcap. Peyton, do something about yourself, please." Her voice was stern and Peyton's color immediately changed, the flush on her cheeks included.

The four of them stood exchanging helpless looks, fidgeting.

A woman shoved through the door and into the house. "We have to do something, Nelda! Now, tonight. We have to—" The panicked flow of her words cut off as she looked to the others in the room. No. As she looked to Shifty. The woman's jaw clamped shut, her eyes widened, and her hands went to her face.

"Mist over the moon," she cursed. "Siofra?"

Shifty was too stunned to answer. She looked from Nelda to Tristan, and then between Peyton and Paxton. Who was this, what was she doing here, and why did she think Nelda could help her?

"Yes, I'm Shifty." Shifty retreated back against Paxton's chest. He placed a hand on her hip, letting her know he was there. "You are?"

"I'm your mother, child." The *hairn* took a step closer to Shifty. Her hand rose, apparently involuntarily, like she was going to reach out and stroke Shifty's cheek. Suddenly Shifty very much did not want this creature touching her. It must have showed in her eyes, because the woman dropped her hand and a look of disappointment flashed across her face.

"Why are you here, Ciarda?" Tristan asked. He wasn't radiating anger or fear, but this was not a tone Shifty was used to hearing from the gentle Tristan.

"Circumstances have changed. We need to hurry."

"Hurry? Where?" Peyton, never one to fear authority spoke, despite the withering look from her mother that clearly said *stay out of this*. Peyton arched an eyebrow at her mother, her nostrils flared, and she made a huffing sound. Her father placed a hand on her shoulder. Shifty could feel Paxton's body shake behind her and she knew he was fighting his inappropriate laughter.

The new woman—Ciarda, her mother—the *sheehairn*, spared the shortest of glances for Peyton.

"Nelda, I'm quite serious. We need to leave immediately."

"Again…where?" Peyton muttered, but only so loud that Shifty and Paxton made it out. This time it was Shifty who had trouble not laughing.

"To *Scath*, child. And we will need you all, I think."

"No, I don't think so," Tristan said.

Ciarda ignored him. "Nelda, there's no time to waste. We must hurry. I will explain on the way. Do I need to remind you of the loyalty you pledged me?"

"I didn't pledge any loyalty and neither did your daughter. Why do we have to go with you?" Paxton's voice was strong, but his hands still did their rhythmic clutching at Shifty's hip.

She gave him what she hoped was a supportive smile. She hoped desperately that her fear and confusion wasn't telegraphed on every pore of her face.

"You've obviously not been taught the ways of your *riocht*."

"My children weren't raised in our *riocht*, by *your* request." Nelda maintained steady eye contact with the other *sheehairn*. "But, we will join you…After I receive a full explanation."

Ciarda looked liked she was going to argue, an imperious expression crossing her features, but it passed. She seemed to realize that Nelda would not back down. This was the best offer she, Ciarda, was going to get. A single nod was exchanged and Ciarda turned on her heel, heading for the back door again.

Nelda gestured for all of them to huddle close. "We have to go with her. She has the power to destroy us if we do not do as she asks. I trust Ciarda. She was the one who asked us to be your protectors, Shifty. Of all the *sheehairn* or banshees that could have summoned us, I believe us to be safest with her. We'll have to go to *Scath* with her. Shifty, stay close to Peyton and Paxton. They understand the magic and traditions of shadow, even if they haven't been raised there."

Shifty nodded. She took Paxton's hand and gave it a weak squeeze.

They made their way as a group out to the back yard, where Ciarda waited to take them to *Scath*.

To her birthplace.

CHAPTER

TWENTY-NINE

Evangeline's panic rose to her throat. If she couldn't stop hyperventilating, she was sure she was going to scream and then pass out.

Lara Keelin stood with her back pressed firmly against it, facing Evangeline. Not that Evangeline would have been any match for the wraith—or for any *Scath* creature, really—but the move made Evangeline feel even more trapped and claustrophobic. As did knowing, *knowing* with all that she was, that there was no reasoning with Lara. There was nothing she could do to talk her out of placing the *cheangal*. She was good and trapped.

She wondered if it would hurt. If her mind would be out of her control. What about her movements? She knew Lara wouldn't be gentle. Possibly she wouldn't go out of her way to hurt Evangeline, but if there was a way to make the process more comfortable, Lara wouldn't employ it.

Lara held her casting rod at her side with a kind of threatening nonchalance. Evangeline couldn't take her eyes off it. What did the *cheangal* involve? Would it be quick? And why didn't Lara speak? The fear boiled up inside Evangeline, clutched at her throat, and told her to do crazy things: leap from the window, or push Lara aside and run down the stairs for freedom. She'd never make it even a foot beyond the front door. Would it be Locke who stopped her?

How could she have been so wrong? How could she have thought he might understand? Was he even capable of caring for her, outside their duty to *Scath*?

Lara lifted her rod and took a single step closer to Evangeline. Evangeline's heart raced. She could feel her nostrils expanding and contracting against the bridge of her nose. Would it hurt? Would it…

It didn't hurt.

When the veil of the spell fell over her, everything dimmed slightly. Her limbs felt just a bit heavier. Her mind just a touch slower. As her thoughts stopped racing, so too did her fear begin to ebb. Just a little. It was still there, tickling at the back of her thoughts, but it was behind a door. She was closed off from her ability to feel it. She knew, vaguely, that this should worry and upset her. But those feelings, too, were closed off in a different compartment.

"Have a seat, Evangeline. It won't be much longer now."

Evangeline walked to the chair she sat in to read. The chair her mother had sat in when Evangeline was a child and read to her. It was where she had learned that knowledge was powerful; where she had discovered her place in the world. Now it was a part of her prison. And she couldn't feel sad. She wondered a little what her expression looked like, if it was as blank as her mind felt.

She and Lara sat in the closed room, not looking at each other. Waiting.

Underneath them, she could hear more people arrive. It wouldn't be long now.

CHAPTER

THIRTY

Shifty's mind reeled. Everything was zipping past her like blurred trees out of the window of a moving car. The short walk to the ley line, its strange glowing fire appearing in the foliage. The feeling of vertigo, and her stomach in her throat, as they stepped over it. She arrived not on the other side of the line but in a whole different world. The redwood trees of her home were groves of birch. The sky was still darkening, but the very feel of the air was different: crisper, colder than home. There was a dense mist around her ankles, different than the fog she knew. It swirled with a luminescence, and seemed to crawl up her legs. She felt that if she reached out and cupped a handful of it the fog would sit on her palm, turning and dipping, folding in on itself.

There was no reflection of light in the sky. The stars were beginning to blink into existence so clearly that she was sure she could make out their color bursts. She walked for a few feet in awe with her head tipped back, trying to take it all in. It was wondrous. Somewhere in her mind she thought she should probably be afraid. But the *riocht*... it made her spirit sing.

Her limbs felt lighter and her joints moved freer. She looked at her hands. Her glamour had dropped with the crossing of the line. She was pure *sheehairn*; from her flesh, hair, to the white *rian* crawling across her skin in elaborate patterns. The marks seemed to be dancing. She felt like *she* was dancing. She had never felt so in control of her being. She looked over at Paxton with her eyes wide, a barely contained grin bursting across her face.

"This is why you have to come home," she said with understanding. "You feel what I'm feeling when you're here?"

He nodded. His face was more restrained than hers, but his amusement at her wonder was still clear. "Yes. We are products of our *riocht*. It isn't merely our appearance that is cloaked in *Talam*."

Shifty moved her arm through the air around her, wiggled her fingers, and smiled wider. "Incredible."

"Think you can rein it in? I mean at least until we know what's going on?" Paxton's voice was gentle. He was not chiding her, he sounded as if he thought there was a real possibility she'd be unable to contain her enthusiasm.

Shifty straightened her spine and took a deep breath of the clear air. Filling her lungs with such purity made her feel even lighter and more present in her body. More in control, as well. She felt confident when she nodded her head. "I'm on it, Pax. I can maintain."

They made their way along a path, past a collection of what appeared to be storefronts and stands. There was a meeting place in the center, a kind of town square. Further on the path the birch trees became denser, the moss and other brush barely parted for their feet. Soon, though, the terrain cleared slightly and Shifty's group traveled by a spattering of homes. It was all so familiar, the homes not so different from those in Duncan Mills. Porches where people could sit and talk. Gates surrounding tidy back yards. So much the same, and yet to her core she could feel the difference in this place. The magic that hung in the air crawled, very literally, on her skin.

Ciarda had walked at a steady pace ever since they crossed the ley line. She looked straight ahead, confident that Shifty and the others were following. They'd made it most of the way through the community of homes when Ciarda came to a halt. Unlike most of the other homes, which were completely dark and had the feeling of being empty, this one had flickers of light behind the drawn curtains. The shadows of dozens of creatures played across their surface. Shifty moved closer to Paxton and whispered into his ear. "Where are we?"

"I think this is your parents' house," Paxton whispered back, his face tightening. He took her hand automatically and they stood side by side, watching Ciarda. She motioned to the elder Devlins and the three conferred for a moment. When Nelda stepped out of the group, she made a similar gesture to Shifty and her own children.

"Just stay close, do as you're told, and trust me. Okay?"

Wide-eyed, terrified, and exhilarated, Shifty nodded.

"Good. Follow me."

Up the stairs, across the porch, and through the door. The eyes of all the creatures hung on them, taking them in. The colors of their skin captivated her; the blue and the green.

And the silver.

The creature stood in the near the front of the room in an place of obvious import, while she wasn't elevated, Shifty could tell she was above everyone else in her presence. A chill passed over Shifty at the woman. With skin the metallic hue of pure silver, and hair just a shade or two lighter flowing down her back like a wave of molten metal, Shifty knew this creature must be a wraith. Power wafted off her and swirled around her. She was the most beautiful creature Shifty had ever seen, and the most frightening.

Without meaning to, Shifty took a step behind Paxton.

There were more of them, the silver beings, scattered in the crowd. Shifty fought her inner voice and remained blank-faced. She wasn't imagining it. They were staring at her. Taking her in. She felt their hunger, knew they were watching her *rian*. She wished her markings would fade so these creatures wouldn't seem so hungry for her.

Finally, after what felt like an eternity, a *sheehairn* male approached them. Shifty had only seen her *hairn*-self fully a couple of times, but she saw herself in his face. Was this her father? Did *hairn* genetics work that way? Would she resemble her parents?

Apparently, yes. As he came to stand next to Ciarda, he placed a protective hand on her shoulder and whispered into her ear. Ciarda turned her attention to the *sheehairn*, then her eyes darted back to Shifty and she nodded her head to her new companion. The interaction had such a feeling of silent communication, of connection that Shifty immediately had her answer.

Her breath quickened. She felt the pressure on her hand —Paxton squeezing it—a reminder to remain placid and unaffected. To keep it together.

"You brought her?" The man asked his mate. What was his name? They'd told her his name. Why couldn't she remember?

"I did. She's everything we believed."

I'm not! Shifty's mind screamed. *I'm not special. I'm just me and I don't know what I'm doing here.* She took a deep breath, hoping the sound didn't telegraph how nervous she was. Her father came closer to her. Paxton held his position. He was unwilling to yield even to a powerful *hairn*. Shifty appreciated it, even as she wondered how smart it was.

"Siofra?"

"Yes, sir." She wanted to tell him that he could call her Shifty, that everyone did, but something deep in her screamed that this was not a good idea.

"Welcome home."

"Uh, thank you."

He smiled at her, though not that warmly, and turned his attention to Nelda and Tristan. "You've done well. Thank you."

Peyton was suddenly beside her. "Am I the only one who doesn't like what's going on here? Are we being dismissed? Relieved of our duties? Thank you very much?" Her lips barely moved, but both Paxton and Shifty heard her. Almost in unison, they shook their heads. "Yeah. That's what I thought. Because right now this feels like the beginning of an epic clusterfuck."

They didn't have much longer to wait and wonder. Shifty's father—Arawn, she remembered suddenly, they'd told her his name was Arawn—stepped onto one of the lowest stairs of the staircase. He waited for the crowd to turns its full attention to him.

"Thank you. As you can see Ciarda has returned. She's brought with her Nelda and Tristan. And my daughter, Siofra. Everything we need is in place. I will need everyone's complete participation once the ritual begins. No deviation. Once the sacrifice is complete we can begin the *aontuet* and then *falt rich drait*—"

His voice went on, but Shifty stopped hearing him. On either side of her Paxton and Peyton went rigid. She swiveled her head between them. Their brightly colored eyes were wide and filling with fear.

"What?" she hissed. "What does that mean? And what sacrifice?"

"*Falt rich drait* is a beckoning spell. It's for *riochtfíos*." Paxton explained, his lips pressed against her ear.

She wanted to ask more questions, but Nelda shot a warning glare at them. In their whispering, they'd missed the last of Arawn's instructions. He was holding out a hand for Nelda to join him on the improvised platform.

"You've brought my daughter home. I can see she's fared well under your guardianship. Her mother and I thank you. We'd planned her arrival slightly differently." He let the words hang between them, not exactly an accusation, but not a pleasantry either.

Nelda's face registered no reaction. "I beg your pardon, Arawn. Had I known you would be summoning the girl…"

"It's no matter." It didn't *sound* like it was no matter. "This way we have your presence at the *aontuet*. An honor we didn't expect." It didn't *sound* like an honor. "Ciarda, Lara, Cecil, can you join us as well?"

A *hairn*, a banshee, and the wraith that had so frightened Shifty moments before filed silently through the crowd and assembled with the others on the stair. Shifty felt her body start to shake. She had a very bad feeling about this. Something terrible was about to happen. Isolation fell over Shifty like a glass cloche on an exhibit, leaving her feeling just as on display and at a distance as she would have been in a museum. She didn't understand any of this. But every instinct told her that her best interests were not foremost among the goals for the evening. Even if they meant her no harm, they were certainly not planning to ask for her to consent to these proceedings.

She turned to Paxton, needing his comfort and reassurance, but Paxton stared straight ahead. Peyton, on her other side, wore a carbon copy of her brother's expression. Shifty fought the urge to bolt. What would she do then? Where would she run? She didn't know nearly enough magic to fight her way from this room, forget about escaping this *riocht*. Even if she did manage to get out of the house, and by some miracle made her way back to the ley line, she had no idea how to get back to the *riocht* where her parents waited. She was very much at the mercy of the beings in this room.

"Lara, Cecil, will you welcome Siofra into your fold?"

Wait! What?

"We will."

"And will you allow Lachlan to join ours?"

"We will."

Who?

Another gesture. Another creature snaked through the crowd. This one was younger—her age—and he was a banshee. He was attractive. Tall, with striking silver hair that nearly reached his shoulders. He mounted the stair and stood between the banshee and wraith.

Paxton's posture was ramrod straight and eerily still. Shifty wondered if someone had somehow taken control of him. She realized with a sinking feeling in the pit of her stomach that he had let go of her hand.

Peyton, though physically only a couple of inches away, radiated coolness and distance. Shifty wanted to wave her arms in front of their faces, beg them to save her from whatever these creatures had planned for her. She was sure that she would be called to that stair next.

"Siofra Wicklow."

Who? Oh. Shifty Gilbert. They meant her. She cleared her throat. "Um, yes?" She wished she could think of something stronger to say, but her mouth betrayed her as her mind reeled.

"Would you please join us? We welcome you home."

Paxton gave an almost imperceptible push on the small of her back. Nelda's eyes bored into hers and Shifty felt her feet carry her forward. When she was steps from the others, her mother fell in next to her and they both joined the group.

"As a community do you approve this *aontuet?*"

This what?

"We do."

Had Paxton said it, too?

"Then it is done. The altar is in place. When the moon is high, we can proceed with the sacrifice. Please make your way there. We shall ready Lachlan and Siofra for their *aontuet.*"

For what?

Slowly the room emptied until only the Devlins remained. Shifty, feeling drained completely of all ability to feel or comprehend, stood on the stair while the others talked.

"Was the human compliant when you left, Lara?" Arawn asked.

The human? Did he mean...? Wasn't she their child?

The wraith who had so terrified Shifty earlier nodded. "She was. There is no way she can resist the *cheangal*. There won't be a problem."

"Excellent."

Arawn crossed the room and uncorked a bottle of an amber liquid. He poured several glasses and passed them around to all the parents.

"I had this brought back from *Talam* especially for this day," he said as he raised his glass. "Many years led to this and I thank you all for your dedication to our cause."

All of them, Nelda and Tristan included, joined Arawn in toasting their glasses and murmured similar sentiments.

"Siofra, you should meet Lachlan. You and he are to be bound this night," Arawn said.

Finally, painfully, her mouth opened and her vocal cords formed a word. "Bound?"

"He means married," a voice said, one not far from her. She whipped her head around. Paxton.

"Married? I can't get married! I have a boyfriend. I live in *Talam*. With Paxton. I'm only a sophomore in college, I have a gymnastics meet in three days. I want to go to Europe. This summer I'm going to coach kids at Jumping Jacks. I'm only twenty. And...And...well, I don't even know him!" The banshee standing next to her merely looked at her and offered her the tilted slit of his mouth in return.

Arawn stepped closer. "You'll have time to know Locke. And as for your *boyfriend*," he said the word as if it were grit in his mouth, "you never should have been allowed to become so attached. Your guardians knew that would never be condoned. Consider it merely a childish dalliance."

Shifty glared at the older Devlins. This wasn't at all what she was told. Her father seemed to be implying the Devlins had known she was to return to *Scath* and be married off like chattle. That they wouldn't meet her gaze only confirmed the new information. Shifty felt the tears prickle at her eyes, and saw the shock in the faces around her. Apparently, *sheehairn* didn't allow themselves these emotions. But she hadn't been raised in their world. They'd seen to that. Surely they couldn't expect her to instantly become one of them. They'd exiled her, and not for the reasons she'd been told. All the information was piling up in her head, but she had no way to sort it out.

"It happened before we could stop it," Tristan explained.

No, it had not! Shifty's brain screamed. She'd fallen in love with Paxton slowly, like a long walk. It was part of what made her so sure of him. And the Devlins knew it.

"But we've spoken to Paxton. He understands, he knew she was never to be his," Nelda said.

"Then he should have kept his distance!" Arawn snapped.

"These things work differently in *Talam*, and we were ordered to fit in," Tristan explained.

Arawn took in a large breath through his nose and clasped his hands together across his middle. By the time he'd exhaled slowly through his mouth, he had apparently composed his thoughts. "I will concede to you on that point. Paxton, we can expect no problems from you?"

Shifty felt her shoulders straighten. Her feet felt more secure under her. Here it came.

"Of course. Shift—Siofra is to be bound to Lachlan. I'm sure my parents will have a suitable match for me."

Shifty gasped. The words carried a physical sting, but that was but a pinprick compared to the blunt force of his tone.

He meant this. She bit into her lip to keep from crying out at the injustice. Her anger was so thick now she could barely see through the haze of it. Her *rian* flared on her arms, so copious they almost consumed her skin.

"Very good. Now, Siofra," Arawn turned to her. "Your mother will be taking you shortly to prepare you for the *aontuet*. You need not be present for the sacrifice, but after the ceremony, we will need your participation. Your magic needs to be contributed to the *falt rich drait*. Don't be concerned, we will tell you what we need you to do. We know you are unaware of our customs and rituals, and that your magic is new to you. It is not complicated."

Shifty stumbled over the words with little care if she pronounced the name for their ritual correctly. "What's the 'fire drill' thing for?"

"It will finally share *riochtfios* with the wraiths," Nelda said.

It was the final straw. The pyramid of information inside Shifty's mind tumbled down. The Devlins hadn't been protecting her. They'd been raising her like an animal for trading. They didn't want to stop the wraiths from gaining power. They were assisting. Shifty and the human child, the child who had been taken from the Gilberts, had been groomed for this day. And as bad as her fate was…realization struck.

They planned to *sacrifice* the human girl. They were going to kill her.

And what could Shifty do about it?

Paxton wouldn't look at her. It seemed he'd resigned to handing her over to another. Nelda had looked in her eyes, and betrayed her; had betrayed her twice now, really. Even Tristan took part in the duplicity playing out at the bottom of the staircase. He'd dismissed her relationship with Paxton as merely a part of their *Talam* cover story.

She'd found the place where she felt alive in her body. She

had discovered she wasn't crazy. And now the very people who'd helped her down the path were handing her over to sinister rituals, ceremonies, and magic. They'd lied to her. Maybe if she'd been raised in this place she wouldn't be so hurt. Maybe betrayal was thought of differently here. But she was not a creature of *Scath*. She hadn't been carefully taught to control her emotions.

The woman she must now call Mother took her hand and led her from the room. She followed. What choice did she have? She was all alone here.

CHAPTER

THIRTY-ONE

"There isn't much time," Ciarda said, ushering her through a door. "Your father and the others will be readying the sacrifice right now."

Shifty watched her mother, saw *rian* appearing at her neck and wrists. Blue like Peyton's. Shifty's mind struggled to remember what they meant. She needed to latch on to something; to focus on one thing she knew. Looking for an answer would keep her from snapping.

Mind magic. It was mind magic.

"Now, child," Ciarda began, "did Nelda cast a clearing spell?"

"A what?"

"Did she remove our spells from you?" The *hairn* sounded impatient, though not unkind. A teacher prompting a child who wasn't keeping up with the lesson.

"Oh. Yes."

"Excellent." She rummaged in her pocked and thrust a small metal object toward Shifty's chest. Without thinking, Shifty took it and let it settle comfortably in the palm of her hand.

Ciarda gave a wary eye to the door and hurried to a chair in the corner. It was only then that Shifty realized they were not alone in the room. Sitting in the chair was a girl with long, dark curls and blank, wide, green eyes. She was pale with a smattering of freckles across her nose. A human. Shifty gazed at her harder, the girl looked like Adara. Except for her eyes. She had Grady's eyes, the exact same shape and almost the same shade.

The human didn't move, didn't make eye contact with Shifty or Ciarda. Her disconcerting stillness made a chill run up Shifty's spine. The girl might as well already be dead. Ciarda rapped the girl's cheeks, not too gently, three times on each side.

"It's in place," she said, or Shifty thought that was what she said. The words didn't travel all the way to Shifty's ears and they weren't meant to.

"I need your help."

"I don't want to help you." Shifty was as surprised as her mother by the words.

"I have to lift the *cheangal*. It's wraith magic, so I can't do it alone. Only you can. It will take *riochtfíos*. It's good you're so angry."

"How do you know I'm angry?"

"Your *rian*, child. They practically scream it. But that's good, we need as much power as possible. Lara Keelin placed this *cheangal* and we have very little time to lift it. Use the coin." She flapped a hand frantically at Shifty.

Shifty looked dumbly, feeling slow-witted, at the round metal object in her hand. "Use it?"

"It will help you channel your magic, conduct it. Focus on it in your hand. Once you have control, the magic contained, you'll need to direct it at Evangeline—"

"Who?"

Ciarda made an irritated, impatient noise in her throat and gestured toward the girl in the chair. "Evangeline," she said.

"Oh. Sorry. What do I do?"

"Lifting the *cheangal* is not complicated. It just takes immense power. You should be able to shatter it. Like a window."

"Why?"

"To sever her ties to this *riocht*. If the *cheangal* remains she will be unable to cross the ley line."

"You want *me* to help her?"

"Yes!" Ciarda seemed to be fighting to control her emotions. She drew in long, unsteady breath through her nose, held it for a moment, and released it in a rush through her mouth. When she spoke her voice held the false calm of someone who has realized they are speaking to an idiot. "Yes, Siofra. I want you to help her."

"How can *I* help her?"

"We have very little time! I want to save Evangeline, and you. But I can't do it without your magic, girl. We have only moments, Siofra. Please. Please, concentrate."

Shifty fought the urge to ask all her other questions, pushing them to the side. She stared at her palm and the coin that lay there. She pushed with her mind. Nothing. Frustration swelled. It was the glamour all over again.

The coin warmed. She heard Nelda's explanation of the magic of this *riocht*, her magic. "*It gains power from the darker elements in the world. Pain, anger, loss. What it is used for is the decision of the user, but the magic itself is dark.*"

Anger, pain, loss. She had those things. Had them in copious amounts. Power swelled in her. Her *rian* branched off into a dozen paths on her wrist and traveled to the center of her palm, surrounding the coin. It vibrated and grew hot. Shifty pushed harder. It felt good, pushing her anger away and turning it into this power.

When the air around her was all but crackling with energy, she looked to Evangeline. A kind of veil separated the girl from the room. It was translucent with a pale yellow glimmer at the edges. There seemed to be an almost grid-like pattern to its surface.

Oh, yeah. You are mine, Shifty thought. She threw the coin and all it contained into the center of the wraith's spell.

It shattered.

Wisps of smoke traveled into the air above them. Shifty heard her mother gasp and saw Evangeline's head snap to attention. The girl opened her mouth, but Ciarda's hand covered it immediately. "No! Don't speak. It's not safe. You understand?"

Evangeline nodded her head, her eyes widening as she peered over Ciarda's hand. Slowly she pulled her hand back and Evangeline sighed. She smiled at her mother, a world of understanding exchanged in their eyes.

Ciarda rushed to the door, opened it, and stuck her head into the hallway. She looked up and down the hall before motioning to the two girls to join her. "Stay close to me and move quickly. Don't make a sound. Understand?"

Ciarda slipped through the door with the girls following on her heels. Together, they scurried down the stairs. The house was now empty; everyone had moved to the altar, apparently. Ciarda led them to the front door, where she spoke in an urgent whisper. "Get to the trees, quickly. Evangeline, you lead the way. Go to the ley line. Get to *Talam*. You'll both be safe there. I'll come when I can," she paused. "If I can."

"What do we do when we get there? To the ley line?" Shifty asked.

"Don't worry, my child. You'll have answers. Trust me. I know that will not be easy for you, today of all days. But, please, trust me." She didn't wait for a response. She turned to Evangeline and cupped the girl's face in her hands. "Evangeline," she sighed. "I love you. Please forgive me." She pressed her lips against the girl's forehead and Shifty saw Ciarda's lower lip tremble as she pulled in a long breath.

"Thank you, Momma."

"Go!" Ciarda threw the front door open and pushed them through it.

They stumbled down the steps and flew toward the tree line. Shifty didn't allow her mind to focus. She knew she couldn't spare the time to acknowledge the fear coursing through her body. She ran with a determination she'd never experienced before, and all the while the other girl matched her pace. When they made it to the trees Shifty looked over her shoulder and peered back into the night. Ciarda was standing in the waning light of the doorway. She raised a hand in their direction. And then she closed the door. They were on their own again.

CHAPTER

THIRTY-TWO

Evangeline's feet pounded, her muscles strained and screamed, and she fought for breath. Her hair flew in the air, beating against her face and working its way into her throat when she inhaled. Though she choked and gagged, she kept running.

She could see the other girl—the *hairn*—in the corner of her vision. Confusion and fear swirled in Evangeline's mind. How were they ever going to make it into *Talam*? Did the other girl know the way to awaken the line? She had broken the *cheangal*, so she obviously had control of complex magic. Linus had been taught to make a line flare, so this girl might have the knowledge as well. Once they crossed the line, where would they turn? Who could help an orphaned human and a *hairn* in *Talam*?

They closed in, the line mere yards ahead, but she didn't dare slow her pace. If her father and the others didn't yet know of her escape, they would shortly, and it would take no time for them to figure out where to start looking. Panic swelled and she forced her feet to go ever faster, sparing only a short glance to ensure she still had her companion.

The path turned and the line lay ahead Just a small distance more and danger would be behind them.

The fog parted around the ley line and Evangeline saw them. Four creatures. *Hairn*. Two male, two female.

Evangeline's heart sank. They'd been cut off. Tears of disappointment swelled in her eyes.

Together, Evangeline and the girl skidded to a halt steps away from the line.

"Are you going to take us back?"

It was the *hairn* who'd spoken, echoing Evangeline's own mind. She sounded bitter and hostile. But more than that she sounded sad, woebegone.

This was a *hairn*? She looked the *hairn* over closely for the first time and wondered how she'd missed it. The girl was clad head to toe in clothing from *Talam*. She wore blue jeans tucked into black leather boots, a gray t-shirt and a black hooded sweatshirt zipped half way up. In her whole life, Evangeline had never heard a *Scath* creature with pain in her voice. She sounded betrayed. Instinctively, Evangeline placed a hand on the other girl's shoulder.

"No. Of course not. We have let the Wicklows believe for years that we would follow their twisted plan. But only so that we could keep you safe and rescue Evangeline," one of the males, the older, answered. He scattered the contents of a pouch over the ley line and it flared.

The younger male approached them and reached for the *hairn* girl. "Shifty. Please. It was the only way. Please."

The girl pulled her hand away and stepped closer to Evangeline whose protective instincts surged again. She gave in to the urge and stepped between the two. The girl—Shifty?— had saved her. She wanted to return the favor. If these *hairn* meant them harm she, Evangeline, would stand and fight if necessary. But did they mean them harm? Evangeline was not so sure. They were not blocking access to the line. If what they said was true, they were trying to help them, but if that was the case Shifty's anger didn't make sense. Evangeline looked from one *hairn* to the other, trying to decide what to do next.

"Shifty, we have to go now," the older female said. Her voice was cold and authoritative. "Evangeline's life is in danger. *You* are in danger. I realize you're very confused and angry. And you have a right to be. But please, we have to go. We will explain everything once we are safe."

Evangeline swiveled her head to the girl they called Shifty. She would follow her lead. They locked eyes, Shifty's strange purple and orange ones and her own green human gaze. In unison they nodded.

Relief like she had never felt swept over Evangeline. "Me too?" She couldn't help it. She needed to hear it. Needed to know they wanted her to join them.

"Oh yes, Evangeline. You too." There was a gentleness in the woman's voice that made Evangeline want to weep.

"Paxton. Peyton. Quickly," the woman said, gesturing the younger *hairn* to cross the ley line. Obediently, the pair did so, the male staring to Shifty with a longing promise. The line flared brighter as they disappeared into *Talam*.

"I'm scared," Evangeline whispered into Shifty's ear.

"Me too," Shifty said back as she took Evangeline's hand. She offered Evangeline a weak smile. "But forward has to be better than what's behind us."

"Go, girls! Now," the woman urged.

They stepped at the same time. The world swirled around Evangeline. She closed her eyes. When she opened them she would be in *Talam*. All alone, a human who had seen books and magazines, had heard radio plays and music, but had no idea what being human even meant. She didn't know where she would live, or if there would anyone be there to teach her how to take care of herself within the depths of this new dimension. But she would be alive, which was more than she could have hoped for when the moon first rose this evening.

CHAPTER

THIRTY-THREE

Shifty's feet hit the ground and her stomach lurched as if she'd missed a step going up a staircase. She maintained her balance, but beside her Evangeline wasn't so sure-footed. She stumbled and pitched forward. Shifty reached out and stopped her from falling, grabbed her near the elbow and gave her a sharp tug. They over-corrected and tipped backward. Nelda and Tristan were right behind them and stopped the pair from toppling backward onto the ground.

Tristan was scattering something along the line, frantic, muttering, and maneuvering a casting rod. There was no reaction, but Tristan put his tools away and seemed satisfied. "It won't keep them out for long. But we can at least make it home and decide what to do from there. We need to get out of the woods."

Nelda nodded. "We need to move fast." She waved her hands frantically, like someone trying to herd chickens through a gate.

Shifty, studiously ignoring Paxton, stared straight ahead as she walked. Perhaps that is why she was able to see them first.

She stopped in her tracks. A kind of seven dwarves pile-up followed. It would have been amusing if Shifty's blood hadn't gone cold with fear.

"What the hell, Shifty?" Peyton asked, rubbing her nose where the impact had been the worst.

"There's someone at your house." Shifty nodded toward the back porch where there were three figures sitting—one on a chair, the other two directly on the floor, their backs against the house—looking out into the back woods. They looked human at first glance, but these were not *hairn*s practiced at glamours. As Shifty peered at them, she felt frozen in place. Peyton yanked on her hand.

"It's all right, Shifty. We know them. C'mon." Draping Shifty's hand over a shoulders to form a leash with her arm, Peyton began pulling her along up the hill. "They're harmless. I promise."

"I'm having a little trouble with your promises. Just so we're clear on that."

"I know, Shifty. I know. But you're going to forgive him, right?" Shifty huffed.

"You're going to forgive him," Peyton said again, more confidently. Even staring at her friend's back, Shifty knew Peyton was smiling.

Shifty didn't contradict her friend, but she wasn't ready to agree with her. Evangeline appeared next to her. Shifty threw her a smile and stopped walking. Peyton recoiled from the sudden tautness of Shifty's arm over her shoulder and joined them. Shifty held her hand out to Evangeline.

"Hey. I'm Shifty."

Evangeline took Shifty's hand in both of her own. "Evangeline." Her voice was not much above a whisper. She cleared her throat. "Thank you so much for breaking the *cheangal*."

"Oh, that creepy web thing around you? Sure. Glad to help."

"Is this your house?"

"No. The house I grew up in is next door. My apartment is across town. This is the Devlins' house. We're safe here. I'm ninety-eight percent sure of that." As the immediate danger faded and the strangeness of her day—and the uncertainty of her life—closed in, she felt nearly lightheaded. It was strangely liberating. "Of course that percentage could drop, depending on who the people on the porch are."

"They are not dangerous. They want to help," Nelda said. She raised a hand over her head and beckoned the badly glamoured group to them.

They were tall, Shifty noticed. They moved with the strange angular grace of their *riocht*. She had an almost overwhelming desire to run with them in the forest, free from glamours, to see what her true *hairn* form felt like full-out. To turn her joints over on themselves and spin and spin for hours. She shook her head roughly. She was standing next to a girl who came within hours, minutes maybe, of losing her life. If her— if *their*, she reminded herself—mother had cared enough to place herself in the path of danger, then it seemed Evangeline had not been raised as a prisoner. So, Shifty assumed, she'd just had to run from her own family. Shifty's cold heart thawed a little. Probably she would forgive Paxton after all.

The others reached them, smiles stretched across their glamoured faces. Their eyes danced. Shifty couldn't figure out what they were so happy about.

"Lenny!" The taller of the two girls chirped. She *chirped*. It was adorable. And who was Lenny?

Evangeline answered, squinting into the darkness. "Igby? Is that you?"

The girl waved her hands in an elegant magician's presentation in front of her face and when she took them away she was *hairn*, and she was grinning. "It's me! And Tresara! And Linus!" She pointed to the two others as she spoke their names. "Oh! Did you want to tell her? Sorry!" She had a bird's voice, but in a wonderful, endearing way, not cutting or sharp. The other two dropped their glamours as well and were revealed to be a rather severe looking banshee girl and a handsome *hairn* boy.

Evangeline's jaw dropped. "How'd you get here? Why? You're going to be in so much trouble! Oh, I am so happy to see you!" She threw herself in the center of them, pulling them to her. And though Shifty could tell it surprised them, they still patted her awkwardly on the back.

"Inside, everyone!" Nelda called. "There's much to explain and I am sure you have many questions. But we have to do it inside where we are protected. The ley line will only remain barred from *Scath* for a few hours and our next steps have to be carefully planned."

CHAPTER

THIRTY-FOUR

Evangeline was so relieved to see her friends that she almost couldn't care that they had put themselves in terrible danger in order to be here with her.

Once they had all been introduced and were safely inside the house, Nelda sent them to the living room, disappeared into her kitchen, and returned with a tray. It held a pot with steam drifting from the spout and cups for them all. She poured and passed them out. Evangeline was bursting to ask a million and three questions, but the aroma from the liquid in her cup wafted up. So familiar and comforting. Her mother brewed these same herbs.

"Just like home," she said.

"Yes," Nelda agreed. "I thought you might like a little something familiar. Your mother, uh, Ciarda and I created the mix together many years ago."

The entire house smelled like *Scath* and the furnishings were not so different than the homes she'd grown up visiting. She did find it settling.

"Are you sure no one is coming after us?" Paxton asked.

"Yes. Quite sure." Tristan laid a hand on his son's shoulder. "I blocked the line. They'll be able to break it, but they will need the moon to set first. After they've overcome my spell once, they'll be able to defend against it pretty easily. This is our shot."

"So, they were going to kill me?" Evangeline felt strange saying the words. She had to thrust them from her mouth and push them all the way out with her tongue. They were bitter.

"Yes," Nelda said.

"Why?"

"The simple answer: for power. Wraiths crave power. They are jealous of our magic, our ability to travel the *riocht*. The only way for them to gain that ability is through a ritual. A ritual that can only take place through a very specific set of circumstances, timing, and events. It is the *Siofra Ascension*."

Nearby, Shifty squirmed in her seat.

Nelda continued, "The *siofra* are *sheehairn* raised in *Talam*, while a human child is raised in *Scath*. This is hardly ever a successful exchange. The glamours and spells alone are complex and daunting. A *sheehairn*'s very being longs for *Scath*. Both beings usually wither and fail to thrive in their adopted *riocht*. In order for a human to survive in *Scath*, the *sheehairn* in *Talam* must be treated as a true child of the parents they are placed with. The glamour must be so good that the parents would never suspect their child was anything but human. That's nearly impossible."

Evangeline felt Shifty grow tense next to her on the couch. This topic clearly made her uncomfortable. Nelda carried on as if she hadn't noticed, though Evangeline was pretty sure everyone in the room had noticed.

"In order for the *Siofra Ascension* to be successful, the children have to be kept alive for over two decades, treated as family, made a part of the community. But more than that, they have to have other qualifications. There are very specific signs. The two of you were born at the same time. Not just the same day, or even the same hour, but within moments of each other. From different mothers and different *riocht*, but with the timing of twins. And the *sheehairn* must have white *rian*. These marks appear almost immediately, their magic is so strong. The other factors of the *Siofra Ascension* are the sacrifice," Nelda cleared her throat and studied the carpet for a moment, letting the words drift into the room. "And the *aontuet*. Directly after the sacrifice, the returned *hairn* is bound to a banshee. But this banshee must be the child of a wraith and a banshee. The *aontuet* includes magic that uses the blood of the sacrificed human. I'm sorry, Evangeline, I truly am. I don't want to upset you."

The horror of what Nelda had just described sat between them like the soupy *Scath* fog. Finally Evangeline managed her way through it. She reached out blindly for one of her friends, but it was Shifty who took her hand.

"Go on," Evangeline said.

"When the ritual is complete, the wraiths have access to the same magic and the same ability to travel into other *riocht* as the other *Scath* creatures do."

"No wonder they want it," Peyton muttered.

"Badly," Nelda agreed. "Planning for this particular shot at the ritual has been in the works since before I was born. Since before my mother was born. The creatures involved in the *Ascension* have been plotting and re-plotting strategies for generations, just waiting for the right combination of events. Tristan and I were placed in *Talam* years before Shifty's birth. The ley lines here in Duncan Mills are strong. So strong, in fact, that we never settled too far from here while we waited for signs that *Talam's siofra* twin would be born. We were to watch over the family and the *siofra*, provide needed potions and spells, and keep the illusion strong until the time of the *Ascension* when she would be returned. But, Shifty, we were never on their side. We've always been working against them, our goal has been to keep you safe, and stop this. They thought they needed a *hairn* strong in potions placed with the *Talam siofra* this time to help ensure her successful maturation. There have been failed exchanges. Both before and after your births. I know of three for sure."

Evangeline shuddered. Had the baby she'd seen been one of these failed exchanges?

"And we crashed their party. Oh, man! They must be *piiiiiiissed*." Peyton drew the last word out until it had at least five syllables.

"Murderously so. And we have to continue to fend them off until the moon finishes this cycle."

"So...that's bad news," Peyton said, louder this time, but just as irreverently.

"Thanks, Peyton, for the stunningly obvious."

"Shut it, Pax."

"So, we didn't stop the ritual just by breaking it up tonight?" Paxton asked, ignoring his sister.

"No." Nelda sighed. "We didn't. The ritual can be done any time in the last two weeks of the moon's cycle, during the first month of the twins' twentieth year. After that, it's lost. Tonight is the first night. There are thirteen more."

"And we can't keep them locked out?"

"I'm afraid not."

"So, it's us against about a trillion pissed off banshee and *hairn*?"

"Peyton. Please!" Tristan finally snapped. "We are all well aware of the...unique way you deal with stress, but maybe put a cork in it?"

"Sorry."

"It isn't just us," Nelda said, as if there hadn't been an interruption. "There's an underground. A rebellion. We do have assistance in the fight. It is how I got Linus, Igby, and Tresara informed and out of *Scath* to join us."

"I don't get it," Linus said. "Why would the banshee and *hairn* agree to help with this ritual? The wraiths are brutal now, and their magic is the strongest in the *riocht*. With more power, they could take over entirely."

Evangeline smiled. Linus, his level head showing through above all else, had been the one to ask.

"They were offered power and wraith magic," Nelda explained.

"Holy sh—" Peyton started, but a single raised eyebrow from her father seemed to halt her.

"They are the minority," Nelda explained. "But they are also the most powerfully positioned banshee and *sheehairn* families. And they were working under a veil. It was not well-known what was happening. If we can keep the girls safe until the close of the cycle, then we can return to *Scath*. If they fail, the families involved might simply give up and turn their back on the wraiths, and keep their current elevated status. It would be like the whole thing never happened. If we wanted to bring them to justice, we would have to expose and dethrone them. Of course, neither option stops them from trying again. But in the generations it would take for all the components to line up again, the hope is that we would also learn better ways to combat it. Hopefully the rebels will always prevail."

"If we live that long," Peyton said. "What?! You were all thinking it."

No one disagreed with her.

CHAPTER

THIRTY-FIVE

Shifty was exhausted by the time she clicked her seatbelt in place and pulled her car into traffic for the short drive to her apartment. She had Evangeline in her passenger seat. Paxton had taken Linus in his truck. Peyton had the other two girls in her car. It had seemed best that they all spend the night at the apartment—none of the creatures from *Scath* knew where Shifty now lived.

Going to her apartment had also shelved the much less pressing worry that Shifty's parents would see and wonder about her car in the driveway next door all night. Or that they would just decide to stop by for a chat. She worried for her parents' safety, though Nelda assured her again and again that it was okay to leave for the night, that she and Tristan would make sure no harm came to them.

The Devlin family had fooled her. Had fooled her even after they'd confessed to the first deception. They'd kept the knowledge of the *Ascension* from her. And she had certainly believed they were prepared to hand her over for the ritual, believed Paxton could easily turn off his love for her. That none of Paxton's deceit had been true hardly mattered at the moment. The betrayal felt real and raw. She wondered if her parents could be just as adept at deception as her best friend, her boyfriend, and their parents.

If they had retained any knowledge known about the exchange, surely that was all they knew. They couldn't have known Evangeline's life was forfeit, could they? No parent on earth could do that. Not even the *Scath* creatures were asked to make this kind of sacrifice; it wasn't a *hairn* being bled dry and used as a spell component. That was only asked of the humans.

Her thoughts shifted to *Scath* itself. Her body had never felt like it belonged to her so much as it had in the short time she'd spent there. But a large part of Shifty still identified as human. It made her feel guilty that more than a small part of her wanted nothing more than to return immediately. She wanted to see what the trees looked like in the daytime. What did the air smell like after it rained. Did it rain? She wanted to stretch the limits of her body. She'd felt just a little of what she could be capable of there, and it was intoxicating. She wondered what being with Pax would be like there, grinning to herself a little and hearing Dr. Miller's clinical voice in her head.

Shifty stifled a yawn. She was clearly becoming giddy with exhaustion, she told herself. She needed to rest, needed to clear her head and think. Needed to be alone, yet she never wanted to be alone again. She needed to be comforted by her friends, the same friends she wanted to lash out at for having betrayed her. She was burning with curiosity about Evangeline, despite the twin-like kinship she felt for her. She was jealous of her because this was her parents' real child, a human, meant to have lived Shifty's life.

Evangeline watched the world flit by outside the window of the car. She knew about cars, she'd told Shifty a little defensively. She'd read about them. Shifty racked her brain for something to say.

"It's not far." *Well, that was lame.*

"Okay. You have room for everyone?"

"We'll make do."

The car went silent again and Shifty let it stay that way. If Evangeline's mind was half as crowded as her own, casting around blindly for small talk would only frustrate them both.

The living room light was on when they got to the apartment, and once through the front door, Shifty and Evangeline found they were the last to arrive. Voices drifted out from the kitchen.

"We made it!" Shifty called, throwing her keys onto the small table by the front door and shrugging out of her jacket. "Make yourself comfortable. Let's go grab a beer with the rest of them. You know about beer?"

Evangeline smiled. "I know about beer. I've never had it. We have ales and mead in *Scath*, though."

"Oh, I know," Shifty said, thinking of Nelda's pink sparkling concoction.

Linus, Tresara, and Igby each sat perched on a bar stool at the kitchen counter. Paxton had his head in the refrigerator and Peyton was planted on the counter, lazily kicking Paxton on the back of his leg. They all looked so normal and comfortable. Shifty felt like she was holding her entire body together by force of will, and they were all sitting around acting as if they were having a poker night.

Paxton glanced at them around the door of the fridge, stuck his head back in, and reappeared with two bottles. He turned on Peyton. "Will you cut that out? Are you ten?" She stuck her tongue out at him, but she stilled her foot. Paxton twisted the tops of the beers and handed one to each of the girls.

"Thanks," Evangeline said, and she took an experimental sip. She grimaced slightly, but took a longer draw anyway. "It's not terrible."

"Everyone have sleeping assignments?" Shifty said, taking a long drink and avoiding Paxton's expectant stare.

Peyton launched herself to the ground. "Yep. I'll put all

three girls in my room, one in the bed, two on the floor, Linus will take the couch, you and Paxton can—"

"Evangeline can sleep in our room with me. Paxton, you can take the floor in the living room, right?"

"Uh, sure, I guess." Paxton sounded more dejected than angry.

"I think Evangeline and I would like some time to talk alone,." Shifty added. She wanted him to feel miserable, but she also had a need to make sure he wasn't wounded. She didn't know if he deserved that kindness, but it was still her instinct.

They said good night and Shifty led Evangeline to the bedroom she shared with Paxton. She closed the door behind them and realized that Evangeline had only the clothes on her back.

"You'll need something to sleep in. I think I have a spare toothbrush in the bathroom. There's a good facial wash by the sink. I hope you don't mind sharing the bed, do you need—Shifty, I'll be fine. We'll figure that out. Let's talk for a while." Evangeline indicated the bed with a simple inclination of her head.

"Oh. Right. Okay," Shifty said.

They sat down, both crossed-legged, and faced each other. Evangeline gripped her beer with both hands. Shifty placed her bottle on the nightstand. She propped her chin on her intertwined fingers and let some of the tension lift from her body. She willed it out. Pulling in strength on her inhale, letting out fear with her exhalation.

"So, you always knew you were human?"

Evangeline nodded. "Oh, yes. A glamour might have made me appear *hairn*, but I would never have moved like them or had their magic. I always believed I'd been abandoned on the ley line, deserted and near death, when my parents found me and decided to take me in."

"Were they good to you?" Shifty realized it might be an incredibly insensitive question, right after the words left her mouth. One of Evangeline's parents had just tried to kill her. But she was helpless to draw the words back, and just as helpless to stop her curiosity.

"They were. They did all they could for me. They gave me the best of everything *Scath* had to offer. I was given access to a lot of the *riocht's* historical information. My father told me if I couldn't be a *hairn*, I could at least understand them, know our culture and our ways. I thought they loved me." She paused and gave her beer a weak smile. "Are your parents kind?"

"They're great. I didn't always tell them what was happening with me, but I wasn't exactly easy to live with when I was a teenager. They always supported me. Never made me feel broken or like I was a disappointment."

"Do they like Paxton?"

"Yes. They approve of him." Shifty added *more than I do right now, anyway*. But only in her head.

"He really loves you," Evangeline said.

Shifty looked up from her fingernails. "How do you know?"

"The way he looks at you. I've seen that look in someone else's eyes." Evangeline's own gaze became focused on a spot over Shifty's head.

"I'm guessing that someone else isn't Linus?"

"No. It isn't Linus."

"Evangeline, I am sure Nelda and Tristan can get more people out. If you think this someone is in danger, you should tell them tomorrow. They could bring him over when the ley lines clear. If he matters to you. If he looks at you that way, he'll want to support you."

"I don't think so." Evangeline's voice cracked and she cleared her throat. She did look at Shifty again, though. That expression broke Shifty's heart. It was the haunted look of a ghost from a gothic romance.

"Did you have a fight?"

"Something like that."

"Look, Evangeline, I may be totally out of bounds here. I don't mean to talk out of school, but from what I've been told, *Scath* creatures are different about emotions than humans. But even so, surely if this guy loves you, he isn't going to want you dead. It's my understanding that *Scath* creatures, even the wraiths, aren't inherently evil."

"You've been told correctly. I don't know if he was always aware of what would happen to me, or if he just picked duty over me when he was told to do it, but I know I was wrong. He doesn't lo—feel the same way about me."

"You can't know until you talk to him," Shifty insisted. "Let Nelda get a message to him at least. Let him know where you are, that you're safe, that there's hope."

"He knows where I am by now."

"How could he?"

"Because he was at the altar when we ran, Shifty. He was waiting to be bound to you."

CHAPTER

THIRTY-SIX

When the sun came up the next morning, everyone at the apartment was at least rested, if not necessarily ready to take on whatever the next days would bring. They loaded into cars and headed out to the Devlin house.

Nelda and Tristan had much more information. And a plan. Evangeline couldn't believe how calm they seemed. Their children were in danger, they risked expulsion from their home... And yet, they gathered everyone in the kitchen and handed out warm beverages—a *Scath riocht* herb concoction to her and her friends, and coffee to Shifty and their own children—like it was any normal day.

"Are we gonna get our debriefing now?" Paxton asked, loping into the kitchen and taking a mug from his mother. He took a seat next to Shifty at the large island in the center of the bright, sunny kitchen. Shifty smacked him in the chest.

"Oh, you're so cool! Are we joining the CIA?"

He winked at her. Evangeline blinked hard. The comfortable affection between them made her heart hurt.

"Are the ley lines down?" Linus asked. He'd been practically jumping out of his skin since they'd awoken this morning.

"No," Nelda answered. "But for the moment, we don't think that's going to be an issue."

"They decided to just let us go? Great! I hope you realize

I'm still not going to my classes today," Peyton cracked.

"No, daughter." Nelda raised an eyebrow and her lip twitched at the left corner. "But we have information about the group trying to perform the *Ascension*."

"Can we give them a cool name?" Paxton asked.

"You have something in mind?" His mother's voice held reluctant indulgence, as if this was quicker than arguing and losing.

Evangeline wanted to be irritated that she wasn't getting to the point quickly, knew she should be afraid for herself and her friends. But she was comfortable here. And it wasn't only that these people were being kind to her, sheltering her from danger. She was fascinated by her surroundings. Her curiosity was taking over, soaking in every moment of this adventure.

"'Right Dirty Bastards' has a ring to it."

"Okay, then. Moving on," Nelda said, but her lip twitched again and there was a hint of a laugh in her tone.

"*Sleacht*." Tristan said. "Just call them that."

"What's it mean?" Shifty asked.

Tristan shook his head, eyes watching the coffee in his mug. "Doesn't matter, it's what they do. It's as good a term as any."

Linus shifted a little in his seat and he became very interested in a loose thread on the cushion of his stool, which was on the side that would ensure he couldn't make eye contact with Evangeline.

Nelda nodded. "Fine. Everyone happy?" She didn't wait for confirmation, though, and carried on speaking. "Here's the thing, the *Sleacht* have been working with the knowledge—and practically the express permission—of the elders of our region in *Scath*. That's a lot of power to have behind them. Many of them are on the Elder Council. But, what they do *not* have is the approval from the *Scath* Council to perform the *Ascension*. The *Scath* Council has the final say, and they do not approve."

"They know?" Shifty asked.

Evangeline saw her reach for Paxton's hand under the counter. Apparently they were on the road to recovery.

"They have been informed, yes."

"That's terrific!" Igby said, her voice cracking on the upbeat. "Oh, Lenny! We can go home soon. "

"Well, it's not that simple, unfortunately. They've been informed, but they aren't willing to believe us just on our word. They require proof."

"Fabulous," Peyton muttered. She slammed a palm on the counter, crossed her arms, and stared out the window, looking mutinous.

Evangeline couldn't blame her. In fact, she felt very much the same. She'd been raised like a lamb for slaughter so they could hand power to the wraiths. Evangeline wished a little bit of faith wasn't too much to ask from the *Scath* Council.

"It's a delicate situation, Peyton. We can't blame them." She shot her daughter a warning look. "The Elder Council and the *Scath* Council work together, so they can't really be expected to act based only on the word of a rebel force they didn't even know existed until this morning."

Another stern look, another jaw snap from Peyton, then Nelda continued. "The good news is that they are taking the situation seriously and have communicated with our Elder Council, as well as the others in the *riocht*. This has forced the *Sleacht* to stop working as out in the open as they have been. Additionally, the *Scath* Council has placed members of the Guard along the ley line that runs through our wood. Getting into *Talam*, at least our part of it, will not be so easy. The next closest entry point is several hours' journey from here. I'm not saying it's impossible, but they can't do it with an army."

Shifty sagged in relief and she leaned on Paxton's shoulder. Evangeline felt as if a very heavy monkey had jumped off her back. She sat a little straighter.

"My mother isn't so easily controlled. We can't drop our guard," Tresara warned.

"No one will drop their guards, Tresara. We will all be on alert. I understand the wraiths, I've been privy to much of their planning, and I know what they're capable of. I don't intend to let them succeed. Evangeline's safety is my highest priority."

"What proof do they want, Mom?" Paxton asked.

"They haven't been specific. Anything we can present to them that would confirm the plan and at least a couple of the participants. *Scath Fios* with the spells and planning. First hand accounts from someone involved with the planning—"

"My mom," Evangeline said. Everyone in the room looked at her and then back to Nelda, collective breath held.

Nelda's face took on the look of a mother who knew what she was about to say was going to hurt, but if she pretended it wasn't, maybe she could absorb some of the pain. "I'm sorry, Evangeline. She won't."

"What do you mean she won't?" Linus spat. "She was the one who got Shifty to shatter the *cheangal*. She stopped the whole ritual. Of course she'll tell them what's happening."

"She won't, Linus. I'm sorry. She won't speak against her *ceile*. She didn't want to see you hurt, Evangeline, she loves you, but she isn't willing to go any further. Tresara, your mother is involved, but as a wraith and a key member of the *Sleacht*, she's not going to take this laying down. Your father was kept in the dark for some reason."

Tresara's smile was faint, but proud. Her eyes shone a little. "Well, yes, he would be. My father thinks my mother hangs the moon. But he also loves me and is extremely fond of Evangeline. They wouldn't have risked telling him about anything that would have hurt her. He's also one of the most law-abiding men I have ever met."

"Do you think he would help us?" Tristan asked, leaning forward on his elbows.

Tresara didn't speak immediately. Evangeline knew she was turning the question over in her mind. Just when Evangeline was sure one of the Devlins would scream from anticipation, Tresara nodded her head. "I think so. If he can. Yes. And I think I know what he can do."

"Your mother's book," Evangeline said. Again with that damnable book. Hadn't they risked their skins enough for it already?

"My mother's *Scath Fios*. That's the one you want. It contains the *cheangal* spell, a sketch of the altar, and the *Siofra* symbol. I don't know what else, but I would bet a whole host of the kind of stuff you need to prove to the *Scath* Council what's been going on."

"And you know where this book might be?"

"Sure. It's in her office. Or it was when I stole it and then replaced it. Third shelf, four books from the left."

"That's really precise," Paxton said.

"My mother is a very precise wraith."

Nelda rinsed her mug and set it down on a towel at the side of the basin. She placed both her hands on the counter and lowered her head. When she finally turned back around to look at them her face was carefully composed. "We'll get someone to speak with your father, Tresara. If he retrieves the book for us, that would be best: he can go into her office without arousing her suspicions. But if he won't—or can't— help, we will have to have someone else retrieve it. Thank you for trusting us with this information. For trusting us with your lives. I will do my best not to let you down."

"So what do we do in the meantime, Mom? Are we to stay cooped up in the house feeling helpless and scared? There has got to be something we can *do*," Peyton said.

Nelda sighed. "I don't want you going too far from the house. The backyard is okay if you're no further than the picnic bench. Don't go near the woods. And stay alert. As for helping, right now the best thing you can do is help our guests with their glamours. Sorry, kids. I know you did your best, but—"

Linus held up a hand, indicating he realized their glamours were sub-par and nothing Nelda had said offended him. "I would appreciate the help. It looks like we might be here a little while, best to fade into the background as much as possible."

"There's nothing we can do to help, really? And not just things you think we can do because they aren't dangerous, Mom," Peyton peered down her nose at her mother.

Nelda placed a hand on her child's cheek. "My girl, no. Help your friends. Teach them about this *riocht*. Help them hide. That's what I need you to do right now. Look out for each other. As soon as we're able to reach Tresara's father or we have more information, I promise I'll let you know what you can do to help. Even if it's more dangerous than I would like."

CHAPTER

THIRTY-SEVEN

The tree line behind their houses had never appeared more ominous. Shifty squinted at the redwoods, imagining she could see *Scath's* mist drifting over the bumps and mounds that made up the beginnings of their roots.

"You're really angry with me." Paxton was behind her, hugging her shoulders and talking into her hair. "That's why you stayed in the house and snuck out here away from the rest of them. And me."

"I really am, Paxton. You let them hand me over to someone else. You didn't trust me with the truth. You let me feel that. After all the other things you've let me believe, let me feel about myself, I just can't believe you could do that to me."

"My parents—"

She broke away and turned to face him. She wanted to slap him. And hug him. Her emotions rolled and crashed in her stomach.

His eyes searched hers, begging for her understanding.

"Paxton, I know why you did it. I know they made you promise. But you made a promise to me, too. You swore you'd never make me question my sanity again. And that's what it felt like. Exactly the same, like I wasn't sane. Like I didn't understand reality."

"I know," he said, his voice breaking. Paxton pushed his hands into his hair and gripped the strands between his fingers so tightly his knuckles went white. He made an animal-like cry in his throat, a warbled sob of an injured pup. "God, Shifty! I know what I did. I know it hurt you. Worse, I knew it would hurt you when I agreed to do it. But they were going to kill that girl." He thrust a finger across the yard to where Evangeline sat on one of the lawn chairs with her knees pulled up to her chest and one cheek resting on a knee. She was near her friends, but not involved with their conversation. "*Kill* her. Saving her. Stopping the ritual? That seemed worth hurting you for."

That brought Shifty up short. She blinked hard. She swallowed harder, pushing her anger down to the second or third step on the ladder of her feelings where it properly belonged. "It is. Of course it is. You're right. You're parents are right. I'm sorry, Paxton. I'm the most selfish being on Earth."

Paxton ran a hand through her hair now. "You're not. I understand. And I am sorry, Shifty. I am. It killed me to have to do that to you again." He cupped her cheek. Shifty placed her own hand over his.

"Okay…okay, Pax. It's okay."

He placed his forehead against hers and gazed into her eyes. "I would do anything to keep you safe. Anything at all," he whispered.

"We're going to be fine. They'll get the book, take it to this *Scath* Council, and the danger will be gone. Then all we will have to do is figure out if my parents were a part of this, what's going to happen to Evangeline, all the things like that. You know, easy stuff."

He let out a chuckle. "Right. Piece of cake."

They stood like that for another moment before they heard Peyton approach. Without breaking their stare, Shifty reached a hand out to Peyton, who took it and squeezed, hard.

"I'm sorry, too, Shifty." She said, her normal flippant, almost prickly tone gone and replaced with a quiet earnestness.

Now Shifty did tilt her head so she could look at her friend. "Nope. No need. We are all fine."

Peyton exhaled loudly. "Glad that's settled. Now, what do you guys think of the new kids?" And just like that Peyton was back, a wise whip letting out its crack.

"Haven't really had the time to think about it," Paxton said. "I guess they're fine. You trust them, Peyton?"

She looked at them over her shoulder. When she turned back to Paxton and Shifty, she was smiling. "I do. I think they look out for her. Coming here? That was a classy move. They didn't have to do that. But they wanted to make sure she wasn't here alone and scared. I know a couple of other people who would do that for each other. We should go up there. Do as Mom asked and help them work on their glamours. Tell them all the extra special secret *Talam* stuff."

Paxton nodded. Picking up their joined fists and pointing them toward the top of the incline where the others were, he asked Shifty, "Shall we?"

She pulled her hand free. "You go ahead. I'll be there in a minute. Just need to clear out my loud brain so I can be helpful."

Peyton and Paxton started toward the others. Shifty walked in the opposite direction, closer to the tree line. The air was clean and clear, just a little crisp, with a slight wind that cut straight through the light sweater she had on. She pulled it tighter around herself and crossed her arms over her chest. She walked to the first row of redwoods, running a hand along the rough, splintering surface of them.

While she did, she remembered some of the exercises Dr. Miller had taught her for dealing with her emotions. Ways of maintaining her control, not letting her feelings own her.

She inhaled slowly through her nose, exhaled through her mouth, and visualized her anger and hurt as dark puffs streaming out of her along with her breath. She placed her back against the tree, tilted her head to the sky and saw, in her mind's eye, her confusion unraveling. It felt good, letting it go. She felt lighter. Like she could focus on helping Evangeline and could be strong for whatever came next.

She took a step away from the tree, ready to go and join the rest. Her vision went dark with pressure across her eyes and her feet were lifted an inch or two off the ground. She was secured firmly against someone taller and stronger. Her vision cleared, but the hand only moved from her eyes to her mouth. She jerked her head from side to side, trying to shake herself free.

A harsh whisper sounded in her ear, hot breath coated her skin. "Don't fight me and I will have no reason to hurt your friends. Nod your head if you understand."

With panic rising in her throat she tried to speak and found she was unable, but she managed to nod.

"Very good. Now, just relax, this won't hurt."

He was walking backward, holding her against his chest in a death grip that kept her immobilized, her feet hovering just an inch over the ground. He moved quickly. As she watched the trees grew thicker in front of her until the Devlins' backyard melted away. A blurry view of the woods swallowed up her friends in the distance.

Just like Paxton, she would do anything to keep them safe, she reminded herself as her fear and doubt rose. She didn't fight her captor. They hadn't traveled far when she heard the shouts. Her friends had noticed she was gone. She believed her captor when he said he wouldn't hurt *her*, but she didn't hold a lot of faith that his promise extended to the people she cared about.

He moved quickly along the woodland floor, especially for someone toting such an awkward burden. When he stopped, it was just as sudden. Her feet touched the ground again, but she was no less a captive than before. Under the grip of his hand, Shifty grunted and growled, hoping to elicit some kind of response.

"I told you I wouldn't hurt you. I'm afraid that was a bit premature. But this won't be too painful."

Shifty didn't even have time to question. A sharp, white explosion of pain at the back of her head, and the world went dark.

CHAPTER

THIRTY-EIGHT

"Everyone just *calm down*!" Nelda yelled over the cacophony of voices.

Evangeline watched as the others stammered to a halt, the words filtering out as if a leaky faucet had finally run dry.

Nelda took a deep breath. When she finally looked up again, her eyes were bright and alert. "Thank you. Now. Tell me what happened."

"They got Shifty," Paxton said. "Pulled her into the woods and disappeared. Crossed the ley line. I thought they were guarded, Mom!"

"They are. But the *Scath* Council only half believes us about the *Ascension*. They are giving us some support, but that doesn't mean someone couldn't slip past with some quick talking. It would have to be someone powerful and well-connected."

"What does it matter who it was?" Paxton shouted. "We have to go after her. Now!"

"We're not going after her. We have to let them keep her. She's essential to the *Ascension*. They won't hurt her."

"Unless the time window closes and they can't use her to gain their power. Then they won't need her anymore."

"That's not going to happen. We will get her. But we have to leave her where she is. I'm sorry." She turned on her heel and walked out of the room.

Evangeline sat in stunned silence and watched them all exchange outraged, impotent glares. Peyton's lower lip quivered and jumped. She seemed halfway between bursting into tears and launching into a tirade against her mother, but as if she couldn't get her mind to engage either one.

Paxton stormed around the kitchen, randomly picking up items and slamming them back where he'd found them. It seemed to do nothing for his mood, and Evangeline wondered how long it would be before he broke something. Her own thoughts were strangely detached, and she supposed she must be going into shock. If you knew you were going into shock could you stop it? Were you actually going into shock if you thought you were going into shock?

"Okay, fuck this!" Paxton threw open the door to the backyard. "If no one's going to do anything about this, I'm going after her myself!" He was out the door before anyone could stop him. After a beat or two, Peyton ran after him.

Alone in the kitchen, Igby, Linus, and Tresara turned toward Evangeline. Their faces clearly telegraphed that they thought she'd know what to do. She was human. This was *Talam*, so some kind of switch must have been flipped in her when they got here. Helplessly she raised her shoulders. "I don't know. But I guess we should go after him, too? I mean we can't let him go into *Scath* on his own, right?"

"You're not going back at all," Igby told her, like she was scolding a small child.

Evangeline huffed. "Did I say I was going? No. I said we should go after him."

Linus, irritated with the lack of action, threw open the door and frantically gestured them through it. "Quit standing there discussing it. Move!"

Igby flinched as if he'd slapped her, but she scooted through the door, Tresara and Evangeline followed, and Linus closed the door quietly behind them.

Peyton and Paxton were standing at the line of trees, arguing. Their voices didn't travel all the way to Evangeline's ears, probably trying not to alert their mother, but they both motioned wildly, limbs slicing through the air. Peyton grabbed her brother's upper arm and began to try and pull him away from the trees. Paxton dug his heels into the damp, soft earth and glared at her. Evangeline moved faster, not sure what she would say to him when she got there, but feeling compelled to try. Linus was right beside her, and the girls were right behind them.

"Pax! You can't just go over the ley line alone, storm up to the house, and demand they hand her over! What are you thinking?" Peyton's voice was soft but not calm, and it held a pleading that broke a piece of Evangeline's heart.

"I'm thinking she's in danger, and I'm *thinking* I can't let her get hurt."

"They'll eat you alive, Paxton. You're only you. She's got value to them, they won't hurt her. She might not be comfortable, and she'll be scared, but they aren't going to harm her. You, on the other hand, they won't have a problem killing." The air became thicker and time slowed. Peyton narrowed her eyes at her brother. "You're the son of their enemies, and you just defied them. They'll crush you. You can't do this. We'll get her back. We just need time to figure out what to do. Please, Paxton. Go. Back. Inside."

Evangeline was sure he was going to bolt into the woods. The clouds overhead darkened. Evangeline thought she heard distant thunder. Finally, he turned on his heel and stalked back to the house. He stormed up the porch stairs and slammed the door behind him.

Peyton let out a long, ragged breath. "I didn't think I could stop him. I feel kind of shitty that I did," she admitted.

"They won't hurt her, Peyton," Linus said. "You told him the truth. He was being rash."

Peyton's eyes flashed with anger. "I know that, Linus." Her words were clipped.

Evangeline looked at Linus, it was clear he had no idea what he'd done to set Peyton off. In his *hairn* mind he was speaking cool logic. Evangeline smiled to herself, hiding it from the others as best she could. So many times in *Scath* she had stood in Linus's shoes: there was a difference between knowing a culture behaved a certain way, and running up against it when it mattered. She placed a hand on his shoulder and grinned even wider when he looked at it blankly.

"You're a weird one, Linus Rafferty."

"What are you talking about?"

"You left your home with virtual strangers, on the word of a woman who might have been lying to you, in order to help out a friend. But you don't hear the sarcasm in Peyton's voice?"

"Why would she be sarcastic? I was just offering assistance. Telling the truth. Surely it would offer some comfort?"

Evangeline shook her head. "Surely," she said.

"Is Paxton going to be okay?" Igby asked.

Peyton nodded. "He's going to be a pain in the ass, but he'll survive. I hope they make a plan quickly and give him a task to keep him occupied. And we need to get her back. She's been through enough." Peyton made eye contact with Evangeline. "You both have."

"What are you going to tell Shifty's parents if we don't have her back before they notice she's missing? I assume they talk to her often?"

"Aw, crap!" Peyton said.

"Maybe it is time to tell them the truth?" Evangeline's voice felt weak. She wondered if it was transparent: her other reason for wanting this.

"They'll have to do something about Mr. and Mrs. Gilbert. Even with her out of the house, they are pretty hands-on. If my mom is right and they aren't involved in this, they'll get frantic quick if Shifty's missing…"

Peyton's voice trailed off and her eyes went behind a cloud. Suddenly, she snapped her fingers.

"I've got an idea. Gotta talk to my mom." She was halfway to the house when she turned back around. "You guys coming, or what?"

CHAPTER

THIRTY-NINE

When she regained consciousness, Shifty could tell by the smells alone that she was back in *Scath*. The next thing she encountered was the headache. It was worse at the back of her skull near her neck, where she'd been clubbed, but the pain spidered out and had pretty well consumed her entire head. Opening her eyes, she found she'd been left in a small but well-furnished bedroom with no windows. She lay propped up on mountain of feather pillows on the bed, a quilt draped over the foot of the sleigh frame. There were two chairs at a square tea table in one corner of the room, and a book shelf against a wall contained what appeared to be leather-bound journals.

She pushed herself up until her back was flush against the headboard. She touched the back of her skull gingerly, and pain flared.

"Son of a bitch," she murmured. Her panic was muted, but still knocked like an arrow at the back of her mind. She might have been foolhardy. Even after the blackjack to the cranium, she believed the voice that told her she wouldn't be harmed any further. If she could clear her head, she might be able to figure out her best play.

She scanned the room again. Only one door. She didn't want to waste her energy and get up, only to find it locked.

And even if it wasn't, what was she going to do? Saunter out the door and make her way to a ley line that she had no idea where to find or how to operate? Nope.

She wasn't restrained and she wasn't in a barren room or cell. She had her wits about her, which told her she had not been placed under a *cheangal*. It didn't seem as if they planned to restrain her or otherwise make her uncomfortable. She doubted they would be giving her a say in what happened to her next, either, but she was getting sort of used to that by now.

She was pondering how best to make enough noise to let them know she was awake when the door swung inward and a face peered around it. Blue, a banshee, and female.

The banshee came in, carrying a tray with a glass of liquid, a bowl, and a towel. Without a word she set the tray on a tea table, moved the entire thing closer to the bed, and perched on the edge of the mattress, close to Shifty's leg. Shifty suppressed the urge to pull away. She didn't want to show outward dislike. Not yet.

"Are you the one who brought me here? I thought it was a man. It sounded like a man."

The woman picked up the towel and dipped a corner of it in the bowl. An orange color began to spread through the cloth. The woman shook it lightly, letting the excess liquid fall back into the bowl. She ran her thumb and forefinger along it, further squeezing it out. She patted the bed right next to her, expecting Shifty to move closer to her on the bed.

"I was there, but not alone. Please. Come close, and I'll tend the wound on your head. My companion got a little over-zealous. I apologize."

Shifty moved to the spot next to the woman. Her head was killing her.

"Turn around," the woman instructed.

Shifty turned so that her back was to the woman. She braced for the pain when the towel made contact with the bump on her head, but when it happened the sensation was a brief, sharp burst of cold, followed by a spreading warmth, and finally the dull ache drained away until it was just a pinpoint at the spot where the fabric was pressed to her skin.

Involuntarily, Shifty sighed with pleasure. She hadn't realized exactly how much it hurt until the pain faded.

The woman chuckled softly. "That's better, then," she said and removed the compress. Shifty turned around so she could see what the woman was doing. The banshee might have helped her, but that didn't mean Shifty trusted her. The woman picked up the glass and held it out to Shifty. "You should have some water."

"Well, that's very nice of you and all, but my mother taught me not to take food or drink from people who knock me over the head and pull me across a magical line into another dimension. So, I think I'll pass, thanks."

The woman's face barely changed, a slight lift at the corners of her mouth, maybe. She held Shifty's gaze, lifted the water glass to her own mouth and took a large sip. Once she had swallowed the liquid, she held the glass out to Shifty again. "It's only water. You'll get dehydrated."

Reluctantly, Shifty took the glass. She had to admit she was thirsty, and the water felt wonderful going down her throat. She took another sip. "Where am I?"

"You're in my home."

"I don't think we've been formally introduced."

"My name is Katarin MacNair. You are meant to be *ceile* to my son, Lachlan." Her face was carefully composed. Shifty wondered who else was listening to them.

"So, arranged marriages and trafficking. You guys haven't quite made it into the twenty-first century, have you?"

"I'm sure we seem," she paused, searching for the proper word, "*different* to you. But this is your home, and you'll adjust to our ways. I think you'll be very happy here."

"Yeah, I'm sure I'll love it once you hand all the power to the wraiths and they imprison us all in their megalomaniacal attempt to take over all the *riocht*. I'd rather you piss off, if it's all the same to you."

"Well, you are up to speed, aren't you?" Katarin's mouth twitched again. Shifty couldn't tell if the woman was amused or irritated with her. Or possibly both; it sure looked like a face her own mother gave her often.

"Sort of, yeah. So, what's your play here? I don't know how to do any magic. I've got no control over my *rian*. And I'm not real keen to help out your husband and his ilk. Add that to the fact you've lost your sacrificial lamb and you've kind of gotten yourself into a pickle here, huh?"

"For the present, but we're working on that."

"What. Am. I. Doing. Here?" Shifty clipped each word in her best disenfranchised youth drawl. "Isn't the *Scath* Council going to give a little more merit to the charges against you if they find out I'm here?" She wasn't sure if this was the best strategy, revealing most of what she knew, but Nelda's instructions hadn't been comprehensive, and she was depending on her wits now that she was alone. She could only hope that if Katarin assumed she was already well-informed, she would be careless with her breadcrumbs.

"Your parents called you home. What's strange about that? Wouldn't any parent do the same if they discovered their long lost child was alive and well? They have the right to bring you home." Katarin's face was so blank as she spoke that Shifty found herself in a kind of awe. She could almost believe this woman believed what she was saying.

"That's very impressive. And how are you going to keep me from disputing this set of erroneous facts?"

"I doubt very much you will be invited to speak to the

Scath Council. But in the event they do wish to interview you, I would think the safety of those you care about in *Talam* would keep you from telling everything you know."

"The ley lines are being watched. You might have found a loophole to force me back here, but you wouldn't be able to use that against the Devlins or my parents." Shifty hoped she sounded more certain than she felt.

"Sure. You're right. For now. But once the moon's phase changes, they will relax their guard. Then, if you don't cooperate, we can exact our vengeance at our leisure."

"Well, that's cold-hearted and unsettling."

"It will get us what we want: your cooperation. Are we in agreement?"

"I don't have much of a choice. I'm a terrible liar, though."

"You should probably work on that. Try to improve." Katarin stood and took a couple steps toward the door. She looked back over her shoulder. "I'll send someone up with some food soon. You must be starving."

"You could just send me home for my supper."

"Well, Siofra, your parents are not quite ready for your return home. Hopefully you will be able to join them for dinner soon."

"That's not the home I meant." Shifty knew she sounded as grumpy as she felt, this time. Katarin's deliberate misunderstanding pissed her off, and she resented showing the woman she'd won even this little victory.

Alone again and with her head no longer throbbing, Shifty hopped out of bed and walked the perimeter of the room, confirming what her eyes had suspected—there was no other door hiding in the woodwork, no boarded-over window. She rattled the doorknob, just for good measure, but it didn't budge.

"Well this is just lovely." She slammed her palm flat against the wall. It made a satisfying smack, but left her no better off than she had been before. She picked up one of the pillows from the bed and buried her face into it. Fabric and padding absorbed a yell of frustration and anxiety. The first one felt so good she tried a second, which bled into a third. She was warming up for a fourth holler when the door opened again.

Shifty jumped at the noise and threw the pillow back on the bed. She backed away from the door, and felt her back come up against the corner of the room. It was somewhat comforting, the solidity of it, until the phrase "backed into a corner" began running through her head. Before she could decide to move elsewhere, the banshee bringing her dinner tray was already inside, and the door was shut behind him. He turned and she looked into the face of Lachlan MacNair. She suppressed a shudder.

"I brought you something to eat." He lifted the tray a couple of inches higher when he spoke, as if she might have missed it.

She didn't say anything.

"I'll just put it here, okay?" He placed it on the same table Katarin had used, and looked up at her for her answer, like he thought she might actually give him one. "She sent up enough for both of us. Thought you might like some company."

As he spoke, he picked up the table and brought it back to the place between the chairs. He pulled out one chair and then the other. "Please. Sit. You must be starving. Mother's a good cook."

Shifty didn't move. He shrugged his shoulders and picked a chair. While he uncovered small dishes and served up portions on both plates, his eyes kept darting up at her. They were not unkind eyes. The food smelled wonderful. Shifty took a step closer to the table.

He smiled. "It's just dinner. I won't hurt you."

Shifty gave in and sat in the chair opposite him. The food

on the plate in front of her did look divine. She picked up her fork and speared what appeared to be a green bean. Did they grow the same crops here? She studied it on the end of her fork, tilted it one way and then the other. She didn't think there was anything wrong with the food, though she wasn't sure how she would tell. He'd obviously been instructed to eat from the same shared serving dishes to put her at ease. That wasn't what was bothering her.

"You hurt her," she said. "Evangeline."

She popped the green bean in her mouth, chewed slowly and did not break eye contract with him.

"You hurt her," she continued after swallowing. "She believed that you loved her. And you turned your back on her. You don't mind if they kill her. Is it because she's human?"

Locke coughed, as if his food had gotten caught halfway down. "What are you talking about? No one was going to kill Evangeline!"

CHAPTER

FORTY

When the front door finally opened, Evangeline found it much harder to take a breath. She was sitting between Igby and Tresara on the couch, but she didn't look at either of them. She stared into the fire grate, trying to lose herself in the jumping flames. Did they know? Had they handed her away willingly? On purpose? If so, did they know what would become of her? Would they recognize her? Would there be a cell memory of sorts, where their very beings called to hers?

She stiffened, steeling herself. The Devlins had decided to talk to them first, try to control the situation to the meager extent it could be controlled. Surely, *surely* they would not have brought them back to the house if it hadn't gone well. Had they even brought them back? She'd have to turn around to peek, but her head felt locked on her shoulders.

There were footsteps in the hallway, but how many sets of footfalls she was hearing? More than two? Only one? She could feel Igby's eyes on her. The concern that wafted off the *hairn* was palatable, but Igby remained silent. She didn't reach out to squeeze Evangeline's knee. For that, Evangeline was grateful. She was sure if Igby touched her, she would crack like a sheet of ice and then collapse into tears. Nothing in her life had ever been as nerve-wracking as this moment. That was a pretty bold statement, considering how close she'd been to death not two days ago.

She heard them come into the room. She felt Igby and Tresara turn. Across the room, Linus and Paxton stood up. She felt like she was back under the *cheangal,* watching the world move around her and make decisions for her.

Four adults walked into the room. They all appeared human. Evangeline heard Nelda offer her parents—*parents!*—something to drink. She watched as they declined and perched themselves uncomfortably on the edge of a love seat, side by side. In their eyes, Evangeline saw her own emotions. Trepidation warred with excitement.

"Evangeline," Tristan said. "I'd like you to meet Grady and Adara Gilbert. Your parents."

Adara Gilbert made a kind of gasping, almost pained sound, as if someone had pulled a breath out of her. And yet, it was an organic, natural sound as well. An *oh* sort of sound, not a word so much as an emotion. Evangeline had it heard before, when she'd been at the birth of a *hairn* child. When the mother had seen her child for the first time. Hearing her own mother make that noise, Evangeline's shell shattered.

Evangeline looked away from the fire, finally, and straight into her mother's eyes. "It's very nice to meet you." She hadn't planned to say it, had not planned to say anything, really. But it seemed as good a place to start as any.

Her mother's eyes welled with tears, and a whoosh of air escaped her. "May I hug you?"

Evangeline stood up and she started to take a step, but her mother crossed the few feet between them before Evangeline's foot could even meet the rug. Adara's embrace was warm and unrestrained. Evangeline curled herself inside of it, while her mother's shoulders shook with suppressed tears. It wasn't long before there was another person in the embrace. She wasn't sure who parted first, but soon she was being held at arm's length. Then she was being passed back and forth between them while they gazed at her. Fingers grazed her face and touched her hair. Voices commented on her eyes (her father's) and her mouth (her mother's).

"We need to talk, I know that," Grady said, gravel-voiced and a little harsh. "I want to tell you…your mother and I… we…We love you."

The wave crashed. Evangeline took her first step away from them. She suddenly wished they were alone. She didn't want her friends to see her emotion, and she didn't want strangers to witness her pain. Their pain was right on the surface, but so was something else. Something that made Evangeline ache, even while her anger started to raise as well. Guilt.

"You *did* know," she whispered.

Grady held up a hand—to explain or to beckon her back, Evangeline wasn't sure—but she didn't step to it. Instead she flailed at his hand, batted it away. Her breaths came erratic and rough, and the room seemed much smaller.

"You knew. You knew. You knew, oh, you knew—"

"Evangeline!" Nelda said, stern and commanding. "Hear them out. Please."

Nelda got the room back in order with a series of stern looks. Several pairs of eyes bore into the Gilberts. Evangeline wasn't the only creature in the room to feel betrayed, and she wasn't alone in her desire for answers, and possibly retribution.

"We were very young when we found out we were going to have you, Evangeline. We were students. Our families were both gone. We had no help." Grady cleared his throat, uncrossed and re-crossed his legs, and reached for his wife's hand. "We wanted you. We were very much in love and we wanted a family. It was just a very difficult time. When you were born, it only got worse. We were desperate. When someone offered us a way…" he took a deep breath, shrugged his shoulders weakly. "We made a deal."

"There's more to it than your father is telling you, Evangeline," Tristan said. "He's being too hard on himself, not painting the circumstances with the most honest brush."

"No. I'm trying to accept responsibility," Grady argued.

"You can do that, but she deserves the whole truth. She needs more than someone to blame." Tristan raised an eyebrow, requesting permission to continue. Grady offered a half nod. "The Wicklows used spell-craft on your parents; influence, mind magic. Now, they couldn't compel them to make the actual trade through magic, since the *Ascension* requires a free exchange. But they were able to make their circumstances seem more dire, the exchange more innocuous, and the loss of their own child not so incomprehensible. Especially with a replacement. They'd still be a family, have a child."

The room was filled with uncomfortable shifting.

"We'd have a family, they told us, but with a chance to make our child's life successful—"

"You sold me," Evangeline said. The realization dawned on her with the bluntness of a sledgehammer. "They *paid* you."

Adara burst into tears and buried her head in her husband's shoulder. "I can't take this. I can't believe you did this, Grady. I can't believe *we* did this."

Paxton's voice was a razor slicing through the air, wanting blood. "You're awfully distraught about this. You've had twenty years to come to terms with it. Seeing Evangeline make it real, suddenly?"

"Son," Nelda said, holding up a hand. "They didn't remember."

"A memory spell," Tristan explained. "We removed it. They made the exchange of their own free will, but with quite a large bit of influence. They—"

"Traded their child for the promise of an easier life." Evangeline's voice held the coldness she'd been taught in *Scath*. "They sold me like a pair of shoes and it was okay because they'd have their own family to ease their pain. They wouldn't have to think about the infant who would grow up to be bled on an altar."

"What?" Grady and Adara spoke together. Both their heads snapped up.

Nelda's expression softened. She tilted her head to her husband and whispered into his ear. Tristan nodded.

"And this place just became officially the weirdest room I have ever been in," Peyton quipped.

"They didn't know about the *Ascension*. They weren't offered compensation to participate in it," Nelda said.

"And how do you know that?" Linus snapped. "They'd hardly tell you."

"Yes, that's probably correct. It is also why we only removed the memory spell, had a brief conversation, and brought the Gilberts here. We were unsure what their complete knowledge of Evangeline and Siofra's exchange was. This is the first they are hearing of the sacrifice."

Adara's face showed abject horror. "Sacrifice?"

"They only wanted me to use for a human sacrifice. You didn't know? Truly?" Evangeline hated to hear the pleading in her voice. She felt it betrayed her weakness, and her need to have a family that loved and wanted her.

"No!" Adara's voice rose an octave. "We didn't know, Evangeline. Of course we didn't. We took money for our child. We exchanged her for another. Agreed to love that child, raise her as our own. Be a family. We made a terrible choice. We did a despicable thing. We were weak, and stupid, and so very young, and desperate. And we loved you. Loved you so terribly we wanted to give you a better life. An extraordinary life. The Wicklows told us that was what you would be given. We never, *never* sold our daughter to be killed."

Evangeline held her gaze for several more seconds, then

shifted her attention to Grady. His eyes didn't waver from hers, and he offered no further explanation. All the words were out in the open, the ugly truths uttered. His eyes told her he would accept whatever judgment she meted out.

She inhaled through her nose, held the air in her lungs, and let it out through her mouth.

"I believe you."

CHAPTER

FORTY-ONE

"Ask your mother. She'll tell you," Shifty insisted, while Locke continued to shake his head. "The *Siofra Ascension* requires the sacrifice of the human twin, a bloodletting. The blood would be used in our *aontuet*. I didn't ask how. I didn't want to hear that I would have been expected to drink it, or rub it...somewhere. What did you think? They were going to pat her on the butt and send her on her merry way?"

"It's not my place to think about it at all." Locke saw her look of skepticism. "It isn't! You have to understand, we don't do that here. We don't question the Elders, we don't decide *if* we want to offer our loyalty. My allegiance *is*. To my *riocht* and to its continued prosperity; to my kind—my fellow *Scath* creatures—and then to my family. Then and only then, after everything else has taken a bite, then I can think of myself. What *I* want. What I think.

"They told me when I was a child that I would be bound to Evangeline, that it was for the good of the *riocht*. I grew up with her, I knew she would be my *ceile*. But it wasn't until a few months ago that I decided to think about how I felt about that, and if I wanted it. I decided I did. Decided I was actually happy about it. I set about making her happy about it as well. I think I was succeeding. I wish I'd started trying with her sooner. If we'd had more time..."

He stood up suddenly and began to pace the room. He was on the third pass when Shifty couldn't take it anymore. "Are you all right?"

"I want to take a walk. Do you want to take a walk?"

"Dude," Shifty said a little warily.

Locke stopped his rapid circuits of the room and peered down his nose at her.

"Okay. Apparently that's not a term you use over here. Noted. Locke, in case you haven't noticed, I'm sort of under house arrest here. I'm not free to come and go as I would like."

"They'll let you go out with me." He held out a hand to her and wiggled his fingers. "Come on."

Shifty realized that sitting in this windowless room, scared, frustrated, and angry was getting her no closer to her goal. And she had to admit she had a burning curiosity about the parts of the *riocht* she hadn't seen, and information was power.

She shrugged her shoulders. "Why not?"

He unlocked the door and led her through it. They were on a small landing at the top of a steep staircase of dark wood. Shifty could make out a faint light several yards below them. The walls on either side of them made Shifty feel claustrophobic, and a sense of vertigo took hold of her. She pitched forward and lost her footing. She would have taken an ugly trip to the bottom of the stairs if Locke hadn't been in front of her. Instead, she ran into his back and he was forced to right them both.

"Are you okay?" he asked, guiding them both down the few remaining stairs, and helping to steady her at the bottom. He held a hand on either side of her, inches from her ribcage like a gymnastic spotter.

"Usually I am much more sure-footed. I don't know what happened," Shifty stammered.

"Don't worry about it. You all right now?"

Shifty nodded. Locke walked her down a short hallway and turned left into a kitchen. Katarin stood to the side of a small copper bowl with a flame beneath it. She had her back to them and she seemed to be peering out the window into the night outside. She dropped something into the bowl, turning it in circles in a distracted kind of way, like she wasn't really aware of what she was doing. She hummed lightly to herself.

"Mom?"

She didn't jump, which made Shifty believe she'd heard them coming.

"Yes, Lachlan?"

"I'm going to take Siofra on a short tour, okay? Maybe walk her through the market? Go to the clearing? We won't be gone long."

"That's fine. Please be home before your father, okay?"

Locke sniffed, and a strange combination of emotions streamed off him. Shifty couldn't translate them. She knew Locke's father was a powerful wraith, heavily involved with the *Ascension* and the *Sleacht*. Was she seeing a chink in his armor? A possible way to get through to him. Did Lachlan MacNair have daddy issues? She could only hope.

"Watch over her," Katarin added. "Those who wish to take her back to *Talam* have freer access to come and go than we do, and they could very well have eyes anywhere you go. You understand me?" Her head moved, like she was going to look at them, but she didn't turn around completely.

"I understand, Mother."

Locke stepped aside and let Shifty go past him. He opened the back door and motioned her through it. She could bolt, and there was a small part of her that considered it. But gaining more of Locke's trust was probably the smartest move at the moment. She was prepared to play it out for a while.

She followed Locke through a gate in a high fence. The air was thick with a pleasant, earthy aroma. Shifty was again overwhelmed by the rightness she felt here. The connection she seemed to make with everything from the scent in the air to the moon twinkling above their heads. It seemed clearer than the moon she'd grown up gazing at in her own backyard. It wasn't just the lack of light pollution in the *Scath riocht*, it was the way her eyes saw here, the way scents smelled. This was her home. She knew she couldn't stay here, and it made a part of her—a larger part than she was comfortable admitting— very sad. It opened a door of longing within her.

"What do you think of *Scath*?" Lachlan asked.

"Actually, you might not believe this, but I love it here."

Locke chuckled. "Of course I believe it. You're *hairn*."

They were on a wide path, unpaved but well-trod for generations, making it as smooth as many of the roads back in *Talam*. The mist wasn't as thick this time as it had been on her last brief visit, and Shifty had the strange sensation that it wasn't as thick because there wasn't as much magical energy being produced tonight. She wondered if the mist wasn't some kind of magical smog.

"So, what color are your *rian*?"

"You are a quick study, aren't you?"

"Much fuss has been made about mine, so I have a vested interest. Don't be too impressed." Shifty was comfortable talking to this boy, and that made her uncomfortable.

"Some of us think the color of our *rian* are private, and take extreme measures to hide them."

"Oh. I had no idea, I'm sorry if I over-stepped."

He shook his head. "No, you didn't. It's a little ridiculous, in my opinion anyway, hiding your *rian*, or trying to. There's one *hairn* here in the village who covers himself from here to here." Locke pointed to the tips of his fingers and the top of his upper lip. "And all the way to his ankles. *Rian* usually only travel as far as your throat, so they are not necessarily difficult to hide, but the slight advantage you might gain in a fight is not worth spending your life as a ridiculed, paranoid fool. But, I have neglected your question. My *rian* are red. I get my power from conflict. I'm a warrior."

The information surprised Shifty, since he didn't seem aggressive. She thought of soldiers as men of aggression, though she knew that might not be fair. War could be a battle of wits and strategy. Often the best generals were level-headed, intelligent, and even in favor of non-violence. Tristan swam into her mind's eye, so kind and gentle, with his red *rian* shining brightly on his skin. Just because Locke was a warrior of the *Scath riocht* didn't make him a blood-thirsty, hostile meat-head with a hair trigger. "Is there an army here? An organization—"

He cut her off. "I know what an army is, Shifty. Maybe you haven't been given a very accurate picture of our knowledge of other *riocht*, their cultures, languages and trends. Pretty cool, huh?"

Shifty spat out a laugh. "Oh my, you are hip! Though 'dude' seems to have eluded you."

Locke tapped his temple with two fingers in a salute. He made a cascading, looping flourish with them and cocked his head to the side. "Again, I seem to have evaded your question. Yes, we have an army. We do not carry firearms and explosives. Magic is our defense. We call our army the Guard." He said the words with reverence.

"Are you a member?"

"Me? No," he scoffed. But there was something deeper there, possibly something he was trying to hide—from her? From himself? "A MacNair a common warrior? A member of the Guard? We couldn't have that! *Lachlan, you must claim your seat on the Council.*" The bitterness was thick, and it brought them both to a standstill. He kicked a rock with a savage force. Meanwhile, Shifty searched for something to say.

"The *Scath* Council?"

"No, though I am sure my father wishes it were so. Our Elder Council. There's a seat on it for me. I'm expected to take it after our *aontuet.*"

Shifty studiously ignored his mention of their union. Thus far, their communication was moving along so well that she didn't want to create a conflict, especially when she didn't know how he could use that against her in both a figurative and magical way. But she had no intention of leaving Paxton behind or being a willing participant in an *aontuet* with Locke.

"So, you're not interested in the Council? You want to join the Guard?"

Locked nodded.

"And Evangeline knew this, didn't she?"

Locke nodded again. Then he straightened and she saw a veil drop over his features. "Up there is our market place and town square. Most of the shops are closed, but there's plenty going on."

They'd entered the heart of the square. The night life in *Scath* was vibrant. *Hairn*, banshees, and a few wraiths stood in groups. Some had food or drinks in their hands. The youth of the community gathered at the borders of the main square. They grinned and laughed, and ran from one group to another shouting to each other. Wherever she and Locke walked, everyone seemed to go out of their way to acknowledge him; nod, lift a finger, even bow slightly at the waist. In the center of the square, a *hairn* body was airborne, executing a perfect tucked triple flip before disappearing into the crowd again. Shifty had no time to comment. The body was back in the air, this time in an upright position that turned into a full front split in mid-air. Then the *hairn* back-flipped out of it. The crowd made an appreciative noise.

Shifty's feet moved closer, drawn inexorably to the joyful movement. She stood on the outskirts of the circle that had formed around the *hairn* acrobat, but close enough that she could still see the entire scene. The *hairn* returned from its most recent pass and stopped about a foot from the ground, levitating. She strained her eyes and made out a thin, vibrating cord. In the same moment Shifty saw the cord, the *hairn* made a death drop onto it and the cord gave a little. The *hairn*'s body dipped with its chest against the line, this time stopping merely inches from the ground. Shifty held her breath until the *hairn* shot upright again and stood straight on the wire for a second before performing a perfect piked dismount.

The crowd applauded. Shifty joined them. A banshee jumped onto the line and began her own routine.

"You look like you're dying to try," Locke said, smiling at her. Shifty jumped; she hadn't realized he was so close.

"Will they let me?"

"Oh, sure, anyone can. It's a community line." Locke gave a sharp whistle through his teeth and gained the attention of the banshee as she finished her first pass in the air. As she stood on the gently bobbing line, she nodded at Locke, and held a hand out for Shifty. Shifty took the banshee's hand and vaulted herself onto the elastic cord. She stood facing the girl, their hands still clasped. Shifty bent her knees and took an experimental bounce. The rope had appreciable give, but it wasn't loose. She smiled at the banshee, unable to help herself.

"Ready?" the banshee asked. "We'll just do an easy one, okay? A jump."

Shifty dipped and released her knees, the cord sprang beneath her and released them both into the air. The wind whipped around them, Shifty's curls flew into the air and around her face. They landed again and Shifty grinned at the banshee. "That's what I'm talking about!"

"Enjoy it!" the girl said and she jumped to the ground, taking a place next to Locke in the rapidly growing crowd.

Shifty threw herself into the air, just a simple flip to test her footing and the depth of the line. Once she felt secure as secure on its surface as she did the balance beam in her gym, she built up momentum with a series of bounces, until she was flying so high into the air it made her gasp with pleasure. She did splits, front flips, and scissor leaps. In between them, she landed on the line on her butt, her stomach, and her hips. She watched the ground approach rapidly without fearing it would make contact with her face. She finished off with a series of three back handsprings and a back round off dismount that elicited catcalls from the crowd. She offered them the traditional gymnasts' dismount posture, but was immediately self-conscious and quickly dropped her arms to her sides.

Locke approached her, grinning widely. "How was that?"

"That was the most exhilarating thing I have ever done! Thank you for waiting."

"It was fun to watch you. You looked like a *sheehairn*."

Shifty, uncomfortable with the assessment, looked for a change of subject. "So, this is what you guys do for fun? Gather in the square and throw yourselves in the air?"

"Well, there's Cilian's," he said.

"Cilian's?"

"You'd call it a pub, I believe." His eyes sparkled now, but it wasn't as real as the hurt she'd seen in them when they'd discussed Evangeline.

"How do you get your information about what goes on culturally in *Talam*?"

"We can visit your adopted *riocht*, Shifty. We bring back books and magazines. We have radio waves here, and if you know how, you can get transmission from the twenty-first century."

"What do you get if you don't know how?"

"Big Band. *The Shadow*."

"The forties? Why is that?" Shifty found that fascinating. Was the delay in the transmission of information because it crossed the ley lines? Or was it that the modern transmissions were only obtained by magic because the realms existed in a different time? Were they in the forties here? Electricity seemed to be limited. They apparently had radios, but did they even work the same way in different *riocht*? Shifty had to stop thinking about it. It made her dizzy, the unknowable complexity of it.

"Magic," Locke said. He held his hands out in front of him with their palms up and offered her a dazzling smile. "We don't question. We just use it."

"I question," Shifty said.

"Yes, I've noticed. So, would you like to have a drink with me? See what a *Scath riocht* pub is like?"

"If it's anything like the last *Scath* activity I tried, I would love to."

They passed a few more people and a couple of shop fronts before Locke stopped at a heavy oak door and pulled it open. The noise was the first thing that Shifty noticed. Most of their walk until the market had been quiet, with just the wind, their voices, and the chirps and scurries of the local wildlife between them. Suddenly the air around them was filled with laughter and raised, boisterous voices. The air was staler, smokier, though it wasn't cigarette smoke. Locke stayed close to her, making it clear to anyone who took notice that he was responsible for her, but he never made her uncomfortable. Shifty's impression was that he hadn't once noticed her in *that* way, and his claim to be committed to going through with the *aontuet* was only lip service. His heart lay with someone else. Not that she minded, since her heart did as well. But she'd been raised as a human. Locke claimed to have loyalty to *riocht*, species, parents and *then* self. So far he had willingly revealed himself to be conflicted about his career, his father, and his *ceile*. And they hadn't even had one drink yet.

CHAPTER

FORTY-TWO

"We've heard from Tresara's father," Nelda told Paxton. He sat in the bay window of his old bedroom and watched the tree line.

"Oh?"

Nelda tapped her son on the leg to make room for her, and sat next to him. She placed a hand on his shoulder and watched the trees with him in silence for a few seconds. "Yes. He'll help us, son. He's going to bring us Lara Keelin's *Scath Fios*. It's a risk for him, but he says he wants his daughter home, and he wants that home to be safe."

Paxton hadn't looked at his mother yet; he found himself unable to look away from the window. "She will never speak to him again, his *ceile*."

"I think he knows that," Nelda said. "Why don't you come downstairs? Your sister is beginning to worry about you."

"I'm not good company. All I want to do is go after her, and you won't let me do that." Shifty's parents were in the living room, but aside from his one outburst, Paxton hadn't spoken to them since they arrived. He wasn't sure why, exactly. He believed them that they didn't remember trading their child for another. He believed they didn't know Evangeline was to be killed. He decided it might be the suppressed joy the Gilberts couldn't quite hide at being in the same room as their child.

Paxton knew they deserved to be happy, he was glad they loved their daughter, and that she was alive for them to love.

But their *other* daughter was in danger, was being held against her will, and that was what mattered to Paxton right now. Getting her back, making sure she wasn't harmed. The Gilberts wanted that too, of course, but they wanted both girls now. In his logical space, Paxton understood that this was fair and normal—as much as anything in this whole situation could be considered "normal"—but he was still angry.

"We can't, son. We just can't. They have a right to her, at least in the eyes of the Council. She's their blood. We can't just barge in and take her back. Once we've proved what they're up to, we will get her back. Do you trust me?"

"Of course I trust you, Mom. When will *Saoi* Keelin have the book?"

"He's going to take it straight to another rebel, and they will take it right to the *Scath* Council. It's safer and faster if he doesn't have to cross the ley lines right now."

"So, it won't be too long?"

"No, son, it shouldn't be too long."

"In that case, I'll just stay up here, if it's all the same."

Nelda stood up and sighed. "Okay. I'll have Peyton bring you something to eat."

Paxton nodded. "Tell me as soon as the *Scath* Council has seen the book. Let me know when they're ready to do something about the *Sleacht* and the *Ascension*. Or as soon as they're ready let me do something about it."

CHAPTER

FORTY-THREE

Shifty had never felt so watched in her life, and she had been in competition at the National Gymnastic Championship the previous summer, with over ten thousand people in attendance

In the *riocht* pub, there were no more than two dozen *Scath* creatures, and Shifty could feel their inspection like it was an insect creeping up her spine. They had the studied disinterest of those who hung on your every word. Locke seemed comfortable with it. He sat casually, his chair leaned back but not quite tipped onto two legs. He held his glass with one hand and rested the other in his lap. He made good eye contact, but didn't hold it long enough to make her feel uncomfortable. Shifty liked him.

"So," she continued with her story, "they diagnosed me with body dysmorphic disorder. It's a disease that affects the way people see their bodies. They can't see themselves the way they really are. They will insist they are fat or their nose is disfigured, that kind of thing. So, that's when they put me on medication."

"Medication to stop you seeing things? Is that possible?"

"Not in my case." Shifty laughed. "They gave me a variety of medications, but one of them was called Lithium—"

"How fast did it kill your glamour?" Locke asked.

"I'd always seen through my glamour; what the medication killed was whatever kept my joints seeming moderately human. They began to bend in ways they shouldn't have been able to, and it wouldn't hurt. But once Paxton could see my *rian*—or, once the *rian* appeared, I guess is more the point— that's when the Devlins knew they had to tell me the truth."

"I would guess so!" Locke shook his head. His silvery locks fell into his eyes, but she could still see his mouth quirk up.

Shifty lifted her glass and downed the last of the amber liquid. It was sweet, but not cloying, with some of the same flavor of hops as the beer she was used to drinking at home. It warmed her throat on the way down and sat pleasantly in her stomach. She'd never been much of a drinker; she wasn't fond of the taste, nor the result, even before she'd been placed on medications that interacted poorly with alcohol. This stuff was different. It didn't make her feel fuzzy and a little sick. She felt sunny and warm, a little lighter at heart maybe, but still in control. She still knew her mind. She held the glass up and wiggled it. "You guys make a fine ale in these parts."

"You want another one?" Locked asked. He reached for the empty glass and collected his own while he was at it.

"No, thanks." She leaned forward over the table so she could be heard only by Locke. "I'm beginning to feel a little bit like a bird in a cage. Can we go? I'm not exactly dying to go back to being locked in a windowless room, but this attention is making my skin crawl a little."

"Absolutely." Locke jumped to his feet and moved behind her to pull out her chair. It was all so very proper that it gave Shifty the almost overwhelming desire to giggle. She issued herself a mental kick, reminding herself she was the one with a job to do here. She followed him through the pub, looking straight ahead to avoid eye contact with her spectators.

The air outside had cooled significantly, and the mist was so thick Shifty couldn't see below her kneecaps as they walked the path. It licked up as high as her elbows. She ran her hands through it, enjoying the ripples as they rolled away from her like tiny waves. "Is this very thick? Or is it always like this at night?"

"No, this is quite thick. There's a lot of magic being performed tonight."

"Because of us?"

He nodded, but didn't say anything else. He put his hand in the pocket of his jacket, fidgeting there while he watched the path intently, on guard. He really was a warrior, she thought.

"Do you see something I'm missing?"

When he looked at her, she could tell he'd forgotten she was there. He smiled. It was a short, small line across his face. "Just a feeling."

His hand, in the pocket of his jacket, still moved. He was holding something, a weapon possibly.

"Can I ask you something, Locke?" Shifty decided to take her shot.

"Of course."

"Do you love Evangeline?"

He stopped walking. Shifty didn't notice until she was a couple of steps ahead of him. She looked back over her shoulder and saw the confused look on his face. "What?"

"Why would you ask me that?"

"It's not that strange a question, is it?"

"Sure it is. What does love have to do with anything?"

"Uh, everything?" Shifty scoffed, as she walked back to stand beside him.

"Even if I love her, what does it change?"

"It can change what you do about her circumstance. Or maybe it doesn't change anything. Maybe you still do what your parents and your *riocht* expect of you. Maybe I just want to know." She didn't allow herself to hope, not just yet.

Locke went completely still and totally silent, his face veiled in thought.

"Locke, you told me you've known Evangeline her entire life. You grew up with her, your families are close. You must know if you love her. It isn't that complicated."

"No one has ever asked me that before."

"That's just sad and disturbing. And you still haven't answered me."

"I do. I think." He nodded his head, as if to himself. "Yes. I do."

"Can I ask you something else?"

"I don't know," he said. But he smiled, and she knew he was giving her permission.

"What are you prepared to do about it?"

"What do you mean?"

"Gee, Locke," Shifty rolled her eyes. "You love her. Your father is actively trying to get her back to this *riocht* so he can have her murdered, in order to obtain magic that would allow him brutal control of the *riocht* you claim to have such allegiance to, and in every other *riocht* he can reach. Your father and Arwan Wicklow are trying to force us into an *aontuet* that none of us wants. Why? Because we are both in love with other people that we may never see again, if our fathers have their way. So...what are you prepared to do about it?"

"You came here on your own to confront me about this, didn't you? My mother didn't kidnap you. She's working with you, isn't she?" Locke accused.

Shifty smiled at him and raised an eyebrow. "Answer the question."

CHAPTER

FORTY-FOUR

The Gilberts and Evangeline had taken over the living room. Everyone else had scattered throughout the house to wait for word from *Scath*. Tristan was in the kitchen when Nelda found him.

"Should we let Paxton sleep?" he asked. "He hasn't eaten."

"Paxton isn't asleep. Nor will he. He's sitting in his old room and staring at the woods." Nelda stood up, her decision made. "Let the rest of them speak. We can have a meeting in the morning. But I owe Pax an explanation."

Tristan whistled through his teeth, a low hiss, like the sound of a cartoon plane crash. "Do you want me to come along?"

"No, dear. He's going to be plenty upset; better if he has one parent he doesn't hate." She tried to sound lighthearted, but she knew as soon as the words were out that she'd missed her mark.

She climbed the stairs to his room and opened his door without knocking. He sat in the same place she'd left him a few hours before. He had his knees pulled up to his chin, and he rested a cheek on his knee as he gazed out the window at the Gilbert's house. One arm was wrapped around his legs, the other hung loose at his side. There was condensation collecting on the other side of his window. Water ran through the fog accumulated there, making a complicated maze of rivulets. It wasn't a particularly cold or wet night outside.

"You can't reach her with a spell, son," Nelda said, as gently as she could. She hated to see her boy in this much pain, hated to be the cause of it.

"I know." His voice was far away. He didn't turn his head to look at her.

"Can I come in?"

"Sure, why not."

She pulled a chair with her as she crossed the room and positioned it so that she faced him, whether or not he wanted her to, and he could see her at least out of the corner of his eye. "I have an update."

"Oh, yeah?" He shifted his eyes; she had half his attention. "Can we go get her now?"

Though she hated to, Nelda shook her head. "No, I'm sorry. Not yet. The *Scath* Council wasn't swayed by Lara's *Scath Fios*. Now, wait!" She raised her voice slightly as she saw his back straighten. "We knew it was a long shot, that it might not work. The *Scath* Council requires rock solid proof before they move to sanction an Elder's Council. The written word, even Lara Keelin's *Scath Fios*, just had too large a hole in it. Too much that could be denied. *Meas* Keelin thinks they believe it is not a forgery, but Lara could claim it was…and who could disprove it? The *Scath* Council doesn't want to go to war with the wraiths."

"So, what do they need?" Paxton asked. Nelda could feel the frustration pouring off him. He was seconds away from bolting for *Scath*.

"Someone who has firsthand knowledge of what is going on. Someone who has heard at least some of the planning of the *Siofra Ascension*."

"So, that's Tresara's dad, right? Or Shifty's mom."

Nelda was already shaking her head. "No, son. It's not. Tresara's father was never a part of the planning; Lara didn't trust him to be supportive. Shifty's mom would be ideal, but she won't do it. Yes, she has first-hand knowledge, but she won't talk to the *Scath* Council. She isn't willing to turn on her *ceile* publicly, isn't prepared to face the dishonor of the *riocht*. She is helping the rebels, doing what she can, but we can give up any hope of her speaking in front of the *Scath* Council."

"So, then, what?" Paxton looked away from the window finally and his eyes drilled into her. She flinched.

"Lachlan MacNair. He's seen enough that he could testify before the *Scath* Council and bring the *Sleacht* down."

"Don't we have the same problem with that guy? Maybe you haven't been listening when Evangeline talks, Mom, but he's pretty damn loyal. A good little banshee."

"His mother thinks he has real feelings for Evangeline. She thinks he is conflicted. They didn't tell certain specifics about the ritual, like the exchange of his intended until the day it was to be performed."

"But he agreed, he was going to be bound to Shifty. I saw him there on the stair, ready to take my girlfriend."

"Yes, he was willing to be bound to Shifty, to turn away from the girl he'd been told his whole life would be his *ceile*, a friend he'd been close to since childhood, and someone he'd developed feelings for. But he wasn't told about the sacrifice. He didn't know they were going to kill Evangeline. *Meas* MacNair believes if he knew about that, he would be first in line to tell the *Scath* Council what he saw and heard at the Elder Council meetings."

Nelda reached out and squeezed her son's leg. "I need to tell you one last thing."

"Oh, do you really?" Paxton sounded disgusted. Nelda knew he distrusted her more each time she turned around, the last few days.

"We have someone, a rebel, trying to convince him to tell

what he knows. She's doing it at a pretty great personal risk. It's very brave."

Paxton's eyes opened wide. She could see the moment it dawned on him; his eyes flared with anger so bright Nelda wouldn't have been surprised if they'd turned red. "You sent her there? You let someone take her?" he whispered, a thin, murderous sound. He launched himself out of his chair. "I'm going after her."

He tried to shove his way past his mother, but she reached up and caught his hand, pulled him back to her side.

"No. You aren't. You could get everyone killed. She knew, son. I asked her to be a part of the farce, allow herself to be abducted and brought back to the MacNair's house. It was *Saoi* MacNair who took her. Shifty was in a unique position to talk to Locke, tell him about the sacrifice, and appeal to the part of him that has feelings for Evangeline."

"I can't believe you."

"It was our best chance, Paxton. And I trust she can do it. Most importantly, I didn't *do* anything. She wanted to go. I know you want to protect her, but you also have to let her be *hairn*. Stand up for her *riocht*, for you. Convincing Lachlan MacNair to testify is the surest way to ensure she doesn't end up bound to him."

"You're painting a pretty rosy picture, Mom. But what happens if she doesn't get this guy Locke to turn his back on his parents?"

"I don't have a pretty answer to that question. If that is the case, we might not be able to get her home. *That* will largely be my fault."

CHAPTER

FORTY-FIVE

Locke hurried up the front steps of his house. If they weren't gone from the house by the time his father returned, "the jig was up." It was Shifty's expression, and Locke liked it because it sounded like something they would say on the radio plays Evangeline loved so much. They needed to get Locke in front of the *Scath* Council. He could give his account of the meetings he'd attended. So he could tell the tale that would have his parents arrested. The idea squirmed in his guts like a poisonous snake. If he and Shifty were caught, they would have to continue along the kidnap-and-extortion ruse Locke's mother had come up with in order to explain Shifty's appearance in the house. And what his father would do at that point, Locke didn't even like to consider. Certainly a quick *aontuet* against their will. And more likely than not the ceremony would be followed by a storming of *Talam* to find Evangeline.

Once inside they found Katarin, frantic and harried, waiting for them. She thrust an object into Locke's hands. "I packed a bag for you. Everything you need is in there. Take Siofra and go. Your father will be back soon. If someone tries to stop you, put up a fight. Magic, weapons, or hand-to-hand, do what you have to do. There's a map in there. A member of the *Scath* Council will meet you at the point I've marked, accompanied by one of the rebels. Tell them everything you've seen. Then you get to *Talam*, to the Devlins' house. It's a safe house, and Evangeline is there. Stay with the Devlins until you've gotten word from the *Scath* Council that it's safe to come back. Do you hear me? Don't come back until you know they've taken steps to stop it."

"Mom—"

"No, not for anything. We knew what we were getting into. We knew the consequences of trying to initiate the *Ascension*. You have to let this happen. Understand me?"

"Yes. I understand." He held her gaze for just a moment and smiled at his mother. "Thank you."

"Now, where's Siofra?" Katarin raised her voice a little, sounding on the edge of panic.

"I'm here, Mrs. MacNair," Shifty called from the front hall. She'd hung back to allow Locke to say goodbye to his mother in private. She entered the room now, but stayed near the door. She looked ready to bolt.

"Will you please tell Evangeline something for me?"

"Yes."

"Tell her that her mother and I made her a promise when she was a little girl. We told her it would never be her. She may not even remember it. And we lost our way for a while. But we did remember our promise. Eventually. Tell her that, please."

Shifty nodded and backed out of the room.

"Oh, okay, good, well…"Locke had never heard his mother at a loss for words before, but she was pacing now, and she seemed unable to come up with a complete sentence. She finally came to stop in front of him and did something she hadn't done since he was a little boy: she cupped his face in her hand, tilted his face forward, and kissed him on the forehead. "Stay safe, Lachlan. Stay alert."

"I will, Mother."

"Go now, I'll keep a good thought for you."

"We'll see each other soon," Locke assured her.

She offered him a weak smile, a mother appeasing the unrealistic optimism of her dear son. He'd seen that smile before. A lifetime ago when he'd insisted a dead bird they'd found in their backyard would be just fine.

"Yes, Lachlan, of course."

He decided to believe her words instead of her tone.

Shifty was standing to the side of one of the tall, thin windows that flanked the front door. Thin, gauzy curtains covered them, and Shifty was holding a corner back so she could peer through. "Ready?"

"Yes. Let's go." He slung the bag from his mother onto his shoulder. Shifty followed him out the door and down the front stairs, into the night.

Once under the cover of the trees Locke stopped to consult the map. He laid it out between the two of them on the floor of the forest, clearing the mist with a wave of his hand. It stayed clear.

"Here, hunker down," he motioned to her.

The map had obviously been drawn in haste, but it was as detailed as they needed it to be. A clear path was laid out for them. Locke followed it with his finger, and then looked up to peer into the trees. He cocked his head to one side and nodded. "I think we're clear for now. Stay close to me. It's not far, where we're going. You're as quick and nimble as I am. I'm not going to slow my pace for you. That okay?"

She nodded.

"Good." He folded the map back up, shoved it in the pack, shouldered the bundle once more, and held out a hand to her.

She looked down at it.

"The mist will get thick. It is the best way to keep track of each other."

She put her hand in his. "Lead the way."

CHAPTER

FORTY-SIX

Shifty went over a low fallen branch in a sprinter's hurdle position, following Locke's lead. The scenery blurred past. Locke's footing was sure; she couldn't detect a note of hesitation from him. She trusted him to get them where they were going, but she had to suppress the urge to ask the where, whens, and whats of their travel and destination. Her fear was carefully tamped down in her lower intestine, where it would hopefully stay until she and Locke were safely at the Devlins' house. She couldn't use it, so she needed it to be out of her way.

She relished the freedom her body felt in this full-out run through her mother-dimension. Her legs felt like they had double the power they had in *Talam*. They contracted and extended seamlessly, pushed into the earth, and propelled her along at a breakneck speed. Shifty felt like she was flying instead of running. She closed her eyes—Locke was leading them, anyway. All she had to do was keep her arms and legs moving to match his pace…and not come up against another branch, of course, but she couldn't stop herself.

The air blew across her face and rushed past her ears. It was the sound of driving through a tunnel with the car window down, a hissing white noise. It was calming, and helped her to shut out all the nagging thoughts and worries. She'd open her eyes in a moment, she would…but the calm, the dark, the noise, it was so—

Locke's hand slipped out of hers.

She hit the ground on her back. Her breath left her in a whoosh, her head ricocheted and bounced on the hard earth. Her eyes flew open. One leg already bent, she brought both arms up to her ears, ready to flip herself back to her feet. An apology was already formed in her mind; she wasn't sure exactly what she'd tripped on, but as the runner with her eyes closed, she was sure it had been her fault.

Until she saw the wraith with the branch in his hand standing over Locke, who was also on the ground, and she realized what had stopped them.

Locke rolled to his side with a groan. He'd taken the brunt of the blow from the branch and he was a little slower to regain his breath than Shifty, who'd only had the wind knocked from her. She completed the flip-up to her feet and positioned herself behind the wraith and she tackled him. She led with her shoulder, wrapped her arms around his waist, and dragged him to the ground. His muscles rippled beneath her arms, all cord and hard steel ropes, she knew immediately that it was only the surprise of her attack that gotten him off his feet. The moment they hit the ground, he rolled, gained control of their position, and hauled her up by her shoulders. He gave her a rough shake, to ensure she was paying attention.

"Hello, Siofra."

She'd heard his voice at the MacNair house, but it was different now. It was like the wind around them, cold and filled with malicious magic. She knew if he didn't need her so badly, he would kill her on the spot. She'd caused him problems, and he didn't allow that. Defiance was unacceptable. He raised a fist, pulled it back—

And was hauled off her.

Locke tackled his father from the side. He used much the same stance that Shifty had a second earlier, but he was one up on Shifty, and his father—he had a knife.

Shifty could barely make out Locke and his father as they scuffled in the mist. She heard blows land, and the grunts and groans that followed. But the fog obscured sound. Shadows around her seemed to tussle. Locke's voice came from all around her.

"You should just run," he taunted his father. "You might still have time to get away before they know what you did. What you tried to do."

Shifty saw them properly then, practically on top of her, and she had to jump out of the way to avoid being injured again.

Frantically, she looked around for a weapon of her own. The branch Cecil had dropped when Locke hit him? It wasn't within arm's reach, and she couldn't see any further than that. She swore under her breath.

"Locke, be reasonable," he called to his son in a voice so calm it chilled Shifty's blood. "You and the girl come back with me now. Go through with the *Ascension*. No one else has to get hurt."

"Except Evangeline?" Locke spat. Suddenly, he was next to in her the mist, he searched the ground as feverishly as Shifty did. "My knife," he hissed to her. "I've dropped it. I'll hold him off, you look for it."

She nodded. She hoped he could see her, but she didn't want to waste the sounds, didn't want to alert Cecil that they were together and unarmed. Locke pivoted on his foot, listening and looking for his father. He bolted into the mist, and Shifty heard him make contact with what she hoped was Cecil and not a tree trunk.

Where was the knife? Elder MacNair was too strong, too quick for her to take alone, and while Shifty was brave, she wasn't stupid. And she didn't have a death wish. They had to get out of this alive. Had to get to the *Scath* Council.

They'd been close, she'd felt it.

There was a firm grip around her arms and chest; it pinned her tightly. She started to kick and buck, until she felt a blade her throat—cold, heavy, and sharp. Cecil had found Locke's knife.

"I have what you're looking for. Both of them," he called into the mist. "Just come out, Lachlan. I won't hurt her. I don't want that. She's the key to *riochtfios*. Why would I endanger that?"

"Don't, Locke! Go, get to the *Scath* Council—" Shifty sucked in a breath as the blade cut deeper.

"No more out of you, please," Cecil hissed into her ear. His breath was hot and angry, but he was still perfectly calm. He pulled her tighter against his body and stood rigid, listening, searching with all his senses for his son. Waiting for him to make an error.

"Now!" Cecil yelled.

Nothing but the swirling of the mist answered him.

He exhaled sharply. He was getting frustrated, Shifty noted with a small bit of satisfaction.

"No?" he said in a lower voice. "You care that much about the human? I think you're getting soft, Lachlan. And I think I know how to convince you."

She felt the knife leave her throat, and then there was a sharp punch to her side. She screamed. She couldn't help it. The pain was exquisite. She'd never been punched before. She barely had time to comprehend the punch when another sensation blossomed· A quick, sharp swipe near where the punch had come. She'd been injured, and thought she handled pain well— broken bones, pulled muscles, severe contusions. This pain had a different quality. It was so pure it was almost clean.

"Shifty?!" Locke's voice was closer. He was giving up his advantage, trying to get close enough to rescue her.

"I'm all right, Locke! Stay where you are. He's just trying to—" She couldn't get any more words out. It hurt to speak, and she couldn't understand why until she felt the warmth spread across her shirt.

Cecil hadn't only gut-punched her, he'd cut her. She couldn't tell how badly she was injured, but she had to assume he wouldn't want her mortally wounded, or even critically. He needed her alive.

She coughed as loudly as she could and seemed to regain the breath she'd lost with the blow to her stomach. She shuffled her feet. She tried to find a twig to snap. Any noise she could make. She knew Locke was there, stalking them…waiting for a time to strike.

"Stop. Moving," Cecil whispered. He dragged the knife up the side of her body and back to her throat. "That wound isn't deep, barely more than a scratch. I can continue to hurt you very badly without killing you, without even coming close. Wounds that can be tended once my son comes to his senses, but while he works through his crisis of conscience, you and I are just going to stand here and wait. Clear?"

"Yes." And it was. She locked her jaw and stood rigid. Her mind raced almost as quickly as her heartbeat.

There was a sickening crack. It echoed in her head and bounced around inside her mind. The arms around her went slack and the body dropped, now just dead weight at her feet. Her knees buckled and she started to follow Cecil to the ground. Locke threw his heavy branch to the side and caught Shifty under her arms. He righted her, but didn't let go of her.

"Can you stand?"

She nodded. "Uh…yeah. Yes. I can."

Locke let go of her and dropped to his knees next to his father's prone form. It took him only a second to locate and snatch the knife. He shoved it into the waistband of his pants, found his pack again, and tugged gently on Shifty's hand. "Can you run? It isn't much farther."

"I can make it. I don't think I can go as fast. What about your father?"

"I'm not sure. I might have killed him. I'm not sticking around to check."

"Locke. I'm—"

"Do not tell me you're sorry. I'm not. He didn't leave me a choice." He tugged a little more urgently. She started moving. The pain in her side was bad, but she had practice at shutting down the part of her brain that protested pain. She'd completed floor routines with broken toes, and this was the same sort of thing. She had to stop her body from caring that she hurt, at least until they reached the *Scath* Council.

The pain eased, she picked up the pace, her breathing evened out. Tolerable. She kept moving

And so it went. Through the darkness and the mist. Air in through the nose, out through the mouth. Trees whooshed past them; leaves smacked her in the face. No pain. One foot down. Pick the other up.

"There!" Locke yelled, exalted. Relief swept over Shifty, she stopped, doubled over, rested her palms on her knees, and sucked in air.

"You're sure?" Shifty could hardly believe it. She'd begun to think that her hope had been foolish, and the trail would never end.

"Yes."

A few yards ahead of them was a gathering circle. Four *hairn*, three banshee, and a wraith sat around a fire pit, a raging fire illuminating their faces. They all looked up at Locke and Shifty's approach. There was no malice in their faces, but they weren't welcoming either. Locke finally dropped Shifty's hand as he walked, and she saw that his fingers crept closer to the knife in his waistband.

Shifty worked to keep her breath even. "Are we doing the right thing? We could still just jump across the ley line, wait out the moon phase with the Devlins."

"It would never work, Shifty. My mother is right to send

us here, instruct us to do it this way. This is the only way to make sure they are held to account for what they did to you and Evangeline."

They were within shouting distance of the group around the fire.

"They might hold you to account as well, Locke."

"I know that. I'll accept whatever they decide. Look, wait for me here. I have to handle this alone."

He didn't wait for her to agree. He just doubled his pace and left her in his wake. She sank down to the ground in front of a nearby tree, far enough that she couldn't hear the voices, but close enough to see the proceedings, and to shout if anyone else arrived to try and drag her back to the *Ascension*. While Locke walked to the *Scath* Council's contingent and his judgment, Shifty sat with her back against a tree, and willed herself not bleed.

CHAPTER

FORTY-SEVEN

When he finally made it back to where Shifty sat against the tree, Locke thought she was unconscious. Her head was tilted back against the bark as if she was stargazing, but her eyes were closed tight. He wondered if he should try and lift her and just carry her over the ley line.

"I'm still here," she said, as if able to read his thoughts.

"Can you walk?"

"Can we leave?" she countered.

"Yes."

She shifted a little, tried to gain her feet, and held a hand out to him. "Then I can walk. Just help me up, would you?"

He hoisted her up, as gently as he could manage. "It's not far."

She let a huff of laughter escape while she tested her weight from foot to foot. "What are you saying, Locke? You think I'm not tough enough to handle a knife slash to the gut? Your father said it could be tended, it can't be more than a slash. We've got to get me to Nelda." She lifted her shirt, exposing the shallow wound. It was steadily seeping blood, but it wasn't gushing. She was hoping to mollify him a little and as she took in the wound, she felt better about it herself. It hurt like a son of a bitch, but it wasn't deep. It looked as if she'd been swiped at by a large, determined dog.

But Locke just shook his head. "Lean on me while we walk. The less you move the wound, the better."

She looked as if she might argue with him, but he put on his most determined expression and she gave in with a sigh. He was pretty sure he felt her relax a little once she'd adjusted her weight so that he was responsible for supporting more of her body than she was. He had to admire the *hairn*; she was made of tougher stuff than he'd given her credit for. She was more *sheehairn* and less human than he'd believed possible for one raised in *Talam*.

Their progress was slow and her breathing worried him, but he kept a steady pace. He'd been telling her the truth, they didn't have far to travel. He managed a fumbled salute to the guards at the ley line while balancing Shifty on one side and his pack on the other. One of them returned it and stepped forward. Obviously the man in charge.

"Lachlan MacNair?"

"Yes. This is Siofra, uh..." he stumbled. What was her last name? "Wicklow," he said finally, feeling as if he was disrespecting her in some way by using that name instead of the one her adopted parents had given her. "I believe you've been given instructions to let us cross?"

"We have. She doesn't look so good. Are you sure you don't want someone to look at her first?"

"No," Shifty said, her voice stronger and firmer than it had been at the clearing. "I need to get back. They'll have help for me there. Uh, thank you, though."

The guard nodded, a brusque, though not unkind, movement. "Very well." He stepped aside. "Are you able to activate the line on your own?"

Locke scoffed. Most of the contraband Evangeline kept hidden in her room, he had obtained for her. "I've been crossing ley lines since I was a kid."

~

Usually Locke didn't give the magic a second thought. Though usually he wasn't toting a badly injured *hairn* girl who was depending on him to get her back to her family. When the line flared, its red reflection felt more like a warning than an invitation. Locke got a better grip on Shifty and took a deep breath, hoping his trepidation didn't show. If it did, she was good at hiding her own, because Shifty gave him a confident smile and lifted her feet at the same time he did.

There was the usual strange, missed-a-step-on-the-stairway feeling, and his stomach raced to meet his throat; the vertigo threatened to knock him and Shifty both off their feet. But when it cleared, they stood in the woods of *Talam*.

He turned his face to Shifty. "You're going to have to guide me from here. I'm not sure where your family lives."

"Straight ahead." She lifted her hand and pointed to a small, dim light peeking through the trees. "The Devlins' house is right through there. My parents' house is next door to that." She surprised him by stepping apart from him. He reached out for her, but she waved him off. "I'm okay. I can make it on my own."

He had a pretty solid prideful streak of his own, so he recognized it when he saw one in others. He knew she didn't want to be seen as having been rescued. He didn't argue, but he stayed close enough to catch her if she stumbled.

Their progression was slower on this side of the line, but Locke was unsure if this was because of Shifty's injury or just the general lack of urgency that came from no longer being pursued by things that wanted to kill them. When they finally made it to the tree line, Shifty offered him a face-splitting grin.

Neither of them wore a human glamour, and in the light *Talam* provided, from homes and the lamps lining the street, he got what he felt was his first honest look at her he'd had since he met her. Now, when she wasn't frightened, running for her life, or using her wiles to convince him to turn on his family, he realized she was lovely. She had a clever sparkle in her eye that promised mischief, but also a softness that spoke of kindness and caring. She was a new concept for him, a human-raised *hairn*, and he hoped he got a chance to know her better.

"Your Paxton is a lucky guy."

"Yeah. Evangeline got a bum deal." She knocked her shoulder into his, and winced.

The Devlins' backyard opened from the woods at a gentle incline. There was a picnic table, and several benches and chairs were scattered around. A collection of bricks were arranged in such a way that they obviously encased a fire quite often. Further up the hill, Locke made out the house; its large deck also housed a variety of items that spoke of a family that spent a lot of time outside together. Items he knew were games, though he'd never played them; a large barbecue; and another table with a set of chairs. It was a space that told a story: a story about family.

That family must have heard them coming up the hill, or someone had been keeping watch at a window, because people came streaming out the back door. They ran across the porch and stormed down the stairs.

"Shifty!" Paxton was the first to reach them. He beat the others by several seconds. He grabbed Shifty around the waist and hoisted her into a bear hug. It made Locke wince just watching it, and he couldn't imagine how she kept from crying out.

"Shit! I've been frantic. I don't know what kind of heroic crap you thought you were pulling, but don't ever do anything like that again."

Locke was pretty sure he didn't even know what he was saying, that he was just expelling all the energy that he'd built up from worrying about Shifty while she was gone. Locke could also tell Shifty hadn't heard a word of it. She clung to Paxton, allowed him to kiss and admonish her, and then she pushed herself just far enough away from him that she could see the others as well.

They were all there: Igby, Tree, and Linus flanked Evangeline, who stood next to Peyton. In a ragged line behind his friends were Nelda and Tristan Devlin, looking relieved and worried in equal parts, and two humans Locke knew had to be Evangeline's birth parents. They looked like Evangeline, a concept Locke turned over in his mind a couple of times to take in the strangeness of it. For all their lives, no one had ever looked like Evangeline. She'd been completely unique.

For a moment no one spoke, as if there was a group inhale—a second to assure themselves this was real. And then the floodgates burst and they all spoke at once. Questions overlapped in a symphony of confused and hysterical waves.

Locke held up a hand to beg that the faucet be turned to a trickle. There was another abrupt silence as everyone's jaws hinged closed at once.

"We will answer all your questions. I promise. But Shifty's hurt. She needs help."

Paxton made a sound of shock and anger. He looked Shifty up and down as best he could, since he was apparently still unwilling to let go of her. When he finally saw the blood stains, now transferring from Shifty's clothing to his own, he groaned. It was an anguished sound, like an injured animal, and it hurt Locke's heart to hear it.

"Shifty, what happened to you?"

She offered a weak smile. "I got in a fight with a wraith. I think I lost."

"Get her in the house," Nelda instructed. "Tristan, Grady, help Paxton carry her. Keep her as still as possible." There was no room to question Nelda; her voice held the authority of one long used to having her orders carried out.

Locke watched, impressed, as the others organized and orchestrated their movements. They had Shifty on a stretcher made of arms, marching her back up the hill to the house. All other questions were on hold. Igby trotted in front of the group, got to the back door first, and held it open. Locke hung back and took Evangeline by the forearm before she could make her way inside.

"I have to go," he told her.

"What?" She stared at him and then shook her head. "No, Locke. No. Don't—"

"I don't want to leave. Not with Shifty hurt…and it's my fault. Not with you in danger…and it's my fault. But I made a promise and I'm going to keep it."

"What are you talking about?" She sounded confused, but not angry. He would take the small victories today; they were probably the only ones he could hope for.

"I told the *Scath* Council what I knew about the *Ascension*. About our parents' plans to carry it out. I owe you an explanation. And I'll give it to you, Evangeline, I will. I want you to understand I didn't know they would hurt you. And I wasn't aware until the end that I was promised to Shifty. I went along with it, and I'll regret that my entire life. But I hope you'll believe that I wouldn't have gone along with a plot to kill you. I wouldn't blame you if you didn't, but it is the truth."

"So stay and give me the explanation," she pleaded. He could see the tears forming on her lower lids. He'd once found it so irritating when she cried. When they were children, her tears had always seemed close to the surface, so easily spilled. Now, he thought they were beautiful. Made from emotion and vulnerability, they meant she cared.

He reached out and wiped one away from her cheek. He

watched it on the tip of his finger with wonder. He rubbed it onto his own cheek, felt its coolness stripe across his face. He wanted it to be a piece of her to carry back with him, to remind him of why he was going back in the first place.

"I can't, Evangeline. They only let me cross over because Shifty was hurt. I swore I'd come back immediately. I have to face the *Scath* Council for my part in the *Ascension*." He drew an uneven breath. "For what I did to you."

Evangeline turned her hand so that she gripped his forearm while he gripped hers. For a moment they were the only thing holding each other up. They locked eyes. Hers full of shock and fear and tears. He hoped his held a steely determination to turn this around, to be loyal to the right things, and own up for his part in his parents' plot.

Her face crumbled first and she crushed herself into his chest. "But you didn't know!" she wailed, her voice muffled by his flesh.

He pressed his face into her hair and inhaled her scent. When he spoke he didn't lift his lips from her hair. "Not that they were planning to kill you. That's true. It is also true that I *did* know they were planning to perform the *Siofra Ascension* and for a long time. I should have done something earlier to stop it. I'm well versed in the law of the *riocht*. I understood my father was trying to gain power to which he had no right, through means against every edict our land has set in place. So, I am responsible. I will accept whatever punishment the *Scath* Council deems righteous."

"They could kill you, Locke."

"I don't think they will," he said.

She was correct, of course, and he had considered it. Furthermore, he didn't think the possibility was as remote as he was making out for her. The *Siofra Ascension* was considered the highest form of treason in the *riocht*. The *Scath* Council was not known for mercy. He extracted himself from her grip and lifted his face from her hair reluctantly, but he knew if he didn't do it then he'd never find the strength.

"I have to go. The *Scath* Council will be in touch with Nelda and Tristan. No matter what happens, there will be a time for us to talk once...they've passed sentence."

"I hate this, Locke. I hate it!"

He placed finger on her lips. "I know."

He leaned forward, even as he wondered if she would push him away. She should. After the trauma he'd put her though. But he had to try. When his lips found hers, she hadn't pulled back, and she responded to the kiss immediately. He didn't let himself fall into the kiss. He knew how easy it could be to get lost in her, and he'd also lose all his will to return to *Scath* if he allowed that. He pulled away and just held her gaze with his again.

He backed up a couple of steps, all the while still watching her. He finally forced himself to turn his back on her. He walked quickly to the edge of the woods, where he turned to find her still watching him, a hand half-raised in a wave.

"I love you," he called.

He didn't wait to see her face, couldn't bear to pause to hear her reaction. He turned and stepped into the woods. He sprinted to the ley line and back to the *Scath* Council's judgment.

CHAPTER

FORTY-EIGHT

In the spare bedroom, the bed had been stripped down to the fitted sheet and Shifty was laid upon it. As Nelda cut her shirt away with a pair of surgical scissors, Shifty wondered why she owned them, but wasn't actually surprised. Nelda seemed to be constantly prepared for any and all emergencies. Shifty understood why they had left her in charge of watching over her as she grew up. It was just the *Sleacht's* bad luck that Nelda had been working against them the entire time.

They'd never had a chance; once Nelda Devlin put her mind to something, it was going to get done. Or not done, as the case may be.

Shifty realized she'd been drifting, letting her mind walk away from the pain and the fear. It was probably the easiest way to cope with what was happening to her, but it also left her out of the decision making, and she was done letting things happen to her. She wanted a voice and a vote.

"How bad is it?" Her teeth were clenched, but she got the question out without screaming. First Paxton jostling her, then exposing the wound to the open air, and maybe even taking her out of *Scath*, seemed to have set it on fire. What had been painful but tolerable in *Scath* now felt as if someone had torn a hole in her side with a red hot poker.

"It isn't good." Nelda prodded at the side of the wound. This time, Shifty did yell out. Paxton, at her other side with both hands holding one of hers, snapped to attention.

"Mom!"

"I have to inspect it to help, Paxton. If you can't handle it, I can have someone take you out of the room until we've finished."

Shifty tightened her grip on him and shook her head. "I'm all right, Pax. But I need you here. I need you to stick this out with me."

Nelda continued to prod at her, the pain shot up one side of her body and down the other. She closed her eyes and clamped her jaw so tightly her teeth creaked, but she didn't yell out again. "It's going to need stitches. I can do that. I have the supplies, but I have to control the bleeding before I can close it. How long ago did this happen?"

"I'm not sure. More than an hour but less than two, I think." It was the closest approximation she could provide, and she realized it could be completely wrong; her concept of time over the last three or four days was shot.

"Has it been bleeding like this the entire time?" Nelda asked.

Shifty tilted her head and peered at what Nelda was seeing. The cut that had looked like a bad animal scratch in *Scath* was now an angry, open wound. The blood that had seeped thickly before they'd crossed into *Talam* had begun to pool next to her on the mattress. "No," Shifty said. "This isn't what it looked like and there wasn't anywhere near this kind of blood."

"When do you think it got worse?"

"Well…" Shifty averted her gaze from Paxton. "When we came over the ley line. And when Pax hugged me."

Paxton punched his fist into his own leg with a ferocity that frightened Shifty and caused Nelda to place her own hand over his.

"I don't like this," Nelda said

"What's wrong?" Peyton asked.

"It's not a particularly deep wound. If Shifty was injured as long ago as she thinks, the bleeding should have slowed, and there should be some coagulation. It's still bleeding steadily. Slowly, yes, but there's no clotting. The fact that it became worse when she arrived in *Talam* makes me believe this is a magical wound. Once she left *Scath*, the spell increased and what was a relatively innocuous injury will swiftly become critical if we don't stop it." Nelda paused for breath and turned to call over her shoulder. "Payton! Please bring me the small amber bottle with the green wax stopper? We can at least do something to ease the pain."

They all listened as Peyton's footsteps clomped up the stairs. She appeared in the doorway, shoved the bottle into her mother's outstretched hand, and retreated back to the hall. Nelda popped the seal off and helped Shifty to swallow the liquid inside. Nelda paused, her eyes rolled slightly up into her head, as if she was looking for a solution on her brain. "Who inflicted this wound?"

"Locke's father," Shifty whispered, and pulled in another raspy breath. She wondered how long it would take before the pain medication took effect.

"I see." Another pause. Another flick of her eyes into her brain's database. "Did he say anything before he cut you?"

"What do you mean?" It seemed like a very odd question to Shifty.

"Tell me what happened. Exactly what he said before you were injured."

Shifty tried to replay the fight in her mind. If Nelda was asking, it was important, and the devil was in the details.

"He was holding me and taunting Locke. He said *'I think you're getting soft, Lachlan. And I think I know how to convince you.'*

Then he punched me in the side, with the knife in his hand."

"But he didn't say anything else? Anything that sounded like a spell?"

Shifty shook her head. "I think I would remember that."

"And you're sure it was a knife?"

Shifty nodded. "I saw it. It was Locke's knife. He lost it in the scuffle with his dad, but I know it was a knife. He had it in his waistband, he'd been carrying it the entire time."

"I think I know the knife, *Saio* Devlin," Evangeline said from her place at the door next to Peyton. "If it would help. He got it at market. We walked home together and he showed it to me. He must really have liked it because it replaced the other knife on his belt after that. Could it be important what knife it was?"

"It could be, yes. Very important. Get Locke." When there was no answer, she looked up and scanned all their faces. "Where is he?"

A cloud floated across Evangeline's face. Tears welled in her eyes. "He left. He went back to the *Scath* Council. They only let him leave so he could get Shifty back safely. He's gone back to accept sentencing." Her voice cracked, but she didn't actually begin to cry.

"I see. Well." Nelda looked at her hands on Shifty's wound, then at Evangeline's face. Shifty knew her well enough to see Nelda wanted to comfort the girl, but she could also see that the situation wouldn't allow for that. "Yes, Evangeline, it would be very helpful if you could describe the knife for me. Could someone get her a piece of paper and a pencil? Any detail you can remember will be valuable."

Peyton rushed from the room and returned in seconds carrying a small pad of paper and a cup full of pens and pencils. She thrust them into Evangeline's hands and pointed to a small desk and chair in the corner of the room. When

Evangeline was done, she handed the pad of paper to Linus.

"Do you remember anything else? You guys saw it, too."

Linus studied her drawing, his forehead creased and he chewed on his lip. "Looks like it to me. I don't think there's anything you forgot."

He handed the picture off to Tresara and Igby, who both took a long look and couldn't add anything either.

Finally, Igby handed the paper to Nelda.

"Thank you. Is this the knife, Shifty?" She held the drawing in front of Shifty's face.

It was more of a dagger, a little blunt, made for sticking and jabbing instead of slicing. The blade was almost the same length as the handle. Both blade and handle had ornamentation on them; symbols on the hilt and one on the blade.

"Yes," Shifty confirmed. "That's it."

"I see."

Nelda sounded strange.

Shifty's eyes had been closing, but she opened them wide again so she could see Nelda's face. It was dark and worried, and then it was a mask of calm. The quick change made Shifty worry more than anything else. Nelda had just pulled that face on, turned off her emotions, and gone completely *sheehairn*.

Shifty knew there were not that many reasons why she would do that. One of them would be because she had bad news. After all the rotten things Nelda had told them in the last couple of weeks and all the crap they'd waded through, if Nelda felt the need to wear the blank face now...how terrible was what she had to say?

"Mom!" Paxton urged. "What is it? Do something! We can't just let her lay her and bleed to death!"

Nelda sighed. She handed the pad to Tristan, who looked at it and then at her in silent agreement. Whatever she'd seen on the page, he saw as well, and understood it to be the same omen.

"One of you say something!" Peyton's voice was high, like barely contained hysteria.

"Stay calm, please." Lifting the picture as she spoke, she said, "If this is the knife that wounded Shifty, we might have a serious problem. The hilt is marked with symbols connected to the *Siofra Ascension*. It was meant to stop wraith magic in other *riocht*. It's a tool of the rebels against the *Ascension*."

"So that's good, right? That's us! We're the rebels! Yay us!" Peyton's voice took on a relieved tone.

"Where did Locke get this knife, Evangeline?" Nelda asked, ignoring her daughter's interruption. "At market, I know, but from whom?"

Evangeline shook her head. "I wasn't with him when he got it. He showed it to me after, but he said he'd been at the knife stand, so I just assumed that's where he'd gotten it."

"Yes, that makes sense," Nelda said. She spoke to herself, which was fine. No one else knew what she was talking about anyway. She was quiet for a time, she tapped her lips with a finger, and chewed on the inside of her cheek.

"What, mother? Spit it out!"

"Because it is a spelled knife. If this blade wounds the *hairn Siofra* twin, the wound won't heal. The blood won't congeal. The *hairn* will bleed to death. The *Ascension* can't be completed. The minute the knife makes contact with a white-*rianed hairn* it blocks her magic. Any of you notice Shifty's got no sign of her *rian*? An injured *hairn's rian* should appear without their control, in an effort to heal. This," she rattled the paper again, "is a very powerful object."

"So, there's got to be a way to stop it!" Paxton's voice had rushed right passed his sister's and he'd arrived at full-blown panic.

"I'm going to do everything in my power. We got very lucky that the wound was shallow, practically superficial, and that the magical effects didn't take hold until Shifty returned to *Talam*. We gained hours that way. First thing we're going to do is thicken and slow this blood by magic. But I can't make any promises. Shifty, I'm so sorry."

Shifty closed her eyes. She couldn't even process the information. "Don't apologize. Not yet. Apologize if you don't find a way."

CHAPTER

FORTY-NINE

Evangeline had never been in a house so quiet that spoke so loudly, in her life. Nelda, Evangeline and Linus were in the library with books piling up around them. Tristan was in the kitchen working on potions for Shifty, anything to slow and thicken the blood. They'd gotten it to a trickle, but still not a sign that it was congealing.

Paxton and Peyton hadn't left Shifty's side in the spare room where she lay. They tried hard to appear upbeat and happy. Grady and Adara alternated between joining the group at Shifty's sickbed and standing on the back porch holding each other and talking in whispers.

Evangeline watched them mourn a child who wasn't gone yet. The more she saw, the more convinced she became that they hadn't lied to her. These people hadn't known they were raising a *hairn*, they'd believed she was their child. The grief and fear Evangeline saw on their faces couldn't be faked. They might have made a terrible, heartbreaking decision when they were tricked or spelled into trading their child, but they hadn't known all the repercussions, and they hadn't even remembered it until Nelda had lifted the memory spell.

Evangeline couldn't be more sure of it. She didn't know why her confidence in them was so strong, but she knew on a cellular level that the belief in her parents was correct. And as she worried for Shifty, and for Locke, for herself, she let go of the remaining doubt, anger, and fear surrounding her birth parents.

Much like the house, Evangeline herself felt like a walking contradiction. Believing her parents to be truthful made her heart sing. And now as she had to watch them face the possibility of losing the daughter they'd raised, and it broke her heart. They had been searching for nearly twenty-four hours. They'd managed to halt the bloodletting to a slow trickle, and Nelda had even gotten butterfly bandages to hold the wound closed for up to twenty minutes a few times. But they knew time remaining was closing. No one had mentioned it, but it was closing in on the time to start saying their goodbyes.

Evangeline felt helpless and wished she could do more. She owed her life to the creatures in this house, and she was watching one of them die for her.

"Tristan!"

Nelda's voice echoed through the house, and the hairs on the back of Evangeline's neck stood up. Nelda had found a hope. Evangeline heard it in her voice. Evangeline jumped to her made eye contact with her friends as they approached the room, silently asking the question no one dared to say out loud.

More practically, though: Nelda had called Tristan. Were they allowed as well? The look that passed between them was unanimous: they didn't care. All of them bolted through the door at the same time, they caught on each other, and pushed their way through as one mass.

Once near their destination, it was obvious the entire house had come to similar decisions. Grady and Adara were rushing from the right side of the hallway arriving from the back porch, and Paxton and Peyton were flying down the stairs, their feet barely made contact with the floor as they approached.

Nelda, in her doorway with a book in her hand, looked unsurprised that she'd attracted a crowd.

"You found something?" Adara asked, her eyes so confident they sparkled. Evangeline gave into the urge to reach for her mother's hand. Adara received her the squeeze, returned it, and gave Evangeline a grateful smile.

"Well. It's not that optimistic…the information," Nelda warned, but none of the faces in the crowd changed. "But, yes. I don't know if I want to get Shifty's hopes up and discuss this in there. Come in here, please. I'll explain what I found."

Everyone gathered around Nelda's desk. She cleared off enough space to allow her to lay the book flat. Evangeline recognized the glyphs as ancient *hairn*. Her mind began to translate them automatically, but so many of them were unfamiliar. The text didn't make much more sense to her than it did to Grady and Adara, whose puzzled expressions still couldn't mask their anticipation. Nelda pointed to a section of text near the bottom of the right hand side of the page.

"This talks about the knife that stops the *Siofra Ascension*. But, it also mentions an elixir. The elixir will reverse the bloodletting of the knife wound."

"So, what's the big 'but'?" Peyton prompted. "I know you too well, Mother. I've heard this guarded voice since I was a tiny girl. You've been hauling it out since the puppy went missing when I was three. 'I hope we'll find Radley, but…'"

Nelda didn't even bother to glare at her daughter.

"The elixir is an ancient recipe. The ingredients, if I can even translate them and update the language to modern plants and spices, well…some of them might not even exist in this *riocht* anymore."

"So we go to *Scath* and get them. No problem," Paxton said.

"Hopefully—"

There it was again: *hopefully*. Now Evangeline could hear it, too.

"How long to translate it?" Paxton asked.

"Well, I don't know. Evangeline and Linus can help me. They make it so much faster. You two are quite the scholars."

Linus was already reaching for the book, Evangeline knew he'd just been waiting for the invitation, and that probably he'd been translating in his head since they got their first look at it.

"Pencil," he said, and held out his hand for one.

She pointed to a cup of them not far from where he stood. Linus could be like that when he was concentrating, he didn't see past the project he was working on.

"Oh. Thanks. Evangeline, what do you think this one is? It looks like a symbol for 'half moon,' don't you think?"

Evangeline positioned herself so she could see what he was pointing at. She did agree now that she looked, but she wouldn't have noticed the similarities without him. Her heart soared, they were lucky to have Linus here.

When she'd been kept home to prepare for her binding to Locke, and the life she'd live as his *ceile*, Linus had begun his career as a teacher and in doing so had honed his skills in a way Evangeline hadn't been able to. And now because of it he would be able to contribute even more to the rescue effort. She leaned on her elbows next to Linus so she could get a closer to the text. They conferred about a couple more symbols, and made a few more notes. Out of the corner of her eye she saw Nelda usher the others out of the room.

On the razor's edge of her consciousness, Evangeline heard Nelda whisper that she would call them back as soon as they knew anything.

Soon Nelda joined them at the desk, picked up her own pencil, and started sketching out her own translation so they could all compare notes. They worked for what felt like hours. A few times Evangeline had to tamp down panic that it was taking too long. Every once in a while another occupant of the house would walk by and peer in the room. A word was never exchanged, but their shadows in the doorway caused a hysterical wave to rise in her throat.

"I think that's s close as we're going to get," Nelda said finally, as she set her pencil to the side. She scrubbed her face with her hands and exhaled with a heavy sadness. "It's not good."

It wasn't.

The elixir was all but impossible to create in modern times, and it needed several days to cure. Evangeline stared at the book, at her own paper, and then at Linus's. She tapped a symbol on his page. It wasn't a symbol she had on her own. "What's that?"

"An *Ascension*-specific symbol." He reached for one of the books they'd been using for reference and began to flip pages, he landed on the one he wanted and stabbed at it with his index finger. "Here. It has something to do with the white-*rianed siofra* twin. I think this symbol," he pointed to the original recipe they'd been translating, "is the same, don't you? I think it is the title of the elixir."

Evangeline was already nodding her head. She felt that her heart might explode before she even had a chance to talk. "I do. I've seen that symbol before!"

Nelda and Linus dropped their pencils on the desk simultaneously, if Evangeline wasn't concentrating on hearing over her pounding heart and breathing in spite of the fact that she felt like someone had a death's grip on her wind pipe, she would have laughed.

"Where?" Nelda asked.

Evangeline reached down the collar of her shirt and pulled on a cord she had around her neck. "That day at the market when the vendor gave Locke that knife? I got a gift, too. I didn't think much about it. People often gifted me silly little things, totems and charms, but this one was pretty. And the vendor who gave it to me was so earnest and sweet." Evangeline shrugged. "I just kept it close like he asked."

She slipped the cord over her head and placed the small totem on the book in front of them. Etched elaborately on its face was the same symbol. It matched the reference book and Linus's translation.

"That's it, isn't it?" Evangeline whispered.

Nelda touched the surface. "Absolutely."

"What good does it do us?" Linus asked, bringing a small bit of doom to the awe that had begun to blossom between the three of them.

"Don't you realize what this is?" Nelda asked, fingering the entire totem itself now, not just the etched symbol.

"It's a totem," Linus said. "Isn't it?"

Nelda picked it up, held it close to Linus's ear and shook it gingerly twice. "It's a container."

A slow understanding spread over Linus's face, his eyes lit up, and a smile took over. "You don't think…"

"I absolutely do think." Nelda's head bobbed.

Evangeline felt like squealing. It took all the restraint she had to keep her voice even when she spoke. "We all think this is the elixir. We all believe it is going to work. But I don't want to get their hopes up."

She thrust her head toward the door indicating the house in general. "I say we make sure it is going to work before we tell them one way or the other. Agreed?"

Evangeline feared she might get an argument from Nelda, who was concerned not only with saving Shifty's life, but also her son's heart. But both Nelda and Linus nodded agreement.

"I'll get Paxton and Peyton out of the room. Then you two can give her the elixir. Just give me just a couple of minutes."

Linus and Evangeline listened carefully as Nelda left the library. When they heard Paxton's voice on the stairs and it was clear he was making his way into the kitchen, they stole up the stairs and into the spare bedroom. Linus shut and locked the door while Evangeline perched on the side of the mattress next to Shifty.

Shifty's breathing was even, Nelda had been allowing her to drink deeply from the amber bottle that sat on the side table. Her eyes were closed. A small stain spread across the sheet beneath her that hadn't been there half an hour before. It wasn't growing quickly, but it hadn't been there at all the last time Evangeline had been in the room. Shifty was bleeding through the covering on the wound. Even with the thickening potions, the blood loss was significant. Evangeline touched Shifty's shoulder, trying her best not to jostle the girl.

"Shifty?" she whispered. Shifty's eyes remained closed. Evangeline gave an experimental shake and raised her voice. "Shifty?"

"Ow," Shifty murmured, her eyes fluttered open, and she blinked. Her eyes were glassy and clear but distant. They were the eyes of a person in a tremendous amount of pain.

"Evangeline?"

"It's me, yes. Is it really bad?"

"It's terrible. Don't tell Pax. I'm trying…" her voice trailed off, she coughed, and her face contorted.

"We think we've figured it out."

Evangeline hadn't really meant to just spit it out like that, hadn't meant to tell her anything that would offer false hope, but something in Shifty's pain made Evangeline's heart hurt and all she wanted to do was fix the *hairn*. Would it really be any harder to die knowing there had been a moment of hope?

If this didn't work, Shifty was going to die. Period.

A glimmer of optimism wasn't going to matter one way or the other in the end.

"We found…a…ah…never mind." Evangeline pried the top off what she had believed was a totem. She was terrified she was going to jostle it, it was a small container so if she slipped at all, she could spill the lot of it and reduce the small chance they did have to a stain on the rug beneath her. "I need you to drink this. Can you lift your head? Wait! Never mind. Linus? Can you come over here and prop up Shifty's head?"

Linus hurried to the other side of the bed and he smiled at Shifty. Ever so carefully, he slid a hand under her neck and lifted her head. She made a small, pained noise, but she managed to assist him in the endeavor. Evangeline placed a bottle to her lips and tipped it. Nothing came out.

Shifty looked down her nose at Evangeline with question in her eyes. Evangeline's heart skipped a beat but she didn't panic. She knew she'd heard liquid in the container when Nelda shook it. Evangeline tipped it further and wiggled it gently. It was an agonizing three seconds until the liquid crested the lip of the bottle and fell onto Shifty's tongue.

"Close your mouth around the bottle. Tip your head back."

Shifty followed the instructions. She grimaced, her mouth quirked around the bottle and she lifted her eyebrows at Evangeline.

"Empty?" Evangeline asked, putting her finger tips on the bottle. Shifty nodded. Evangeline plucked the bottle, recapped it, and slipped it back around her neck. "How do you feel?"

"Ow," Shifty said and her eyes closed again.

Evangeline looked across Shifty's body to Linus. "How long?" she mouthed.

He gave an elaborate shoulder shrug.

They could call for Nelda, but Evangeline wasn't sure Nelda would have any better idea about the elixir's time to efficacy than they did. In addition, Nelda was in the kitchen with Paxton trying not to get his hopes up.

So they waited.

Shifty's eyes didn't open, but her chest continued to rise and fall regularly.

No change.

The doorknob wiggled, and then a knock. "Linus? Evangeline? Open the door."

Linus crossed the room quickly. He flipped the lock on the doorknob with his thumb, and let Nelda into the room.

"Any change?" she whispered.

"We can't tell," Linus told her.

Nelda knelt by the side of the bed so that Shifty's wound was at eye level. She touched the bloodstain, and rubbed her forefinger and thumb together. She didn't find an answer there, apparently, because she lifted the bandage from Shifty's wound. Linus and Evangeline leaned in, each of their faces on either side of Nelda's hand.

The wound was knitting.

It wasn't fully closed, but there was thick, coagulated blood on the bandage and beginning to form over the wound. A trickle of new blood seeped at the opening, but didn't flow over it, and it wasn't streaming onto Shifty's skin. Nelda held a finger on her lips, warning them not to jump to conclusions.

"Shifty? Can you hear me? It's Nelda, hon."

"Mmmmmhmmmm."

"How do you feel?"

"Mmmmmm...itches." Shifty's eyelids opened. Her eyes were immediately focused. Her voice was still weak when she spoke, but it held a bit of light that hadn't been there seconds before. "Itches. It's healing! I'm not going to die, am I?"

Nelda pushed a strand of the *hairn's* beautiful, bright hair out of her eyes. "No, honey. I don't think you are."

EPILOGUE

FIVE WEEKS LATER

Shifty peered over the back of the couch to watch Evangeline pace the floor of the mud room. Evangeline had been walking the same ten foot stretch of linoleum for half an hour. It was amusing, but Shifty was starting to worry about her mental stability.

"Pax, make her come sit down. She's making me nervous. I'm not supposed to be upset. I'm still healing."

Paxton choked on the soda he'd been sipping and sputtered into the hand he'd raised to catch any liquid that sprayed through his nose.

"How long are you going to milk that?" he asked. "I saw you do a string of half a dozen back handsprings in the backyard yesterday."

Shifty looked guilty. "Oh. You saw that, huh?"

He grabbed the big toe of her bare foot. She sat with her legs stretched across the cushion and she was pressed against his body. They lay head to feet like little kids at a sleep-over.

He wiggled her toe again. "Yeah. I saw that, you big faker," he teased.

She giggled.

"Can you still make her stop? If she wears a path in the floor our parents will think she's flipped."

"She's worried. Leave her be."

"Yeah!" Evangeline called form her position by the door. After about every five passes of the hallway, she would stop and peer out the window. "Leave her be."

Shifty rolled her eyes, leaned a little closer to Paxton, and lowered her voice. "She must know it could be hours still. And she called us to come over at the crack of dawn."

"She's probably still not sleeping well on her best days. I understood it when Igby, Tree, and Linus had to go home after the moon phase changed. She needed a bit of an adjustment period. But that was three weeks ago. You talk to her more than I do, is it getting any better?"

Shifty took a sip of her own drink and set it back on the side table, carefully resting it on one of her mother's coasters. She nodded as she swallowed. "She's still having those dreams. She ends up with my mom in her room a lot of nights. Our folks took her shopping for furniture and decorations for her room. She says it's perfect and feels like home, but that's not enough when you wake up in a cold sweat and are sure someone is there to slit your throat. The curtains you thought were pretty in the store and the cool poster you thought was so soothing? Not going to hug you and tell you it was a dream.

"Mom doesn't mind. I do hope that if this goes the wrong way today it won't make them worse, though, the dreams. Thanks to my folks unearthing her original birth certificate so she's legit as a citizen and Peyton's pretty bit of mind magic at the admissions office, Lenny is supposed to start her classes at the start of the semester. It would probably be much easier to get a linguistics degree without the cloud of a broken heart and an imprisoned boyfriend hanging over her."

"You think it's going to go bad?"

Shifty considered the question carefully. She didn't know much about the *Scath* Council's tribunals. Only what she'd read while preparing to testify about what she had seen and done, about what she knew of the *Siofra Ascension*. She hadn't been able to gauge the reaction of the eight council who'd taken her testimony. They'd asked her questions and she had answered them. She'd tried to tell them how Locke had saved her from his father. How in the end he'd made sure she was safe. She implored them to believe that he had not known the full impact his actions would have on the *riocht* and that as soon as he had comprehended it, he'd switched sides.

Their faces had remained impassive. *Scath* creatures were maddening that way—experts at controlling their emotions—and as much as she knew that, it was the thing about them that made her feel as if she'd never be one of them. She had been raised by human parents, been taught in *Talam* schools by human teachers, gone to a psychiatrist; all of whom had instructed her to get in touch with her emotions, learn healthy ways to express them, and deal with them. She didn't think she would ever be able to consider herself a full *sheehairn*. She'd begun to describe herself as a hybrid. Genetically she was a *sheehairn*. Emotionally she was human. It didn't seem like such a bad deal to her.

"I don't know, Shifty. I have trouble trusting them to remember anything other than that he was involved in something against *Scath* law. I think they need to give a lot of weight to Locke's actions once he knew about the sacrifice."

Shifty listened to his thoughts. Typical of his *hairn* nature, it made sense in a cool, logical way, but she wasn't convinced.

"My mother's actions didn't count for much," she said. "They locked Ciarda away right along with Arawn. Locke's mother, too. All the members of the *Sleacht*. Did you ever find out what that meant?"

Paxton nodded. "It's dark. My father was obviously upset that day. It means slaughter."

"Well, isn't that peppy?"

There was a sound from the hallway, a kind of high-pitched squeak. Paxton and Shifty jumped and suddenly remembered they'd been waiting for one thing all day. Paxton pulled out his phone, ready to text Peyton the minute they had information. Peyton, who had traveled to Washington, D.C. for three days with the debate team, but had threatened slow and painful deaths to Paxton and Shifty if they didn't keep her caught up on the *Scath* Council's proceedings. If she could have hooked up a closed circuit TV in *Scath* and started a local affiliate for CourTV, she would have.

"Is there someone coming?" Shifty got up from the couch, she was careful not to say 'he' or 'Locke' as they didn't know who would be sent if the Council didn't rule their way, and Shifty didn't want to say anything to put Evangeline more on edge.

Evangeline didn't answer her. She threw the deadbolt, flung the door open, launched herself out of the doorway, across the porch, and down the back stairs. She was stealing down the lawn at nearly *hairn*-speed when Shifty and Paxton finally made it to the doorway.

He was walking out of the trees with had a pack on his back. Locke lifted a hand to Evangeline, who leapt at him. They saw him wobble as she made contact, wrapping her arms around him, her legs around his waist. He steadied her, held her to him as she snuggled her face into his neck.

A smile spread across his face.

Though still yards away, Evangeline's voice carried. "I've been so worried! They said they would issue a judgment today, but it's been hours, Locke! And you weren't here...no sign of you from the trees. I was sure I wouldn't get a chance to... to...you didn't give me a chance to say anything when you walked away. I was so scared I wouldn't get to tell you. I love you. I love you, Locke. Please tell me you get to stay. They aren't going to imprison you? Punish you? They know you did the right thing in the end, don't they?"

Locke carried her to the foot of the deck's stairs. He set her on her feet and smiled at Paxton and Shifty, who were sitting on the lowest step. Paxton had an arm around Shifty's shoulders. They'd stopped walking when they heard Evangeline pouring her heart out. While it would have been impossible not to overhear her, Shifty didn't want to be right on top of them during what could possibly be the only time they would have together for a long time.

Evangeline was bouncing on the balls of her feet, manically shifting her weight. She couldn't take her eyes off of Locke.

Paxton pushed Shifty a little further over on the step. "Take a load off, man. That pack looks heavy."

Locke dropped the bag at his feet, looking grateful to be free of the burden. He sat down on the stair and pulled Evangeline onto his lap. The four of them sat, no one speaking, the sun warming them as they shared smiles.

"That's a big bag," Shifty observed.

"It is," Locke agreed.

Evangeline made a frustrated bark. "Are they keeping you, Locke? I can't take this anymore. What did they say? What was their judgment?"

Still Locke didn't speak immediately. He looked into Evangeline's eyes, ran a hand along her cheek, and kissed her. It wasn't a long or noisy kiss, but it was full of such tenderness and intimacy that Shifty found herself looking away to give them privacy.

When they parted, Locke cleared his throat. "They aren't going to imprison me."

Evangeline clapped her hands over her mouth and a muffled, joyous scream emitted from her. Shifty felt a weight lift from her shoulders. Paxton clapped Locke on the back.

"That's great! Congratulations."

Locke nodded his head. "Yes, it is good. Thank you."

"So, that's it? You're free." Evangeline sounded as if she could barely believe it.

"Well, that's not exactly it." Locke sighed. "The *Scath* Council took into account that I finally did work to stop the *Ascension* and that I'd stood up to my father when he attacked you, Shifty."

Shifty looked at the ground. She knew there hadn't been a lot of love between Locke and his father, but that didn't mean Locke wanted his father dead.

That's what had happened.

Though it hadn't turned out to have been the blow to the head as Locke thought at the time. Ironically, he'd gotten cut with the knife during the struggle. His wound, though immune to the magic that had nearly killed Shifty, had been extreme. He'd bled to death before anyone had reached him.

"Don't look like that, Shifty. He got what was coming to him. If he hadn't tried to stop us, he'd still be alive. As far as I am concerned, he killed himself."

"That's nice of you to say, Locke."

"I mean it." He did sound adamant, so Shifty let it drop.

She lifted her eyes to let him know she wouldn't interrupt again, and he had the floor.

"So, they thought my actions were worth commending. But the fact of the matter is that I did know about the *Ascension*, and I did assist in the planning. They couldn't let that kind of disloyalty go unpunished." He drew a wavering breath in through his nose. "My standing offer to have a seat on the Elder's Council has been rescinded and I will not be welcome to join the Guard. My loyalty is not pure and proven."

"Crap. Locke, I'm so sorry," Shifty said. When he'd talked about the Guard that night at the pub she'd seen his eyes light up. Watching that, it was like seeing someone who understood what they were supposed to do with their life; who they were supposed to be when they grew up. She hated to see this rug pulled out from under him this way.

Locke gave a kind of half shrug. He pushed a strand of Evangeline's hair behind her ear. "I couldn't have joined anyway."

"Why?" Paxton asked.

"Because the *Scath riocht* isn't safe for Evangeline. As much as I am a creature of *Scath*, my place is where she is." He squeezed her tightly.

Her eyes glistened. She kissed the side of his face and rested her forehead against his temple.

"Do you think your parents would put me up, Paxton?"

"Of course they would. They're having empty nest syndrome and they love a stray. They've agreed to stay here and watch over Shifty. We can all go back and forth and visit *Scath* to make sure Shifty gets the things she needs to thrive. We've been working with her magic. She isn't a half-bad *hairn* after all! Surpris—ow! Hey!" He rubbed a spot on his arm where Shifty punched him. "She's got a mean left hook, too. Anyway, yes, I'm sure my folks have a spare bed for you. You have a plan?"

Locke nodded. "I do, yes. I talked to Linus quite a bit when I was waiting to hear. He came by for at least one meal a day. Anyway, you know how that guy is about researching a subject once he gets interested. He had an idea if the *Scath* Council didn't lock me up, they might decide something like they did. When that happened, he didn't want me getting depressed. '*You want to be with Evangeline anyway,*' he told me a million times. Evangeline is going to be in *Talam*. A twenty-year-old human. We knew young people went to a much more organized and formal learning environment than ours in *Scath*. So, Evangeline would be going to college. If I got a handle on my glamour, there was no reason I couldn't relocate to *Talam*. If your parents can help me get documentation?"

He looked at Paxton again.

Shifty was surprised it hadn't occurred to her that of course the Devlins had to know how to obtain items like these. They'd been living in a *riocht* populated by a different species—they had to know a forger.

Paxton gave Locke another nod. *Of course they would help him*, it said. Locke didn't even need to ask.

"Great. I can still join a Guard. Someone told me recently that *Talam* had an army." Locke grinned at Shifty. "I'd still be a soldier. And I'd still have the *ceile* I want. I think it is a pretty good compromise."

He jostled Evangeline on his lap happily and gave her a quick peck on the cheek before continuing, "I was worried. None of them, Linus, Tresara, or Igby would tell me much about your feelings, Lenny. They would only say 'just don't worry about it.' They told me they saw you, came around here for family dinners on Sundays. Told me you were healthy and that I shouldn't dwell on it. I'm pretty sure they'd decided among themselves that they didn't want me to know how you felt about me. What you thought of my telling you I loved you. Just in case I was imprisoned. I can understand that. And I would live through the last five weeks all over again if I could see your face like it was when you ran at me. Hear you tell me you love me."

She leaned close to his ear. "I love you," she whispered, and she nuzzled his ear.

Shifty wouldn't have been surprised if they had both started purring.

"Wow. I thought *we* were gross," she joked to Paxton.

"I know, right? They are going to give us a run for our money. Peyton isn't going to want to be around any of us!"

"This is going to be so strange," Locke admitted. "Living in *Talam*. You'll help me learn what I need to do? What I have to know to avoid discovery, illness and—"

"Don't worry about it," Paxton assured him. "It's old hat for us, we'll help you. There are more *hairn* and banshee living here than you would believe. It isn't so hard to fit in. The worst part is going to be telling the Gilberts the daughter they just got back is dating the refugee next door."

Shifty laughed and it felt good to her psyche, but hurt her body. While the bloodletting had stopped relatively quickly, the damage the blade had done remained. She'd needed stitches and there had been some nerve and tissue damage. Her side ached off and on, her skin would go into uncontrollable twitching spasms, and she knew it might never be the same as it had been before the stab wound.

"I'll work to win them over. Let them know they can trust me. I know what it felt like when I thought I might be locked away from her, when I didn't know how she felt about me. I'm willing to go to pretty extreme measures not to feel those things again."

Shifty snuggled into Paxton and let her mind wander. She allowed the memories to play in her mind's eye without having to decide how they made her feel. Some would still leave her in a cold sweat, same as they did Evangeline.

She knew who she was now. She knew *what* she was. She understood that everyone who had lied to her had done it to protect her. Knew that there would be times she would still be angry with them for it. She would no longer have to believe she was crazy or that her own body was rejecting her. It would be different now, here in this *riocht*, with this human girl as her sister. They would have struggles. There were always struggles. But what couldn't they face now? They'd already been through hell and come out on the other side.

After sharing that, it was easy to share silence.

ACKNOWLEDGEMENTS

As with any project of the heart, there are so many people without whom this never would have happened. I owe them all so much more than a mention on paper, but that's what I have to offer.

First, my family, Grace and Eric, there were nights when hearing them laugh outside my office door was the only thing that kept me going. My mother, Claudia, whose pride and belief has never wavered. My sisters, Sydney and Courtney, for being... well, sisters. I love you both immeasurably. My father, Paul and step-mother, Louise for love, support, and escapes for family time. My step-father, Duncan, the best Bopa in the world, and a consummate listener. My aunt Connie for bragging on me to strangers. My aunt and uncle, Darrell and Karen, who have helped me to see that most stories are about family. Their love and support means more than any of them will probably ever know.

The words on these pages wouldn't be nearly as coherent as they are if it wasn't for my editor, good friend, and other half of my brain, Gabrielle. She will probably never know how many times she pulled me back from the edge. She's honest and fair, and never cruel or mean-spirited.

Jamie, copyeditor extraordinaire. Your comments made me smile, and more importantly, made me think. I was scared to hand *Shifty* to a stranger, and lucky that a thoughtful and caring friend sent her back to me. Thank you so very, very much.

My beta readers and good friends who kept me honest along the way, Dan (the best fake brother ever), Christine (we really are going to open that pub, café, or have that podcast, my partner in book crime!), Scott (without whom Shifty might have had a different name), Bridget Ruth (and her kitty pics!), Becky (shut your pie hole), and Betty the book slut.

The family I chose along the way that have always stood by

me: Sabrina and Aminika, my oldest, dearest and most loyal girlfriends ("I never had friends again like I did when I was 12, Christ, did anyone?"—okay, we were 15, but the sentiment is the same, they've been there since the beginning), Ilka and Tawuna for movie nights and wine when I thought my brain might fall out of my head. Patrick for old personal jokes, and Clara for the newest ones. Erika for a shelter from the storm, free coffee and always having chocolate. Steve and Matt for so much more than indulging Gabrielle and me while we participated in shenanigans, but for that as well. Sally, for almost thirty years of smileys both concrete and from the heart.

Fellow writers can pull you back out of it like no one else. Frank, you'll probably never know how many times you saved me from the data entry want ads! Leah—that WAS my beer. Marie Who Needs Therapy and Derek the Waffle King for taking a huge swipe at my impostor syndrome and making me feel like someone might care what I say. My crit partner, Brandon for his kind words, and the not so kind ones that I needed probably more, for understanding on the bad days, and a kick in the butt when I cried wolf.

Everyone should have people as completely biased in their love and support as I do. But these are mine. I'm afraid you'll have to find your own.